She rode the West looking for a man she swore to destroy. She found something more dangerous... a man to love.

D0199267

"YOU CAN SAY NO," TRACE MURMURED IN A STRANGE THICK VOICE, HIS GAZE FOCUSED ON HER LIPS.

But Sam couldn't speak at all. Merely breathing was struggle. She stared up at him, lost in some timeless space that she hadn't known existed. Helplessly she gazed into his narrowed predator's eyes and saw a tiger watching her. A kaleidoscope of swirling hypnotic amber reached to engulf her and her head spun dizzily.

When his lips touched hers, a warm liquid surge exploded through her body. His kiss was deliberate and unhurried. It astonished her that his mouth was soft; she hadn't expected that at all. She noticed that he closed his eyes.

When his mouth released hers, Trace gazed into her startled eyes for a long moment, then he smiled. "I'll get the horses."

Sam couldn't move. She was twenty-three years old, prided herself on being tough and ornery as a pole cat.

But Sam Kincade had just received her first kiss.

And it devastated her.

ALSO BY MAGGIE OSBORNE

THE WIVES OF BOWIE STONE

Published by
WARNER BOOKS

THE SEDUCTION OF SAMANTHA KINCADE

MAGGIE OSBORNE

WARNER BOOKS

A Time Warner Company

WARNER BOOKS EDITION

Cover design by Diane Luger
Cover illustration by James Griffin
Hand lettering by Carl Dellacroce

Warner Books, Inc.
1271 Avenue of the Americas
New York, NY 10020

Ⓦ A Time Warner Company

Printed in the United States of America

First Printing: September, 1995

10 9 8 7 6 5 4 3 2 1

CHAPTER

* 1 *

As always, Sam Kincade was looking for a man. Zeke Slattery wasn't the man she'd been thinking about for twelve years, not the man she'd been seeking for the last five years. But he was the man she was hunting right now.

According to recent information, Slattery could be found at Dogtown—which wasn't much of a place, Sam thought as she turned her horse down Main Street. Situated on the treeless plain near the Kansas–Colorado border, Dogtown wasn't more than a bump on the face of the prairie, a watering hole for bad guns and the men who wore them.

The saloon, where Sam was headed, was the only two-story building aside from a sorry-looking hotel at the bottom of twin ruts that passed for a street. The establishments bordering Main sagged toward the sunset, losing the battle to stand upright against the relentless prairie wind.

After tying Blue to a crowded rail in front of the

1

saloon, Sam tossed back her poncho and checked her gun belt. She spat on her hands, then slicked back a mop of short hair and shoved her hat firmly into place. Hitching her shoulders up, she thrust out her chin and donned a spit-in-your-eye expression. After glancing up at the rising moon, she swaggered into the Dogtown saloon like the boy she pretended to be.

The stink of liquor, sweat, and tobacco juice rolled forward in a thick wave. Near the staircase a harried piano player thumped out tunes that nobody recognized, dribbling cigar ash over yellowing keys. A group of silent tight-faced men pressed around the faro bank. Occasionally one of the players at the poker tables flicked a glance toward the whores running up and down the stairs like painted yo-yos spinning along a cowboy's string. Saloons didn't vary much from one dirt town to another.

Sam elbowed through the men crowding the bar rail and a couple of the whores gave her the once-over, then decided she was just a kid with a small poke and lost interest.

She gave the noisy room a slow scan. When she thought she spotted Zeke Slattery, Sam edged toward the poker tables and leaned one shoulder against the wall, taking a sip of her beer. It was flat and tasted like cat piss, but if she wanted to blend in, she had to drink the stuff.

After double-checking that no one was paying her any attention, she drifted closer to the poker tables, mentally comparing the faces scowling at the cards against the face on the wanted poster folded in her pocket.

The man she guessed to be Slattery didn't take long to call trouble to himself.

Grinning triumphantly, he reached to the center of the table to gather in a pile of money. His whiskery smile froze when one of the other players threw down his cards and shouted.

"How the hell many aces does this deck have anyway?" A spray of spittle flew over the table. "I got an ace, that cowboy has an ace, and you got three aces! You want to explain that before I kick your ass from here to kingdom come?"

"Are you accusing Zeke Slattery of being a cheat?" Slattery's eyes narrowed into glittering slits.

Slattery's own words nailed him. The reeking lard-belly with the dirty face fuzz was indeed the man Sam was after. Moving away from the fracas, she headed back to the bar as the men at Slattery's table jumped to their feet yelling accusations and threats.

The bartender and a man the size of a freight wagon rushed across the room and wrestled Slattery and the other players toward the door. "Settle it outside!" the bartender shouted. He pulled the swinging doors shut and posted the freight wagon beside the door to make sure the brawl stayed in the street.

Sam leaned her elbows on the bar and listened to the ruckus erupting outside. Glass broke nearby. A volley of gunshots sounded. If Slattery survived the enraged poker players, she figured he'd return to the saloon to pick up his pride. But he'd leave Dogtown before sunup. Slattery was a man on the run, and Sam's job was to guess the direction he would run next.

Being good at what she did, she already had an idea where he'd head, except he wasn't going to get there. If the poker players didn't get him, she would.

The layer of sawdust covering the floor was thin enough that she heard a pair of boots approaching her. Sam turned her head and glared at a large ruddy-faced man who looked as if he intended to shove her aside.

"I'm in this spot and I ain't moving," she announced coldly. Straightening, she eased back the edge of her poncho, letting one hand drop casually to the butt of the Colt holstered at her waist.

"Oh for God's sake." The man gave her a disgusted look, then spat a wad toward the nearest spittoon. "Ain't nothing more annoying than a green kid looking to make a name for himself."

Ignoring him, Sam glanced toward the door in time to watch Slattery swagger inside, brushing dust off his hat and looking mean enough to kick a dead man. A cut on his lip leaked blood into his whiskers. A deep gash opened across his forehead. He walked to the far end of the bar and shouted for a shot and a beer. There was no sign of the other poker players.

This would be a good time to move out and take up her position, Sam decided. She could toss out her bedroll and grab a few hours' sleep before Slattery showed up and the action began.

After swallowing the last drops of cat piss, she

dropped the tin mug on the tray of a passing bar girl and gave the saloon a final scan to make sure she hadn't missed anything. Two sets of features grabbed her attention.

The first face belonged to Kid Gally, a nineteen-year-old punk laboring to build a name by robbing stages up Laramie way. So far Gally hadn't killed anyone, so the bounty wasn't as lucrative as that offered for Zeke Slattery, who had murdered at least five people—six if you counted the preacher who had died of heart seizure while Slattery pistol-whipped him. The preacher stuck in Sam's craw like a lump of gristle. She was going to enjoy watching Slattery hang.

The second face wiped her mind clean of thoughts about Kid Gally and Zeke Slattery. This man's presence made Sam feel lightheaded and shaky inside. He held himself apart from the saloon scene the same as Sam, and in the instant their eyes met, she remembered all she hated about the tiger-eyed man. That hatred had driven her from the time she was a young girl.

But as quickly as a white-hot rage scalded her innards, Sam realized this man was not Hannibal Cotwell. He reminded her of Cotwell, but the physical resemblance wasn't as strong as she had initially thought. Cotwell was barrel-chested and stocky; this man was lean, almost elegant. Cotwell's features were coarse, his mouth sensually cruel, whereas this man's profile was sharply aristocratic, his mouth fuller and more handsomely shaped. The man sitting by the door of the saloon didn't have a mass of scars disfiguring the right side of his forehead.

But the eyes were the same. Sam would never forget those strangely compelling amber-colored eyes.

Sucking in a deep breath, Sam shoved blindly toward the door. She hadn't seen Hannibal Cotwell in twelve years, though she'd been searching for him almost that long. He would be in his mid-thirties now, older than the man beside the door.

"Get out of my way," she snarled at a cowhand, elbowing toward the night air outside, commanding herself not to run.

The man who reminded her of Hannibal Cotwell thumbed back the brim of a black Stetson and watched her approach, one dark eyebrow quirking slightly.

By the time Sam had moved close enough to notice his dandified jacket and the heavy gold watch chain looped across his waistcoat, her nerves twitched with tension. It was his eyes. The way they followed her made her stomach churn. That predatory gleam was scorched in her memory.

Fire and frost surged in her blood as she pushed through the saloon doors and stepped outside, filling her lungs with a gulp of chill night air. She discovered her Colt gripped tightly in her hand, but didn't know when she had drawn it. She only knew she wanted badly to return to the saloon and kill the man beside the door, wanted it so much that she shook with the urge.

"Damn it!" Her knuckles whitened as she gripped

the gun. Her back teeth ground together. Groaning, she pressed the butt of the Colt against her poncho and the scar beneath her rib cage.

"It isn't Cotwell!" she told herself again and again. Forcing herself to place one boot in front of the other, she made herself walk away from the gaslight spilling through the saloon doors. When she found Blue, she leaned her forehead against the horse's neck and cursed beneath her breath.

Lately she'd been conjuring Cotwell in every shadow. Impatience and frustration ate her alive every time she picked up his trail only to lose him. Desperation was beginning to make her imagine him lurking in every town she rode through. It was a damned wonder that she hadn't shot some poor bastard who had the misfortune to resemble Hannibal Cotwell.

What stuck in her craw was knowing he was still out there, murdering, thieving, leaving a trail of blood and destruction. Like quicksilver, Cotwell slid through the fingers of all those who had tried to capture him, including Sam.

"Someday," she whispered through clenched teeth. Someday she was going to get him. And Cotwell was one outlaw she was not going to bring in alive.

Swinging her leg over Blue's saddle, she rode down Dogtown's dark deserted Main Street, heading east toward an eroded gully she had scouted on her way in to town. Slattery had ridden in from Laramie, and since she figured he wasn't fool enough to return to Denver, she reasoned Dodge City was his next likely destination.

Two miles outside of town, she located the gully and led Blue down the side, out of a chill night breeze. She staked him, removed her saddle for a pillow, and shook out her bedroll. But sleep didn't come easily.

She kept recalling the amber-eyed man who resembled Hannibal Cotwell, and the nightmare his look-alike had inflicted on the one she loved most. When she did finally doze off, she whimpered in her sleep.

Dogtown was too small and insignificant to be on the gaming circuit. If Trace Harden had been in Dogtown to enrich himself, he could easily have cleaned the pockets of every rube in town; there wasn't a skilled sharp among them.

That didn't stop the locals from challenging him. Those who had heard of him, and there were a few, wanted to boast that they had won a pot from Trace Harden. But it didn't happen. Instead of taking their money and then dealing with the accusations of cheating that would inevitably follow, Trace had turned aside the challenges. He'd hired on with the saloon proprietor to deal faro, accepting the insultingly low salary of five dollars for an eight-hour shift because he needed to be in the saloon where the locals and strangers gathered. That was where he would pick up the information he sought.

At this wee hour the saloon was almost deserted. Two cowboys were sleeping off a big night, laid out on the sawdust floor like a pair of corpses. The piano man had departed, thank God, and all the girls were occupied upstairs except Mattie. The bartender half dozed behind a scarred mahogany counter.

Trace sat alone at one of the poker tables, amusing himself by cutting aces out of a deck. These were the new double-headed cards that meant a man no longer had to turn his hand right side up to see what he had. In Trace's opinion, the new rounded edges were less of an improvement.

"Don't know how you do it," Mattie Able said, sliding into a chair across from him with a look of admiration. She smoothed a limp auburn tendril off her forehead. "You still look fresh as a daisy."

"I don't believe I've ever been compared to a daisy," he answered, smiling and extending the deck of cards. "Cut. If you pull a face card, I'll buy you a drink."

Her tired eyes lit with surprise and pleasure. "Well now. A drink would be right welcome." After he shuffled, she cut the cards and flourished a queen with a triumphant grin.

"Atchison! Bring the lady a brandy smash." Trace folded the queen back into the deck. "I'll have another sarsaparilla."

"You ain't a drinking man?"

"I have been and will be again." He offered another smile, meeting her eyes squarely and ignoring the mounded flesh straining the seams of her mended costume. The gaslight flickering overhead revealed a face that was tired but younger than Trace had guessed. Life, and the way Mattie Able lived it, had taken a toll. The freshness of youth and innocence had fled, and soon the remaining traces of prettiness would follow. But her eyes were a fine vibrant brown, and the luxuriant mass of copper-colored hair pinned beneath a dusty feather headdress was clean and shining.

Trace scowled at the glass Atchison set on the poker table before her. He pushed it aside and narrowed his eyes. "That's tea. Take it away and bring the lady a brandy smash like I ordered. Miss Able isn't working. This is an after-hours conversation between two friends."

"Lady?" Atchison sneered. "Huh!"

Mattie ignored the slur and stared at Trace. "Now that's damned fine of you!" She considered a minute, then arched a penciled eyebrow and flicked a speculative glance toward the staircase. "The night ain't over. This could be work . . . I'd give you a good price . . ."

"I'm tempted," Trace lied, glancing at her full bosom and pretending to consider. "Ordinarily I'd leap at an offer from such a handsome woman . . ."

"But?" She leaned forward over the brandy smash that Atchison slammed down before her.

"But I've temporarily sworn off liquor and women," he confided sadly, looking down at the kings he cut out of the deck with his left hand. He transferred the cards to his right hand and shuffled the boards between his long fingers.

"Oh." Disappointed, she raised her glass and took a dainty sip. "Why would you do a fool thing like that?"

"I'm looking for a man. I don't want any distractions until I find him." He'd been waiting a week to sink the hook, baiting it with admiring glances and polite words. Early on he'd learned that Mattie was his best chance. Rumor suggested that she had the information he sought.

"Who're you looking for?" She hesitated. "Maybe I can help out."

Reaching across the table, he covered her hand with his, gazing into those fine tired eyes with genuine gratitude. "I'd be obliged if you could, ma'am."

"What's his name?" It had been a long time since any man had touched Mattie with clean nails and an uncallused palm. A long time since she'd had a one-on-one with a clean-shaven, clean-smelling, great-looking man.

"Hannibal Cotwell." Abruptly Mattie withdrew her hand, and her expression tightened. Trace knew he'd drawn the high card.

"I've been wondering about you," she said after a lengthy pause. "You got them same tiger eyes like Hannibal, same quiet voice, too. You don't look like him, not exactly, yet you do."

Trace's stomach constricted into an icy knot. His hands felt like clumsy blocks of wood. He fanned the cards across the felt and reached for his sarsaparilla.

"I'd give twenty dollars gold to learn where I can find Hannibal Cotwell."

Mattie set down the brandy smash. "Something you need to know. Hannibal and me, well, we got an understanding, if you know what I mean." She frowned at the staircase and pulled her lower lip between her teeth as if a sudden memory pained her. "Leastways we used to before . . ."

"I heard it a little differently," Trace commented gently when her voice trailed. "I heard that you'd as soon shoot Hannibal as look at him."

"Maybe." Her frown deepened. "Are you a lawman?"

"No, ma'am." When she continued to regard him suspiciously, Trace spoke in his most convincing manner. "I assure you Hannibal will want to meet with me when he hears that I'm looking for him."

"Well, he won't hear it from me," she said flatly, her face expressionless. "Hannibal was here a while back, but he's gone now. I don't know where he is."

After a lifetime in the gaming world, Trace could spot a bluff when he saw one. Striving for patience, he let the conversation dwindle. If he pushed her as he wanted to, she would dig in her heels and then he'd never learn the truth.

Flexing his shoulders, then his fingers, he pretended a yawn and glanced toward the windows and the gathering dawn as if it didn't matter if she told him where Hannibal was hiding out. He'd dealt the hand; now he had to wait while Mattie decided whether to play the cards.

"I think I'll wander up to the hotel and see if the cook is awake yet. I'll be back before your shift ends."

"Thank you for the drink," she said stiffly.

"My pleasure, ma'am."

He nodded politely, then donned his coat and hat and stepped outside into the shadowy murk of predawn. A couple of outlaw types were shouting drunken challenges at each other at the end of the street, but otherwise the town still slumbered, gathering its strength to face another broiling day.

The hotel dining room was deserted except for an itinerant preacher who made a habit of accosting other guests and muttering about charity when he wasn't staring into the bottom of a bottle. He'd roused the cook and was waiting impatiently for his breakfast.

Trace took a seat at the end of the table, ignoring the preacher, and considered the contrary ways of women. Mattie might decide to point him toward Hannibal, or she might not. He couldn't predict her decision any more than he could predict which number would drop out of a keno cage. He liked women and generally women liked him. But he didn't pretend to understand their ways.

For instance, he'd been puzzled by the woman who had wandered into the saloon earlier in the evening, rigged out like a boy. At least he thought it had been a woman. Her disguise, if it was a disguise, had been effective enough that he couldn't be entirely certain of gender.

But if she was a woman, Trace couldn't begin to guess what had inspired her to tog out like a male and enter a rough saloon. Considering her manner and how she had handled herself, he'd put money on the line that she was no stranger to turbulent surroundings. That wasn't the first time she had bellied up to a saloon bar and tossed back a beer.

He'd spotted a couple of similar strange creatures in Deadwood and another in Dodge. What amazed him was that such women seemed to believe that cutting their hair and stepping into a pair of denims transformed them into males. More amazing yet, was that most of the world did look at them and see a smooth-cheeked boy. If a woman wasn't wearing skirts and frills, if she talked tough and could handle a sidearm, then she must be a boy. A pretty boy, maybe, fit for teasing and crude comments, but a boy nonetheless.

When it came to women, Trace preferred them dainty and feminine. He liked piles of silky curls that tumbled to a tiny waist when unbound. He admired the seductive sway of rustling skirts and the promise of lacy French corsets and smooth dark stockings. He was attracted to society belles who smelled like flowers and wore pearls in their small ears, women of grace and charm and delicate, fragile movements.

Those were the attributes that had drawn him to Etta.

The instant her image rose in his thoughts, regret and fury slammed through his stomach. He pushed aside a plate of ham and potatoes swimming in grease, his appetite gone. The old preacher opened bleary eyes and cast a covetous look down the table.

"Take it," Trace growled, shoving his plate away. Standing, he walked out of the dining room, pressing one hand against the letter folded in his waistcoat pocket. He imagined the scent of lilacs, the perfume Etta had worn the last time he saw her.

Blinded by a rush of hatred and shaking with the enormity of his failure as a man, he rushed outside and strode toward the dark prairie.

It was dawn before he returned to the saloon and sat at one of the poker tables, watching Mattie come down the staircase followed by a grinning cowboy.

She waved the cowboy out the door, then sat across from Trace, but she wasn't as friendly as she'd been before she learned he was looking for Hannibal. She watched with wary eyes as Trace idly rifled a deck of cards.

"I've figured out who you have to be," she said abruptly, shifting her chair out of a bar of dawn light.

Trace lifted his head, surprised by the anger sharpening her tone. "I'm Trace Harden out of Kansas City. Until recently I owned two of the finest hotels and gaming establishments in the west. None of that is a secret. After my wife died, I sold everything and headed to the territories."

The anger left Mattie's eyes in a flash. Her gaze widened and she jerked upright in her chair. "Your wife is dead?"

"May she rest in peace," he said evenly, staring down at the cards.

"Your wife's name was Etta," Mattie said, her lip curling. She spoke Etta's name as if the word scalded her tongue. "How did she die?"

Trace fumbled a shuffle, something he hadn't done in years. He lifted his head and stared hard. "Where is he, Mattie?"

"I thought so. You're Hannibal's half-brother, ain't you?"

His throat closed and he felt like he was choking. "I need to find him. Where is he?"

"I ain't telling you nothing about him until I know why you're looking for him." She leaned forward and frowned into his eyes. "I need to hear your story first. Especially the part about your dead wife."

Trace gave her a bare-bones version of the truth, picking and choosing what information he decided to reveal. Ultimately he told her that he and Hannibal had urgent matters to discuss regarding their late mother's estate.

He did not tell her that he had sworn to kill his brother.

Light frost rimed Sam's saddle when she woke. The sky was shading to pink in the east, telling her that she hadn't overslept and missed Slattery. To make sure, she crawled up the side of the gully and peered through the shadowy light, searching for a horseman moving on the prairie.

Satisfied, she slid back to the bottom of the gully and watered Blue, then moved him to a patch of thin spring grass, making sure the walls of the gully were high enough to conceal him from the sight of anyone approaching.

Waiting was the hardest part of bounty hunting. Waiting for information, waiting for confirmation, waiting for the quarry to make a mistake or return to a favorite haunt, waiting for the trap to spring, waiting to discover if this was the time her luck ran out.

The sun popped over the horizon and she spotted a lone rider moving through hillocks of sage and low brush. If fortune smiled, the rider would be Zeke Slattery.

Glad the sun was behind her and wouldn't glint off her spyglass, Sam raised the eyepiece and scanned the prairie. It was Slattery all right, and he was alone. His ugly bearded face filled her vision.

He was red-eyed and half drunk, swaying in his saddle and wearing a brooding expression, as if he were replaying the night's poker hands in his mind.

There were pros and cons to taking an intoxicated man. Liquor made a man quicker to rile but slower to react—easier to surprise but occasionally harder to subdue.

Rolling on her back, she worked a folded sheet out of her pocket. Dead or alive was the information she wanted to confirm; it was two hundred dollars either way. Not all of the wanted posters listed victims, but this one did. She looked hard at each name, wishing she knew something about them. All she knew was that Slattery had shot them dead.

Sam flipped back on her stomach and sighted her

rifle over the edge of the gully. Like her lawman father before her, she didn't waste a glimmer of compassion or compromise on criminals. She made it her business to hunt them down like the vermin they were. She liked to think that the scum she hunted would destroy no more families after she was through with them.

When Slattery rode within target range, Sam steadied her elbows against the ground, planted the rifle butt against her shoulder, sighted, and squeezed off a shot, grinning broadly when she heard Slattery scream and saw him lurch forward to grab his thigh.

"Damn all!" she whispered happily. She'd made a spectacular shot, lucky as hell. She'd managed to wing him in the thigh without wounding his horse. If her father had been alive to witness this, pride would have popped the buttons on Daniel Kincade's vest.

Slattery whipped his pistol up and peered wildly around him, hampered by the sun rising full in his ugly face.

Sam closed one eye, aimed, and fired, so charged up by her previous good fortune that her shot went wild, missing Slattery altogether. She loaded and fired again, amazed to see her second shot spin the pistol out of Slattery's hand. A frown clamped her eyebrows. The shot looked as spectacular as the first, but it wasn't. She'd been aiming for the broader target of the bastard's shoulder. But hell, she'd take whatever luck came her way.

Jumping to her feet, she ran toward him. "Hands in the air! Don't move. Not a twitch or you're dead."

It was imperative to move fast, while he was still shocked by his injuries and surprised by the ambush.

"Take your rifle out of the scabbard and throw it down. Do it now!"

"Who's there?" he shouted, squinting into the sun. "Damn it, I'm shot!" He cradled his pistol hand against his slack belly and stared down at the blood starting to soak his pants leg, blinking in disbelief. "My hand's shot and my leg's shot."

"You're going to be shot dead if you don't throw down that rifle." Sam planted her boot heel and sighted on his chest. She had him now and her body knew it. Fire blazed in her innards. Blood pounded in her head. She felt taller and stronger than she had five minutes ago. The satisfaction of swinging justice's sword made her feel powerful enough to chew her way through a mountaintop.

Slattery swore down at his wounded leg, then slowly he withdrew his rifle from the scabbard and dropped it to the short prairie grass.

"Who the hell are you?"

"I'm Sam Kincade working for Judge Mockton out of Denver."

Almost disappointed that he'd given up so easily, Sam approached close enough to kick the rifle aside so Slattery couldn't drop from his horse and lunge for it.

"Get off your horse. Do it now."

Slattery examined his leg and hand, then gazed down the barrel of Sam's rifle before he grunted and dismounted. Immediately he sank to the ground, gripping his thigh above the knee.

"Jesus. I'm bleeding to death."

"You might," Sam agreed, although she suspected he wouldn't. While his hands were close together on his thigh, she snapped a pair of figure-eight manacles around his wrists, cuffing him easily and efficiently. When Slattery realized what she'd done, he howled and tried to jerk free of the iron wristbands. Finally he gave up, as Sam knew he would, and glared at her with a poisonous gaze of pure hatred. Sam removed the key to the manacles from her pants pocket and held it up for Slattery to observe.

Slattery swore between his teeth.

"You paying attention?" She flung the key to the manacles as far as she could out onto the prairie. "Don't go thinking about jumping me and getting the key. It's gone."

After exchanging her rifle for a pistol, she moved behind him, jammed the barrel of the Colt against his thick neck, and gave him a quick pat-down, checking for concealed weapons. A careless bounty hunter was a dead bounty hunter.

Slattery raised his head and blinked at her. "Jesus God! You're jest a goddamned kid!"

She knew what he was thinking, the same thing they all thought at this point. First came shock. Then the first hot pang of humiliation as his pea-sized brain leapt forward to forecast the laughingstock he would become when it became known that Zeke

Slattery had been apprehended by a boy who hadn't yet taken a razor to his chin.

Sam fetched Blue out of the gully and strapped Slattery's saddlebags over her own. "Stand up and get mounted. We're riding to Denver."

After satisfying herself that she hadn't overlooked anything that might prove perilous later, Sam mounted Blue and, leading Slattery's horse, headed northwest across the high prairie. If they rode straight through and didn't stop either night, she figured she could deposit Slattery at Sheriff Ainsley's jailhouse door about noon the day after next.

As usual after a successful capture, Sam felt buoyant and euphoric, certain that Slattery's victims smiled down over the rim of heaven, applauding her actions on their behalf.

Unfortunately the euphoria seldom lasted for more than a few brief hours. Then a sense of depression dropped over her like a lead cloak. Zeke Slattery was not Hannibal Cotwell. She'd removed one murdering viper from the landscape but not the worst one, not the one who had haunted her day and night for twelve single-minded years.

There was nothing to see on the prairie except endless earth and sky, nothing to do but listen to Slattery groan, nothing to think about except the past and the might-have-beens.

If Hannibal Cotwell hadn't ridden into Cottonwood, Kansas, that day twelve years ago, what kind of life would Sam be living now? She couldn't visualize herself as a wife or a mother. She wouldn't know how to be a woman if she tried. More important, she didn't *want* to be one.

She'd been living as a male so long that she couldn't remember what it felt like to be female. All she knew was that women were dependent, powerless creatures, helplessly drudging through life at the mercy of a man's whim. Just thinking about it made her shudder.

Turning her thoughts toward Denver, she cheered herself by anticipating Judge Mockton's praise when she brought Slattery in. Her great-uncle would treat her to steak and oysters at Clarion's, and he'd tell anyone who would listen that his nephew was the best damned bounty hunter in the west.

For a few hours Sam would feel as if someone in this miserable, lonely world cared about her.

CHAPTER
* 2 *

Immediately prior to her monthly curse, Sam felt as mean as a snake in shedding season. What she most resented was the regular reminder that regardless of the image she presented to the world, regardless of how she ignored and tried to deny the truth, she was a woman. Being forced to acknowledge this hated fact made her want to whack the hell out of somebody.

Tired, hungry, and mad at the world in general, she kicked open the sheriff's door and strode inside, jerking a thumb over her shoulder.

"Slattery's in the street tied to his horse. He needs doctoring. I need my money." She glared at the sheriff. "What I don't need is any of that crap that you think passes for wit."

"Hello to you too, Kincade." Sheriff Ainsley leaned back in his chair and grinned at a deputy propped against the wall picking his teeth. "What do you think? Is Kincade here the meanest kid in the

23

west?" Standing, he ambled to the window and peered out at Slattery, who was hunched over his horse's neck scowling at a knot of curious spectators.

"How old are you, Kincade?" the sheriff asked after a minute. "Sixteen? Seventeen?"

"Old enough to mind my own business," Sam snapped. Going directly to the bench against the far wall, she sat down and tugged off her right boot. She turned the boot upside down and shook it over her hand.

"It occurs to me that by the time you're my age, you're going to be a legend," the sheriff commented, still peering out at Slattery. "If you live that long."

The compliment surprised and mollified Sam somewhat. The real key to Slattery's manacles dropped out of her boot and she tossed it to Sheriff Ainsley's deputy. He pushed off the wall and sauntered outside to untie Slattery from his horse.

"I'll take my money now," Sam said, stamping her boot back on.

The sheriff opened a desk drawer and tossed her an envelope. "The judge wants to see you. He's got another job for you."

Sam swore. "He can send somebody else. I'm taking a few days off. I got personal business to attend to." She had a headache and the onset of cramps. She was hungry and she hadn't slept in more than forty-eight hours.

The sheriff grinned and gave her a sly look. "That business wouldn't have nothing to do with Millicent Snow, now would it?"

Whatever the sheriff alluded to was a mystery that Sam was too tired to pursue. "Tell the judge—"

"Tell him yourself, he's your uncle."

"Great-uncle," Sam corrected, as if the distinction mattered to anyone but her.

She knew Sheriff Ainsley thought being related to Judge Horace Mockton gave Sam easy entrée into Denver's social and political circles, and granted her access to special favors. Actually, the judge usually appeared surprised and a little suspicious whenever Sam presented herself, as if he'd forgotten she existed.

Having learned how little the judge knew or cared about family connections, Sam was no longer surprised by his reaction. If Horace Mockton had known there were two Kincade children, he'd forgotten about it years ago. From the first, the judge had accepted the story that she was Samuel Kincade, the boy who had really died when Sam was a toddler. Sam had never known her brother.

Neither had the judge. Nor had he ever set eyes on his niece, Sam's mother, nor made contact with his relations in any way. If Sam's grandmother hadn't mentioned a brother, no one would have known who Horace Mockton was. The judge wasn't what anyone would call a family man. Sam felt closer to her horse than she felt to her only surviving relative.

Right now, irritated and tired, Sam half-wished she had never come to the Colorado territory to seek out Judge Mockton. The only time the judge took notice of her was when she got her name in the newspaper for capturing scum like Slattery or when he needed her for a special job.

She watched the deputy drag Slattery down a short hallway and kick him into a cell. "Have you heard any new information about Hannibal Cotwell?" she asked the sheriff as she always did.

"Someone fitting Cotwell's description robbed the assayer's office in Leadville a week ago," the sheriff answered. "He and his gang got away clean."

"Damn!" Sam heaved a depressed sigh and stared at the floor. Until Cotwell dangled at the end of a hangman's rope, her life would remain poised between the past and the future. She couldn't turn backward and she couldn't move forward. Revenge was the only thing that could set her free. But sometimes she felt like she was chasing a ghost.

With a population approaching twenty thousand, Denver was the largest metropolis within five hundred miles. Despite a nationwide depression, the town continued to grow in fits and starts. Five years earlier Sam had used her first bounty money to buy a little brick house, well outside the city proper. Now neighbors were beginning to encroach and smoke from the gas works obscured her view of Mount Evans. A saloon and a feed store had sprung up within shouting distance of her front porch.

She stopped at the saloon to pick up her mail and the free lunch that came with the price of a beer. While a couple of old miners filled her in on town gossip, she skimmed a week's worth of mail. The only item of interest was a note from the judge inviting her to Clarion's for oysters and venison when she returned. A reply wasn't necessary. By now the judge would know Slattery was in the sheriff's custody. He would be expecting Sam at seven.

Feeling more depressed by the minute, Sam dropped Blue off at the corner stables, then walked a block to her house.

It was obvious that Mrs. Riley, the woman who cleaned for her, had stopped by recently. The furniture smelled of lemon wax and the ice chest was full.

Tired and crampy and wishing she didn't have to go out for supper, Sam filled a couple of buckets from the well in the yard and set the water on the stove to heat for a bath. While she waited, she sat at her kitchen table and ate a slice of pie. The silence was so complete that she could count the minutes ticking off the mantel clock in her little parlor.

It would have been nice to have someone waiting for her safe return, someone interested in the tale of Slattery's capture, someone who gave a damn about the small details of her life.

A long sigh lifted Sam's chest. Since she couldn't risk having her gender discovered, she didn't work with a partner and she didn't encourage overtures of friendship. Which left her . . . alone. And that's how she preferred it, she thought defensively, blinking angrily at a sudden shine of tears.

But sometimes . . . sometimes a deep loneliness settled in her bones and made her ache all over.

Sometimes she felt like weeping for absolutely no reason at all.

Ostensibly Clarion's was open to the public, but the menu placed the restaurant satisfyingly out of reach of all but the upper echelon of Denver's society. Ordinarily Sam would never have stepped inside had it not been for the judge's occasional invitations.

Henri, who claimed to be a genuine Frenchman, smiled thinly and bowed as Sam entered the luxurious splendor of oriental carpets, crystal chandeliers, and polished mahogany.

"Judge Mockton is waiting in the club room," Henri murmured, trailing a critical eye over Sam's evening attire before he offered a grudging nod of approval. She wore spit-shined evening slippers beneath dark trousers and a jacket purchased readymade. But her tie was good-quality black silk against a snowy linen shirt. She surrendered her hat and gloves, then followed Henri to the club room, which smelled pleasantly of cigar smoke and gas jets.

Judge Mockton raised a hand in greeting after Sam discovered him sunk in one of the wing chairs facing the hearth. An orange halo glowed around his head, an illusion created by firelight shining on the ring of hair surrounding his bald pate. The thought of a halo crowning a man as ruthless and scheming as the judge was humorous enough that Sam shook the judge's hand with a genuine smile.

"Congratulations, boy. Heard you brought in another killer. Sit down, sit down. Walter, bring my nephew a whiskey."

Other than sharing similar blue eyes and a small stature, Sam couldn't identify any family resemblance between herself and the judge. She was lean and slender whereas her corpulent great-uncle was nearly as round as he was tall. Her skin was smooth and tanned; his florid complexion reflected the ravages of a half century of rich foods and strong liquor. The judge had never revealed his age, but Sam guessed him to be on the far side of fifty. It was hard to say. His small eyes were lively and sharp, but an ash-colored beard and mustache obscured the lower half of his face.

"We have two items to discuss," the judge announced, being a man who came directly to the point. Sam guessed neither item had anything to do with Slattery's capture. The judge leaned forward in his chair, eyes glittering like blue marbles. "I want you to return to Dogtown immediately."

"If you're after Kid Gally, send someone else. I'm only interested in Hannibal Cotwell or outlaws wanted dead or alive."

"I want you to bring in a man named Trace Harden. And believe me, you're interested." The judge regarded her with smug expectancy, the way he always did when a scheme had simmered to perfection and he was prepared to reveal a portion of his self-proclaimed brilliance. "Mr. Trace Harden is Hannibal Cotwell's half-brother." Grinning, the judge watched Sam jerk to attention. "And he just happens to be the only creature on God's green earth that Hannibal Cotwell gives a flying damn about."

Sam bolted upright so abruptly that her whiskey sloshed across her knee. She didn't notice. "I didn't know Cotwell had a brother," she said in a thick voice.

"My informant swears it's true. They had the same mama, different papas. It seems Harden used to own two luxury gaming establishments in Kansas City which he sold after his wife hanged herself."

"His wife *hanged* herself?" Sam stared. A man had to be rotten to the liver to drive his wife to suicide.

"As of a week ago, Harden was dealing faro in Dogtown, nosing around for information as to Cotwell's whereabouts."

"I saw him," Sam said abruptly. A tiger's predatory gaze rose in memory. She recalled the man sitting near the door of the Dogtown saloon. Suddenly her collar felt two sizes too small. Her pulse slammed in her ears. This was the best lead she'd run across since she launched her personal quest for revenge.

She leaned forward, eyes hot with eagerness. "Is Harden looking to join up with his brother?"

The judge tented stubby fingers beneath an ashy fringe of beard. "That's hard to guess. My informant claims Trace Harden is wealthy and he's never landed on the wrong side of the law. That anyone knows about, at least. On the face of it, it doesn't seem logical that he'd turn his back on a respectable life and join up with Cotwell. He doesn't need the money, that's for certain. On the other hand, why else would he be looking for Hannibal? Birds of a feather . . ."

Sam rubbed her temples, remembering that she had wanted to shoot Harden because he reminded her of Cotwell. She wished she had followed her instincts. Any brother of Hannibal Cotwell's had to be guilty of something. Wives didn't hang themselves for no reason. But she had to remind herself that Harden was more useful alive than dead.

"There's a problem," she said finally, hating herself that she felt compelled to raise an objection. "If Harden isn't charged with any crime, how do we justify bringing him in? And what's Sheriff Ainsley going to do with Harden after I throw him in the jailhouse door?"

The judge's pitying look annoyed her. Settling deeper into the upholstery, he focused on the flames jumping in the hearth.

"Let us suppose for a moment that it's true that Trace Harden is the only person in the world whom Cotwell loves. And let us suppose—just suppose, mind you—that Trace Harden gets himself convicted of a hanging offense. You're a smart young sprout, so you tell me what happens next. Do you think Hannibal Cotwell is going to allow his beloved brother to hang?"

Sam gripped her whiskey glass so tightly that her knuckles whitened. "I like this," she said quietly as the scheme dropped into place. She stared at the judge. "Hannibal rides in to rescue his brother, but he walks into a trap."

"You get your revenge; I get another step closer to the United States Senate. Voters love tough law-and-order judges." The judge smiled with pleasure and laced his fingers over a silver waistcoat.

"There's still a problem." Sam frowned. "Trace Harden hasn't broken any law that we know of, let alone committed a crime that he can be hanged for."

The judge waved a hand in airy dismissal. "I've got a man who will swear Harden stole a horse and shot down its owner. The story won't hold up in court, but it doesn't have to. All we need to do is keep Harden in jail long enough for Hannibal to hear of the arrest and accept the probable outcome. Hanging."

Sam hesitated. She hated Hannibal Cotwell with an intensity so consuming that it had altered the direction of her life, hated him so deeply and utterly that she shouldn't care what happened to his brother. If Hannibal Cotwell's brother hanged, he hanged. So what? Cotwell deserved to lose someone he loved just as Sam had lost someone she loved. An eye for an eye.

Unfortunately, Sam was also her father's daughter, and as such she cherished a passionate respect for the law. Her father would never have arrested an innocent man, would never have bent the law to serve his own purpose. Any suggestion, however oblique, that he manipulate justice would have insulted and outraged Sheriff Daniel Kincade. The memory of her adored father and the attitudes he had imparted prevailed over her hatred for Hannibal Cotwell.

"You don't know how much I detest having to say this," she said in a choked voice. "But I won't take part in hanging an innocent man." Not if she wanted to live in her own skin. Not even, damn it to hell, if the man to be hanged was Hannibal Cotwell's brother, a man who very probably deserved a noose around his neck. Unfortunately, the law was clear on this point. You couldn't hang a man merely because you believed he was bad to the bone.

The judge flicked his fingers in an irritated gesture. "The chances of Harden being an innocent are less than zero. But he won't actually hang. That's not the plan."

Sam leaned back in her chair and considered. There were rumors that Judge Horace Mockton used his courtroom to punish enemies, whispers that he dispensed his own brand of questionable justice. However, she could imagine no advantage in actually hanging the bait that would lure Cotwell within range of capture.

"I want your solemn oath that you won't hang an innocent man." As a precaution she needed to hear him swear it.

Offended, the judge frowned. "I told you. What we have now won't hold up in court. Therefore, Harden won't actually hang unless I can dig up proof of a legitimate crime and substantiate his guilt."

Assured, Sam dismissed Trace Harden and savored the anticipation of watching Hannibal Cotwell swing. Her fists clenched and sweat dampened her temples. Her imagination erected a gallows as vivid in her mind as the memories that had been eating her alive for twelve seemingly endless years.

"Trace Harden isn't going to linger in Dogtown

forever," the judge pointed out, interrupting her reverie. "Best you be leaving at sunup."

The only thing giving her pause was the inconvenience of her monthly curse. But she'd be finished with all that by the time she returned to Dogtown. By then, she'd be in fighting form. Sam nodded.

"Agreed."

"Excellent. Now to the second item. There's a matter we need to discuss before Edwin Snow and his daughter arrive." The judge checked his pocket watch against an enameled clock on the mantel. "They'll be here soon."

"The Snows are joining us?" A skiff of disappointment fanned Sam's tone. She'd secretly hoped for a private dinner, just her and the judge. While she'd bathed and trimmed her hair for tonight's dinner, she'd daydreamed about the judge inquiring after Slattery's capture, or maybe soliciting Sam's opinion about one of his cases.

"How old are you, boy?" The judge sipped his whiskey and regarded her with a speculative gaze.

"Twenty-three." Uncomfortable, Sam fiddled with her tie. Questions regarding her age or appearance tended to alarm her.

"Five years ago you showed up on my doorstep swearing that your sole aim in life was to capture Hannibal Cotwell and see him hanged. You said you wouldn't rest until Cotwell paid for destroying your family."

Sam ground her teeth and turned her face toward two men playing chess near the doorway into the restaurant. Unconsciously, she pressed her arm against the scar beneath her ribs.

"That's right," she said between her teeth.

"If our scheme works, Cotwell is going to hang very soon. So . . . what are your plans afterward?" The judge studied her. "You know and I know, there isn't any future in bounty hunting. You're already making a name for yourself. Won't be too long before every outlaw in the territory starts shooting baby-faced boys, thinking they're you."

"I haven't thought about it," Sam admitted, a sudden edge appearing in her voice. The future was a blank-faced void. Since capturing Cotwell had long since assumed the likelihood of a life-long quest, she hadn't considered what she would do once she achieved her vow of revenge.

The judge's eyelids dropped a notch. "Well now . . . you might start thinking about banking." When Sam's eyebrows lifted in puzzled surprise, the judge leaned forward and tapped her knee, lowering his voice. "Edwin Snow and I have been discussing your future, son. Edwin is prepared to make you a vice president of his bank, at a vice president's salary I might add. And you know that big stone house on Fourteenth Street? The one with the iron grillwork? Yours, if you want it. And a carriage, too. I'm working on a matched set of bays to go with the deal."

Sam's mouth opened in astonishment. She watched the judge fall back in the wing chair with a triumphant smile.

"Why in blazes would Edwin Snow make me an offer like that?"

"Use your bean, boy! Why do you think? Millicent Snow practically crawls up your bones every time she sees you! She's too damned ugly to interest any of the young sparks in her own social class, so her daddy is going to have to buy her a husband. Everybody in town knows Miss Snow has set her sights on you, boy."

Sam dropped her empty whiskey glass. Horrified, she sucked in a breath and stared hard at the judge.

"That is lunacy," she managed finally. "I can't possibly marry Miss Snow!"

"I don't see why not. An opportunity like this doesn't come along every day, not even for a handsome young sprig like you." A cold glitter frosted the judge's eyes. "You haven't gone ga-ga over one of those doxies down on Blake Street, have you?"

"My God! I . . ." The blood rushed to Sam's head and she felt dizzy. "Millicent Snow! My God. She's . . . I can't possibly . . . I mean, we're both . . ."

"A man with your limited prospects can't be choosy when it comes to a wife. This chit is an heiress, for Christ's sake. All right, Miss Snow has more of a mustache than you do, and a nose to rival Pike's Peak. So turn out the lights when you crawl into bed. Set up one of Miss Fannie's girls on the side." A shrug adjusted the judge's heavy shoulders.

"I can't," Sam whispered. Shock washed the color from her face and pinched a white ring around her lips. She couldn't recall the last time she'd had cramps this bad.

"You can and you will marry Miss Snow," the judge stated firmly. "Once you think this through, you'll see that you just fell into a pot of gold, boy. You just found a gilded future. By the time I finish pounding out the details with Edwin, you're going to be rich beyond your wildest dreams. And all you have to do is marry Millicent Snow and give Edwin a grandson. Preferably with your nose and her mustache. Give me one good reason why any man with a brain in his head would walk away from a sweet deal like this!"

"I . . . oh my God!" The proposal reduced Sam to appalled stammering. Worse, it was crystal clear that a refusal would irrevocably damage the tenuous relationship with her only relative in the world.

"You think about it, boy, although I don't know what the hell there is to think about, and you come up with the right answer. It's time you settled down, and this is the best offer you're ever going to get. You have no fortune, no social connections, no prospects, and no future. If you think you're going to inherit anything from me, you're wrong. What I don't spend in this lifetime, I'm leaving to Miss Daisy Shakowski and her daughter." A plum-colored flush darkened the judge's heavy cheeks. "The best I can do for you is set you up with an heiress wife. And you should thank your lucky boots that I found one who don't seem to care that all you got to recommend yourself are those pretty-boy good looks and a great-uncle who's respected and feared in this town!"

"Judge—"

"Shut up. Here they come." Standing, the judge

arranged a benign smile on his face and stepped forward to kiss Miss Snow's gloved hand. "You look especially lovely this evening, my dear."

Miss Snow batted her big brown eyes at Sam over the judge's shoulder. "Good evening, Mr. Kincade," she cooed. Now that Sam was paying attention she realized Millicent sounded gooey and lovesick. A blush rushed upward from Miss Snow's plump satin bodice. Her silky mustache appeared especially dark and fulsome tonight.

"Oh my God," Sam whispered, swaying on her feet. She wished to heaven that she was not having her period. She was never as mentally sharp during her time of the month. There had to be a way out of this mess that she wasn't immediately seeing.

"Sam! Heard about Zeke Slattery, congratulations." Edwin Snow pumped Sam's hand as the judge led Millicent into the restaurant. "Did the judge speak to you about a certain delicate matter?" Edwin inquired, leaning near Sam's ear.

"Yes," Sam croaked. There wasn't enough air in the restaurant. She was strangling.

"Excellent!" Edwin placed an arm around Sam's shoulder. "Once this Cotwell matter is resolved, I want you to stop by the bank and study our operation. I think you'll be pleased with your office. I can't say that you were my first choice, Kincade. But that's neither here nor there." He cast a fond gaze at Millicent, who glanced back over her shoulder to throw Sam a melting look. "Whatever my little girl wants, she gets."

CHAPTER
* 3 *

Mattie Able rolled out from under the cowboy who snored on top of her, lit a cigar, and gazed at the cracks in the ceiling plaster. The walls were so thin that she could hear Big Sal working next door, and noise drifted up from the saloon below.

She had a lot to think about now that she knew Etta Harden was dead. Mattie drew on her cigar and searched for patterns among the cracks splintering the ceiling. Yessir, she had things to ponder and things to decide.

Eventually Trace Harden was going to find Hannibal, tell him about Etta's death, and show him Etta's parting letter. Mattie wanted the satisfaction of watching Hannibal read the last letter Etta had written to her husband.

Darling Etta, the belle of Kansas City, that paragon of respectability, that shining example of all a true lady should and ought to be. Precious Etta's last act had been to write a letter that aimed a bullet straight at Hannibal's guts.

Mattie knew this for a fact because she had bribed the desk clerk at the Dogtown Hotel to sneak into Trace's room while he slept. Alf had read Etta's letter and then he'd told Mattie what it said.

Shifting her head on the pillow, Mattie studied the old bureau leaning against the wall, thinking about the nest egg hidden in the bureau's secret drawer. She had saved enough money so that if she wanted to, *really* wanted to, she could go to Hannibal and warn him about Trace. She could be there for him.

Mattie smoked and listened to the cowboy's snores and let a tear trickle down her cheek. She and Hannibal had shared some good times together. Deep down, where it didn't show too much, Hannibal cared for her. She just knew he did. And fool that she was, she couldn't help hoping that maybe she still had a chance with him.

'Course, like her ma had always told her, she didn't have a lick of sense when it came to men.

By the third day, Mattie Able's absence began to concern Trace. He was too disciplined, too professional, to let her disappearance distract him while he worked the crowded faro table, but the instant his shift ended near dawn he positioned himself at the bar rail and waited for the saloon to clear out.

"Busy night," he commented to Big Sal and Fat Annie after the last cowboy stumbled outside into the morning's glare. "I imagine you ladies will be glad when Miss Mattie returns to work."

"Mattie's gone and she ain't coming back," Big Sal snapped. "Couldn't even wait until Atchison found a replacement, that's how big a hurry she was in. Never give a thought to Fat Annie or me! Or how we was short-handed to start with!"

Fat Annie jerked down the window shades against the harsh morning light. "It ain't enough that we got to serve drinks, dance if they want to, and sweet talk 'em—"

"And clean up afterward! Now I ask you—when are we going to find time to go upstairs?"

Trace straightened and the smile slid from his lips. He'd hoped Mattie had been suffering from her monthly indisposition or from the spring ague. For all he knew she might have been holed up in a love nest with a new man.

"Where did Mattie go in such a hurry?" The sudden churning in his stomach suggested he knew the answer.

"Why ask me, I ain't her mother!" Big Sal slammed the lid over the piano keys and waved furiously at a puff of rising dust. "All I know is my best black hat went with her!"

Trace shifted his gaze to Fat Annie, clenching his fists at his sides. He stared at her, not trusting himself to speak.

"Alf over at the hotel drove Mattie to Julesburg to catch the train." Fat Annie carried a tray filled with empty mugs to the bar and dropped it next to Atchison, who didn't look up from the newspaper he was reading. She leaned against the bar, closed her eyes, and blew the hair off her forehead with a heavy sigh. "I'll wager my Sunday garters that she's chasing after that no-good Cotwell."

Atchison spoke without glancing up. "If she's that stupid, then she deserves to get her teeth knocked out."

"Cotwell broke her arm," Big Sal chimed in. "He almost broke her ribs. He blacked her eyes a couple of times. Tossed her down the staircase." Spreading her hands on wide hips, she threw back her head and shouted at the tin ceiling. "But she *loooooves* him! Alf over at the hotel is plum moony about Mattie, but she won't give 'im a tumble. It's Hannibal this and Hannibal that."

"Alf ain't exciting." Fat Annie covered a wide yawn. "Some women just ain't interested in a man lest he's dangerous."

"Ladies." Trace stepped forward, his voice as tight as his shoulders. He forced his jaw to relax. "Did Mattie take the train to Cheyenne or to Denver?"

They stopped talking and studied him curiously. Big Sal winked. "Well, well. You sweet on Mattie?"

Fat Annie was quicker to grasp the point. She shoved past Big Sal and examined Trace's taut expression. "What's the information worth?"

Trace slapped a gold half-eagle on the bar and covered it with his palm. "I heard Cotwell walked out and left Mattie in Dogtown. She swore she hated him."

Both women laughed. Fat Annie grinned at him. "Honey, you don't know cow flop about women. Mattie hates him all right. As much as she loves him."

Trace rubbed a hand over his jaw, scrubbing at his frustration. "I'm looking for Hannibal Cotwell." He'd wasted too much time trying to be discreet. "If Mattie Able ran off to join Hannibal, I need to know where she went. North, south, east, or west." He lifted the gold piece and turned it slowly in a bar of sunshine.

"Wait here," Fat Annie said. "Alf will know."

"I get half! It was my hat she stole," Big Sal shouted as Annie cut out the door and pelted down the street toward the hotel. She lifted an eyebrow and studied Trace. "If you're looking for Hannibal Cotwell, then I hope you're as good with a gun as you are with a deck of cards. Cotwell's been known to shoot first and ask questions later. After he's robbed the body."

Trace smiled, the effort wooden. "I appreciate your concern, ma'am. I'm confident I can handle myself well enough when the need arises."

"You better be right." Sal lifted her foot and placed a high-heeled boot on the nearest chair seat, showing off a long, thick expanse of leg and mended black stocking. "Guess you'll be leaving us." She cast a covetous glance at the gold piece shining on the bar. "If you're interested in one for the road . . ."

Fat Annie's reappearance spared Trace the necessity of a refusal. She puffed in the doors and thrust out her hand for the gold eagle. "Mattie took the train to Denver, but Alf says she wouldn't tell if that was her final destination or if she was leaving out of Denver for someplace else. He thinks someplace else, but he don't know why he thinks it."

Trace flipped her the gold piece, then informed Atchison he wouldn't be working at the saloon anymore. Pursued by Atchison's shouts of anger, he stepped into the morning sunshine, swore in frustration, then turned toward the hotel.

His mind raced ahead of his steps, assessing the damage Mattie could do by reaching Hannibal before he did.

Gradually his thoughts calmed. Mattie would tell Hannibal that Trace was looking for him. No harm there. She would tell him that Etta was dead. But Mattie Able didn't know why Etta was dead.

Knots rose along his jaw and he felt a wave of heat blaze behind his eyes. Made dizzy by a flood tide of hatred and betrayal, Trace stopped in front of the hotel and leaned against a porch post.

Every minute he spent in Dogtown was wasted. The sooner he started for Denver, the better chance he'd have to pick up Mattie's trail. First, he'd sell his horse to the blacksmith, who had made him an offer. Next, he'd catch the stage to Julesburg and pick up the train. Then, he'd—

"Hey! Trace Harden!"

Lifting his head, he thumbed back his hat and squinted into the sun. Damned if it didn't look like the boy–woman he'd seen in the saloon over a week ago. Curious, Trace stepped to one side, attempting to minimize the glare falling full on his face.

In daylight, he felt certain that she was indeed a woman. Either that, or she was the prettiest boy he'd ever seen. She was small like a boy, standing about five foot four in her boot heels. A few strands of dark hair dropped from her hat, falling to the bottom of her earlobes. Sweat and dust streaked her sunburned face, but the shape was pleasing. Her mouth was full-lipped, her teeth straight and white. A woman's thick dark lashes framed a pair of periwinkle eyes. But the expression was anything but feminine. Those remarkable blue eyes glittered with hatred, as chill and unyielding as slate.

"Who are you?" he asked, making no secret of his curiosity. "How did you know my name?"

"Come around to the back of the hotel. I want to show you something." She stepped off the boardwalk, turned left, and disappeared behind the hotel. There was nothing back there except open range and the prairie-dog village from which the town took its name.

Trace sighed. Of course he recognized one of the oldest tricks in the book. Only a sucker would follow her. Just as he would have to do if he wanted to discover who she was, how she had known his name, and what was going on here.

Irritated by his curiosity and by the implication that this hard-eyed pretty-boy thought he was a rube, Trace withdrew a derringer from his inside coat pocket. He flexed his shoulders and shook the weariness from his body before stepping off the end of the boardwalk and turning left.

He saw two horses. Before he fully realized that one of the horses was his, he spotted the boy-woman out of the corner of his eye. She was gripping her rifle by the barrel, swinging the butt toward his head. In an instant he grasped what was about to happen, but he hadn't time to react.

Pain exploded through his skull as he dropped to the ground like a hundred-sixty-pound rock.

Sam was always surprised by how easy it was to ambush a man. All she had to do was hit first and hit hard. Even when they expected trouble it wasn't all that difficult, she thought as she picked up Harden's derringer and stowed the sissy gun inside one of the flaps of her saddlebags. She had already stripped his hotel room and packed the items she had decided he required, leaving behind the rest. He wouldn't need fancy duds where he was going.

To avoid possible trouble, she had paid Harden's hotel tab and his board bill at the stables. And because she'd paid, she had experienced no difficulty gaining access to his room or fetching his horse.

She sat on the ground in a sliver of shade and leaned against the back wall of the hotel, her Colt in her lap, and waited for Harden to regain consciousness. Patience was a boon to a bounty hunter and a quality Sam continually nurtured. Pulling out her pocketknife, she cleaned her nails, watched Harden, and waited.

He was one good-looking son of a bitch, she had to grant him that. Better looking by far than his murdering, scum-sucking, whore's son of a brother. If it hadn't been for those smoldering tiger eyes, Sam would have sworn the two men couldn't possibly be related.

Even sprawled on the ground with his face in the prairie dirt, she could see that Harden had a patrician profile. Because he was clean shaven, she noticed a handsome mouth that hinted at secrets and sensuality. That mouth promised much but gave away nothing. After studying him for a full ten minutes, Sam decided that most women probably considered Trace Harden dangerously attractive. Most likely they gazed into his eyes and felt a fiery little tingle race through their insides.

Sam twitched, sat up straight, and stared at the flat horizon. Did Millicent Snow look at *her* that way? The possibility made her gag.

She swallowed hard, shoving down a surge of anxious panic. The looming threat of Miss Snow was a problem she would address after she had delivered Trace Harden to Sheriff Ainsley. Right now she couldn't bear to think about it. Besides, she needed her full wits focused solely on the problem at hand.

Harden groaned, spat dirt out of his mouth, then rolled to a sitting position. He squeezed his eyes shut, gave his head a shake, then discovered he was

wearing iron cuffs when he tried to explore the knot
rising on his skull.

"What the hell?"

"See this?" Sam called his attention to the key she
thrust under his nose. "This is the key to your wrist
manacles." Standing, she wound up, then hurled the
key toward the prairie-dog village, watching it spin
and flash in the sunlight. "Don't go thinking you're
going to jump me and set yourself free. The key is
gone. Stand up, Harden. Do it now."

"That was a crazy irresponsible thing to do!" he
shouted furiously, swinging a stare from the prairie-
dog village back to her. "Who in blazes are you?
And what the hell do you think you're doing?"

"I'm Sam Kincade working for Judge Mockton
out of Denver. There's a bounty on your head and I
aim to claim it. I'm taking you to Denver to stand
trial for killing a man and stealing his horse. You're
going to hang."

"*What?*" Harden struggled to his feet. "That's a
damned lie! I haven't killed anyone, and I've never
stolen a horse!"

"Yeah, well there's an eyewitness in Denver who
swears that you have. Get on your horse. Do it now."

"The hell I will!" He stared at her, then turned and
stumbled toward the street.

Sam stepped forward and jammed the barrel of the
Colt against his spine. "Pay attention because I'm
only going to warn you once. If you try to resist, I'll
shoot you dead, Harden. I'll do it without a minute's
hesitation or remorse. In fact, I'm just itching to kill

you because I know who you are. You give me the tiniest little reason, and I'll blow your kneecap into a thousand bits of bone. That's where we'll start. You got that? Now you climb up into that saddle and you sit still while I tie your boots to the stirrups. I'm in a real bad mood, Harden, so you do exactly what I say and you do it now, understand? Or I'm going to shoot you just to make a point."

"You're making a mistake, Kincade. I haven't broken any law. I'm not the man you're looking for."

"You're exactly the man I'm looking for. And now I've found you, so get your butt on that saddle. You're going to Denver or you're going underground. Your choice."

For a long minute Sam thought she would be obliged to shoot him. She stood on tiptoe, scowling into his furious amber eyes, feeling the trigger tempting her forefinger. When she looked into his eyes, she saw Hannibal Cotwell. And she wanted to shoot him.

"Denver," he said, squinting at her. He bit down on his back teeth and glanced at the wrist cuffs, then toward the prairie-dog village. Finally he swung his gaze toward his horse. "I had a money pouch in a hole in the mattress."

"I found it," Sam said shortly, insulted that he thought she was an amateur. "The Denver sheriff will hold it for you. You'll get your money back if you don't hang." And if Sheriff Ainsley wasn't tempted to confiscate the pouch for his own use. Which, based on previous experience, didn't seem likely. As

Sheriff Ainsley viewed it, relieving prisoners of encumbering personal goods was a side benefit of his job.

"Denver," Harden repeated in a thoughtful voice. Then, to Sam's surprise, he nodded and managed to mount his horse on the first attempt. He rested his cuffed hands on the saddle horn and gazed down at her as if he were calling the shots. "It isn't necessary to rope me. I'm willing."

"Yeah, and I'm the Queen of England," Sam sneered. She tied his boots to the stirrups, tossed his hat up to him, then mounted her own horse. "Head out. Now. I'm right behind you and so's a bullet, so don't try anything."

Trace Harden gave her such a long speculative look that it made Sam powerfully uneasy. She had an uncanny impression that those strange tigerish eyes gazed through her poncho and saw the form beneath. She raised the Colt and aimed it at his kneecap.

"What are you waiting for?"

"This is a mistake. I haven't committed any crime. But I'll accompany you willingly because I planned to go to Denver anyway." His expressive lower lip curled. "I'll straighten this out with someone who knows what the hell he's doing."

"That would be Judge Horace Mockton," Sam informed him with a tight smile. "The judge knows exactly what he's doing." She almost laughed. "Go. Do it now."

If Harden thought she trusted his little speech about acquiescence, he had sadly misjudged Sam

Kincade. The likelihood of Sam trusting a man was about equal to the likelihood of her ever hanging a skirt on her hips. It would never happen in this lifetime.

Sam would have preferred to ride directly to Denver without stopping, but she'd ridden straight through to Dogtown, which meant she hadn't slept a wink in more than forty-eight hours. When she caught herself dozing and swaying in the saddle, she swore and reluctantly decided they would have to halt for the night.

"We'll camp over there," she shouted forward to Harden, "by those chalk bluffs."

The outcropping offered shelter from the wind that swept unimpeded across the prairie, and the rocks would retain the sun's warmth. Spring on the high plains meant sunny and pleasant days, but nighttime temperatures still plunged into the thirties.

"Off your horse, Harden. Do it now," Sam said after she'd selected a sheltered campsite. The old fire ring was where she remembered; there was even a leftover stack of sage branches and buffalo chips.

"You don't have to tie my feet," Harden objected, watching her advance with her Colt and a length of rope.

"Pick a spot and sit down." Ignoring his protests, Sam tried his ankles together.

When she had Harden secured, she watered the horses and put them on a tether line, then she lit a

fire as the sun dipped to the west and the temperature
began to drop. She hung water and coffee pots over
the fire, threw out their bedrolls in front of their saddles, then sat on a rock to rest a minute while she
waited for the water to boil

"I didn't steal a horse and I didn't kill anyone,"
Trace Harden insisted, examining her across the
flames licking the bottom of the pots. "Therefore
there isn't any eyewitness. This is a frame. The question is why?"

Sam dropped a lump of pocket soup into the water
and gave the pot a stir before she opened two tins of
beans. That she had to feed Hannibal Cotwell's
brother made her throat swell with resentment. The
brothers might look different, but she knew they
were molded from the same twisted material. She
didn't mind one bit using Harden to get Hannibal.

"Stop looking at me," she snapped, using her
elbow to wipe dust off two tin plates.

"You said you knew who I was. If that's true, then
you know I'm no killer."

"Ha!" Lifting her head, she gazed into Hannibal
Cotwell's amber eyes. She was just itching to boast
about the judge's plan, to inform Harden that his
beloved brother was finally going to bite the rope.
And if the judge could dig up any evidence, Harden
would join Cotwell at the gallows. After considering
a minute, Sam decided the plan wouldn't be jeopar-
dized if she scratched her itch. There was no way
Harden could warn Cotwell about the trap.

"You're Hannibal Cotwell's brother," she said, biting off the words between her teeth. Merely speaking Cotwell's name released a flood of bile into her stomach.

"So that's what this is about." Harden watched her pour soup into a pair of dented tin cups and lifted his manacled hands when she took him a serving. "Thank you."

Thank you? Sam stared at him through narrowed eyes. This was the first time she'd heard those words from one of the brutes she'd captured. Moreover, her emotion and temper had been running so high that until now she hadn't noticed the south in his voice. His accent was slight, but it was there and she gave herself a mental kick for failing to take note earlier.

"The last I heard it wasn't a crime to be someone's brother."

"We're talking about Hannibal Cotwell!" The words burst out of her like pressurized water spurting from a geyser. "He's robbed trains and stages. He's robbed banks and individuals. He's raped women. He's murdered at least eighteen people and left their families devastated!"

Trace Harden met her blazing eyes over his untouched soup. "Hannibal's done those things," he said in a quiet voice. "I haven't." He studied her with a thoughtful expression. "But if you're thinking of using me as bait to lure Hannibal . . ."

"Maybe. Maybe not!" It startled her badly that he was clever enough to immediately spot the plan. No longer hungry, Sam tossed her soup over a clump of sage. "I know you're the only thing in this world that Hannibal cares about!"

Trace Harden stared at her. "Why the hell didn't you tell me this in the first place?" The tension left his body, but his expression hardened. He leaned forward and his eyes were so like Hannibal Cotwell's that Sam's stomach twisted in knots. "I want Hannibal dead as much as anyone! If your plan has a chance in hell of working, then I'll cooperate in every way."

"Right!" But the conviction in his voice and expression startled her. "Tell me why you would help drop a noose around your own brother's neck."

"I have reasons."

"What are they?"

"They're personal," he said between his teeth.

He was too clever by half, Sam decided. He'd had her going there for a minute. But this was a professional gambler, a man who made his living by hiding his emotions and bluffing. She was too smart to be suckered by a handsome face and a handful of improbable lies.

"You can untie my feet. I'm not going anywhere." He gazed toward the empty twilight prairie. "You and I share the same goal."

In answer Sam raised her poncho to show him that her gun was within quick and easy reach. "That's right," she snapped, patting the handle of the Colt. "You aren't going anywhere."

After they ate the beans, she scrubbed out the soup cups and the plates with a little water and loose sand, then she poured herself a cup of coffee and sat beside the fire. Ignoring Harden, she turned the pages of the book she'd taken from her saddlebags.

"Now that's a surprise," he commented after a while. "I didn't figure someone like you would be reading Voltaire."

"Shut up." She stared at him over the pages. "Just because I'm a bounty hunter doesn't mean that I'm a savage."

"Is that so?"

"If you spent as much time alone on a horse as I do, you'd want to fill your mind with interesting things to think about too."

"Wasn't it Voltaire who said if God didn't exist, man would have to invent Him? That isn't an exact quote, but it's close." Leaning his head back on his saddle, he gazed up at the early stars burning bright holes in the sky. "What's your opinion, Kincade? Does God exist? Or did we invent Him?"

Sam was so astonished that she almost dropped her book into the flames. No one had ever requested her opinion except her parents. And that had been so long ago that she wasn't even sure she remembered correctly. The preacher and his wife who raised her from age eleven to adulthood certainly had not been interested in hearing her thoughts. And the judge could care less about any opinions except his own.

"Why do you want to know what I think?" Her voice sounded strained and peculiar even to her.

Harden lifted his head to peer at her from beneath the brim of his hat, then dropped his head back on the saddle and gazed at the velvety sky, his manacled hands folded on his stomach. "I used to think God was just another name for Lady Luck. I'm not so sure anymore. Do you believe in the concept of final judgment, Kincade?"

Amazed by the question, Sam paused before she answered. "If we're judged by our deeds, then I doubt you and I are going to gain entrance through the pearly gates."

Leastways that was her impression after seven years of listening to Preacher Moss and his wife bludgeon her with talk of hellfire and brimstone and the hopelessness of sinners like herself ever making it into heaven. Exactly what her childhood sins might have been was never clear. But Preacher Moss made it plain as day that Samantha Kincade was doomed to perdition.

That being the case, Sam figured she couldn't make things any worse by running away, passing herself off as a male, and seeking revenge against Hannibal Cotwell. She had left Cottonwood, Kansas, the day she turned eighteen and she hadn't suffered a minute's regret, hadn't thought about Preacher Moss or his sharp-tongued wife from that day to this.

"Do you think children can be guilty of sin?" she asked. According to the preacher's wife, childhood years were the devil's playground. For Sam, those years had been dull, tightly restricted, and burdened from dawn to dusk with labor. During her teens there had been a few periods of vague, undefined longings that she suspected might have been the devil's work.

Otherwise, if Old Nick had tried to tempt her, she'd been too exhausted to notice.

"I think adults are far better at sinning than children ever could be," Harden commented sharply. "What's your opinion?"

"Well . . ."

Abruptly, Sam stopped talking. She bolted upright and gave her head a violent shake, trying to knock loose the craziness clouding her brain. Part of her seized on this conversation and desperately wanted it to continue. She wanted to explore her ideas and she wanted to know Harden's thoughts.

Shock widened her eyes. This was Hannibal Cotwell's brother! Was she so lonely and needy that she could crumble like last year's taffy when some manipulative slick casually requested her opinion? Was she that damned easy to flamdoodle?

She squeezed her eyes down tight and spoke through clenched teeth. "That's enough talking. Shut up and go to sleep."

Disgusted at herself, Sam banked the fire, then slouched over to her bedroll, well away from Harden, suddenly remembering how tired she was. Tomorrow they wouldn't stop to camp. They'd ride straight through the night and reach Denver before supper the next day. The sooner she removed herself from Trace Harden's sly seductive ways, the better.

And seductive was the right word. She couldn't stop thinking about Harden's voice. It curled inside her head and murmured, requesting Sam's opinion about this or that. It plain appalled her to recognize just how eager she was for company and decent conversation.

Confused and agitated, Sam bit her tongue to stop from calling over to Harden and asking when he had read Voltaire and what else he had read that he might recommend and what did he think about Colorado's bid for statehood and did he like oysters and was there such a thing as an honest game of poker? Her hands clenched and she ground her teeth in an effort not to call out.

His voice drifted through the darkness, deep and full and rich with whatever meaning Sam wanted to find there. "You're a woman, aren't you, Kincade?"

Sam jumped to her feet like a bolt of greased lightning. Her Colt dropped into her hand, and she stood over him, aiming the barrel square at his chest.

"Are you calling me a sissy pantywaist, mister?"

"No," he said calmly, gazing up at her. "I'm calling you a woman."

His accusation was shocking and unprecedented. Blindsided, Sam had no idea how to respond. Sweat appeared on her forehead despite the chill night air. She depended on the fact that most people focused so narrowly on their own concerns that they tended to accept others at face value. No one had ever before suggested that she wasn't what she pretended to be.

"I ain't no woman," Sam shouted. "Could a woman capture killers and haul them in to justice? Would a woman ride God knows how many miles alone across the prairie? Or ride into a wide-open mining camp?" Sputtering, ranting, she waved the Colt and listed a half dozen things that women didn't do, but which she had done.

Darkness, anger, and a peculiar hot feeling pulsing behind her eyes blurred Trace Harden's face into a pale blob near her boots.

"There's an easy way to prove your manhood," Harden suggested when Sam finally paused for a breath. She identified a strong current of amusement flowing under his tone. "Drop your pants."

She couldn't see his face, but she heard a chuckle in his voice and it enraged her. She ached to shoot him, not because he was Hannibal Cotwell's brother, but because he'd guessed the truth and because he was laughing at her.

"I don't have to prove a damned thing to a no-good scum wad like you!" Grinding her boot heel into the dirt, she stomped back to her own bedroll. Swearing, she made herself shove the Colt back into the holster. "Drop my pants! You pervert!" When he laughed, she cussed him soundly, then rolled into her bedroll and turned her back to him.

As exhausted as Sam was, Trace fell asleep long before she did. She lay rigid in her bedroll, staring at a dark clump of grass, trying to sort out the emotional turmoil she'd experienced from the first moment she'd heard Trace Harden's name.

Sam overslept. When she finally jumped out of her bedroll and spun in a circle of panic, the sun was blazing overhead and already hot enough to blur the horizon with shimmering heat waves.

"Good morning."

Whirling, she discovered Trace sitting near the firepit, smoking one of the thin, fragrant cigars that gambling men seemed to favor. Somehow he'd managed to untie his ankles. And the wrist manacles hadn't prevented him from poking up the fire or making a pot of coffee.

Sam swore. It was no thanks to her that he was still here and not miles away by now. She studied the spring grass that stubbled the plains like new green whiskers and she tried to guess how far Harden could have traveled while she slept on unaware.

"How did you get your feet untied?" Her heart beat erratically as she contemplated the disaster that might have been.

"Coffee's ready." He lifted his manacled wrists. "It would be more convenient if you poured."

Sam sat on a rock across from him and rubbed a finger over her teeth to clean them, staring at the stubble darkening Harden's chin and jaw. She would have given everything she owned to boast a few honest whiskers on her own chin. Sighing, she poured out two cups of coffee, grudgingly pleased to discover that Harden apparently didn't favor morning chat any more than she did.

"Do you want something to eat?" she inquired after she finished her second cup of coffee and could bear conversation. Her tone and an impatient glance at the sky made it clear that she would prefer to skip breakfast and get moving.

"No thank you."

"Good." The wrist manacles made him useless as far as any help with breaking camp. But Sam was accustomed to working while the outlaw in her custody sat on his duff and watched. Standing, she stretched her muscles, then lifted Harden's saddle with a grunt and carried it toward the horses.

After stumbling over a dead rabbit, she swung the saddle up on the gelding's back. Skittish, the horse rolled his eyes and danced away from her before Sam could fasten the cinch. Damn. Some mornings nothing went right.

A whirring erupted near her boot but Sam was focused on settling Harden's horse and she didn't register the significance of the rattling noise until a jab like a hot needle struck her lower leg. Startled, she leapt back and gazed down. Horror widened her eyes as she recognized a diamond-shaped pattern on the back of the snake coiling to strike again. Swiftly and instinctively, Sam whipped out her revolver and shot the rattler's head off.

"Kincade?" Harden stood, frowning toward the sound of the shot.

The Colt dropped from her fingertips and Sam stared down at her leg. Blood and straw-colored venom slowly soaked into her pant leg. Beneath the material, her skin burned as if a branding iron sizzled into her calf.

"No," she whispered. Horror darkened her eyes almost to black.

Somewhere far, far in the distance, she heard the gelding pawing at the prairie, heard Harden's saddle slide to the ground. Dry mouthed, her heart skipping and pounding, Sam lowered herself abruptly to a patch of grass. With shaking hands she found her pocketknife and ripped the blade up her pant leg from ankle to knee. Until she actually saw the puncture wounds, she hoped and prayed that she was only imagining the white-hot pain spreading toward her kneecap. The sight of twin fang marks paralyzed her.

"Lie back. We've got to get your boot off before the swelling starts!"

Sam blinked at Harden like he was an apparition that had materialized out of sweat and fear. "It was a rattler," she said stupidly, as if he couldn't see the snake's body not a hand's reach from where he knelt. "It's a draw. I killed him and he killed me."

When Harden jerked off her boot, a fiery sunburst of pain rocketed up her leg, momentarily blinding her. Choking and blinking furiously through pain-scalded tears, Sam only dimly perceived Trace Harden's surprise when he saw the key fall out of her boot. He understood at once what it was.

"Here!" He moved up beside her and thrust the key into her trembling fingers. "Open the cuffs. Do it, Kincade. If I'm going to help you, I need my hands free."

Pain and panic paralyzed her thoughts. She couldn't quite work out what he was asking. "What?"

His jaw clenched and his eyes glittered. "Damn it! Do what I'm telling you. Open the cuffs!"

Her hands shook so violently that she dropped the key, then missed the keyhole. When the cuffs finally fell beside the dead snake, Harden didn't even glance down. He thrust out his hand.

"Now your pocketknife. Give it to me."

He was going to kill her. It required all of two seconds for Sam to decide that she would far, far rather die from a slit throat than suffer the agonizing death that inevitably resulted from a rattler's bite. Venom poisoning was the most hideously painful death she had ever witnessed.

The decision made, she pressed herself flat on the ground and raised her chin to expose her throat. "Make it quick. Do it now." She didn't want time to ponder regrets or grieve about all the living she was going to miss. Self-pity had never been Sam Kincade's style; she didn't want to die badly.

A swift sting slashed across her leg, overlaying the fiery pain creeping corrosively beneath her skin. Gasping, strangling on scalding tears that she was powerless to halt, Sam shoved up on her elbows in time to see Harden fling the pocketknife behind him. She dashed the embarrassing tears aside and stared at a bloody X he had carved between the fang marks.

"Do you have any whiskey in your saddlebags?"

"No." Sam's eyes glazed over at the question. Whiskey was the only known remedy for snakebite. And she didn't have any.

"This is going to hurt like hell."

Harden lifted her leg to his knees, then bent his head and sucked hard on the wound.

Sam screamed. The pain was so intense that she thought she would faint or go insane. Blinded by tears of agony and terror, she struggled against waves of red and black just to remain conscious. Harden spit out mouthful after mouthful of blood thinned by yellowish venom. The pain of his sucking clawed at Sam's sanity, as unbearably painful as the scalding hot needles that stabbed and flowed beneath her skin. She screamed until her throat was raw and her voice shattered into hoarse ragged gasps.

"I've done the best I can," Harden announced finally, lowering her leg. He wiped his mouth across his sleeve. "All I'm getting is blood now. No more venom. There's no way to tell how much of it I got out. Probably damned little."

Shaking, Sam fell back on the ground and licked her lips, beginning to experience the excessive thirst characteristic of fatal snakebites. Nausea gripped her stomach, and her fingers trembled like dry twigs. Yellow acid boiled and bubbled in her veins, eating her flesh, chewing toward her thigh with molten teeth.

"Harden," she rasped, struggling for breath, unaware of the tears that fell off her cheeks and created little pools of mud beside her head. She blinked up at the heat-white sky, her pulse hammering like a kettle drum in her ears. "Have you ever heard of anyone surviving a rattler's strike?"

He looked away. "No."

"I haven't either."

The truth immobilized her. She was going to die, no way around it. And she was going to die in one of the most hideously painful ways imaginable. At the end she would lie soaked in her own sweat and vomit, paralyzed and laboring for every shallow breath as her lungs began to shut down. She would lose her vision, the use of her kidneys, and finally her mind. She would end screaming and begging to die.

"Please," Sam whispered, not sure if she was asking Harden to stay with her so she wouldn't die alone, or if she was asking him to shoot her now and spare her the unthinkable suffering that lay ahead.

Trace Harden's shadow fell across her as he stood, He gazed down at her for a long unreadable moment, then he turned and walked toward his horse.

CHAPTER

* 4 *

Acold spring rain stirred the street below into a gray stew of mud, manure, tobacco juice, and slops. The oozing muck sucked at boot heels and buggy wheels and overflowed the loose boards laid down as a walkway in front of the Imperial Hotel.

Hannibal lifted the curtain away from the window and gazed through the rain at a farmer kneeling in the mud laboring to clear heavy clods from a wagon wheel. In the room behind him Mattie Able nervously bounced on the hotel mattress, making the rusty bed springs sing like night music. A smell of wet wool wafted from her travel skirts. Water dripped from the sodden brim of her hat.

"Ain't you going to say nothing?" she asked finally, still testing the spring in the mattress. "Ain't you glad to see me? Glad I spotted you out of the train window?"

In the past her voice had usually exerted a soothing effect, but this afternoon the expectation glowing in her dark eyes grated on his nerves. Lately everything seemed to scrape his gizzard—the weather, missing the train, this jerk-water town.

Pueblo wasn't much larger than Dogtown, but Pueblo boasted a town marshall and an ongoing struggle for respectability. Hannibal didn't like towns in the best of times, and he especially disliked small towns where a stranger stood out like a badge on a lawman's vest. Such visibility was dangerous.

If Mattie Able hadn't bounded out of a passenger car and flung herself on him, he would have boarded his train and been fifty miles away by now. That he'd let her distract him to the point of missing his train kindled a slow flame of anger and disgust deep in his chest. If a snitch fingered him to the marshall, he'd have only himself to blame. And Mattie.

Letting the curtain drop across the window panes, Hannibal turned back to the room and straddled the only chair, studying Mattie in the rainy afternoon shadows while he tried to decide how much fault she bore for his predicament.

Once he had believed that Mattie Able was the prettiest whore east of the Rockies. But things had changed since his last trip to Trace's house in Kansas City.

"Hannibal, honey? Why're you staring at me like that?"

"What were you doing on the train to Santa Fe? Where did you think you were going?"

"I was going to the Holborn ranch to find you."

Giving him a coy smile, she unpinned the soggy hat and tossed it aside. The watery light dimmed her copper hair, deadening the highlights and dulling any shine.

"How did you know about the Holborn ranch?" he demanded sharply.

"You told me." She sat still and gave him an uncertain look.

Hannibal smashed his fist against the chair rail and swore. Damn his drunken hide. Liquor and a woman's body could unlock a man's lips faster than a load of powder could blow a safe. Though it was obvious that he must have, he didn't remember spilling anything about his hideout near Santa Fe.

Even if he'd told her, there was no way he could have anticipated that she would brazenly seek him out. That she had taken it upon herself to chase after him infuriated him. Because of her, he'd missed his train and now he would have to risk another day in Pueblo.

"You're going back to Denver tomorrow morning," he ordered. "You can stay there or return to Dogtown. It doesn't matter to me." He shrugged and rubbed the scars on his forehead. Whenever the weather changed, the scars near his eye irritated him. "There's nothing for you in Santa Fe."

Mattie smoothed her wet skirts around her, not looking at him. "I thought maybe the ranch could use a woman's touch. I'm a pretty fair cook. I know how to iron and put up a wash. I'm a hard worker and I don't complain much. I thought maybe you wouldn't mind having me around."

Hannibal hated woman-talk. A year ago he would have swatted her across the room for being an annoyance. He would have used his fist to remind her not to ask or expect anything from him. Now he amazed himself by experiencing a small skim of understanding for the plea in her eyes. He'd learned how it felt to yearn in the soul for something as far out of reach as a new beginning.

He did something he seldom attempted; he repressed his temper and tried to be straightforward. "I've been honest with you, Mattie. I told you that I don't want you anymore. You and I never amounted to much anyway."

He thanked God that the boys had gone ahead to the ranch. Pride would have forced him to silence anyone who overheard him talking this slop. "You've got your regulars, and I've got . . ." He stopped and ran a hand through his damp hair. "You and me . . . it was just a passing thing," he said, irritated that she didn't know. "Nothing important."

"Oh Hannibal." Mattie's eyes sparkled with amazement. "I never expected to hear you talk like this, open and all." As his gaze became a menacing glare, she added, "I love you, Hannibal. I think you care about me too."

"Aren't you listening?"

Any suggestions of sympathy vanished. He considered smacking her for making him sound like a pantywaist. The only reason he didn't hit her was because he wanted to avoid a ruckus that would draw attention. Standing abruptly, he reached in his jacket and removed the pouch of gold coins he'd robbed from the assayer's office in Leadville.

"Be on the morning train to Denver," he growled. Jamming his hat on his head, he tossed a couple of double eagles on the bed as he passed to the door. "There's enough for the room and a train ticket home. Board is included in the fare."

He was pressing the latch when she jumped off the bed and shouted, "Your brother is looking for you. Trace showed up in Dogtown, asking questions! I came to warn you!"

The blood rushed out of his head and he froze. Trace had never come looking for him. There could only be one reason why he'd come now.

When Hannibal turned back to the room, his eyes burned with a dangerous yellow flame. "If you're lying . . ."

The murky light grayed Mattie's powder and rouge; her lips were white. She clutched her wet skirt in both fists. Her expression wavered between fear and determination.

"I ain't lying! Trace told me he sold out his establishments and he's searching for you. The way he said it . . . Well, he ain't looking for a happy family reunion."

Hannibal nodded once, then made it back to the chair before he collapsed. Rolling his head backward, he stared at the shadows flitting across the ceiling, "Christ!"

Trace knew.

The sudden guilt of being found out squeezed Hannibal's chest.

In his whole sorry life Hannibal Cotwell had cared for only two people. That's all. No one else. And only two people had ever cared about him. He'd betrayed one of them.

Dropping forward, he massaged the scars on his forehead, swearing. Trace was the only person in the whole universe who had stuck by him and still cared about him. *Trace.* His kid brother had idolized him throughout their childhood, admiring him, emulating him. He had always believed there was something in Hannibal worth caring about. Of all the people in the world whom he could have betrayed, why had it been Trace?

"Did you tell Trace about the Holborn ranch?" he asked after a minute.

"No," Mattie said, looking insulted.

Facing Trace again was going to be one of the hardest things he would ever do. Acknowledging that he was glad it wouldn't happen soon added a feeling of shame.

"I can see you got some thinking to do," Mattie murmured, patting his shoulder and peering down at him. "I'll go downstairs and fetch us some supper."

Appalled by her sympathy, Hannibal tried to backhand her for witnessing his guilt, but he couldn't summon the energy to raise his arm.

In Hannibal's dreams, he appeared first as a child, confused and frightened, desperately trying to please his stepfather and inevitably failing. In the dreams Charles Harden's fury grew by leaps and bounds, unstoppable, building a deep dread in the child Hannibal's terrified mind, a helpless despair, the knowledge of his own powerlessness and insignificance.

His stepfather loomed as a dark giant with a heavy hand while his mother faded to a shadowy consort. Trace looked nothing like the Trace of reality. In the dreams, Trace was golden skinned, and yellow haired, and Hannibal was sick inside with envy of his brother's angelic demeanor. Sometimes Trace appeared wearing a princely crown, and in those dreams, Hannibal shook with hatred, wanting the crown and despising his brother for having it.

The dreams always began the same way, with Trace imploring his father not to beat Hannibal, and the boy Hannibal cringing in desperate hope that this time his brother's plea would be successful.

While Trace pleaded, Hannibal stared in frozen terror at the bullwhip writhing in Charles Harden's fist, hearing only the sick pounding of his own heart. In the dream the whip looked as long and lethal as it had in reality. But in the dream, he didn't know in advance that Trace's pleas would fail, so his despairing hope deepened his fear.

"Tie his wrists to the post!" came his stepfather's command, each word like a gunshot.

At this point in the dream, Trace always disappeared. And Hannibal was alone, trying to blink back tears of dread and terror. And he always asked the same confused, humiliating question.

"Why, papa? What did I do wrong?"

The question increased his stepfather's rage. He could hear the sound of Harden's boot heels striking the courtyard flagstones, hear the whip snaking forward. And he didn't know why, didn't know how he had failed this time, or what he could have done differently to earn a smile instead of the lash.

Even in the dreams, the pain of the whip biting into his bare back was excruciating. Once again, he experienced the warm gush of blood streaming down his spine and sides, felt the shock of flesh tearing and splitting. Sometimes he relived the agonizing moment when the tip of the lash had curled around and slashed his eyelid.

In the strange way of dreams, he aged between each blow of the whip, growing from age six to twenty-one. His body filled out, muscle grew, scars replaced scars. And his hatred intensified. The lashing continued, as did the mocking sound of Charles Harden's satisfaction. It went on and on and on until pain and rage brought Hannibal gasping out of sleep, ashamed of the moisture in his eyes.

Mattie raised her head out of the blankets and peered through the cold darkness toward the window. No wonder the air was frigid. Tumbling flakes of spring snow pelted the frosted panes.

She burrowed deeper beneath the covers and pressed herself close against the scars that crisscrossed Hannibal's naked back, listening to his drunken snores and inhaling the whiskey fumes that stirred around his head. He'd been as drunk as a man could get when they finally went to bed. But the only thing that mattered to Mattie was that he didn't shove her away.

He needed time. Mattie knew that. He could take as long as he wanted; she had all the time in the world. She was patient and she would wait.

Hannibal muttered something she couldn't make out and jerked the blankets over his shoulder. Mattie curved herself around his body and wished he would reach for her.

All the way from Dogtown, she had passed the time by thinking about what she knew and how much she would tell and when. Now, an hour before dawn and still sleepless, she berated herself for her cowardice. She'd made a mistake, not telling him everything immediately.

But his temper had intimidated her. She had feared that Hannibal would beat her senseless because she was the carrier of bad news.

She pressed her forehead against his back and closed her eyes. Maybe it was better that Hannibal didn't know exactly why Trace was looking for him. Let him think what he wanted. She could always tell him later that Trace's wife was dead.

Mattie decided she'd just wait and let events unfold. Besides, it was always wise to hold back a little something just in case things didn't work out the way she hoped.

* * *

By early afternoon the sun had melted the light fall of snow and warmed the air, but the thin sunshine wasn't warm enough to dry the mud in the streets.

Mattie stood at the window gazing across the river toward the depot, inhaling the stink of the mud and a nearby tannery.

"Yes sir, it's turning into a fine day," she repeated.

Hannibal had dressed, but so far he hadn't spoken a word, hadn't touched the breakfast or lunch tray she had carried upstairs from the hotel dining room. He sprawled on the bed like a man fresh shot, staring at the ceiling. Mattie had gazed at enough ceilings in her time to know there were no answers up there.

"It's pretty near time for our train," she announced brightly. Dipping her head, she peered into the bureau mirror and pinned on the hat she had boosted from Big Sal. The brim was rain-warped and the velvet cherries squashed, but it was still serviceable.

Hannibal swung his boots to the floor. "You're not coming with me," he said in a tired voice.

"It's a long walk to the depot," Mattie reminded him, tucking his razor and soap into her tapestry bag. She didn't care that he hadn't shaved this morning. What mattered was that the Denver train had come and gone hours ago. Satisfied that she hadn't overlooked anything, she closed the tapestry bag and straightened. "We should get started. Better a minute early than a minute late."

He slapped her against the wall as casually as he would have swatted a fly off his jacket. "You're not going to Santa Fe."

Mattie slid down the wall, her face ablaze, her ears ringing. A minute passed before she realized there had been no fire or real conviction behind Hannibal's slap. It hardly hurt at all. She'd been right. This had to mean that he cared for her, at least a little.

"I'm going with you."

She picked herself up, dusted off her skirts, and straightened her hat. She considered searching through the tapestry bag for powder to minimize the mark on her cheek. But there wasn't time if they were going to catch their train. After pulling on her gloves, she gripped the handle of her bag and dragged it into the hotel corridor.

"I'm not taking you with me."

Progress with men occurred in small increments. Mattie took it as encouragement that they had progressed from "You're not going" to "I'm not taking you."

Bent over, her fanny wagging in the air, she dragged the tapestry bag toward the staircase.

When she looked back, Hannibal was standing in the doorway of the room, scowling with an expression that told Mattie he wasn't seeing her at all. Shocked by his appearance, she straightened and studied him in the dim corridor light.

He was only thirty-five, but he looked older, like a busted-up old cowboy who had taken one too many kicks. Dark stubble peppered his jaw and the whites of his eyes were reddened. The news about Trace had hit him hard.

"Hannibal, honey," she called softly, her heart

flowing toward him. Despite the knot of scars on his forehead and the scar that pulled at his eyelid, he was a handsome man, rugged and dangerous looking. "Would you mind giving me a hand with this here bag?"

He stared at her for a full minute before he walked forward and kicked the tapestry bag down the staircase. Without a word, he shoved past her, stamped down the stairs, and strode across the tiny lobby.

Mattie hurried after him, smiling inside where he couldn't see. Yes sir, she thought, following him toward the bridge, skimming her bag along the surface of the mud. Given a little time things were going to work out just fine.

CHAPTER

* 5 *

A hand lifted Sam's head and the lip of a tin cup clicked against her teeth. She swallowed the water frantically, greedily, desperate to quench a thirst that could not be appeased. As the cup disappeared from sight, she was again half crazed by thirst, weeping and begging for another sip.

Her mouth tingling, she dropped back on the sweat-soaked horse blanket beneath her and gazed through a yellow haze at the canopy of interlocking branches curving above her.

Wait. Blinking through a feverish sweat, Sam strained to lift her head and stared hard. Those weren't sage branches and strips of sod above her. With rising horror she realized she was peering at a ceiling formed out of writhing, twisting, nesting snakes. Snakes as small as finger bones to snakes as thick as her wrist. Brown snakes and yellow snakes,

78

and snakes colored gray and silver. They slithered, spitting and hissing, amassing to spring down on her.

Choking and paralyzed with terror, Sam turned her head and vomited. She tried to scream, but she fainted instead.

On several occasions she glimpsed an angel, but she couldn't be certain if he was real or a delirious fabrication. A white collar framed his bearded face. His hands were cool as he bathed the sweat and vomit from her naked body. She wanted to ask where his wings were as she couldn't see them, but her tongue was too swollen to form coherent speech. He murmured words she couldn't understand, holy words she guessed, but she didn't have to comprehend his angel language to understand he was trying to help her. Sympathy and encouragement beamed in his brown and gold eyes. Sometimes she was so deeply grateful not to be dying alone that she gripped his hand and wept as helplessly as a newborn.

Eventually the day arrived when Sam began to realize that she was not going to die as she had expected, or as she had wanted during the worst of her agony. The yellow haze slowly faded from her vision and she recognized the underside of the lean-to in true colors of brown and gray and pale silvery green. Now she identified the sweet pungent scent of sage. Her mouth stopped tingling and no longer felt painful or numb. Thirst continued to plague her, but not as urgently as before, and she had ceased vomiting. She was no longer naked but dressed in her spare set of clothing.

Breathing deeply, she thought she smelled roasting meat and saliva flooded her mouth. Surely the hint of an appetite signaled that she had passed the crisis point.

"Lift your head." As she heard the deep, soothing voice of her angel, his hand slipped behind her shoulders and supported her back, helping her rise.

The bland taste of pocket soup disappointed her. She was hungry for real meat, though she suspected her stomach wouldn't retain solids yet. It was frightening to discover how weak she was. The effort to steady the cup, even to swallow, made her tremble and left her exhausted.

After finishing the soup, she fell heavily back on the horse blanket, sweating and panting. A damp cloth wiped her face, lips, and the dribbles of soup leaking down her throat.

"Well I'll be damned," Sam croaked, looking up. A rush of amazement and embarrassment provided a small burst of energy. "I thought you left me to die."

The sudden rasp of her whisper caused Trace Harden to jump as if she'd lashed him with a willow whip. He sat beside her and stared. If it hadn't been for those amber-colored tiger eyes, Sam didn't think she would have recognized him. A ragged dark beard and mustache concealed his lower face. A wave of dust-darkened hair dropped over one eye.

"You're going to make it." He sounded incredulous. "It must have been the rabbit." When he noticed her confusion, his beard shifted in what might have been a smile. "I'm guessing the rattler struck a rabbit shortly before it struck you. Therefore you didn't get a full injection of venom."

Sam couldn't follow what he was saying. Her mind was stuck on the surprising revelation that he hadn't run off, and on the dawning embarrassment that she had mistaken Trace Harden for an angel.

"You saved my life," she whispered, too weak to do anything but gaze up at his bearded face. He wore a ruffled white shirt lined with dust. No jacket, no tie. And, of course, no wings. Struggling, Sam tried to square her delusion of Trace Harden as an angel with her conviction that he had to be an outlaw as unprincipled and ruthless as his brother.

"Tonight we'll try solid food. Venison stew." When he read the question in her tired eyes, he added, "Animals come to the spring. Food hasn't been a problem." A smile crinkled his eyes. "I borrowed your rifle."

Sam fought through tides of weakness and exhaustion to frame a question. "How . . . long?"

"We've been here eight days."

The shock of losing eight days was nearly as great as the dismay of realizing she owed her life to Hannibal Cotwell's brother. With her mind spinning, Sam closed her eyes and curled on the horse blanket, almost instantly dropping into a restless sleep disturbed by prickles of receding pain.

By the next afternoon she was able to sit up, and could concentrate for longer periods. When Harden joined her beneath the lean-to to escape the heat of the afternoon sun, Sam looked down and bit her lip. Her cheeks turned crimson.

"I was naked for days," she whispered. All morning she had been thinking about Trace Harden observing her naked body, touching her. Outrage formed her first response, followed by grinding mortification, and finally a warm fluttery uneasiness that she couldn't put a name to.

Clasping his arms around his knees, Trace leaned against a corner pole and gazed outside at their campsite. "It was easier that way to keep you clean and cool."

An angry sigh depressed her chest. "Well, I guess you know the truth now. You were right about me," she admitted.

Humiliation burned her cheeks and she couldn't have looked at him if the fate of the world had depended on it. It made her feel peculiar and resentful, knowing a man had seen her naked.

A deeply disturbing sense of vulnerability troubled Sam's mind. She'd never felt so exposed or defenseless in her life. The man sitting beside her had seen her helpless, weeping, at her absolute worst. He'd held her life in his hands; he still did for that matter. Because of his intimate knowledge, Sam was forced into an unavoidable closeness that she had never experienced with another living human being.

And there was something else that was equally distressing. Because she knew Trace had seen her as a woman, Sam suddenly felt an acute awareness of him as a man. She inhaled the sharp sensual scent of male sweat, studied his beard out of the corner of her eyes, stared at the long length of muscle beneath his pant leg, noticed the tension in his thigh.

These simple observations increased the fluttery strangeness she felt inside, a nervousness that was raw and wanting and tight and feverish. It was exciting and frightening at the same time, and it made her feel unsure and awkward in his presence.

"If you're up to some conversation, I'm more than a little curious why a lovely young woman would tape down her breasts, chop off her hair, dress as a man, and choose to be a bounty hunter. I'm also curious about the scar on your side. It looks like an old bullet wound."

Sam felt him studying her. To provide an outlet for her nerves, she plucked at the fuzz balling on the horse blanket. She swatted a fly, concentrated on a bead of sweat that rolled down her neck and then soaked into her shirt.

"It's a long story," she said finally, speaking in a low voice.

"We'll be here until you're strong enough to ride. Which won't be anytime soon," Harden pointed out.

He passed her a canteen, then tilted his head back and mopped a handkerchief over his throat. Sam stared at the cords rising on his neck, feeling a sick fascination. Every tiny gesture he made seemed vastly interesting and worthy of attention. She couldn't imagine when this had happened or why.

Dropping her gaze, Sam swallowed the tightness constricting her throat. "Are the horses all right?"

"They're fine."

"There's plenty of water?"

"It rained about a week ago and replenished the spring."

Sam wondered if venom still pickled her brain. That might explain the effect his hands were having on her. The shape of his palm and the elegant length of his gambler's fingers seemed wildly erotic, his movements sensual. These strange thoughts came from a person who had never before characterized any man as even remotely enticing. But she kept picturing his hands on her naked skin; she wished she could remember his touch. Sam gave herself an irritated shake. What the hell was the matter with her? She had to halt these crack-brained thoughts.

"Listen . . . it's not my fault that I'm a woman. I didn't ask to be one. Are you going to tell everyone?"

"Tell me something." Raising an eyebrow, he met her sidelong gaze with a look of curiosity. "How many outlaws have you brought in since you've been a bounty hunter?"

"One hundred and thirty-four. Not counting you," she said proudly. "And I only had to kill two of them."

Harden stared, then threw back his head and laughed. "Not one of them guessed you were a woman?" he asked, grinning at her.

Sam stiffened and narrowed her eyes. "Did you know? For sure?" He had fine teeth, straight and as white as a Chinaman's shirt. With a sinking feeling,

Sam realized she enjoyed his laugh too. The sound reminded her of thunder and gravel rolling together.

"I suspected from the first time I saw you."

"Well, no one else has," she huffed, jerking upright. "I'm damned good at what I do! If I hadn't got snake bit, your butt would be sitting in the Denver jail right now!"

His grin widened. "If it came out that a hundred and thirty-four outlaws had been captured by a mere slip of a girl, those men would never live it down."

"I'm not a mere slip, damn it!" The starch faded from Sam's gaze and her shoulders slumped. "I knew this would happen. You're going to tell, aren't you?"

Trace hesitated, then shrugged. "I'll keep your secret."

Relief lightened Sam's mind before she remembered that she couldn't trust Trace Harden. He was Hannibal Cotwell's brother, for God's sake, by association and definition a liar, a thief, and probably a murderer. But if she couldn't trust the man who had saved her life when he didn't have to, who hadn't escaped when golden opportunity came knocking, then who in the hell could she trust? Lifting her hands, Sam rubbed at the confusion throbbing in her temples.

"I'm tired," she announced abruptly, stretching out on the horse blanket and pointedly turning her back to him.

Once the trap was sprung and Hannibal was captured, then her goal would be accomplished and she'd be free to begin her real life. The problem was she didn't know what her real life might be. She wouldn't live as a defenseless woman, that was certain. She wished to hell that Trace didn't know about her. Sam was almost asleep, lulled by the afternoon heat and the drowsy buzzing of flies, when Harden spoke again.

"It requires tremendous courage to confront hardened outlaws, and a lot of skill to subdue them. What you've accomplished would be impressive for a man. For a woman, it's damned amazing." Sam heard a smile lighten his voice. "Remind me never to play poker with you. You can bluff better than anyone I ever ran across."

Surprise and a burst of pride popped Sam's eyes open. She didn't receive so many compliments that she knew how to handle them, so she didn't roll over to look at him. She held herself as still as a dead man until Harden left the lean-to.

Oddly, the professional praise wasn't the compliment that kept jumping around her thoughts. The comment she replayed like a mysterious echo was: "a lovely young woman." No one had ever directed such a statement to Sam Kincade. It had never even entered her thoughts that anyone might consider her lovely. She didn't want them to. Therefore, it puzzled her greatly that she yearned to ask Harden exactly what there was about her that he considered lovely. Had he made an empty off-the-cuff remark, or did he really see something in her that truly might be considered lovely?

"Oh God!" Disgust exploded from her lips.

Bounty hunters were not lovely. Gunslingers were not lovely. People obsessed by revenge were not lovely. Sam didn't want to be lovely. She wanted to be a man. She wanted to be the roughest, toughest, meanest pistol-packing, sod-blasting SOB who ever flung a murdering pig-butt through a jailhouse door. Still . . .

Maybe, she thought, Trace was referring to her naked body. She hadn't observed another woman's nakedness so she didn't know how she compared. For all she knew, it could be possible that she had a lovely body. Stranger things had happened. She wished she could think of a non-humiliating way to ask him.

Moaning, Sam ground her forehead against the hot and prickly horse blanket. She had never felt so confused in her life. If these were the kind of emotions a woman had to endure, then she was right not to be one.

The continued delay while he waited for Sam to regain her strength created a restlessness as frustrating as an itch that he couldn't reach. By now Mattie Able's trail would be as cold as old ashes. Reluctantly, Trace accepted that his best hope of seeing Hannibal pay for his violence and betrayal, was to offer himself as bait and rely on Judge Mockton's trap.

He stopped reading aloud and set aside Sam's volume of Voltaire's writings. "How trustworthy is this Judge Mockton?"

"In what regard?"

"In regard to my neck. If I understand the plan you outlined, it might be necessary to conduct a sham trial. If so, your plan works only if I'm sentenced to hang. The verdict is a foregone conclusion." He considered the back of her head. "It strikes me there is a very real chance that I could actually hang. This might be a good time to mention there's a limit to the extent to which I'm willing to commit to this scheme."

She was sitting in the opening of the lean-to, her back propped against a saddle, watching the wind ruffle the wildflowers that had burst into bloom during the past few days. When she turned to answer, her jaw-length hair, shining with brown and gold highlights from a recent wash in the spring, swung back to expose a strong, clean profile.

"You won't hang. You have my word on that," she promised.

Trace studied her. "I guess I have to rely on your word."

"My word is my honor. It's as good as gold. I know I said I was taking you in to be hanged, but that was just scare talk. Actually hanging you is not and never was part of the plan. That is, unless the judge can unearth a legitimate hanging offense. Which you swear he can't, so you don't need to worry."

"I've never done worse than brace a game or two. And that was years ago."

She nodded. "Well, there you are. Besides, the judge isn't going to hang the man who saved the life of his only relative."

"Ah." One of the pieces of the Sam Kincade puzzle fell into place. "So that's how a woman got hired as a bounty hunter."

She frowned when he made reference to her sex. "You're wrong. My great-uncle doesn't know I'm a woman. He thinks I'm my dead brother. The judge wasn't real pleased when a relative he didn't know about showed up on his doorstep asking for work. If I ran into real trouble, I'd like to believe that he'd support me—grudgingly—but I'd be repaying him for the rest of my life."

"Your uncle never questioned your assertion that you were male?"

Having seen her naked, Trace now found it incredible that anyone could be fooled. He forgot that he had been willing to accept her as a boy. Everything about her now seemed abundantly female, from her narrow wrists and ankles to her full lips and the sensual curve of her throat. Unfettered by the ridiculous bands of cloth he'd discovered wrapped around her chest, her breasts thrust against her shirt, her nipples prominent as she sat in the lean-to's entrance and the wind molded flannel to skin.

Her slow recovery exposed a softness that he hadn't suspected in Sam Kincade. Occasionally he believed he caught glimpses of the young woman she might have been had life treated her more kindly. When this new, oddly vulnerable Sam Kincade smiled at him, his chest tightened and he saw her as a vital, desirable woman.

Feeling an uncomfortable stirring, he frowned and looked away. Since earliest childhood he had been surrounded by striking women, first in his father's gaming establishments, later in his own. Women who understood the power of beauty and the female body, who employed the charms of lace and ribbon and satin and silk to alluring advantage. Such examples of femininity had formed his preference.

Never had he conceived the puzzling possibility that he might be attracted to a woman so alien to all he admired and considered desirable in the fair sex—a rough-hewn woman with hacked-off hair, blunt speech, bold mannerisms, and the habit of meeting his eye as squarely as a man. Sam didn't possess a single feminine charm that he had noticed. She was in fact an enigma as intriguing as a new pack of cards. Perhaps that was why she was beginning to fascinate him.

"When I was eleven," she said suddenly, speaking in a low voice and staring at the far horizon, "my mother and I went to the jailhouse in Cottonwood, Kansas, to take supper to a prisoner. My father was the town sheriff. He'd captured one of the men who'd robbed the Cottonwood bank."

She fell silent for a full minute. "I adored my father. I wanted to be just like him. He taught me to fish and to shoot. To ride and to think. He and my mother used to argue over how he dressed me and treated me like a boy, like Samuel, my brother who died."

Looking down, she picked at her fingernails. Trace had to lean forward to hear. "My father wasn't at the jail when my mother and I arrived. Neither was the deputy. While we were waiting, Hannibal Cotwell and three members of his gang burst in the door and freed the man in the cell."

Restless, she lifted her head again and gazed at a single cloud hanging motionless in the sky. "They were mean drunk. Hannibal and two of his men raped my mother on top of my father's desk while I watched. When it was over, my mother slid to the floor. She slumped there crying and saying over and over that she wished she were dead." Sam drew up her shoulders and the air hissed out of her in a long, angry sound. "So Hannibal shot her."

Trace nodded, his mouth tight. She told the story simply, reducing it to the flat essential elements. But he heard the emotion shaking her voice.

"I swore to my mother as she was dying that I would avenge her death."

"You're sure the outlaw was Hannibal?" It disgusted him to realize that even now, he fought the idea that his brother was capable of such atrocities.

She whipped around to face him, her eyes blazing blue fire. "He was looking at me while he raped my mother! I'm damned sure it was Hannibal! I'll never forget those eyes! After he killed my mother, he shot me too." An unconscious hand pressed the old scar on her side. "It's no thanks to him that I'm still alive."

Turning away, she crawled out of the lean-to and stood, facing the mountain caps rimming the horizon. Her fists curled into tight balls at her sides.

"My father blamed himself for not being in the office when Hannibal came, and for not posting a deputy. He blamed himself for my mother's death. Three months later he stretched out between her grave and Samuel's and blew his brains out. People said he did it because he loved her, as if killing himself was romantic and admirable. As if he owed it to her or some damned thing. Except, what about me?"

Trace watched her whirl to face him, her face reddened with the effort of telling, her eyes shattered by remembered pain.

"Was it romantic and admirable to leave me all alone? Didn't he owe me something? Those men would have raped me too except they thought I was a boy because I was wearing my fishing overalls. Nobody seemed to notice that I got shot too. I needed someone to care about me, to tell me why . . ."

"Sam—"

"That's why I detest Hannibal Cotwell! That's why I won't rest until he's dead! He destroyed my family. He did it as casually as tipping a howdy-do. I'll bet he doesn't even remember what happened on that day twelve years ago in Cottonwood, Kansas. He raped her and he killed her, Harden, and he never even knew her name! He didn't care that Jenny Kincade was shy and gentle and sang songs while she cooked. He didn't know that she read Voltaire and Rousseau or that she played the piano. And he might as well have fired the bullet that killed my father! He destroyed all of us."

"What happened afterward?" Trace inquired after a period of silence.

"No one knew I had any relatives, and I didn't remember the judge until I found some of my grandmother's letters. But that was years after the killings. Preacher Moss and his wife took me in after my father died. They didn't want to, but it would have looked bad if they'd ignored their Christian duty and let me starve on the streets. In me they got a servant and someone to preach and shout at, and I got something in my stomach and a roof over my head." She shrugged. "It worked out for all of us."

She crawled back into the lean-to, out of the sun, and lay down on the horse blanket, flinging an arm over her eyes. "I swore I'd track down Hannibal Cotwell and kill him if it took the rest of my life. Hating Cotwell kept me going during those years with Preacher Moss and his wife. Hating him has kept me going since. Hating your brother is why I became a bounty hunter, because the job gives me movement and information and a chance to find him. Despising Hannibal Cotwell is the fire in my belly that burns me alive and gives me a reason to face each day. I won't rest until I spit on his grave!"

The intensity of her hatred scalded the air inside the lean-to. But Trace had gazed through the window she had opened, and he had seen her wounds and glimpsed a deep and painful loneliness. He touched her shoulder, then left her to reassemble her shell in privacy.

"My leg's still stiff and sore," Sam remarked two days later. "But I should be able to ride. We'll head out in the morning."

She tilted her cards to the light of the fire, then fanned them out on the ground with a shout of triumph. "Four sevens beats your full house!"

"Damn it!" Scowling, Harden watched her scoop up the pebbles they had designated as dollars. "I knew I shouldn't play poker with you."

"If we were playing for real money, you'd owe me more than two hundred dollars!" She grinned, rubbing it in. "Deal 'em."

He'd guessed correctly. Sam was as hard to read as the sands of time, a natural player. She didn't betray a flicker when she studied her hand. And she'd won several hands without any covert assistance from him. Gathering the cards, Trace tapped them back into the box.

"I'm not playing another round against someone who's coasting the longest lucky streak I've seen in a year of Sundays," he announced with mock bitterness.

"Lucky streak my fanny!" Eyes shining, she grinned at him. Her pleasure made her appear about sixteen years old. And heartachingly lovely. "The trouble is, no one's going to believe that I beat Trace Harden in a fair game."

"My mind was on other things," he growled, reaching for the coffee pot.

"Whooee," she laughed, falling back on the ground and smiling up at the stars. "If that isn't a lame excuse, I never heard one. What were you thinking about so hard that you forgot to deal yourself a couple of aces off the bottom? I know you can do it. I've watched you practice. You can make those cards sit up and whistle Dixie."

"I told you. I never cheat." He clasped the hot tin cup between his palms and gazed into the flames. "If you want the truth, I was thinking about Hannibal."

She sat up abruptly. "I was wondering when you were going to tell your story," she said levelly.

He hadn't lied. Hannibal was never far from his thoughts. The same fire in the belly that drove Sam drove him too. Whenever he had a moment free from distractions, as during the long silent days waiting for Sam to die or recover, Hannibal towered in his mind, shoving his thoughts down dark corridors.

Several minutes elapsed before he spoke. "Hannibal's father died when Hannibal was four," he said, speaking to the flames. "Our mother remarried and I was born on Hannibal's fifth birthday." He watched the firelight reflecting on the black and metal sides of the coffee pot.

"Where was this?"

"My father owned three gaming establishments in New Orleans. We had a house overlooking Lake

Pontchartrain, and a townhouse in the French Quarter. Hannibal and I grew up exploring the back bayous in the summer and chasing through the alleyways of town during the cool season. We knew where the swamp deer mated and where Monsieur La Bouge kept his high-yellow mistress."

Memories of childhood overwhelmed him, as vivid as the flames. He could see the room he and Hannibal had shared at Five Oaks; he remembered the pranks they had played on the servants, and how they had snuck away to discover the hidden nooks and crannies of old New Orleans, its sins and delights. Trace had possessed an unerring nose when it came to sniffing out that which would most excite and thrill two boys with a daring sense of adventure.

But when they were caught, it was Hannibal who bore the punishment for their transgressions.

Trace covered his eyes. Only dimly did he recall Sam, sitting before him in silence. He spoke to himself.

"It's a terrible thing to be the favored son," he said quietly. "A terrible guilt to watch another be punished for your crimes, small boyhood crimes redressed by a man's punishment. My father hated Hannibal. It wasn't until four months ago that I understood the possible reason. I found a portrait of Hannibal's father in my mother's effects. Hannibal is the spitting image of my mother's first husband."

A hundred examples of his own favored status depressed his thoughts. One would serve for all.

"When I was sixteen and Hannibal twenty-one, we

pawned three of my mother's silver spoons and took the money to the Chat Chat with the idea that we would win our fortunes. At my mother's request, my father had forbidden us entrée to the gaming tables, but we thought we would not be recognized at Monsieur Renault's establishment." Glancing toward a coyote's howl, Trace gazed into the night. "My father came for us. He tied Hannibal to a post in the townhouse courtyard and lashed him until . . ." He shook his head, unable to put the horror of it into words. "Hannibal will bear the scars from those beatings for the rest of his life."

"And you?" Sam asked.

"I was petted and praised as my father's natural heir. The escapade was lauded as amusing proof that I was destined to follow my father's successes, that my future lay in gaming. I told my father it was I who stole the spoons, I who persuaded Hannibal to accompany me, I who conceived the idea to disobey our parents' wishes. The truth didn't matter. Hannibal was lashed just short of crippling; I was rewarded with motherly kisses and fatherly pride. That's how it was throughout our childhood." He let a silence develop. "Hannibal could have hated me for being the favored son, but he didn't."

The night of that last beating, guilt had driven Trace to his bed with a sickness of spirit and a fever he had tried to pretend was as agonizing as stripes laid deep across a bloody back. Hannibal's screams shrieked through his nightmares, echoing from dozens of beatings almost as brutal and debilitating

as the one in the courtyard, and equally as undeserved.

"Hannibal never understood. Who could? He tried
to please my father for so many years," Trace continued in a low voice. "Finally, understandably, he gave
up. The beatings began when he was a child and
ended that night in the courtyard. The day his back
healed to the extent that he could walk without lau-
danum and the aid of a cane, Hannibal beat my father nearly to death and then he rode out of New
Orleans. He joined the Confederacy, but he deserted
a few months later. He never found a place for himself."

"Poor Hannibal," Sam said coldly, her voice shaking with anger and sarcasm.

Trace's head snapped up and his vision cleared.
"There are reasons why people become who and
what they are," he said sharply. "Can you say for certain that you aren't riding around the west dressed as
a male because you wanted to please your father
when you were a child? Because he wanted a son
and you're still trying to be the son he wanted? Or
could you be hiding in pants because once you were
mistaken for a boy and that mistake saved you from
being raped alongside your mother?"

"Shut up, Harden! Just shut the hell up!"

"Maybe Hannibal rapes women in an effort to
punish a mother who never interceded on his behalf.
Maybe he kills men who remind him of Charles
Harden. Hannibal stopped feeling, stopped caring
about anyone or anything years before you were

born. Trust and justice and kindness and fairness and all sense of human decency were beaten out of him before he was into long pants. And why? Because he was guilty of resembling a dead man, his father. Because he wasn't the favorite son. I don't excuse what my brother became. There is no excuse. But there are reasons."

Sam's fist flew out of the night so unexpectedly that Trace had no time to prepare. The blow knocked him off the rock he was sitting on, spilled cold coffee over his vest and pants. He raised a hand to his jaw, probed his back teeth with his tongue.

"Don't you dare defend Hannibal Cotwell, you son of a bitch," Sam shouted, standing over him shaking with fury. "I don't care what happened to Cotwell when he was a child. I care what happened to me when *I* was a child! I don't want to hear about your guilt and I don't want to hear apologies or excuses for your evil animal of a brother! He's a scourge on the earth! I don't care how he got that way, I just want him dead!"

Trace grabbed her ankle when she tried to kick him and he jerked her to the ground. Rolling on top of her, he pinned her wrists against the dirt.

"Listen to me," he said between his teeth, his eyes burning in the starlight, his mouth inches from hers. "I want Hannibal dead as much as you do! For years I made excuses, defended him, blindly looked the other way. I remembered the boy and refused to see what the man had become! I was wrong. Is that what you want to hear? That I believe he's as evil as you do?"

She bucked under him, twisting and turning beneath the weight of his body. The heat of her hatred seared into his groin. Her breath was hot and hissing against his face.

"Sam, listen to me! Hannibal raped my wife! He held her prisoner in our home while I was in New Orleans settling our mother's estate. He sent the servants away and he raped her again and again for two goddamned weeks. He used her and made her pregnant. My *brother* did that! Because of what Hannibal did to her, Etta hanged herself!"

Sam stopped struggling and went quiet beneath his body, staring up at him with eyes so dark they looked black.

"There's no excuse, no justification. No possible forgiveness. He has to pay for what he did to my wife."

Trace rolled off of her. Hands trembling, he removed Etta's letter from his vest pocket and thrust it into Sam's fingers before he strode out onto the ink-dark prairie.

"Etta wasn't as blind as I was. She recognized that Hannibal was a ruthless outlaw. But at my insistence, she welcomed my brother into our home. She helped me create a safe haven for him. And she paid for my blindness with her life."

He pulled a hand down his face, then jerked on his beard until his jaw erupted in pain.

"My wife chose suicide rather than life with a

rapist's child in her body. She couldn't bear to face my pain when I learned the brother I had defended and welcomed into our home was as evil as everyone recognized except me. It's all there, in the letter she left beneath her wedding ring."

Silently, Sam carried the letter closer to the fire and tilted it toward the light. Etta Harden's spidery handwriting flowed across three pages. The letter corroborated Trace Harden's obvious pain.

Etta's missive began with a detailed account of how Hannibal had forced her at knifepoint to dismiss the servants, how he had raped her again and again until she bled in her marriage bed and wept for mercy. She had pleaded that he remember his love for Trace and Trace's unflagging loyalty when all others had forsaken him, and Hannibal had laughed. He had beaten her and threatened to take her to a place where Trace would never find them. When she had feared pregnancy and wept for her beloved husband's loss of honor and her own shame, Hannibal had struck her and insisted that Trace was so trusting and stupid he would never question the child as his own.

On the last page she begged Trace to forgive her for lacking the courage to live as a constant reminder of Hannibal's treachery, for choosing death rather than shame and a memory too agonizing to endure. Specifically, she implored Trace to forgive his brother for her abuse and death, and not to hunt Hannibal down like the mad animal he was and kill him as he deserved.

After reading the letter through a second time, Sam let the pages fall shut along folds that had been creased so many times the paper had begun to tear. Carefully she placed the pages on a rock near the fire and anchored them with Trace's coffee cup.

Etta's letter was as lethal as arsenic. Surely, she must have understood that her story, and the inflammatory words with which she chose to relate it, would send Trace out to kill the brother who had destroyed his wife, regardless of her saintly request for forgiveness.

Sam didn't buy it. Etta Harden wanted Hannibal dead by her husband's hand. Rage simmered beneath the meek words begging Trace to forgive his brother for that which was unforgivable.

In no way did Sam fault the woman for wishing Hannibal dead. Hannibal's crime against Etta and his own brother demanded blood payment. But the manner in which Etta manipulated her revenge—by pleading against it—left a sour taste in Sam's mouth.

Before she crawled into the lean-to she spoke quietly to the black silhouette standing tense and alone on the night-dark prairie.

"I'm sorry, Trace." She drew a breath. "We'll leave for Denver at sunup. We'll ride straight through without stopping."

CHAPTER

* 6 *

They rode across the rising prairie side by side, the intimacy they had shared during the preceding two weeks diminished with each silent hour that passed.

Sam watched the mountains growing taller against the sky as the land lifted and the miles rolled beneath the horse's hooves. Whenever Trace's gelding moved ahead of her and she was forced to look at him, rancor made her eyes burn.

She deeply resented that Trace had placed the image of Hannibal as an abused and rejected child in her mind. Her imagination now painted a sad portrait of a confused boy seeking approval and affection where only indifference and punishment could be found. Sam despised the ghostly outlines of sympathy that struggled to gain substance when she thought about Hannibal's youth. Until a few days earlier, it had never occurred to her that Hannibal Cotwell had even been a child with parents and a

103

family. To her, he had sprung full-blown into a ruthless and merciless rapist killer.

Not until they halted in late afternoon to stretch their legs and boil some coffee and soup did Sam realize she was nursing her resentment, employing it as a brake against the growing attraction muddling her thoughts.

After miles of pondering strange new feelings—and hotly remembering the weight of Trace's body on top of hers—Sam concluded that her fascination with every detail about Trace Harden could only be due to gratitude. Naturally she'd feel grateful toward the man who had saved her life, and her gratitude would lead to curiosity and an inevitable bonding caused by their unique circumstance. Finding a name for her peculiar sensations offered vast mental relief. Unfortunately, doing so didn't extinguish Sam's feverish emotions.

Humming beneath his breath, Trace watered the horses and staked them, then he stretched out on the ground and accepted a cup of coffee.

"Don't be too hard on your father," he remarked after a period of silence.

"I beg your pardon?"

"You can't guess how it feels to be responsible for a wife, to swear you'll protect and keep her safe, then not be there the one time she needs you most. It's the worst failure a man can experience; the sense of guilt is crippling."

Sam stretched her neck against her hand. "You

didn't put a gun in your mouth and pull the trigger. My father did."

"I can understand how he made that choice." Trace watched her rub her sore leg, then lean to the fire and give the soup a violent stir. "Have you ever loved anyone, Sam?"

"I loved my parents."

"Since you were an adult?"

She shrugged. "I don't let anyone close to me."

Despite the agony of her battle to survive the snakebite, the time spent with Trace had been the best two weeks of her adult life. There was something sad in that. It didn't say much for the quality of her so-called life. Worse, she suspected that from now on her life would divide into the time before Trace and the time after Trace.

"Then you don't know the extent of your father's loss, or his sense of failure, or his guilt. Don't judge Daniel Kincade until you've walked in his boots."

"I don't recall requesting your advice," Sam snapped. It appalled and angered her to sense how important Trace had become, how difficult it was going to be to say good-bye.

Turning her back on him, she faced the distant mountains and thought about his remarks. Trace made it sound as if he were discussing Sam's parents, but she guessed he was talking about Etta and his own guilt. A sharp jab of jealousy pierced Sam's chest. All this talk about love and guilt made her wonder what it would be like to love someone enough to feel half insane at their loss, to be so devoted or so deluded that it seemed reasonable to put a gun in your mouth and pull the trigger, or to sell everything you owned and ride west to avenge the loved one's honor. She half-wished she felt that powerfully about someone. Or that someone felt that strongly about her.

These yearnings were so bizarre and so foreign to everything she was that Sam gave herself a shake and laughed out loud.

Trace lifted an eyebrow, waited a moment, then asked, "What will you do when the trap is sprung and Hannibal is in custody? What's next for Samantha Kincade?"

"Don't call me Samantha!" she objected sharply, her smile snapping into a glare. After shoving a tin cup of soup in his direction, she settled on the ground and frowned into her own cup. "Actually, I wish you hadn't asked those questions. They remind me of a problem that I wish would go away."

"If you don't want to discuss it . . ." he said with an elegant shrug, then frowned when she mumbled something. "I'm sorry, I didn't hear?"

"I said my great-uncle insists that I marry Millicent Snow. It's a serious problem." She scowled, daring him to utter a word. "Edwin Snow—that's Millicent's father—has offered me a position in his bank and a house on Fourteenth Street. If I don't marry Millicent, my great-uncle will be disgraced and angry. He'll disavow me. And Edwin Snow will be so furious he'll have me tarred and feathered and run out of Denver on a rail. If he doesn't have me shot first."

Trace choked on his soup, coming up sputtering and wiping his chin. "The judge wants you to marry a woman?"

"The judge believes I'm his nephew," Sam reminded him sourly. She studied Trace, who was clean-shaven again, and glared at the twitch of his lips. "Obviously, I have to do something to stop this. You're a man, tell me how to break an engagement."

"You're engaged? You let it go that far?" His voice sounded choked and peculiar, like he was swallowing air.

"It wasn't my doing," Sam snapped, her eyes narrowing. "The judge worked it out with Millicent's father. They didn't discuss it with me until everything was arranged. Damn it, Harden, if you laugh, if you even snicker, so help me God I'll put a bullet between your eyes! Just tell me how to get out of this!"

Trace clasped his hands around an upraised knee, tilted his head back, and sucked in his cheeks, looking at the sky. "Well, let's see. An engagement is a serious commitment. How far have you compromised this young woman, Kincade? Have you kissed her yet?" The minute he said it, his chest started heaving. Sam heard snorting sounds of suppressed hilarity.

"Go to hell!" she spat.

"I think you're stuck. You'll have to make an honest woman of Miss Snow." Covering his eyes, Trace fell backward, giving in to shouts of helpless laughter.

Sam stared, glaring daggers at him. Then she couldn't help herself; she smiled. Truly, it was a ludicrous situation. Finally, she too was laughing helplessly.

"What does this Millicent look like?" Trace asked, wiping his eyes.

"Blonde, plump—"

"A beauty!"

"Hardly. She has a mustache that sits on her upper lip like a little wire brush!"

"Excellent! One of you should have facial hair!"

They rolled on the ground laughing, holding their sides, shouting jokes and ribald comments, until tears flowed from their eyes and left them weak and gasping.

When the spasm finally passed, they lay on the ground, hands pressed to aching stomachs, smiling at the sky.

"I have to tell you, Sam Kincade, I've never met anyone remotely like you. Knowing you has been an experience I'll never forget."

Sam's fingers locked together and tightened over her stomach. In her whole life, she'd never received as many compliments as in the past two weeks. The pleasure of it all glowed inside her.

"I don't despise you," she admitted after a minute, staring hard at the sky and trying to offer a compliment back. "It's your brother I hate."

Reaching for her hand, he squeezed, continuing to hold her hand on the ground between them.

"Trace? When we get close to Denver or if we encounter anyone, I'm going to have to cuff you and tie you in the saddle. I'm sorry, but this ruse has to look real."

Neither of them stirred. They remained on the ground, holding hands and watching the clouds drift toward evening.

"I guess I won't see you again after the hanging." The words came hard. Sam hadn't had a real friend since childhood. The thought of leaving him closed her throat.

"Whose hanging? Mine or Hannibal's?"

"Hannibal's." She dug an elbow in his ribs. "You aren't going to hang. You have my solemn oath on that." They should saddle up and ride while some daylight lingered, Sam knew it. But the tingle of his hand holding hers pinned her to the ground.

"Sam?" A long pause followed. "I think I want to kiss you."

Sam's heart stopped in her chest, then thundered into a gallop. Her mouth went so dry that she couldn't speak. Suddenly it seemed that her body weighed four times more than it had a second ago; she couldn't move.

"Why?" The word rasped out of her throat like a tiny explosion mixing a whisper with a croak.

"I don't know. I keep thinking about you being naked." His hand tightened painfully around her fingers. "The strange thing is, I didn't think much about it at the time. But I've thought a lot about it since."

Absolute paralysis stiffened Sam's body. Not a muscle twitched; she couldn't breathe.

Trace shifted onto his side and lifted himself up on one elbow, gazing down into her face. Sam's eyes fastened on his, widening with apprehension and sudden anxiety. She dug her fingernails into the sod and hung on. Her heart hammered so frantically that she thought it might fly through her chest. When she felt his breath bathe her lips, she was sure it would.

Trace stroked her cheek, his fingers light and feathery, exploring the contour of her jawline. Immediately Sam's stomach clenched into a hot knot. Her chest collapsed in a gasp that surprised her because she hadn't realized she was holding her breath.

"You can say no," Trace murmured in a strange thick voice, his gaze focused on her lips.

But Sam couldn't speak at all. Merely breathing was a struggle. Gripping fistfuls of prairie dirt, she stared up at him, lost in some timeless space that she hadn't known existed. Helplessly she gazed into his narrowed predator's eyes and saw a tiger watching her. A kaleidoscope of swirling hypnotic amber reached to engulf her and her head spun dizzily.

She twitched and dug her fingernails deeper into the sod when his lips descended and touched hers. A warm liquid surge exploded through her body. A fingertip at the corner of her mouth teased her lips open and she gasped at the pleasure of mingled breath. His kiss was warm and deliberate and unhurried.

It astonished her that his mouth was soft; she hadn't expected that at all. She noticed that he closed his eyes, and his thumbs caressed her jawline, sliding to her throat.

When his mouth released her, Trace gazed into her startled eyes for a long moment, then he smiled. "I'll get the horses."

Sam couldn't move. She lay flat on the ground like a discarded heap of old clothing, listening to her pulse pound, sensing the feverish rush of blood bubbling around her body.

She was twenty-three years old, prided herself on being as tough and ornery as a pole cat, thought of herself as a male, and pretended to be as knowledgeable and experienced as the next man.

But Sam Kincade had just received her first kiss.

And it devastated her.

When Sam finally wobbled to her feet, weak-kneed and trembling, she was too nervous and embarrassed to even glance at Trace. Gratitude was a damned bewildering emotion.

"Good luck with Millicent," Trace murmured as Sam swung out of her saddle in front of Sheriff Ainsley's office. There was enough traffic and shouting in Denver's streets that he doubted he'd be overheard, but he spoke quietly. "I know you'll work it out. I hope your future is everything you want it to be."

"Same to you, Harden," Sam said shortly, her gaze flicking over his cuffs, the ropes tying him to his saddle. She cast a furtive glance toward the sheriff's window, then looked up at him, catching her lower lip between her teeth. "Look, thanks for saving my life. I . . . I'm very grateful." She looked like she wanted to say more, but she swore instead, then jammed her hat brim down to her eyes, turned on her boot heel, and stalked into Sheriff Ainsley's office without a backward glance.

A strange woman, Trace thought, noticing that she didn't allow herself to limp although her leg was still sore. All traces of softness had disappeared within the last few minutes. She had donned her boyish persona as if stepping into a disguise, adjusting her features to fit. Her eyes narrowed into a spit-in-your-eye challenge; her shoulders squared; her chin jutted; a swaggering braggadocio appeared in her step. Watching the transformation made him ache, made him wish he could wave a wand and restore her to the young woman she should be.

Neither of them had mentioned the kiss throughout the night-long ride nor all the last day. On reflection, Trace regretted kissing her because his impulse had placed a strain between them. Sam hadn't spoken fifty words from that moment until this one.

He had no idea why he had experienced a compulsion to take her in his arms. Sam Kincade was not remotely similar to the type of women he usually desired. Prior to the snakebite, he hadn't even thought of her as a woman. He'd thought of her as a stubborn, pig-headed, dangerous, and largely annoying threat whose gender had not figured in his assessment.

But once she'd begun to recover, her softness and vulnerability had reached something in him. And the memory of her nakedness haunted his thoughts. Trace had observed countless female bodies in his time, but he could truthfully say that he had seen few to compare with Sam Kincade. Her small body was perfectly proportioned, her skin taut and smooth. There wasn't an ounce of fat on her muscled frame, just flowing curves and trim lines. Her breasts were as small and as perfect as rose-tipped globes. Recalling her naked and flushed with fever, her skin glistening beneath a dew of perspiration, made his fists clench and his stomach feel hot and tight.

When the sheriff and two deputies followed Sam outside, Trace brought his attention sharply into the present. He'd been concentrating so intently on the memory of Sam as a desirable woman that it came as a surprise to note the men accepted her as male. It was less of a surprise that they stared at him with menace defining their scowls.

"So this here is Hannibal Cotwell's little brother, huh?" The sheriff thumbed back his hat and sneered. "Don't look too dangerous to me."

One of the deputies untied Trace and dragged him off his horse, letting him fall in the dirt street. The deputy kicked him to his feet. Trace swung toward Sam, who returned his angry glare without expression. He had assumed the sheriff was privy to the judge's scheme. Obviously, he had erred.

"Throw him in a cell, Darrel, and don't be none too gentle about it." The sheriff skimmed a threatening gaze over Trace's dark suit and silver waistcoat. "We don't coddle murderers and horse thieves in Denver, mister. You'll beg to hang just to get out of my jail." He dropped a hand on Sam's shoulder as the deputy shoved Trace toward the door. "Good job, Kincade. He have any money on him?"

"His goods are in his saddlebags." Almost absently, she kicked Trace below the knee as the deputy dragged him past her, following the kick with a nod that seemed to say good riddance.

Trace shot her a pained look before he was hurled into the sheriff's office, then hauled down a filthy dark corridor. When he heard the cell door clang shut behind him and picked himself off the floor to inspect his primitive accommodations, he decided he must have been out of his mind when he agreed to this plan.

"Harden isn't like Hannibal Cotwell," Sam insisted, repeating herself. "I'm telling you, Judge, Trace Harden saved my life! He could have escaped, he could have shot me with my own gun, but he stayed and tended me. Are those the actions of a ruthless outlaw?"

"It sounds to me like you been flimflammed, boy." The judge snapped his fingers and after-dinner brandies and cigars appeared. With a sigh of pleasure, he leaned back in his chair, clipped the end of an expensive cigar, then lit it with irritating ceremony and inhaled deeply. "If you ask me, Clarion's is as fine an establishment as Bart Grand's place in San Francisco."

"Harden wants to see his brother dead as much as we do. I told you his story. Cotwell raped Harden's wife so brutally that afterward the woman hanged herself."

"Maybe." Judge Mockton patted his belly and puffed contentedly on his cigar. Tonight the gray fringe that surrounded his head and flowed into beard and mustache resembled polished metal. "On the other hand, the man's a professional gambler. His livelihood depends on convincing folks that he's holding threes when he's holding aces. Or vice versa." A fuzzy eyebrow tilted toward his bald pate. "It ain't like you to go soft, and that worries me."

"All I'm saying is we were wrong about Harden." Frustration reddened Sam's face. She pulled at her heavily starched collar and shifted uncomfortably beneath the tight wrapping that flattened her breasts. Throughout dinner she'd sensed that she wasn't getting through to the judge. If anything, the more she defended Trace, the more the judge inclined against him. "You didn't find any outstanding charges against him, did you?"

"Not yet."

"Well, you won't. The only crime he's guilty of is being Cotwell's brother."

The judge inspected the ash growing on his cigar.

"Some would say that's enough to hang him right there."

"We agreed that Trace Harden won't actually hang," Sam reminded him sharply. "He's bait. That's all." She waved at the cigar smoke with an angry gesture. "If you frame him and then hang him, it's murder, plain and simple."

"I ain't going to hang his butt. It's Cotwell we want, not his fancy-pants brother." The judge settled back in the wing chair and studied Sam with annoyance. "You're worrying me large, boy. Gullibility ain't a desirable quality in a banker."

Sam froze. A low breath squeezed out of her chest. "If you're referring to Miss Snow," she said, frowning, "I've been thinking about that situation . . ."

" 'Course I'm referring to Miss Snow, and your future." The judge's small eyes hardened. "Plans for the wedding are going ahead full steam." Ash dribbled across his vest when he waved a hand. "The wedding dress has been ordered from Paris. Edwin is refurbishing your office at the bank. I've offered my services to Mrs. Snow regarding the guest list. The only thing you have to do is name the day and show up."

Sam suppressed a sigh. Why did this subject always come up when she was feeling crampy, her woman time almost upon her? "And if I don't?" she asked angrily.

"I wouldn't go making threats if I was you." The judge returned her stare. "Me and Edwin has gone to a lot of trouble to reach an agreement. Edwin wants Millicent to be happy; I want Edwin in my back pocket. If you jilt Miss Snow, her outraged father won't lose no time avenging his little girl's honor. Your life won't be worth a sneeze, boy." Tilting his head back, he frowned at the ornate ceiling. "As for me . . . I wouldn't take kindly to you repaying my patronage by wrecking my political plans, which involve Edwin Snow and his bank and my campaign financing. I'd be pissed—mighty pissed—if you were to bring shame down on your head and mine after all the maneuvering I've done on your behalf. Are you seeing the picture here, boy? You don't want me for an enemy, believe me."

"Seems I ought to have an opinion about who I marry or if I marry. Don't I have a say in this?" Sam felt a vise tightening around her chest, and her stomach rolled over. Cigar smoke made her feel nauseous when she was approaching her cycle.

"Well now, I don't reckon you do. I don't see where you have any complaint either. In fact, a little gratitude wouldn't be amiss."

If she'd actually been male, Sam might have been grateful indeed for the judge's manipulations. As it was she felt helpless and doomed. She didn't have a notion in her head how to stop the juggernaut flying toward her. She couldn't possibly marry Millicent Snow, but if she didn't, Millicent would be humiliated, her father would come after Sam with a battery of gunslingers, and the judge, her only relative in the world, would despise her and God knew what he might do for revenge.

Sam rubbed her temples. "I'm damned if I do and damned if I don't."

"That's exactly how every bridegroom has felt since time immemorial, boy. You'll settle down once you've tied the knot." The judge inspected a gold pocket watch. "It's Saturday night," he said by way of explanation. "Miss Daisy's expecting me."

"All I am to you is a pawn in a political game," Sam said bitterly. "You're using me to ensure Edwin Snow's financial support."

"For which you will be handsomely rewarded," the judge noted with infuriating complacency. "Politics is all that counts." He rubbed his hands together and barely restrained himself from crowing. "Statehood is coming, boy, and soon. There's opportunity and wealth waiting for a man with influential banking connections and for the man who puts Hannibal Cotwell's neck in a noose. We're going to do both."

Sam wrenched her mind from the appalling specter of Millicent Snow. "Suppose Hannibal doesn't hear that we've got his brother in the Denver jail awaiting trial for a hanging offense?"

"If Cotwell's in the Colorado territory, he'll hear. An announcement will appear in the newspapers tomorrow morning."

"Suppose Cotwell has left the territory?"

The judge shrugged. "Trace Harden ain't going anywhere. We can wait as long as it takes."

Sam tapped her fingers on the chair arms and considered. "Maybe I ought to ride up to Leadville and nose around a little. Maybe someone up there knows where Cotwell went after he robbed the assayer's office. I don't like leaving this part of the plan to chance. If we knew where he went after Leadville, we could make certain he gets the word about his brother."

The judge's narrowed eyes issued a warning. "You'll stay right here in Denver. Mrs. Snow is hosting a garden party tomorrow afternoon. You're expected."

Learning about the garden party solidified Sam's intention. "I'm going to Leadville tomorrow," she stated flatly.

The judge studied her through a blue curl of smoke. "Shaming Miss Snow will make a lot of people very angry. Do you want that kind of trouble, boy?"

"You can tell Miss Snow there's nothing more important to me than seeing Hannibal Cotwell hang," Sam said between her teeth. "That's my first priority; it always has been. You know that as well as anyone."

"Make up your mind to it. You *will* marry Millicent Snow."

"Or what?"

"Or face consequences that you don't even want to think about."

Sam stood, straightened her dinner jacket, then strode out of Clarion's. She couldn't wait to get out of town.

*   *   *

The altitude in Leadville caused newcomers to wheeze and pant and suck hard for each breath. Until adjustment came, one shot of whiskey packed the same wallop as two shots at a lower altitude. Old-timers watched new arrivals with envious and sour grins as the newcomers dropped unconscious on saloon floors, finding oblivion at half the price.

After ten days, Sam's headaches disappeared and she could breathe without fearing her lungs were about to collapse. She balanced her morning coffee on the porch rail of the Ore House and drew in a long, full breath of chill bracing air.

The hillsides were pocked with shafts, yellow-gray slag heaps, and denuded acres of rotting tree stumps. In town the saloons and dance halls stayed open twenty-four hours a day. Even at this early hour, Sam could hear music and shouts drifting from Main Street. There didn't seem to be an hour in the day that some miner wasn't celebrating new wealth while another despaired over losing everything he had once valued.

It was a raw, wide-open town, as ugly as greed, a ramshackle torn-earth blot on what must have once been a marvel of nature.

Sam could see how Hannibal Cotwell had been drawn to Leadville. The assayer's office was one of the richest in the territories. The town's saloons still buzzed with talk about Cotwell's daring daylight robbery. Depending on how a man's luck was running, the miners discussed the robbery with varying degrees of outrage or admiration. Some speculated that Cotwell had escaped with millions' worth of gold dust and silver bullion; others insisted his gang had made off with only a pittance.

Sam inclined toward the pittance theory since the assayer had shipped his wares to Philadelphia only the day before Cotwell struck. Cotwell's gang must have been disappointed by their haul. The question was, where was Cotwell now?

She thought she knew.

She'd located an old miner with a fondness for liquor and talk who claimed one of Cotwell's men had once been his partner in a played-out claim near Central City. Four bits' worth of whiskey had bought Sam an avalanche of anecdotes about young Marsh Crisp and how he'd gone bad. Another four bits bought the information that yes, Marsh Crisp and the old miner had shared a few pints and a few stories when Crisp was in town with Hannibal Cotwell. The drinks and Sam's urging had coaxed the old miner into revealing more than he might have otherwise.

Sam finished her coffee, then she mailed a copy of the *Rocky Mountain News* containing the announcement of Trace Harden's capture, posting it to Marsh Crisp at a saloon in Santa Fe. She fervently hoped Crisp would share the news with Hannibal.

Finally, reluctantly, she turned her thoughts toward the long arduous journey down the mountains and back to Denver. By the time Sam returned, she would have been gone almost three weeks. The cherry and apple blossoms would have faded from Mrs. Snow's garden, to be replaced by an array of early annuals.

Maybe by then she would stop thinking about Trace's kiss, stop trying to recall exactly how his mouth had felt pressed against hers. Or maybe she wouldn't, she thought with a sigh. It was hard to forget something that cataclysmic.

Forcing her thoughts to more immediate problems, Sam saddled Blue and pulled the cinch tight, deciding grimly that it was time to face the music. Time to tell the truth and dump Millicent Snow back in the judge's lap. There was going to be hell to pay when the judge learned his nephew was actually his niece, and therefore the wedding was off.

After six days of tedious riding Sam reached the outskirts of Golden, fatigued and saddle-sore and feeling as mean as an injured bear. The first thing she spotted was a poster nailed to a pine at the edge of town. Reining hard, she leaned to read the small print beneath a hasty portrait that was unmistakably Trace Harden.

The poster announced a public hanging. Trace Harden, convicted murderer and horse thief, would meet his maker on May fifth. Sam bolted upright in her saddle, her fatigue forgotten. A swift calculation revealed that today was either May second or May third, she wasn't sure which.

Urging Blue into a trot, she passed through Golden, noticing several more posters announcing the upcoming hanging. By the time she reached Denver, lying low over Blue's neck in a full gallop, the posters were as ubiquitous as the mosquitoes hovering above the banks of the city ditch.

Dismounting in a whirl of dust in front of the courthouse, Sam took the stone steps two at a time.

"What the hell happened?" she shouted, bursting

into the judge's second-floor office. She waved the poster she'd pulled off the pine tree. "What kind of double cross is this?"

The judge leaned back from his desk, his judicial robe fluttering like the wings of a bat. Calmly, he raised the lid of a humidor and selected a cigar, offered one to Sam, and shrugged when she refused with a torrent of swearing.

"Get your hands off my desk and sit down." He waited until she did. "Now just how long did you think I could delay hanging a condemned man?"

"Harden was framed! We agreed he would not hang! I gave him my word."

The judge shrugged again and examined her flushed features with a bland expression. "Even Cotwell don't seem to care if his brother hangs. 'Course we still got three days for the plan to work."

"Cotwell isn't in the Colorado territory. Even if he gets the newspaper I sent, there's no way he could arrive here in time to believe he has a chance to rescue his brother!"

"Well then, I guess Trace Harden hangs." Indifference rippled the judge's bat wings. "I'm not happy about this, you understand, but the newspapers have been pushing this thing from the start. There wasn't anything I could do."

A dizzying ringing erupted in Sam's ears. She leaned forward in disbelief. "You have to stop this!"

Mild amazement raised the judge's eyebrows. "Now you know I can't interfere with a hanging. Do you want me to meet with the governor and request a pardon because I let a jury convict a man on evidence you and I cooked up?" He rolled his eyes. "Aside from the possibility of you and me going to jail, if that isn't political suicide, I don't know what would be!"

Sam fell back in her chair, trying to swallow the panic lodged in her throat. "Why did you try him in the first place? We agreed the trial would be indefinitely delayed."

"Obviously you haven't seen a recent newspaper. Sheriff Ainsley bragged to the news hounds that he had Hannibal Cotwell's brother in custody. That was what we wanted, good for our plan. Except the newspapers jumped on the story. The headlines started screaming for swift justice." He waved his hand. "We had to have a trial. Now the verdict's in, and we have to have a hanging. It's as simple as that. You can blame the press."

A flash of insight slammed across Sam's chest. "You always knew it was possible that Harden might actually hang," she said softly. She had been a naive idiot to swear to Trace that it couldn't happen. Her passion to capture Hannibal had blinded her to the obvious.

"Of course there was always that possibility." The judge shifted his cigar from one side of his small mouth to the other. His eyes cooled. "You knew it too."

A sick pit opened in Sam's stomach. Maybe she had known. "You can't let an innocent man hang," she repeated stubbornly, sensing the plea was futile. "Isn't there any way to stop this?"

"Our witness at the trial could recant his testimony and his eyewitness identification. But he's somewhere in Mexico now. Or, the governor could offer clemency. But that won't happen because the newspapers support the verdict and the governor isn't about to get the newspapers mad at him by pardoning an outlaw everyone in town wants to see hanged. Or, our plan could still work and we capture Hannibal Cotwell, then reveal that Harden's conviction was a ploy to trap Cotwell. But that won't happen because you tell me Cotwell can't get to Denver in time to get himself trapped."

Sam stared at a point in space. "So Trace Harden is going to hang and there's nothing we can do to stop it."

"Not that I can see."

She swung her eyes to his expressionless face. "You don't seem overly concerned."

"Can't say that I am, boy. Have you forgotten this is Hannibal Cotwell's brother? Just how innocent do you think he really is?"

"I gave my word that he wouldn't hang," Sam whispered. "I promised."

The bat wings shifted in another elaborate shrug. "In three days it won't matter who promised what to whom. Trace Harden is going to bite the rope and that's the end of that. Good riddance, I say. That's what you should be saying too."

Sam closed her eyes. Trace Harden had saved her life. He had kissed her.

She couldn't believe that he was going to die. And it was her fault.

CHAPTER

* 7 *

*A*hot wind rustled across the sage and past thorny fingers of cactus, stirring the air just enough to heat fraying tempers already strained by boredom. Hannibal mopped rivulets of sweat from his face and throat and spit a chili seed over the porch rail. The Mexicans insisted that eating hot peppers balanced the system and made a person feel cooler. It was a stupid idea and Hannibal had half a mind to shoot the next Mexican he saw. His mouth burned and flames roared in his stomach.

Tilting his chair back on two legs, he leaned against the porch wall, fanning his face with his hat as he watched Mattie fight the wind to hang out a wash. Without paint and dressed in an apron and calico, she didn't look like a soiled dove. She could have been a rancher's wife with two babies in the house and supper on the stove.

Frowning, he shifted his gaze toward the barn where Marsh Crisp and the boys were target shooting old whiskey bottles. He couldn't summon the energy to join them. After a while he looked back at Mattie.

She was a good old girl. He supposed they got on well enough. If things had been different, maybe he and Mattie could have gone somewhere and made a fresh start. Maybe the Northwest, where no one had heard of either of them. He tried to imagine what they would do to make an honest living and couldn't think of any respectable skill that either of them possessed.

He couldn't continue this life forever. The strain of continually being on the dodge was a life better suited to young men with fire in their bellies, no cares and a firm belief in their own invincibility. Men who thought as he had not too long ago, before he came face to face with the aimlessness of his life, the wasteland behind and in front of him.

Mattie carried the empty wash basket up the porch steps and paused beside his chair. "I'm curious about something." Angry dark eyes stared down at him. "Were you disappointed when you discovered a lady's no different from any other woman?"

"Shut up," he said wearily. "I told you not to talk about Etta."

"Why shouldn't we talk about her? She's here, ain't she? Standing right between us." Mattie shifted the basket on her hip. "So. Did it surprise you to learn she was no different than me?"

"Don't be stupid. You're as different as whiskey is from cream."

"No we ain't, Hannibal. She used men too, just

like any whore. The only difference is that I'm honest about it!"

He shot out of his chair like a bullet, but he wasn't fast enough to catch her. When he lunged toward the door, he spotted Marsh Crisp leaning against a porch post, watching.

"Woman trouble, Cotwell?"

"Mind your own goddamned business." Bending, he picked up his hat. Someday soon he was going to wipe that cocky smirk off Crisp's arrogant face.

"That's a fine piece of woman," Crisp drawled, leering into the house. "Mighty fine. If you're looking for someone to take her off your hands . . ."

"What do you want?"

Crisp looked him up and down, his gaze lingering on the nest of scars above Hannibal's right eye. The flicker of a challenge drifted across his expression like the shadow of a cloud as he relaxed against the porch post and folded his arms.

"The boys are bored and restless. Billy's talking about riding into town for a little action. Sounds like a good idea."

Hannibal shifted his gaze toward the ruts leading across ten miles of arid dirt and cactus. Boredom fractured unity and got men killed. He didn't like it that Crisp had spotted the problem before he did.

He studied Crisp, trying to remember if he'd been that sure of himself when he was in his twenties. "You're not calling the shots around here."

"Didn't say I was," Crisp answered easily. "You got a better idea, all you got to do is say so."

"Riding into town just to raise hell isn't smart." He thought a minute. "You remember the last time we were down here? How the Lyman brothers humiliated Mule Joe?"

A twitch of interest tugged Crisp's mouth. It didn't matter that Mule Joe had been thoroughly disliked or that he'd gotten himself killed down in Mexico in a fight over some whore. For a brief time, Mule Joe had been one of Cotwell's boys.

"Them Lyman brothers need to be taught a lesson," Crisp suggested, a slow smile opening along dusty creases.

"That's what I was thinking." It was something to do. "You tell the boys to saddle up. We'll nose around town and see if anyone knows what the Lymans are up to lately."

The prospect of violence improved his spirits. Still spitting chili seeds, he entered the house and walked to the kitchen, peeling off his sweat-soaked shirt. Mattie set down an iron, shoved a limp curl off her forehead, and watched him pull on a fresh shirt.

"You know why I fell in love with you?" she asked right out of nowhere.

Not bothering to answer, Hannibal bent over the basin on the table and washed the dust off his face.

"First of all, I like the way you talk, all proper like, and soft most of the time. But mainly it has to do with the first time I ever seen you. You was standing outside the Dogtown saloon watching two drunk cowboys torment an old yellow dog. You walked up to them cowboys looking mean as grave dirt, and beat 'em so bad they didn't come back to town for a month. I thought you was crazy to take on two men. Finally I figured out it was about the dog. Next time I seen you was three months later and you still had that dog."

He paused, pressing a towel to his face. Sometimes he missed old Mick real bad. They'd ridden together for three years until the damned fool ran under the wheels of a stagecoach.

"Ma always said a man treats his woman like he treats his animals. I seen how you treated that old yellow dog and I knew you was good under all that mean."

"Your ma was wrong. I never hit old Mick."

"You threaten a lot and wave your fists around, but the only times you hit me is when you're drunk or when I make you really mad." She touched a fingertip to her tongue, then to the iron. When the metal didn't hiss, she placed that iron on the cooktop and removed a hot one. After arranging a shirt sleeve just so, she applied the hot iron, leaning over it. "Did you ever hit Trace's wife?"

He could shout at her, could threaten her, could backhand her across the room. But she kept coming back to Etta, kept picking at the scab. Nothing he did or said stopped her.

"No," he said finally, scowling.

"You still think about her, don't you?"

A great weariness fell over him. He didn't know what was wrong with Mattie that she went out of her way to make him hit her. His hand shot out and he slapped her hard enough that she dropped the iron and fell against the hot cookstove. When she pushed herself off the burner lids, her palms were red and fiery and tears welled in her dark eyes.

"Etta thought she got a dangerous man when she married a gambler, least that's how I got it figured," Mattie said in a little voice, blinking at the tears hanging on her lashes. "But Trace was too decent to involve his wife in his professional life. So she started playing dangerous games with other men."

"Goddamn it, Mattie!" Nothing did any good. He had a notion that he could beat her senseless and she'd wake up talking about Etta. "For Christ's sake just let it go!"

She looked up at him, her eyes wet and shiny with tears. "Oh Hannibal. Don't you see what she did? She turned Trace against you!"

Hannibal stared at her in amazement. She was just begging him to choke the life out of her. "Nothing could ever come between me and my brother." He wished he felt as certain as he sounded.

Mattie tilted her head. "You don't know what she might have told him."

Fury darkened his face. If he'd believed it would do any good, he would have flung her through the window into the yard.

"I'm not denying there's trouble between my brother and me. But Trace and I will work this out."

"I don't think so," she said softly, sounding sure of herself.

The anger that surged through his body was so

powerful that Hannibal didn't dare touch her for fear that he would kill her. He tied his bandanna with shaking fingers, then caught up his hat.

"You better go, Mattie." He sounded as if he were strangling. "If you stay here, you'll make me beat you within an inch of your life. You know where the money is. Take what you want and get out."

"Not yet," she said thoughtfully, resting her burned hands on the table and watching him. "I ain't ready to give up yet, not while we still got a chance." She hesitated. "I got something to tell you."

"No you don't."

Mattie followed him through the house and stood on the porch while the boys brought the horses up from the corral. Marsh Crisp wore his pearl-buttoned shirt and Billy Jones had shaved. The young one who never talked had polished his silver belt buckle so that it flashed in the sun. Burt was already drinking, waving a bottle around and slapping his thigh in eagerness to be gone.

Marsh Crisp tipped his hat to her and smiled. "Can I bring you something from town, Miss Mattie?"

"If you think of it, I wouldn't mind having a piece of nice-smelling soap."

Crisp's dancing eyes lingered on the swell of breast showing at her opened collar. He glanced at Hannibal's back, then winked at her. "I'll remember," he promised.

Mattie stepped back from the dirt kicked up by the horses' hooves and watched them ride out. She tucked her sore hands in the folds of her skirt, out of the hot wind, and squinted at the billow of dust moving toward Santa Fe. God, she hated it out here. She missed the excitement of a town, the noise and laughter in the saloons, the companionship of other women, a reason to paint her face and wear pretty clothes.

Love plain wrecked a woman, she thought unhappily. You waited endlessly for a man to start loving you back, drudging and working like a dog all the while. And what if he never did?

Turning back into the house, she returned to the kitchen, glared at the irons, then poured herself a generous splash of whiskey and carried it to the window where she could see the wash flapping in the wind.

She had almost told him about Etta's letter. She'd come so close. Next time she'd do it, too. It was time to find out if there was any real hope for her future.

Hannibal hooked his boot on the bar rail and downed half a mug of warm beer in a single pull. Out in the plaza a Mexican band celebrated a wedding by playing the same loud tune over and over again. The hot peppery scent of the marriage feast invaded the cantina. Hannibal decided he hated Mexican music and he *hated* the stink of roasting chilies.

"Over here!" He pointed at his mug and shouted to the bartender above the noise. "Leave a bottle of whiskey too."

When half of the whiskey was gone, he finally let himself think about Trace, remembering Five Oaks and their early years. The only good thing about growing up in Charles Harden's house had been Trace. He'd be crazy, or dead, if it hadn't been for his brother. Lord, the things they had done together, the trouble they'd gotten into. A smile twitched across his lips. Anyone watching in those days would have predicted that Trace would be the brother to run up against the law, that Trace would be the one to go bad and drift through life with no ties and no purpose.

But Trace had made a success of himself. It was Trace who had the big house and the prosperous businesses, the trips to Europe, and a beautiful society wife.

He scratched his fingernails over the scars mounded on his forehead. If he was half the man he thought he was, he wouldn't wait for Trace to catch up to him, he'd ride out to find his brother. He'd face up to what he had done to the only man who ever gave a rat's ass whether Hannibal Cotwell lived or died.

Shoving his glass to the floor, he took a long pull straight from the neck of the whiskey bottle.

Eventually Trace would find him. Then what? He wished he knew what Etta had told his brother, wished he knew what she wanted him to do.

The worst of it was that he wasn't sorry that he'd bedded his brother's wife. How could Hannibal regret the happiest two weeks of his life? If he had a chance to live those two weeks again, he'd jump at the opportunity to do it exactly the same way.

He could still see Etta brushing her wheat-colored hair with long, slow strokes. He could feel the caress of those silken strands falling across his naked shoulder. If he lived to be one hundred, he would never forget the glorious moment of astonishment and delirium when he finally understood that she wanted him too. A passion followed so hot and intense, so blinding that he had been maddened beyond caring about consequences. The memory of those stolen moments with Etta towered in Hannibal's mind as if nothing else existed. Every treasured second remained as real to him as his heartbeat.

Poisoning his memories like venom in honey was how he had betrayed his brother. Worse, if there had been the slightest possibility that Etta could have been happy living an outlaw's life, he would have taken her away from Trace just as she begged him to.

He shook his head in sick amazement. He would have done it. Not only bedded his brother's wife, but taken her too. He would have hated himself, he would have flogged himself with guilt, but he would have done it. The only thing that stopped him was Etta's happiness. He couldn't give her a lady's life or the luxuries she deserved and took for granted. Regardless of what she claimed, she needed those things.

Closing his eyes, he tried to picture Etta Harden hanging wash in the wind, wearing a soiled apron and a calico dress. He couldn't see it. She belonged on a pedestal, not in a kitchen or a wash room. And in the end, their betrayal of Trace would eventually have soured their love and their passion for each other. His love for his brother had given him the strength to return west without Etta. But there wasn't a day he didn't think about her, miss her, yearn for her.

Hannibal wished to God that Trace had never found out that he and Etta had betrayed him. But somehow he had. That had to be the reason Trace had sold his businesses and was looking for him. Eventually they would have to confront each other.

Marsh Crisp elbowed up to the bar, his eyes sparkling with excitement. He spoke out of the corner of his mouth. "Word has it the Lyman brothers mortgaged their ranch and bought a mess of Herefords. Seems they plan to fatten 'em for a season, then run 'em up the trail and sell 'em off for a fortune. What do you think about that?"

He was tired and too old for cattle rustling, too sick-spirited to want anything but to be left alone.

But a man led or he followed. And his boys weren't likely to follow a self-pitying SOB who wanted only to drink himself blind. Wasn't that what Crisp was waiting for? For Hannibal to lose his edge? Then Crisp could set himself up and ride off with Hannibal's boys.

The bartender leaned over the counter. "Are you Marsh Crisp?"

Crisp's eyes snapped into a squint. "What's it to you?"

"If you're him, you got mail. A newspaper."

"Well give it over." With a puzzled look, Crisp shook out the pages. "It ain't even a recent paper."

"Are you going to sit around reading? Or do you

want to rustle up some steaks for supper? Go get the boys," Hannibal ordered, spinning some coins across the countertop. A man did what he had to.

Crisp grinned and tossed the newspaper back to the bartender. "What're we gonna do with them cows once we steal 'em?"

"Who cares? We'll butcher as many as we want and give the rest to the Mexicans, or we'll turn them loose on the open range, or maybe we'll use 'em for target practice."

It was something to do. Something to take his mind off Etta and the knowledge that Trace would eventually find him.

Once the feud flared up with the Lyman brothers, life at the ranch improved, Mattie decided. It was nerve-wracking, wondering if the Lyman brothers would sneak up on them again, but there hadn't been any sign of them since the gunfight last week. And that hadn't amounted to much when all was said and done. Burt got winged and one of the horses went down. A couple of windows got shot out, but that was the extent of it. The Lymans took the worst of the fight. One of their boys got killed and Josiah Lyman caught a bullet in the thigh.

The feud gave Hannibal and the boys something to talk about, get mad about, plan for and scheme over. Purpose energized everyone's step and Mattie had even overheard the boys laughing out in the barn. The best part was that Hannibal wasn't sitting around staring into space, drinking and brooding. He joked occasionally, slapped her on the bottom, and almost seemed like his old self.

The moody moments reared up less frequently. Mattie was starting to feel confident that she was actually winning. And she knew exactly what would put her over the top.

When Hannibal knew the full truth, he would hate Etta Harden. And he would turn to Mattie, happy to find her waiting. She was glad she had waited until the right moment to reveal the whole truth.

This was the time, she decided, summoning her courage. The night wasn't too hot or too cool. They had made love earlier and it hadn't been bad. Not great yet, but decent. They were getting along better.

"Hannibal, honey? You ain't asleep, are you?"

"What is it?"

"I been thinking," she said. "I been thinking that you deserve to know the truth. About Etta. I should have told you before."

His muscles stiffened under her palms. "You didn't know her. You don't know anything about her. Will you for Christ's sake forget about her?"

Mattie sucked in a breath and held it, then let it slowly release. "Etta wrote a letter. Trace carries it in his waistcoat."

He flipped on his back and shoved her hands away from him. "Are you claiming you know what's in a letter Etta wrote?" he demanded.

"I saw your brother reading something over and over. I was curious so I paid Alf down at the Dogtown Hotel to find out what it was. Alf read the letter while Trace was asleep and memorized every word so he could tell me what it said."

"For Christ's sake, Mattie! How could you?" He was quiet for a long minute. "What did Etta's letter say?"

"She was no good, Hannibal. I know her kind. She was a destructive force who strewed wreckage behind her."

Hannibal sprang on her in frustration and shook her until her teeth knocked together. "What did the letter say!"

Mattie swallowed. She could see his tiger eyes burning down at her through the darkness.

"She told Trace with her dying words that you raped her! She swore you beat her and raped her. Said you laughed when she told you that she was pregnant."

Shock blanked his eyes. Then he frowned in confusion. "Dying words? Pregnant? What the hell are you talking about?"

"She said you told her to foist the baby off on Trace, that Trace was too stupid to know it wasn't his."

Hannibal's fingers gripped her shoulders so fiercely that she gasped in pain. "She's not dead! Damn you, Mattie, you're lying!"

Mattie peered up at him in the darkness. "I ain't. You know I never lied to you. Etta's dead. She hanged herself."

Horror twisted his features. She felt the tremor that shook through his body. "No," he whispered. "No!"

Swinging his legs off the side of the bed, he stared at the wall for a full minute, then dropped his head in his hands. "Tell me everything she said."

Suddenly wishing that she hadn't started this, Mattie repeated the letter word for word. At the finish, she swallowed hard and raised her chin. "I guess when she turned up pregnant, she didn't see any way out except to kill herself. But that wasn't enough for her, not your Etta." Hatred roughened her voice. She had never despised anyone like she despised Etta Harden. "She wanted you dead too. So she sent Trace to kill you for her."

"Did she say that in her last words?" Mattie had to strain to hear him. "That she wanted me dead?"

"No, she asked Trace to forgive you. But she said it in a way that you knew she meant the opposite. The words she used made you think of a shotgun being loaded and aimed. She was evil, Hannibal, can't you see that? You would never have laid a hand on Etta Harden if she hadn't seduced you. It was her who didn't care about Trace, not you. And with her dying words she made herself sound wronged and honorable while she was writing words to set brother against brother, words to send Trace out to avenge her death. Ain't no husband could read that letter without vowing to kill the man who raped and beat his wife and made her hang herself."

Reeling, Hannibal stood up and fumbled in the dark

for his pants. After pulling them to his waist, he stumbled through the darkness toward the door.

Mattie rose on her hands and knees. "Etta never loved you! She used you to hurt Trace, except things went wrong and she got pregnant. She lied about you, she swore you raped her, she filled your brother with hate toward you, and she sent him to kill you!" A sob ripped through her shout. "I'm the one who loves you! Can't you see that? Not Etta, me! Hannibal, please! Come back!"

He fell out of the door onto the dark porch, picked himself up and staggered down the steps. Rocks and bits of broken glass cut his bare feet as he walked toward the nearest pasture. Shock and agony numbed his senses.

Etta was dead. By hanging, the worst death imaginable. She was gone, and she had lied about what they had meant to each other. The pain of it slammed into him like a spike driving into his chest.

She was dead. And so was the child they had created together. She had accused him of raping her. And now Trace wanted to kill him.

In torment, he searched in the darkness for a sharp rock that fit comfortably in his palm. Gripping the stone, he sank to his knees and smashed the rock against his forehead over and over as he had done when he was a child, whenever pain and rejection had become too great to endure.

CHAPTER
* 8 *

You can't possibly know how much I detest the fact that I'm arguing to save Hannibal Cotwell's brother!"

Pausing, Sam drew a long breath. The problem didn't look any better after a sleepless night thinking about it. In fact, she was having great difficulty getting past the fact that Hannibal Cotwell had wiped out her family, but here she was arguing and planning feverishly how to save what was left of Cotwell's family.

Judge Mockton chomped on a cigar and narrowed his eyes in irritation. "How many times do I have to repeat this? There is nothing anyone can do to stop Harden from hanging. It's too late! He's going to swing the day after tomorrow and that is that."

Already Sam could see that saving Trace Harden's life was going to cost her everything in the world that she valued. It wasn't fair. A lesser person than herself would shrug and walk away. Let the slick son of a bitch hang, and enjoy the pleasure of knowing

142

Hannibal would suffer when he heard his brother was dead.

That's what she wanted to do in the worst way. But she couldn't.

"I gave him my word that he wouldn't hang," she said to the judge for the hundredth time.

Trace Harden had saved her life. And he had kissed her. To her everlasting regret, Sam still flushed every time she remembered that kiss, which was often. Those were the incontrovertible facts. Personal integrity demanded that she not allow Harden to be hanged. In order to live with her conscience, she had to save his butt.

Damn it anyway.

"Edwin Snow has reserved box seats for the hanging, and you and I are expected to join him and his lovely daughter. Who, by the way, is getting so allfired pissed at your neglect, that you can just forget about the set of matched bays. You're in trouble, boy. You got some making up to do."

Sam leaned forward and gripped the edges of his desk. "There isn't going to be a hanging. And there isn't going to be a wedding between me and Millicent Snow!"

The judge studied her fiery expression. "I can see you got yourself all riled up, and now ain't the time for a reasonable discussion. But if you jilt Millicent Snow, Edwin is going to hang your hide on the bank wall. If he don't, I will." He dropped back in his chair and let his warning sink in. "So you just forget about Trace Harden."

Sam had tried everything legal. There was nothing left except drastic measures and the demise of life as she knew it.

Trace's untouched supper tray was still on the floor of the cell when Sheriff Ainsley let Sam into the corridor. Trace was stretched out on top of a wooden door supported by two sawhorses, his ankles crossed, his gaze fixed on the log ceiling. He wore the same clothing he'd worn four weeks ago when Sam had turned him over to the sheriff.

"I was wondering when you would show up to gloat," he said, keeping his scowl on the logs overhead.

Sam hooked a chair leg with the toe of her boot and dragged the chair next to the cell bars. The stench back here was enough to gag a cat.

"I didn't come to gloat."

"What I detest most is how damned gullible I was. Me! I could have ridden off and left you to die, but I hung around like a greenhorn rube waiting for you to get well enough to bring me in and frame me." A heave of disgust lifted his chest. "You and the judge must be laughing your rotten heads off."

"Listen, Trace—"

"You'll be gratified to know that you outbluffed me every step of the way, Kincade. I didn't figure this out until the trial actually began. That's when I realized there never was a plan involving Hannibal, and if there had been, it wouldn't have succeeded.

Hannibal hasn't escaped capture all these years by being stupid. He would have smelled a trap from a hundred miles away. I wish I had inherited the same ability."

Acid poured into Sam's stomach. "I didn't lie to you. We thought this plan would work and we'd get Hannibal." She spread her hands. "But the newspapers got involved, everything escalated, and . . . things got out of hand."

"Thanks for setting me straight. I'm sure recalling your honesty will be a great comfort when they tighten the noose around my neck and spring the trapdoor." He swung his legs to the floor and sat on the door, hatred blazing in his narrowed eyes. "Let's see, how did you put it? Your word was your honor, as good as gold, you said. I could depend on you. There was absolutely no danger of me being hanged. Well, I'll tell you something, Kincade. I deserve to hang—not for stealing a horse and shooting the owner, but for being so goddamned stupid."

"I'm sorry things went bad, but—"

"Oh, well that makes it all right then. As long as you're sorry, I'll die a happy man."

"Will you shut up and stop feeling sorry for yourself? I'm trying to talk to you!"

He sprang to his feet and lunged forward, gripping the bars so tightly that the blood drained out of his knuckles. "If you think I'm going to accept dying with a wave and an oh well, you're crazier than I think you are. I'm not ambivalent about being hanged. I'm feeling as black as a spade flush!"

"You're starting to make me mad," Sam said, glaring and coming to her feet. "Is that a good idea, Harden? To piss off the one person in this whole territory who wants to save your sorry hide?"

"In the last six weeks I've been hit on the head with a rifle butt, kicked, handcuffed, and tied to my horse. I've been thrown in this filthy jail, beaten, then tried for murder, and two days from now I'm going to hang by the neck until I'm dead." His tiger eyes shot daggers through the bars. "Can you guess what all these catastrophes have in common, Kincade? You!"

Sam gripped the bars, her hands just below his. A wave of furious heat radiated off his body and enveloped her. She thrust her face toward him.

"Yeah, well you're about to ruin my whole life and everything the name Kincade stood for!"

"I should have known better than to believe anything that came out of your mouth. Etta was the same. Little lies, she called them. Little lies to smooth things out. The problem is, little lies turn into big whopping lies, don't they, Kincade?"

Sam ground her teeth so hard she could hear them gnashing together. "I gave my word that you won't hang, and I mean to keep that promise!"

The scornful twist of his mouth stated clearly that Sam had put him in this place, and he didn't believe for an instant that she would get him out.

"It really fries my butt that you called me a liar! I ought to let them hang you for that!"

Trace spoke through clenched teeth. "I'm sure the

honorable judge, your scheming uncle, would be happy to add name-calling to my list of crimes."

"Just shut up, Harden. Before all hell breaks loose, there's some things I want to say to you."

"There is absolutely nothing you can say that I want to hear. So get out, Kincade, and let me spend my last hours in peace."

Sam fumed, trying to remember why she was doing this. "Don't you walk away from me, or I'll start thinking you're as stupid as you said!"

He returned to the bars, bringing with him a ripe odor that made Sam's eyes water. His amber eyes blazed down at her. "Just shut up, and leave. I wish I had never laid eyes on you."

"Yeah?" Sam thrust out her chin. "Well I wish I'd never laid eyes on you! You have ruined my life!"

"Incredible. I'm going to hang, but *your* life is ruined."

"That's right!" She gripped the bars and stood as close to him as possible, not backing off an inch. "Let me tell you something. My grandfather Mockton was a marshall. My grandfather Kincade was a lawman and my father was a sheriff. All of my life I have respected and revered the law. If nature hadn't cheated me and made me a female, I would have been a lawman too. It's the only thing I ever wanted to be!"

"Is there a point to this story?"

"The point is," Sam hissed, "I never in my worst nightmare suspected that I would go against the law! Breaking the law goes against three generations of belief and honorable living! If I'm going to betray everything my family and I held dear, if I'm going to throw away my history, my reputation and my life, then I damned well expect a whole lot of gratitude from you! Is that clear, Harden?"

He frowned. "Not even a little bit. I can't think of a single reason why I should feel grateful to you."

Sam rolled her eyes and ground her teeth together. "It's too late to stop the hanging. I'm going to have to break you out of here. That makes me an outlaw and I damned well resent it!"

"Is that right?" A flicker of curiosity stirred in his amber eyes. "And just how do you plan to do that?"

"I'm going to burn down the jail."

It was appallingly easy. At half past midnight, Sam threw two buckets of kerosene over the alley wall of the jail, then lit half a dozen oil-soaked torches. Two she tossed on the roof, the others she placed along the bottom of the log wall. The kerosene ignited and the wall erupted into an impressive sheet of flame.

She led Blue and a fast mare around to the front of the jail, tied them loosely, then ran into the sheriff's office, where a single deputy was dozing at the desk.

"Fire! The whole back wall's on fire!"

The deputy awoke with a jerk, looking around with wild eyes.

Sam unhooked the ring of cell keys from his belt and gave him a shove. "Quick! You sound the alarm, I'll get the prisoners out. Send someone for Sheriff

Ainsley! We'll need extra men and a bucket brigade. Move it, Deputy! Don't you smell the smoke?" She shouted enough orders to confuse a regiment. An excited voice yelled outside. "Go!" she shouted. "There isn't a minute to waste!"

She found the key to the corridor without much trouble, but the keys to the cells were a different matter. She fumbled through three keys before she found the one that opened the first cell. The prisoner stumbled out, rubbing sleep from his eyes and sniffing at the smoke that seeped through the chinks in the log wall. He gave Sam a grin, then ran down the corridor.

"The other cells are empty," Trace remarked. He leaned against the bars, arms folded over his chest, watching as she tried one key then another in the lock on his cell door. "I didn't think you'd actually do this."

"Here." Sam thrust an extra pistol through the bars. "Shoot anyone who comes through the door." Swearing, she tried another key in the lock, releasing a hot breath when the mechanism squealed open. "Move!"

The deputy and two men came running in the door as Sam and Trace burst out of the corridor. Sam whipped out her Colt.

"Stand aside, Deputy." The deputy's mouth dropped open in surprise, then snapped tight in fury. "I mean it, Darrel, get out of our way or I'll shoot, I swear it."

"You'll hang for this, Kincade!"

"You'll have to catch me first," she shouted over

her shoulder. The challenge was sheer bravado. She felt sickened by what she was doing.

They dashed for the street, mounted on the run, and galloped past the courthouse and around a throng of people running toward the blazing jail.

"Where to?" Trace shouted over the clanging of fire bells.

"I've got a bolt-hole outside Golden. Follow me!"

Now Sam was a fugitive. Bounty hunters would be after her. She had betrayed everything her father had believed in. She didn't know if it was the night wind or the end of an honorable life that forced tears from the corners of her eyes.

They reached Sam's cabin in the hills above Golden shortly before dawn. Exhausted, they brushed dust and twigs off two hard cots and flung themselves down to sleep.

When Trace awoke, rays of thin mountain sunshine poured through the curtainless cabin windows and past the open door. Pushing himself to a sitting position, he looked around at a sparsely furnished single room. A sagging cookstove occupied one corner, surmounted by two crooked shelves. A pair of wooden chairs flanked the hearth. Dust coated the crude furniture and bare plank floor. The air smelled of pine and mouse droppings.

When he looked toward the table, he discovered Sam cradling a coffee mug, staring at him.

"I despise you," she said, her tone as flatly conversational as if she were commenting on the June sunshine pouring through the doorway. "I truly and totally despise you." She brought the coffee mug to her lips. "I wish I had never met you. I wish you and your brother were both dead."

Trace stood, stretched, took a dusty mug from the shelf above the stove and poured himself a cup of the coffee bubbling in a dented pot. He carried his cup to the window and examined the pine-studded side of a mountain.

"Hannibal destroyed my past; you destroyed my future." He tasted the strong coffee and made himself swallow. "For the rest of my life I'll be a renegade, looking over my shoulder. Dodging bounty hunters, waiting to be shot in the back."

"Yeah, well it's better than being hanged."

He didn't say anything.

"What kind of future do you think I have?" Sam snapped, swiveling in her chair. She flung a hand toward the door. "You can bet everything you own that posters are going up all over the territory saying: Sam Kincade, wanted dead or alive. The judge isn't going to take this embarrassment lying down. My only relative in the world is going to move the earth to put my neck in a noose! Thanks to you, I've lost everything I've worked for, including my only relative, and now I've got a price on my head!"

"I didn't ask you to burn down the jail." Trace focused on a creek that tumbled out of the hills, swollen by the spring melt.

He listened to the sound of teeth grinding together.

"How else was I going to keep my word? For your information, Sam Kincade is not a liar!"

Turning, he studied the crimson pulsing on her cheeks and the anger blazing in her blue eyes. Considering all that she had done to him, it gave him enormous satisfaction to learn her life was as wrecked as his.

"You and your uncle frame me, jail me, convict me, damn near hang me, and you have the gall to blame me for your troubles." Angry sparks shot from his own furious gaze.

"I blame you because you saved my life and made me owe you! You made me swear that you wouldn't hang. For all I know, the judge is right. Maybe you deserve to hang for some crime we don't know about!"

"Let me understand this," he said, his eyes hot. "You would have preferred it if I'd let you die out there on the prairie?"

She gripped her coffee mug until her knuckles turned white, thinking about it. "No," she said finally, an exasperated sigh lifting her chest. "I won't be ready to die until I've put a bullet in Hannibal Cotwell's head." When she looked up at him, she blazed as brightly as the mountain sunshine. "But it's your fault that I'm an outlaw on the run! Right now I'd like to beat the stuffing out of you!"

"Which is exactly what I'm considering doing to you!" Trace said, speaking between clenched teeth.

She stood slowly, her hand dropping to the Colt strapped at her waist. "Yeah? You and who else, Harden?" A challenge glittered in her eyes. "Come on. You want a fight? You found one. Make your move!"

He actually started toward her, his hands knotted into fists, before he remembered she was a woman. Shocked, he stopped a foot in front of her and studied her expression.

No softness curved along her jawline. Her eyes were as challenging and unyielding as a man's. Her chin jutted as if presenting a target. The lips he had once kissed were tightened into a thin sneering line. To his astonishment, he felt a slight stirring and a challenge. This woman needed taming.

The instant he halted his advance, Sam hit him hard in the stomach. She would have followed with an uppercut to his chin if Trace hadn't caught her wrist. Swearing, his stomach aching, he twisted her arm up behind her back, his movements lithe and fluid enough to have pleased the sparring master of his youth. Still cursing, he removed the Colt from her holster and tossed the pistol on the table.

"Let me go, you bastard!"

"If you keep struggling, you'll hurt yourself." Looking around the one-room cabin, he tried to decide what to do with her. As he might have predicted, she ignored his advice, thrashing and trying to twist out of his hold. All she accomplished was putting additional pressure on her arm. He winced at her gasps and sharp cries, but she didn't stop fighting him.

Releasing her arm and spinning her to face him in the same motion, he grabbed her and threw her over his shoulder before he picked up the Colt. She beat on his back with surprising strength as he carried her outside into the pine-scented warmth of the sun.

None too gently, he threw her in the creek.

CHAPTER
* 9 *

S tay there until you cool off," Trace ordered, taking a seat on the creek bank and squinting at Sam over the barrel of the revolver.

She sprawled on the creek bed, water fuming around her body. Sputtering, she shoved wet hair out of her eyes with a furious gesture, then shouted curses at him. "You better not sleep, Harden! The minute you close your eyes, I'm going to kill you!"

"No you're not," he said, beginning to calm down. "If you wanted me dead, all you had to do was wait a day and the governor would have obliged you."

She struck the surface of the water with her fists, splashing a family of curious marmots who watched from the opposite bank. "I hate you!" she shouted. Glaring at the sky, she slid down in the water until only her knees and her profile were visible.

"I believe we've established that you and I detest each other." Trace didn't recall ever hating a woman before. Of course, he'd never met a woman like

154

Samantha Kincade. If he were honest with himself, however, hate was probably too strong a word. At this point he wasn't sure what he felt. "What is this place?" he asked, gazing back at the ramshackle cabin and the piles of gray boulders but keeping the Colt pointed at her nose.

The log cabin sat at the end of a narrow valley, so secluded and surrounded by thick stands of pine and aspen that a rider could have passed within yards of the door without suspecting the existence of a dwelling. A slag heap spilled rock and rust-colored dirt about a hundred yards up the mountainside on the far side of the creek. The mine hadn't been worked in years; pine saplings and rabbit brush sought a footing in the slag. When Trace raised his head, he saw a series of steep ridges climbing toward the snow-capped peaks towering above the western horizon.

"Two years ago I brought in an outlaw named Barrel Bob. He'd killed an old miner. The miner's widow gave me this place out of gratitude the day Barrel Bob bit the noose. This place is mine. No one knows about it."

Trace studied her chattering teeth and a grim smile curved his lips. "Seems you aren't so tough when you don't have surprise on your side."

"Just shut up." Scowling, she lifted her chin out of the water. "I'm freezing to death. When are you going to let me out of here?"

He lowered the gun. "You can come out if you're willing to behave yourself and act like a lady."

Splashing into a sitting position, she stared at him, then shoved back her wet hair with a laugh. "You know better than that. I couldn't act like a lady if I wanted to, which I sure as hell don't. Besides, I don't know how."

Trace could not imagine Sam Kincade twirling a parasol, flirting with a fan, or daintily pouring tea. She possessed the sensual curves of a woman and the harsh mind-set of a man. He had never met anyone like her.

Floundering in the icy flow, she tried to stand, slipped back into the water, then crawled toward him, lifting a cold-reddened arm toward the bank. "Give me a hand, will you?"

The conditioning of southern manners caused an automatic reaction. He reached toward her without thinking. In a flash she'd jerked him into the creek and scooped the Colt out of his hand as he fell forward. He landed on his hands and knees, gasping as the icy water shocked his system. When he turned his head, she was dripping on the bank of the creek, smiling coldly above the barrel of the Colt.

"What were you saying about me using surprise to my advantage?" An eyebrow arched toward her hairline. "Whatever it was, I expect you were right."

Trace started to stand, but she fired a bullet into the water in front of his nose. "What the hell do you think you're doing?" he shouted. "That was too close."

"You aren't coming out of there until you've had a wash. You stink to high heaven. I'd know you've been in jail just by the stench of you. Peel off those reeking clothes and wash them against the rocks."

Trace sat on the rocky bottom of the creek and folded his arms across his chest. Christ, the water was icy. He spoke through teeth clenched against the chill.

"I'm not taking my clothes off in front of you."

"Yeah, you are." She aimed over her forearm and fired another shot. The bullet parted the threads of his jacket atop his shoulder. "The next one goes between your eyes," she said, pleased by his startled expression.

"Where did you learn to shoot like that!"

The smile vanished from her lips. "My pa taught me. Get out of those stinking clothes, Harden. Do it now."

Glaring at her, he eased an arm out of his jacket. "I'm only doing this because I need a bath."

"Damned right you do."

"Not because you ordered me. I don't take orders from a woman." Angry, he scanned her dripping poncho and the denims plastered to her hips and legs. "If you had any sense, you'd get out of those wet clothes. It can't be over fifty degrees up here."

"I'll worry about me; you worry about you." But she was shivering, he noticed while he took off his vest and shirt and tossed them on the creek bank. It occurred to him that if she had less control, a shiver could have caused the last bullet to go through his shoulder. A grudging hint of admiration pulled his lips into a scowl. He didn't know two men who could handle a gun as well as she did. That made him angry.

"Go up to the cabin," he demanded, his voice tight with anger and cold. He threw his boots and socks toward the bank.

"I don't take orders either." She ran a finger down the barrel of the gun. "Let's see how you like having a stranger see you naked."

"All right," he snapped, standing up. "Maybe it's time you had a good look at what a real man looks like." The buttons at his waist resisted the wet loopholes, but he got them open. Watching a red flush begin at her throat and climb upward, he pushed down his trousers with hard angry movements, then kicked them over a rock protruding out of the water.

As brazen as brass, Sam stared at him, her gaze starting at the wedge of sunburned skin at his throat, then moving to the glistening hair sprinkled across his chest. Her fingers rose to her own chest in an unconscious gesture before she dropped her gaze to his waist and hips.

She swallowed hard, then followed a crisp arrow of dark hair down to the nest between his thighs. Staring at her and swearing, Trace clapped a hand over his cold-shrunken privates. Sam scrambled to her feet and pointed the gun at his chest, her hand shaking.

She tried to speak but couldn't.

Ignoring her, Trace turned aside and bent to splash water under his arms and over his chest.

The cold was intense. His bare feet were turning

bluish red beneath the water. But the pleasure of washing off layers of jail-house grime outweighed the shock of the cold and the discomfort of performing his ablutions in front of Samantha Kincade. Scooping up a handful of bottom sand, he scrubbed it over his chest and shoulders, working the gritty abrasion against weeks of unwashed skin. When he next glanced at the bank, he noticed that Sam had fled.

Shivering with cold, she bolted for the cabin and the change of clothing tucked inside her saddlebags. Hastily, she stripped out of her wet denims and shirt, found a dusty, mouse-nibbled towel to dry herself, then jerked on clean clothing, not taking time to tape down her breasts because she didn't know when Trace would return.

She could hear him singing now, and it irritated the hell out of her. He wanted to make her think the icy water didn't bother him, that he was actually enjoying a wash in water only a degree or two above freezing.

Biting down on her back teeth, Sam combed her fingers through her wet hair, then walked to the cabin window. By leaning far to the right, she could spy on him.

He was lying flat on the creek bottom, splashing water over his face and hair and singing at the top of his lungs.

"When Johnny comes marching home again, Ha rah! Ha rah!"

When he stood, Sam sucked in a sharp breath and held it until her chest burned, watching him shake the water out of his hair. Looking up at the sky, he ran his hands over his chest and waist, wiping the cold water off his body.

Sam gripped the windowsill with her fingers, her own body tensing with sudden heat. Over the years she had seen a man's naked leg or arms or chest. Thinking she was a boy, outlaws had peed in front of her and she had glimpsed naked buttocks and the front of them too. But this was the first time she had seen an entirely naked man.

Trace Harden was the most beautiful thing she had ever seen. The mere sight of him took her breath away. Staring at his body made her feel as if she were strangling in hot molasses.

His skin was paler and smoother than she had expected, and his shoulders and thighs were more muscular than she had supposed a gambler's would be. Sunlight caught in the dark hair that sprinkled his wide chest and clung like a pelt to his legs and thighs. Cold water had turned his buttocks to rosy marble.

Except for a missing fig leaf, he reminded her of the picture of a naked archangel she had once discovered in one of Preacher Moss's bibles. The picture had disturbed her greatly all those years ago, and the sight of Trace Harden disturbed her greatly now. She kept looking at the place where the fig leaf would have been, feeling her face grow hot as a tingling sensation spread through her stomach and lower parts.

Sam had lived in a man's world long enough to

know about sex and how things worked between men and women. Until now, reports of sexual encounters had impressed her as fantastic and faintly humorous. As hard as she tried, she hadn't been able to figure why men and women would want to roll around naked together. It had seemed to her like a silly and embarrassing waste of time.

But now, watching Trace rub his hands over his body, wiping the water off himself, she swallowed hard and found herself remembering his kiss and the heat that had exploded through her belly.

Her mouth dried and a tremble appeared in the fingers that gripped the windowsill. Wobbling, uttering a curse word, she pushed away from the window and tottered toward the chair at the table. Sitting there in a feverish trance, Sam tried to imagine what it would feel like to kiss someone while both parties were naked. When she realized what she was straining to imagine, a molten wave of embarrassment scalded her throat and cheeks.

"Ha rah! Ha rah!"

She jumped to her feet and looked around wildly as she heard him coming toward the cabin. Clothes! Where had he put his saddlebags? She'd packed him an extra set of clothes. Her gaze settled on the pile of leather beside the door and she dashed toward it, jerking at the flaps with shaking fingers. A sound almost like a sob rasped out of her throat when she found the right pocket. Jumping up, she ran to the door and threw out a pair of wrinkled but clean trousers and a white shirt.

Naked as a newborn, Trace gave her a hard stare, then bent to pick up the pants and shirt. Sam ducked inside the cabin and flattened herself against the wall, pressing a hand against the pounding that erupted behind her rib cage.

"Get hold of yourself!" she whispered, reminding herself that Trace Harden had ruined her life, and she hated him. She didn't know what was happening to her, but she knew he was to blame for these strange, hot half-sick, half-exhilarated sensations racing through her body, and she didn't like it.

Walking to the stove, Sam poured a fresh cup of strong black coffee, and tried to work up her temper. What she needed now was a dose of the anger she had felt earlier. But she couldn't find it.

Releasing a breath, hot with embarrassment, she sat down at the table as Trace came inside, smelling of water and sunshine. He walked to the stove, poured a cup of coffee, then sat at the table across from her.

"Here's the way I figure it," he said, keeping his gaze steady on a cobweb above the doorway. "We catch some fish, eat, then you go your way, and I'll go mine."

Sam moved her chair into the wedge of sunlight pouring through the window. The place where a fig leaf should have been kept leaping into her thoughts. "Where are you going?" she asked in a low voice.

A shrug lifted the shirt clinging damply to his shoulders. "Back to Dogtown, I guess." He combed his fingers through his wet hair. "Maybe Mattie will return. Maybe someone else will show up with news of Hannibal." Accusation darkened his eyes. "This detour has been costly in more ways than one."

Instantly Sam stiffened. A head jerk indicated the creek. "I thought we were through fighting."

His amber eyes glittered in the sunlight flooding the cabin. "I don't usually treat women roughly, and I apologize. I don't want to fight with you. I just want to get away from you. The sooner the better."

"That's fine with me," Sam agreed sharply. "But going back to Dogtown is just plain stupid! First, you'll have to ride through Denver, and someone is bound to recognize you. You can bet the town is plastered with wanted posters."

Trace gazed at the sunshine teasing red highlights from her short dark hair. Minutes ago she had appeared as tough as a boot, now, she made him think of a young girl dressed in her brother's clothes, fresh faced and rosy, as appealing as four aces. A flush of discomfort stained his throat as he recalled her inspecting his nakedness. And he remembered the first time he had seen her naked. He looked at her now, and pictured the lushness of her body, the warm curve of breast and hips.

"You're afraid of your own womanliness, aren't you?" he asked softly.

Her eyebrows shot up and red circles flamed on her cheeks. "I'm not afraid of anything!"

"You're afraid to accept yourself as a woman."

"Fear has nothing to do with anything! There's nothing about being a woman that I want to be. I like being independent, Harden. I like making my own decisions. I don't want some puffed-up male telling me what to do or undermining me until I think I can't take care of myself."

"It's a man's duty to protect the weaker sex and take care of her. Most women appreciate being cared for."

Sam threw out a hand. "That's what you want every woman to believe. And that's why I don't want to be one! I sure as hell don't want to depend on some man! You want an example?" Her eyes glittered. "Remember your wife Etta's letter? About how Hannibal kept her and raped her for two weeks?"

"Keep Etta out of this," Trace warned, his eyes narrowing.

"Can you imagine some SOB trying to keep *me* prisoner for two weeks?" A hard smile curved her lips. "Ha! Don't you think I'd have found a weapon in that house and a chance to use it? You bet I would have! I wouldn't have been sitting around helpless, waiting for some man to rescue me!"

In fact, Sam had begun to wonder if Etta Harden had been as destructive to herself as she was proving to be to others. How driven toward dark impulses had the woman been? Did she feel a need to wound or shock those who cared about her? How much responsibility did Etta bear for what had happened to her? And exactly what *had* happened to Etta Harden?

Trace rose from his chair, a dangerous glint in his eyes. "Etta wasn't like you. She was a lady."

"That's my point. A set of attitudes comes with the petticoats. Save-me-I'm-so-helpless attitudes. Well, I don't think like that and I never will. I make a far better boy than I'll ever make a woman!"

He started to argue, then closed his mouth. Clenching his teeth, he strode past her and out the door. "I'm going to build a fish trap," he called over his shoulder. "See if you can coax some life out of that old cookstove."

While he worked on the creek bank, building a trap out of twigs and leaves, Trace surprised himself with the realization that it would be difficult to ride away from her. Although Sam Kincade was about as defenseless as an army arsenal, something in him wanted to protect her whether she liked it or not.

Despite the lushness curving beneath her shapeless poncho, Sam was more man than woman, independent, bold, fearless, and combative. As a boy, she could move in the world with some degree of acceptance; as a woman she would have been considered an unnatural creature, avoided by both sexes. He felt a pang of sympathy for this defensive lonely woman who fit nowhere.

Rocking back on his heels, he stared unseeing at the water rushing down the mountainside. Why was he drawn to her?

Part of the reason, he decided reluctantly, was a growing respect for her courage and capabilities. It took a lot of guts to chase after outlaws, courage to confront them, and skill and daring to bring them to justice. He knew men who wouldn't have dreamed of exposing themselves to such risks.

Also she was easy to travel with. Sam pulled her own weight, didn't complain, did what was required efficiently and without fuss. Never would he have expected Etta to cope with the cabin's old stove, nor would he have left Etta alone, unprotected, in the cabin. Etta wouldn't have known the first thing about camping on the prairie, or how to saddle a horse or care for it. There was no way on earth that a woman like Etta could have staged a successful jailbreak, or would even have thought of making the attempt in the first place.

Finally, Sam was beautiful. The longer he knew her, the more beautiful she became, even dressed in boy's clothing. He didn't understand this, and he didn't like thinking about her glowing skin or periwinkle eyes, or the curving body beneath that shapeless poncho.

Trace stared blindly at the twig he turned between his fingers.

Had Etta been so completely helpless that she couldn't have defended herself or found some way to signal for help during the two weeks that Hannibal abused her? Two weeks was a long time. There must have been a few hours when Hannibal was drunk or asleep. Surely there would have been one or two opportunities for a resourceful person to escape or shout for assistance. She could have set the house on fire. She could have thrown something through a window. She could have struck Hannibal with the poker or gotten a knife from the kitchen.

Now that Sam had sunk a barb of doubt in his mind, the questions wouldn't leave him alone.

Surprisingly, she was an excellent cook.

"That was the best trout I've ever eaten," Trace said truthfully, picking up the tin plates and placing them in a bucket of creek water. "Thank you for the meal."

Sam frowned suspiciously. "You caught the fish. All I did was pick some wild onions and throw everything in a skillet." After a pause she jutted her chin and added, "I like to cook." She said it defensively as if admitting to a secret vice, glaring a challenge at him as though she expected him to laugh and would pounce on him if he did.

He'd never met anyone so prickly about compliments. Trace poured them both another cup of coffee, then glanced toward his saddlebags and changed the subject. "Did you by any chance bring along some money?" If he departed in the next hour, he'd have enough daylight to ride out of the foothills without mishap. "I'll wire you any amount you're willing to lend. With interest."

"Everything happened so fast that I didn't have time to dig up my cache. But I've got enough money to stake us for a few days," she said, studying the surface of her coffee.

That caught his attention. "Us?" he asked, frowning. "There is no us, Kincade."

"I've been thinking."

"We despise each other, remember? And with good reason. Because our paths crossed, both of our lives are ruined."

"We've been looking at this all wrong," she insisted, ignoring his comment. Lifting her head, she met his stare. "Hannibal Cotwell is to blame for everything that's happened. It's his fault that you and I met, his fault that our lives are ruined. About the only thing that hasn't changed for you and me, is that we still want Hannibal dead. Would you agree?"

Trace frowned at the lamplight smoothing the lines between her brows. "If this is leading toward a suggestion that we join forces, forget it. I don't trust you any farther than I can throw you."

She tilted her head and examined his face with a thoughtful expression. "I guess that makes us even. I don't trust you either. You and Hannibal have the same bad blood."

"So why are you hinting at a joint effort?"

Tapping a fingernail against her teeth, she studied him for a long moment before she answered. "Basically, the judge had a sound plan about using you for bait."

"And you know where Hannibal is," Trace guessed, speaking slowly.

"I might." She pursed her lips and studied the ceiling.

Trace leaned his arms on the table and scowled.

"Why should I trust you? For all I know, you and the judge planned to hang me right from the first."

"Would I have wrecked my life getting you out of jail if we'd planned to hang you all along?" she demanded, bristling.

"Maybe the jailbreak was a ruse," he considered, thinking out loud. "Maybe you're marking our trail so Sheriff Ainsley can follow us right to Hannibal, where he hangs both brothers."

"That's not a bad idea," Sam snapped, "but there was no backup in case the first scheme failed. If Sheriff Ainsley has someone looking for us—and undoubtedly he does—it's because we're outlaws, thanks to you."

"From my point of view, it's thanks to you," Trace said, speaking between his teeth.

They glared at each other across the table.

In the ensuing silence, they heard the cry of a night bird, heard a small animal wiggling through the brush beside the cabin wall. A loose rock skittered down the slag pile.

"I don't like teaming up any better than you do," Sam said finally. "But we'll both have a better chance of killing Hannibal if we have some backup. I doubt his men are going to stand by and let me or you gun their boss down. There's going to be a fight. We'll have a better chance of coming out of this alive if we have some help."

He tapped his fingers on the tabletop, looking at her. "I'll have to think about this."

She waved a hand. "Think all you want, but do it

fast. I'm going out to settle the horses for the night. When I get back, I expect you to make a decision. I plan to leave at sunup tomorrow. If you're going with me, we need to make some plans."

After a minute, Trace walked to the window and leaned against the sill, watching her lead the horses to the creek through the deepening twilight shadows.

If he agreed to travel with Sam Kincade, he was a bigger fool than anyone had ever suspected. They didn't trust or like one another. They were both outlaws; wanted posters would blanket the west in a matter of days. Instinct warned him to travel alone.

On the other hand, Sam Kincade was the best shot he'd ever seen. She didn't shy from danger, and she wasn't afraid to pull a trigger. Moreover, she was right about Hannibal's men. Undoubtedly, there would be a gunfight. Plus, he believed her hint that she knew where Hannibal could be found.

Finally, he felt an odd bond with this strange woman, as if destiny had linked them and slowly drew the chain tighter. This was the only way Trace could explain his difficulty in freeing himself of her. Each time liberty beckoned, something happened that slammed them back together.

He was still brooding over his decision when she returned to the cabin, listing the pros and mostly cons of a partnership.

"Well?" Planting her fists on her hips, she studied him. "What's it going to be?"

"Tell me something. Are you going after Hannibal whether or not we join forces?"

"Of course," she said, frowning. "Killing Hannibal Cotwell is my life's purpose. I'm not giving up just because of a few setbacks. I can't see you giving up either. Besides, what else do we have to do?"

He considered. "We'll let luck decide it." After fanning a deck of cards across the table, he swept them up and shuffled, then slapped the deck in front of her. "If you draw the high card, I'll join up with you. If I draw the high card, we go our separate ways."

"Did you rig this deck?" she asked suspiciously.

He gave her a pained look.

"I've seen you draw an ace at will. You can't do that unless you've set up the deck."

Angry, he resisted an urge to walk out the door and wash his hands of her. "I know every method of cheating ever invented. If I didn't, my gaming establishment would have gone bust in a matter of days. But I myself do not cheat." Except when it was necessary. "Draw, damn it. Let's get this over with."

Sam placed her hand on the deck. "Is this how you always make decisions? On the luck of the draw?"

"Sometimes," he snapped.

"I don't care if you come with me or not," she said, fingering the deck. "In fact, I'd rather travel alone."

"Just cut the cards."

"The only reason I suggested joining forces is because I'll have a better chance to kill Hannibal. Taking an extra set of guns is a business decision, that's all."

"Let's get this straight right now," Trace said, leaning forward on his palms. "You aren't going to kill Hannibal. I am."

For an instant their eyes locked and held. Then Sam signed and threw out her hands. "I don't care who kills him, I just want him dead!"

"Then cut the damned cards."

She turned over a four of hearts and Trace smiled, knowing she believed she had lost. "This is a stupid way to make a decision!" she said angrily, staring at the card.

He shot his cuffs and flexed his fingers, toying with her. He'd made his decision fifteen minutes ago. There was no way he was going to allow Sam to ride into Hannibal's hideout outnumbered, outgunned, and alone. Hannibal and his men would cut her down in three seconds.

"Just get to it! Cut!" she said, glaring.

Grinning in anticipation, he turned over the deuce of clubs, then pretended to stare in disbelief, his smile fading. "I don't believe this. Odds are, I should have beat you."

A wide grin showed a flash of white teeth. "At least I know you didn't cheat."

He fell back in the chair and stared at a point in front of him, making his defeat appear genuine. Finally he sighed and lifted his gaze. "All right, we travel together. This was your idea, how do you propose we trap the tiger?"

To his surprise, she briefly closed her eyes and a shudder of pleasure shivered down her body. Trace had seen that response before. Frowning, he tried to remember where, his eyes flaring slightly when he recalled that every woman he had ever made love to had closed her eyes and shuddered with pleasure in the early moments of seduction.

"You're asking my opinion?"

"Yes," he said, frowning. Sam didn't respond to compliments, but she shuddered with pleasure when a man requested her opinion. He pulled out a chair and straddled it, arching a puzzled eyebrow and wondering if he would ever understand her.

Sam couldn't help giving him a radiant smile. It didn't occur to her that she was slowly succumbing to a seduction Trace Harden didn't even know he was conducting.

CHAPTER
* 10 *

*I*t took some time for Sam to discover her first mistake.

Her second mistake was allowing the smoke to curl up from the cabin chimney while she cooked the trout. Sam's third mistake was walking to the creek the next morning to rinse out the coffee pot before she packed it, and thereby heedlessly exposing herself to anyone hiding in the brush on the far side of the water.

Later, Sam decided her carelessness had occurred because she had been unsettled and preoccupied by trying to sleep in a small enclosure with Trace Harden tossing and turning only a breath away. Initially, she tried to convince herself that it was the absolute darkness, the high mountain silence, and the day's heat trapped inside the cabin that made her so restless and kept her awake.

But eventually, listening to the cot creak beneath Trace's weight, discovering that she was trying to match her breathing to his, she had reluctantly con-

ceded the truth. She couldn't sleep because her feverish brain spun images of Trace's naked body in her
mind, like a wheel turning up the same nick with
every revolution.

She had burned with a desire to see Trace's body
and she had yearned to kiss him again. Every time
Sam looked at him, her gaze dropped to his full,
well-shaped lips and she craved another kiss. After a
lot of thought, Sam had decided to kiss him back if
he ever felt moved to kiss her again.

That wasn't going to happen, she thought sourly.
They were together because of expediency and a nod
from Lady Luck. Sighing, Sam approached the
creek, shaking the grounds out of the coffee pot.

She had started to bend toward the rushing water
when instinct raised the hair on the back of her neck.
Dropping the coffee pot, she straightened and felt a
jolt of adrenaline kick her nerves into full alert. Edging back her poncho, Sam checked her gun belt and
glanced uneasily toward a pile of boulders.

"Who's there?" she shouted across the creek.

Tense and expectant, she scanned the aspens and
dense undergrowth running down to the water on the
far side of the creek. The tumbling, rushing water
obscured lesser sounds, but she could still hear the
rustlings of a man crouched in the wild currant
bushes. Sam slid the Colt out of the holster and
gripped it in her hand. She wet her lips and edged
closer to the willows feathering out from the base of
the rocks. Someone was out there, watching her. She

couldn't spot him, but she felt his presence like an icy wind.

"Show yourself!" she shouted, skipping her gaze along the dense tier of currant bushes. "I know you're there!"

A bullet smacked into an aspen a few feet behind her right shoulder, and Sam dove into the willow thicket, her heart pounding. As bullets pinged off the granite boulders between her and the creek, she recognized a potentially fatal mistake.

She was trapped behind the rocks with no way to escape that wouldn't leave her exposed. The instant she crawled out of the willows, the gunman would have her in a clear line of sight. And the boulders that had protected her made it impossible for her to get off a shot without flaunting herself as a target. Teeth grinding, she struck one of the rocks with her fist. This was a fine fix.

A guttural shout yelled from across the water. "Edwin Snow sends his regards!" Two bullets splintered into the rocks.

And that Sam realized, brought home her first mistake. She had told Millicent Snow about the cabin.

Swearing, she lifted her arm and shoved her gun barrel over the top of the rocks, firing blindly, then sat down to reload. The bullets were wasted. She couldn't see the gunman, didn't know if he was still hiding among the currants or sneaking across the creek and moving up on her. The next volley appeared to come from Sam's right, which was a bad sign. If she was correct, then her situation became more perilous. The change of firing direction indicated the gunman had indeed crossed the creek and was edging toward the cabin, cutting off any hope of a dash for shelter.

Although the effort was futile since she was shooting blind and didn't know where the target was, Sam thrust her gun barrel between a cleft in the boulders and fired until the Colt clicked down on empty. A hail of answering bullets cut through the aspens and willows, showering her with twigs and bits of leaves.

She'd guessed right. The gunman was now on this side of the creek, between Sam and the cabin. In minutes, he'd be in front of her, and she'd be pinned like a brooch on a spinster's breast.

Crouching at the base of the boulders, Sam frantically patted her pockets, looking for more ammunition. Sweat ran in her eyes, and she dashed it away with an impatient gesture. Damn. The rest of her ammunition was in her saddlebags, already loaded on Blue.

Sliding down the ragged boulder, she sank to the ground in the midst of the willows and drew her knees up. The useless Colt dangled in her fingers. It was beginning to look as if her luck had run out.

"I got you now, Kincade." Pleasure and triumph rang in the gunslinger's shout coming from the clearing in front of the cabin. She was trapped.

"You done messed up, boy. You shouldn't have jilted a banker's daughter. That gal's papa is mighty pissed." A bullet chunked into the rocks near her head and chips of flying stone nicked Sam's cheek. "Mr. Snow's offerin' one thousand smackeroos to the man who brings in your scalp. I mean to have that money, Kincade."

Shock turned Sam's eyes a deep navy color. Edwin Snow wanted her scalp? A prickle ran over her skull as every hair on her head shrank in horror. If by some miracle she managed to escape this particular gunslinger, the promise of a thousand dollars would incite others besides professional bounty hunters. Every man in the territory would be looking for Sam, hoping to lift her hair.

She aimed her Colt at the sound of his voice and pulled the trigger, hopelessly listening to the hammer strike on empty. Venturing outside without adequate ammunition had been another mistake. A deadly one. Disgusted at herself, Sam grimaced and let the Colt drop out of her fingers.

It wasn't dying that made her so furious; it was dying like this. When she'd thought about meeting her maker, she always thought it would happen in the service of justice. She'd pictured herself going out in a blaze of glory and righteousness while fighting lawlessness and destructive forces. That kind of end would have suited her just fine. In fact, she'd half expected that she would die when the final confrontation came with Hannibal Cotwell.

But to die because she had jilted Millicent Snow was too ignominious and too ludicrous to bear. Just thinking about it made her want to scream.

The sound of the gunman approaching the willows told Sam that she had about two minutes to live. That gave her one minute to review a basically eventless life, and one minute to mourn all the exciting experiences she would never encounter.

Trace waited beside the cabin window, watching in the shadows as a bearded man waded the creek, firing steadily at the willows and boulders where Sam must have taken cover. Trace realized at once that she would be trapped against the rocks.

At first it puzzled him when she ceased firing. Then he remembered that she had packed her ammunition in the saddlebags. She was out of bullets.

Gripping the gun Sam had tossed him back at the jail, he stared at the gunslinger until his eyes burned, silently urging him to continue circling until he placed himself between Trace and the willows where Sam was hiding.

"Come on, come on, just a little farther," he muttered beneath his breath.

The last thing he needed was for Sam to get herself killed on his watch. First Etta, then Sam.

His gaze narrowed on the gunslinger.

Patience was crucial in his profession, as was timing. But patience never came easy. When he judged the moment had arrived, a breath of relief eased past his tight lips. Moving silently, he slipped to the doorway and risked a quick glance outside.

The gunman was nearly where Trace wanted him, his back to the cabin, moving stealthily toward the rock pile.

Without making a sound, Trace glided out of the

doorway and into the forest. Advancing from pine to pine, he paused only when he heard the gunman taunting Sam with a description of how he intended to peel her scalp off of her skull.

The moment provided Trace time to consider what he would do when he came up behind the gunman. He was a gambler, on occasion a dangerous and bad-tempered gambler, but he wasn't a killer. Although he had experienced more than his share of unpleasant situations and he had never backed away from a fight, he hadn't yet found it necessary to kill a man.

A man swearing to scalp a woman deserved to die, and Trace was prepared to oblige. But when he stepped out of the aspens directly behind the gunman, he discovered he couldn't shoot a man in the back. Instead, he raised the butt of the pistol and smashed it down hard behind the bastard's right ear. The man dropped to the ground like a crumpled feed sack, sprawling at Trace's feet.

"Come out, I've got him," he called to Sam. Bending, he picked up the gunslinger's weapons, then turned the man over with the toe of his boot. Edwin Snow had chosen well. The gunman was an ugly brute who looked as if taking a scalp wouldn't trouble him more than skinning a rabbit.

Sam stood behind the willows, then pushed through the branches, moving forward until she stood over the gunslinger's body. "You sure took your own sweet time!" she said angrily. "Another minute and I'd have been shoveling coal into the devil's furnace."

Trace pinned her with a long level look. "I distinctly recall you swearing that no one knew about this cabin."

A flush of crimson stained her throat. "I forgot about telling Millicent."

"So we can add a woman scorned to your ever-expanding list of enemies. And her father." They both eyed the unconscious gunslinger. "What do you suggest we do with your lady's avenger?"

"Kill him, of course," Sam snapped, wiping at the nicks that stung her cheek. "Didn't you hear him? He was going to *scalp* me!" A shudder convulsed her shoulders. "Go ahead. You've got the loaded gun. Kill the bastard."

Trace leaned against a tree trunk and considered. There was no uncertainty in his mind that he'd do society a favor by firing a bullet through the gunslinger's heart. This man would have brutally killed Sam as undoubtedly he had others, and he would have scalped her without a qualm. Straightening, Trace walked forward, aimed at the man's chest, then hesitated. He let the barrel drop, spun the pistol in his hand, and presented the butt to Sam.

"I prefer to make my killings at cards, not by shooting an unconscious man. If you want him dead, you kill him."

Sam stared, then accepted the gun. "You've never killed a man, have you, Harden?"

His lips pressed in a line. "I won't hesitate a second to kill Hannibal if that's what you're thinking."

"Just my luck." She flipped out the chamber,

checked the load, snapped it shut, and adjusted the grip in her palm. "I get a partner who's afraid of guns."

"Give me that!" Trace snatched the gun from her hand and fired rapidly at the gunslinger, tracing his outline in the pine needles and dirt. Just as quickly, he reloaded and angrily tossed the pistol back to Sam. "I didn't say I was afraid of guns or couldn't use one. And I didn't say I couldn't kill a man. But I won't kill one who's unconscious and unarmed!"

The shots woke the gunman. Sitting up groggily, he lifted both hands to his head, then blinked at the blood on his fingers and swore viciously.

Sam steadied the barrel of the Colt across her forearm and aimed dead center between the gunslinger's eyes. One minute passed, then another. "Damn it to hell." Sighing, she lowered her arm and glared at Trace. "There's rope in the cabin."

They left the gunslinger gagged and tied to a chair inside the cabin. Maybe someone would come looking for him, maybe a miner would stumble across him by accident, or maybe he would eventually work himself free. Then again, maybe not. Regardless, Sam figured they had given Edwin Snow's hired gun a better chance than he had been willing to give her.

Biting her lips, she urged Blue up a steep, rocky incline, thinking about those moments in the willows when she had believed she was about to die. Astonishingly, the thing she had most regretted was that she had never known a man in the biblical sense and had believed at that moment that she never would.

Sam looked at Trace, riding in front of her, and experienced again the sudden aching emptiness and a sense of loss. It puzzled her deeply that her regrets in the willows had centered on woman things. Recalling those thoughts made her feel peculiar inside.

They completed the arduous journey over the mountains as swiftly as possible, departing each campsite before dawn and not dismounting until evening shadows became too dense for the horses to proceed safely.

On the morning of the eighth day, Sam crawled out of her bedroll with a groan. Every muscle in her body was sore, aching at the prospect of another day in the saddle.

After walking in circles to work the stiffness out of her snakebit leg, she built up the fire she had banked the night before. She warmed her hands against the predawn chill and watched the stars fade against a pink and lavender sky. When the last star winked out, Sam filled the coffee pot at a nearby stream, then hung it over the fire pit, fried some bacon, and stirred up some biscuits in the bacon grease. The food smelled like heaven in the high mountain air, improving her spirits.

"Isn't it about time you told me where we're going?" Trace called. He adjusted a mirror hanging on a pine branch, then pulled his jaw tight and drew a straight razor through a film of soap. A sharp backward gesture shook the soap off the blade, then he leaned to the mirror again and thrust out his chin.

Sam's mouth dried as she watched him scrape the

razor up his throat. If anyone had suggested a month ago that Sam Kincade would go mushy inside at the sight of a man shaving, she would have laughed until her sides burst. The realization that she was changing was sobering. Something fundamental was shifting inside, she could feel it.

"Sam? Are you listening?"

Giving her head a shake, Sam tore her gaze from the sprinkling of dark hair on Trace's naked chest and blinked down at the pale lump of biscuit dough sitting in the skillet. "Sorry. What were you saying?"

Trace rolled his eyes, then tilted the mirror. Morning sunlight flashed down the razor blade. "If you don't trust me enough to tell me where we're headed, perhaps we should reconsider this partnership."

"In my line of work, trusting a man can get you killed."

"You aren't a bounty hunter any more." He glanced at her, then pulled a towel from around his neck and wiped the last of the soap off of his face, leaning toward the pine to inspect his jawline in the mirror. "You're an outlaw. We both are. I've saved your life twice now. Your lack of trust is becoming insulting."

"I might have recovered from the snakebite on my own," she insisted, not believing it for a minute. If she hadn't known Trace saved her life, she wouldn't have busted him out of jail.

"I've thought about it," she said after a moment. "Despite the affront to the law, breaking you out of jail was the right thing to do. I didn't have a choice, not really."

To escape detection, the route Sam had chosen was arduous, through the mountains, rather than out on the flat. During the previous week of hard riding, she'd had time to wage a civil war in her mind. On one side of the battle was her deep inbred love and respect for the law. On the other side stood her conscience and personal integrity which rode above the law in this instance.

"No," she conceded with a sigh, poking at the fire. "I couldn't have let you hang, not if I wanted to live with myself. I gave my word. Regardless of the consequences, I had to burn down the jail."

"And I'm grateful that you did." Frowning, Trace slipped on his shirt. "Are you aware that you have an annoying habit of changing the subject whenever it suits you? This conversation began with me inquiring about our destination. Perhaps you would care to comment on that subject?"

Sam placed the skillet over the coals. "All right, here's the way I see it. Shortly after our arrival, we're going to find Hannibal, or he's going to find us. You say what you have to say and then you kill him. Afterward, I take his body to the local sheriff, claim the bounty, and instruct the sheriff to telegraph the judge. I tell the sheriff and the newspapers that getting Hannibal was the judge's plan and give him the credit for our catch."

"You plan to give the judge all the credit?" Sitting on a rock, Trace reached for the coffee pot and a rasher of bacon.

"Only if he agrees to issue pardons to both of us in

exchange for capturing and killing Hannibal, and for praising his cleverness to the territory newspapers."

"Do you really believe your great-uncle is going to clear our names?"

"I don't see why not. This plan gets him off the hook too. He can boast to everyone that your trial and the jailbreak were staged as part of a master plan to lure your brother into thinking that he had nothing to fear from us. We had to do it this way in order to get close enough to kill him." Her chin thrust forward defensively. "Do you have any better ideas?"

"Not at the moment." The morning sun lit his amber eyes, turning them translucent and making Sam think of honey. "What about Edwin Snow? How do you plan to get Snow to call off his fire?"

"I haven't figured that out yet," she said, frowning. "But I'm working on it."

"Sam . . . when will we get wherever the hell it is we are going?"

Sam drew in a deep breath, hating it that she had to trust him. "I figure we'll break out of the mountains about mid-morning and ride into Pueblo shortly after suppertime."

"Pueblo," Trace repeated.

"We'll leave the horses in Pueblo, then proceed to La Junta by train, then on to Santa Fe by stage."

"How do you know Hannibal is in Santa Fe?" Trace looked up at the snow fields still capping the high peaks even though it was early summer.

"My informant claims Hannibal has a hideout on a ranch about ten miles outside of town. Unless he's moved on, that's where he was headed when he left Leadville."

They finished breakfast in silence, then Sam packed up the campsite while Trace saddled the horses.

"We'll stay in Pueblo overnight," he announced as Sam tied their supplies behind her saddle.

She paused and glared. "Too dangerous. The last train leaves at nine o'clock. I figure we can make it if we don't dawdle on the trail."

"How do you plan to buy train tickets? I went through your poke last night, and you barely have enough money to buy a decent meal."

Sam gasped. "You went through my poke?"

"A few hours at the faro or poker tables and I can guarantee that we'll depart Pueblo with a sizeable bankroll."

"You went through my poke?" Sam repeated, her voice spiraling into an accusing high register. "And you wonder why I don't trust you?"

Neither of them mounted. They stood beside the horses, taking each other's measure. "Where I come from," Trace said, watching her, "there's an unpleasant name for a man who depends on a woman to pay his expenses. I prefer to pay my own way. Unfortunately, Sheriff Ainsley confiscated everything I owned. He can have my gold watch and extra clothing, but I need to replace the money. I can do that at the gaming tables."

"Are you crazy? Do you think the Pueblo sheriff and his deputies won't be watching for us? And what about Edwin Snow? God knows how many hired guns he has out there!"

"By now, everyone will think we've left the territory."

"I say we jump the train as it's leaving the station. We don't need money to ride in a cattle car."

A pained look tightened Trace's jaw and his eyes narrowed. "I am a civilized man, Kincade. I don't hitch rides in cattle cars. I travel in a first-class coach. When you join up with me, that's how you travel too."

"You're suggesting we board publicly with the other passengers?" She blinked in astonishment, then her face snapped down on itself. "Why don't we just hang our wanted posters around our necks in case there's someone out there who hasn't read the newspapers and doesn't recognize us? Or we could paint targets on our foreheads. No, Harden. No, *nada*, not a chance. We are not going to take any stupid risks."

"I've been sleeping on the ground for a week, eating unidentifiable meat that's either charred or half raw, and I haven't had a hot bath for longer than I can remember." He stared at her. "I plan to remedy that. And I am not going to turn my back on an opportunity to put together a respectable stake."

"Then it looks like we've hit an impasse," Sam stated when her eyes began to burn from glaring. "I say we high-tail it out of Pueblo while we still have our skins. You say we flaunt ourselves for the sake of a hot bath and a purse. Short of splitting up, how do you suggest we resolve this conflict?"

"The usual way." Reaching into his jacket pocket,

Trace removed a deck of cards, not taking his eyes off Sam's angry face. In a flash the cards were blurring through his fingers in a speed shuffle.

"High card decides," he said curtly. "Draw."

"I hate deciding something this crucial on the luck of the draw!"

"Would you prefer to toss a coin?" He stared into her eyes. "It will have to be your coin since I have none of my own."

Fuming, Sam paced up and down beside Blue, then she muttered and thrust out her hand. "Give me the damned cards." She cut them, hesitated, chewed her lip, then glared at Trace and cut again. When she turned over a jack, a broad smile of relief curved her lips. "Looks like we play it safe."

"It ain't over until the piano man slams down the lid." Taking the cards from her, he shuffled again, fanned the boards, then snapped them into a block. Without looking down, he cut the deck, then held the upper half face out so Sam could see the card. "What is it?"

"A queen! Damn all!" Furious, she kicked a rock down the mountainside. "Best two out of three. Shuffle again."

"No. You lost," Trace said pleasantly. A satisfied grin exposed white, white teeth. A sparkle danced in his tigerish eyes. "Accept it like a lady, Kincade."

"Go to hell!"

Fuming, Sam tossed herself up on Blue's back and headed down the trail without a backward glance.

The only thing she knew for certain was that he

hadn't cheated. She had watched him like a hawk. At least she didn't think he had cheated. Of course, Sam didn't really know what to watch for. But she did know how clever those long fingers were with a deck of cards. He could have cheated, she thought, chewing her lip.

He must have cheated, the bastard. But since she couldn't prove it, any accusation she made would sound like sour grapes. Frustrated and angry, she decided it would be a cold day in hell before she fell for his cut-the-cards trick again.

They made better time than Sam had predicted, coming down out of the mountains well before noon and arriving at the outskirts of Pueblo before dusk.

Ignoring Sam's muttered protests, Trace located the gaming district south of the river with unerring instincts. After running a practiced eye down the noisy street, he chose a hotel only a few blocks from the Santa Fe station, tilting his hat brim to inform Sam where they would be staying.

She made a sharp hissing noise between her teeth and he followed her gaze toward a collection of papers tacked to the front of a saloon. At once he saw their names on the posters. In consolation, he decided the pencil-drawings of their faces bore only a slight resemblance to reality. The artist's conception depicted them as hardened criminals. Trace looked like a brute and the artist had given Sam a mustache.

"I hate being on the wrong side of the law!" Sam said hotly, jerking her hat brim down to her eyes.

"Relax. No one is going to recognize us from the pictures on those posters."

Sam had reached the same conclusion. But overconfidence had almost brought her down a few days earlier.

Trace stopped before the Glory of Pueblo Hotel. "You take the horses to the stable and arrange for long-term boarding. I'll get us a room."

"Two rooms," she corrected sharply.

"As in divide and conquer? I don't think so. Mr. John Bellings and his nephew, Tom, will be sharing the same quarters." Swinging off his horse, Trace handed the reins to Sam, then gazed down the dirt street, noting which saloons and gaming halls attracted the most action. "We'll have time for a bit of supper and a bath." The prospect of an all-night session overrode any saddle-weariness he may have felt. A spark of anticipation danced in his eyes.

Sam planted her boots in front of the hitching rail. "I'm not sleeping in the same hotel room as you."

He laughed, his mind already down the street at the tables. "I don't plan to sleep tonight. You'll have the room to yourself. After you stable the horses, it would be helpful if you would find out what time the earliest train leaves for Santa Fe."

She squinted up from under her hat brim. "Are you giving me orders?"

"Suggestions, Kincade. Merely suggestions." He brushed the travel dust off his shoulders and lapels and glanced at the door of the hotel. "Still smarting over losing, are we?"

Without a word, Sam angrily turned and led the horses toward the stable on the corner. She was plain worn out from the emotional upheavals of spending twenty-four hours a day with Trace Harden.

Sometimes everything he did irritated her almost beyond endurance. Then, in an about-face that happened for no discernible reason, everything he did enthralled her.

She loved it that he often requested her opinion; yet they seldom agreed on anything. She daydreamed that one night he would roll out of his blankets and slide under hers. The idea excited and frightened her at the same time. Sometimes he made her happy just by smiling at her; other times he made her so furious that she itched to shoot him.

The conflicts that went hand in hand with knowing Trace Harden exhausted her. To her deep shame, and for the first time in her life, Sam Kincade was experiencing lust.

Lust was the only explanation to account for some of the strange things she couldn't stop herself from doing, such as sneaking down to the stream when Trace washed up after a long day of hard riding. She had spied on him and studied every part of his body, often disappointed that he only removed his shirt to wash and not his trousers too. When it was her turn in the creek, she worried that he might be spying on her also. At the same time, she hoped that he was.

There was more. Lately, she'd discovered herself

accidentally brushing up against him, then trying to analyze the thrill of heat that resulted from his touch. It was a strange hot weak feeling that sapped her energy and made her feel spongy inside, but it felt good too. She didn't know how that could be, but it was. For a time she wondered if making her stomach do flip-flops was something Trace did on purpose, so she kept stumbling into him trying to spot exactly what he did that made her break out in goosebumps and feel hot all over. But it was like the cards. She couldn't catch him at whatever he was doing.

As a result of being around Trace, her nerves were turning into a giant snarled ball. Short of parting company, which she didn't want to do yet, Sam didn't see what she could do about the mounting attraction that left her feeling helpless and vulnerable and wildly off balance.

After she boarded the horses and instructed the farrier to sell them if she didn't return within sixty days, she spent twenty minutes saying good-bye to Blue, just in case. Then she checked on the train schedules and, trying not to call attention to herself, hurried back to the hotel.

The clerk informed her that her uncle was in room sixteen, and Sam climbed the stairs, edging around two men who were fighting. They took up the corridor, while a half-dressed woman hung out of a doorway and watched, shaking her fists and shouting incitements.

After taking a moment to rub her temples, trying to soothe the headache building behind her eyes,

Sam opened the door to room sixteen, stepped inside, and stopped short.

Trace sat in a fragrant tub in the middle of the room, happily puffing on a thin dark cigar and choosing oysters from a tray placed within reach. His dark hair curled in the steam, his cheeks were freshly barbered and pink. Soap bubbles glistened on his shoulders and chest.

Sam's posture sagged and she stared at him. He was the most handsome man she had ever laid eyes on, so powerfully virile and male that he simply took her breath away.

When his amber eyes swept over her, Sam felt as if her knees had turned to dust. Disappointment strangled her as his gaze moved beyond her to the men fighting in the corridor.

A hot violent longing seized Sam. Suddenly she desperately wanted Trace to look at her as a woman, wanted him to gaze at her with those dangerous tiger eyes and crave the same mysterious closeness that she did. To her horror she realized that right now, this very minute, she yearned with all her heart to be a beautiful, desirable woman who could drive men mad with a single glance.

Trace leaned his head against the back of the tub, looking at her through eyes made sensual by the pleasures of steam, smoke, and oysters. "Come inside, Kincade, and shut the door."

CHAPTER
* 11 *

"ow are you paying for all this splendor?" Sam demanded.

"With a glib tongue and a promise that if we skip out, the proprietor may sell our horses."

"It didn't occur to the proprietor that if we skip out, we'd probably do it on top of our horses?"

Trace dismissed the question with a soapy wave. "He mentioned something about posting a guard at the stables. So. Did you find out if there's an early train?" Closing his eyes, he drew on the cigar with a groan of pleasure.

Sam moved past him and leaned beside the window, one hand gripping the butt of the Colt as if she expected the Pueblo sheriff to burst through the panes at any second. When Trace opened one eye and studied her, her surly expression confirmed that her mood had not improved.

"The next train to La Junta departs at six tomorrow morning. We take a stage from there."

"Excellent! Couldn't be better." A bath, a decent cigar, and an array of civilized food had rejuvenated him. When the chambermaid returned his jacket and trousers, brushed and pressed, and the ready-made shirt, vest, and tie he had ordered, he would feel like a new man. He'd be prepared to challenge the local gamesmen and relieve them of a small but adequate fortune.

"Would you care for some oysters?" he inquired, feeling relaxed and expansive. "There's also meat and cheese."

Shooting him a glare, Sam shook her head. Something sorrowful and almost accusing pinched her expression, suggesting he had somehow disappointed. Maybe she had wanted the tub first. "I'll dry off after I finish this cigar, then the tub is yours."

She tossed her hat toward a peg on the wall, pushed a hand through her short hair, and sat down on the edge of the bed, testing the springs. "What am I supposed to do while you're out fleecing the gullible?"

"Get a good night's sleep," he suggested, puzzled as to why she seemed so sullen. "One of us should be alert in case of trouble on the train. I plan to sleep most of the way to La Junta."

Anger darkened her eyes. "It doesn't bother you in the least to bathe in front of me, does it?"

Actually, he was becoming more uncomfortable by the minute, aware that he was naked and she was not. "We've been traveling together long enough that I'd say we know all there is to know about each other." He paused, then conjured another lie. "You look like a man, talk like a man, shoot like a man, ride like a man. As far as I'm concerned, Kincade, you are a man. I don't feel at all as if I'm bathing in front of a woman." He moved his shoulders in what he hoped would pass for an indifferent shrug.

Traveling with Sam was indeed similar to traveling with a man in several respects. But Trace was acutely aware that she was a woman. He had, in fact, intended to be out of the tub before she returned, but he'd lost track of the time.

He had been unable to think of her as male since he had seen her naked while he nursed her back to health. Though several weeks had passed, he couldn't forget kissing her. And he couldn't recall her lush curves without feeling a stir between his own thighs. Occasionally, he wondered if something was wrong with him that he could burn with desire for a woman who resembled a boy. Other times he looked at her, and was angered that she wouldn't allow herself to be the beautiful woman that nature had intended.

"I've been thinking," Sam began, frowning.

He recognized that tone of voice. It signaled something to follow that he wasn't going to like.

"Part of Etta's letter doesn't make sense." Lifting her head, she met the resistance in his stare.

Trace's hand stopped on the way to his mouth and he returned a slice of roast beef to the platter. "Sam, I need full concentration tonight. I don't want to discuss Etta."

"Etta said Hannibal held her prisoner for two

weeks. And she claims when she discovered she was pregnant, Hannibal laughed and told her to pass the baby off as yours. Right?"

Trace scowled. Sam did this sometimes, raised a subject that opened an abyss between them. Yet he was glad to focus on something other than the ripe curves concealed by her dusty poncho, even if it meant talking about Etta.

"The timing puzzles me," Sam continued, ignoring his warning. "A woman gets pregnant in the middle of her cycle." Pink circles blossomed on her cheeks and she gazed steadily at the rug beside the bed. "Do you understand?"

Trace tilted his head with a sigh, inspecting the tin ceiling. "I've been married, Sam. I've known a lot of women. I understand a woman's body functions and how pregnancy occurs."

"All right, then." The pink climbing her throat deepened to scarlet. "Hannibal rapes your wife in the midst of her cycle, keeps her prisoner for two weeks, then rides out of town and heads west." She tilted her head and frowned. "When did Etta discover she was pregnant? When and how did she inform Hannibal?"

Trace's head snapped down and he glared at her. A cold knot formed in his chest. "Say that again."

This time he listened carefully. When Sam finished, he extended a hand. "Etta's letter is on the side table. Would you hand it to me, please?" His voice sounded harsh and frozen.

Although he knew every word, could quote the pages verbatim, he reread Etta's letter, this time focusing differently. With a shift in perspective, he saw at once that Sam had posed a legitimate question.

"I don't understand," he said eventually. Having forgotten Sam, his mind circling, he stood and wiped soap bubbles off his chest and hips. He stepped out of the tub and toweled himself dry. Sam scooted to the window and pressed her forehead against the glass, gazing down into the street.

"I missed this," Trace admitted, wrapping a dry towel around his waist. Lighting another cigar, he drew on it absently and without pleasure. Either Hannibal had been with Etta longer than two weeks, long enough to discover the pregnancy, or he had stayed two weeks as she claimed but departed without knowing she was pregnant.

Silently Sam passed behind him and opened the door to admit the chambermaid. The girl handed Trace's clothing to Sam, then threw Trace a smile and departed. Still without speaking, Sam extended a store-bought shirt and Trace interrupted his pacing long enough to thrust his arms into the sleeves.

Averting her eyes as he dropped the towel and pulled on his trousers, Sam selected a wedge of cheese, then stuck her finger in the bath water to test the temperature. "You must have loved her very much," she commented in a thin voice. Instantly, she felt flustered, but Trace was too preoccupied to notice.

Sitting on the side of the bed, he reached for his boots, then paused, remembering the first time he had met Etta Mayfair at a reception in New Orleans given by her aunt, Miss Hettie Mayfair. Intoxicated and made arrogant by a recent high-stakes win at the tables, Trace had attended the reception without an invitation, confident of his ability to charm Miss Hettie should she chastise him.

Had Etta not been Miss Hettie's niece, and had he not been feeling devilish enough to tease Miss Hettie, Trace probably would have overlooked Etta among the pastel beauties gracing the reception. Though she was pretty and her blonde hair impressed him as exceptionally abundant and luxurious, her flat Kansas accent grated and she was too bold for his taste. He lavished attention on her largely to tweak Miss Hettie.

Before the afternoon ended, Miss Hettie was furious at him, and Etta Mayfair was his for the taking. By then, he was fascinated by her. Unlike the society misses of his acquaintance, Etta Mayfair exhibited a bold and reckless nature. A teasing sexuality simmered behind eyes as green as sea water.

"That was four years ago," he said, unaware that he spoke aloud. He stared at the boot in his hand and a faint smile curved his lips. "She raised a scandal when she pursued me."

Alarmed and disapproving, Miss Hettie had summoned Etta's brother to come at once and take Etta home to Kansas City before she compromised herself beyond redemption.

But Miss Hettie was too late. Etta had come to Trace's bed one hot damp afternoon, not caring if the servants knew, and she had undressed in front of him so seductively that he had assumed she was experienced until he thrust into her. Afterward, she had stretched her naked body in the dim shuttered light and informed him with a satisfied smile that now he would have to marry her. Drawing a finger down his chest, purring like a cat, she had informed him that she always got what she wanted.

"So you married her," Sam said, speaking in that same peculiar strained voice.

Trace glanced up and frowned, startled to realize he'd been remembering aloud. He must have spoken in an engaging manner because Sam hadn't moved from the edge of the tub. The wedge of cheese was poised mid-way to her mouth.

Jerking on one boot, he reached for the other. "Whatever else I am, Kincade, I'm a gentleman. Of course I married her. At that point I would have moved the earth to marry her." Her manipulations had been amusing, but unnecessary.

"Her family objected?"

"To state it mildly." After stamping his heels into his boots, he tucked the new shirt into his trousers and donned a burgundy striped waistcoat. "To appease the Mayfairs, I took Etta back to Kansas City and built a home near her family's estate." He adjusted a string tie in the mirror. "They were horrified to have a professional gambler as an inlaw. They blamed me for Etta's death." He hesitated, staring into the glass. "And justly so. If it hadn't been for me, Etta would never have encountered a man like Hannibal, much less have welcomed him into her home. And Hannibal would not have had access to her."

"Are you certain about that?" Sam inquired quietly, returning the untasted cheese to the oyster platter.

"What does that mean?" Trace asked sharply.

"I'm not sure," she said thoughtfully, studying him.

"I am sure," Trace snapped, settling his hat firmly on his head. Without requesting her consent, he took Sam's poke from the top of the bureau and tucked it into his jacket pocket. "Etta led a sheltered and genteel life, protected first by her family, then by her husband. I deliberately kept her from any contact whatsoever with my gaming establishments. Under normal circumstances she would never have encountered a criminal element. But I exposed her to Hannibal. I am to blame. I insisted on opening our home as a safe haven for my brother because I wouldn't turn my back on him. I was, in fact, happy to see him when he visited." A look of pain and disgust distorted his features. "I refused to accept what Hannibal had become because I bear part of the responsibility for how he turned out."

"That is ridiculous!"

"I know that intellectually," Trace said, tapping his forehead. "But in my heart, I remember being the favorite son. I remember the sound of the lash biting into Hannibal's back, never into mine." He stared at her. "He should have hated me, but he didn't. I was the only person he said good-bye to when he left New Orleans."

"It wasn't your fault that—"

"On nights when I can't sleep, I wonder how Hannibal's life would have turned out if I had never been born. Or if we'd had the same father. I wonder if I could have said or done something that might have made things easier for him or changed the path he eventually chose." A frustrated breath escaped his lips. "I know you don't understand. Hell, I don't really understand it myself."

"You didn't kill Etta, Trace."

"But I'm responsible for her death. I told Hannibal he was welcome in our home at any time. And I left her alone with him."

"Did you know Hannibal would arrive while you were away?"

"That doesn't matter."

"So you didn't know. Trace, you didn't leave Etta without resources. Her family was nearby. There was a house full of servants. Presumably she had friends close at hand."

"Etta wanted to accompany me to New Orleans, but I refused." He reached for the door latch. "I settled our mother's estate in two weeks, but I remained in New Orleans for another month and a half. I visited old friends, raised hell, enjoyed myself. I was in no hurry to return to Kansas City." His tiger eyes glittered. "I didn't write to Etta, I didn't give her a thought. And while I was entertaining myself with cards, food, and nightly frolics, my brother was holding her prisoner and raping her."

Sam returned his stare.

"I provided lavishly for my wife, but I failed her in every other way. The only thing I can do to make amends is kill the man who destroyed her. And that," he swore, speaking between his teeth, "I will do!"

The door slammed behind him.

Sam stared at the door and wondered who he meant. To hear him tell the tale, one could almost suspect that Trace believed it was he who had destroyed Etta.

Once Sam recovered from the uncomfortably sensual awareness that she bathed in the tub only recently vacated by Trace, she gradually relaxed and ate the remainder of the oysters, cheese, and slices of roast beef. While she languished in the water, soaking the grime of travel and camping out of her pores, she contemplated Trace and Etta's story.

The more Sam learned about Etta Harden, the less she cared for the woman. On reflection, she didn't share Trace's conviction that Etta would never have met a man like Hannibal if Trace hadn't opened his way. Instinct told Sam that Etta craved danger and excitement and if she hadn't found it through Trace, she would have found it elsewhere.

When the water cooled and Sam's skin began to wrinkle, she stopped frustrating herself by posing questions without answers, climbed out of the tub, and toweled dry. But before she stepped into fresh corduroys and slipped on a loose man's shirt, she stood before the vanity mirror, timidly examining her body.

Usually she avoided reminders that she was not her father's son. But this evening, she inspected her breasts and hips. The only thing to compare herself with were the naked Venuses hanging over many saloon bars. A discouraged sigh eased past her lips. She was not nearly as voluptuous as a ripe saloon goddess. No come-hither invitation teased behind her lashes. After a critical evaluation, she finally decided her breasts were full enough and well shaped, but on the small side, and her hips were too slim. The patch of brown hair curling between her thighs embarrassed her to contemplate so she abruptly shifted her gaze to her legs. Again . . . too slender. And they were muscular rather than soft looking. Finally she made herself inspect the old bullet wound below her ribs. It was small but pink and puckered, ugly enough to draw attention away from her more acceptable features.

Sighing, Sam wondered if Trace would have sped to the window and looked away if she had been the one rising naked out of the tub instead of him. Or would he have stared at her with that slow smoky gaze that made her shiver inside and wish it had been her in his bed on a hot, damp New Orleans afternoon?

Good Lord. Where were these crazy thoughts coming from?

Raising a fist, she smacked her forehead and groaned aloud. Why was she tormenting herself? To Trace, she was merely a nuisance inflicted on him by a shared goal and a cut of the cards. Hadn't he flat told her that as far as he was concerned, she was a man? That's how he saw her. The same as the rest of the world saw her.

Grimacing, Sam turned away from the naked image in the mirror. Sitting heavily on the edge of the bed, she dropped her head into her hands.

After struggling for years to put all female things behind her, here she was yearning for a man—a certain man—to gaze at her and see her as a desirable woman.

This confusion was so ironic that she felt like laughing. Or weeping.

In truth, how could any man find her desirable? She'd worked for years to expunge any hint of femininity, and she'd been successful. No man was ever going to move the earth to marry her.

Throwing herself across the bed and gathering the pillow to her body, Sam burst into sobs, weeping as she hadn't since her father died.

Perhaps all the softness hadn't vanished after all.

She slept until five, then hastily dressed and left the hotel. Since the gaming district never slept, Nugget Street was as crowded and noisy at dawn as it had been at dusk. Three cowhands raced their ponies down the main thoroughfare, whooping and waving whiskey bottles, trading ribald insults. A half dozen soiled doves strolled the boardwalk, seeking a last tumble before turning in. Two lolled against a hitching post, eating fried sausage and comparing the men who moved from saloon to noisy saloon. Music blared from one pair of swinging doors and crashed against tunes thumping out of the saloon next door.

Sam adjusted her gun belt and tugged down her hat brim, then went in search of her partner. After checking two saloons, she found Trace in the third, seated with his back to the wall, playing a game of silent, grim-faced draw poker. Thick cigar smoke hung in choking layers beneath a blackened ceiling. Puddles of tobacco juice turned the sawdust slippery underfoot. A sweating piano man hammered the ivories, surrounded by a group of drunken cowboys croaking songs about lost loves and wasted lives.

Choosing a spot near the door, Sam leaned against the wall and awaited an opportunity to catch Trace's eye. The men he was playing with appeared red-eyed and ragged after a long night. Trace, however, looked as fresh as when he had left the hotel room, aside from a sprinkling of new whiskers. The only sign of agitation was a tie slightly askew, and he'd shoved his hat to the back of his head, letting dark curls tumble over his forehead.

One by one the men at Trace's table folded and pushed back in their chairs with snorts of disgust. When he finally glanced toward the door and noticed Sam, all players were out except Trace and a man the size of a coal cart. Frowning, Sam jerked the brim of her hat toward the door. The sun had climbed well above the horizon; she was starting to worry they would miss the train.

Trace kept his expression professionally blank, but his mouth twitched in a small movement to indicate he understood.

"I believe that's it, gentlemen," he announced, fanning out his hand to reveal a straight flush, which beat the four of a kind his opponent threw down with a stream of cuss words. Reaching, Trace gathered a substantial pile of gold coins toward his waistcoat.

"Hold it!" The man who'd held four of a kind stared hard at Sam. "I saw that kid by the door send you a signal." He glared over his shoulder, focusing on one of the drunken cowboys swaying near the piano. "That's how it was done! The cowboy signaled the kid, then the kid signaled you. Put down that money, you snake-eyed cheat, unless you want a bullet between your eyes."

But the money had vanished into Trace's jacket, and Trace was halfway to the door, astutely placing other patrons between himself and the man shaped like a coal cart.

"Git out of the way," the coal cart shouted, swearing. "Give me a clear shot or git shot yourself!"

"Fancy that. He didn't look like a sore loser," Trace murmured, his eyes sparkling as he passed Sam and pushed rapidly out of the saloon doors. "Shake a leg, Kincade. Trouble's right behind us."

Sam was already moving. They hit the boardwalk at the same moment, spinning into the summer sun and breaking into a run. A bullet whistled past Sam's ear and furrowed into the boardwalk in front of her boots. The window of a dance hall exploded on her right. Whipping out her Colt, Sam jumped between two wagons parked before a gaudily painted doss house.

"I'll cover," she shouted to Trace. Rising over the wagon bed, she fanned the hammer three times in rapid succession, noticing the coal cart had been joined by two friends. They dodged among the horses tied in front of the dance hall. Heads popped out of second-story windows and Sam heard laughter and shouts of encouragement, but she couldn't tell who the encouragement was meant for. After a minute she couldn't hear anything but gunfire ringing in her ears and the crack of bullets smacking into the wagons.

Waiting until she reached a count of fifteen, she drew a breath, flexed her muscles, then darted out from the wagons and ran like hell, pounding down the boardwalk, keeping close to the buildings. Ahead, Trace leaned around the corner of the stables, firing steadily toward the coal cart and his friends. Sam skidded around the corner, gulped for breath, reloaded, and then changed places with Trace. He ran toward the depot, a block away.

A train whistle split the morning air and the stink of coal smoke wafted toward Nugget Street. The furious losers had advanced to Sam's first position and bobbed up, firing over the wagon beds. She kept them pinned until she judged Trace had reached the depot, then she whirled and took off running as fast as she could. Shouts erupted behind her, then she spotted Trace crouched in front of the station steps, firing at the corner.

Sam flew past him, up the steps and through the door. Boots pounding, she raced by a startled porter and burst through the back doors onto the boarding platform. With her heart in her throat, she discovered the train had pulled out and was picking up speed as it chugged down the tracks.

There was a split second to exchange a glance with Trace as he came flying through the station door, his jacket flapping behind him, then they both leapt off the platform and ran as hard as they could down the tracks, chasing the train.

"Not . . . going . . . to . . . make . . . it!" Sam gasped, her eyes fixed on the caboose.

In a burst of energy Trace pushed past her, his breath rasping from his lungs. Making a huge effort, he managed to catch the bumper rail of the caboose. He swung up and scrambled for a foot hold. Spinning, he leaned out over the bumper, extending a hand toward Sam, who was running flat out for all she was worth, praying she wouldn't fall over a trestle.

"Come on!" Trace shouted. "Damn it, Kincade, pump those legs! You can make it!"

Legs working, chest burning, Sam mustered the final effort, stretching out her hand. Her reaching, clutching fingers brushed Trace's fingertips, then a gap widened. Sweat rolled into her eyes and she stumbled. The race would have been lost if Trace hadn't lunged forward, caught her by the wrist, and swung her up against his straining body. Arm aching, boots flying, Sam scrabbled for a secure spot to settle her weight, clawed her way over the railing and fell to the floor of the caboose platform. Heart pounding, she clutched Trace's legs and dragged him back over the rail, where he dropped down beside her.

Panting, chests heaving, they leaned against each other and watched as the coal cart and his cronies burst out of the station onto the boarding platform. The men fired wildly at the receding train. Puffs of dust exploded along the tracks but the caboose had rolled out of range.

Grinning in triumph, Sam and Trace pulled to a sitting position on the tiny caboose balcony, catching their breath, shoulders and hips touching. Already Pueblo was retreating into the distance. An ocean of high prairie flowed past them.

"I hope the pot was worth almost getting us killed," Sam gasped when she could talk. Her heart was pounding so hard that she thought it would fly out of her chest. But Lord, it felt good to win, and to be sitting beside Trace, feeling the solid warmth of his body pressed against her side.

Trace sucked another deep breath, then patted the pouch inside his jacket pocket. "Believe me, it was well worth it."

"You're lucky your sore losers are lousy shots," Sam said, letting the wind cool her blazing cheeks.

"You're lucky that I have long arms." Trace closed

his eyes and inhaled the fresh air, lifting his face toward the sun.

"This whole thing was a dumb risk. You could've lost, and someone could've recognized us."

"I told you it would work out."

Sam glared at his grin. "I hate it when you sound smug." He rolled his head toward her and gazed into her eyes.

"That was some action back there, Kincade. Smooth as clockwork. If I'm in another gunfight, I hope to hell you're there beside me."

Surprised, Sam returned his admiring gaze, falling into sunlit amber, her nose not an inch from his. Suddenly her heart started pounding again and her breath hitched in her throat. "You handled yourself pretty well too," she said in a low voice. "I think you winged one of them."

"It was amazing now that I think about it, like we'd rehearsed who was going to do what and when."

"I know," Sam whispered, close enough that she could see each individual lash rimming his eyes. "I felt like I was reading your mind. I knew just when you'd reach the corner, trusted you to cover me, and I knew when you made it to the depot."

His gaze traveled across her cheek, settled on to her lips.

"When I ran onto the platform, I knew you were going to jump and chase the train."

Sam swallowed convulsively. Being this close to him made her feel dizzy. She wished sweat hadn't plastered her hair to her forehead and cheeks, fervently wished she were beautiful, wished she dared raise a trembling hand and stroke his soot-stained cheek.

"You're a remarkable person, Sam Kincade," he said, speaking to her lips. "I think—"

But she wasn't to discover what he thought. The door of the caboose kicked open and a stern conductor loomed over them, a shotgun cradled in his arms. "Stowaways? Or paying?" he demanded, inspecting them with glittering small raisin eyes.

Gripping the railing, Trace pulled to his feet. He almost extended a hand to assist Sam, then checked the impulse. With only a slight hesitation his hand continued upward to open his jacket enough for the conductor to glimpse the fat pouch inside.

"We prefer first-class accommodations, my good sir," Trace said grandly, brushing soot from his sleeves as Sam hauled to her feet. "As my partner and I have misplaced our hats and our luggage, we'll require your assistance to obtain fresh clothing and other sundry items. I'm confident you have soap and razors aboard. Has breakfast been served?"

The conductor examined them, considering the promising bulge in Trace's jacket. "Right this way, sir," he said finally. Lowering the shotgun, he waved them inside.

Sam held Trace back for an instant, nodding toward the pouch in his jacket pocket. "Did you cheat to win that?"

Amusement sparkled in his eyes. "I never cheat,

Kincade. You should know that by now." He shot his cuffs and entered the caboose.

She followed through three crowded cars, then into a luxury coach, thinking about what Trace had said to the conductor. He had promoted Sam from nephew to partner. And he thought she was remarkable.

Her shoulders squared and a swagger appeared in her step. Things were looking up, by God.

When she recalled that moment sitting on the tiny caboose balcony, that moment when for one thrilling instant she had believed he was about to kiss her again, a warm shiver tickled down Sam's spine.

CHAPTER

* 12 *

At this point no one remembered why the feud had started. That the Lyman brothers had humiliated Mule Joe a year earlier was forgotten. And Hannibal's boys hadn't rustled enough beef to knock a hole in the Lymans' herd, besides which the Lymans were no strangers to rustling themselves. Blind hatred fueled the feud and kept it alive because angry men needed a place to spend their hate or risked turning it inward.

Hannibal lay stretched on the dirt behind a clump of sage and cactus, feeling like a chunk of meat roasting on a spit. Shoving back his hat, he wiped sweat off his forehead, then glanced at Marsh Crisp, Billy Jones, and the kid who didn't talk. They all lay flat on the ground, silently enduring the wait beneath a blazing white sun.

Breathing hot dust and the sour tang of his own sweat, Hannibal swung his gaze back to the Lymans' ranch house. The walls were adobe brick shaded by mesquite and scrub oak. The faint splash of a court-yard fountain tinkled through the shimmering silence, just loud enough to hear. If the Lyman brothers were inside, the bastards were taking their ease in cool comfort—probably laughing about how Burt had taken off last week, diminishing the number of Hannibal's gang to three plus himself.

Rolling onto his back, Hannibal twisted open his canteen, wet his bandanna, then mopped his face and throat. The water was warm and smelled tinny, about as refreshing as bathing in lava.

"I'm turning to a crisp," Billy muttered, lifting his forehead away from the hot dirt. "Hell ain't no hotter'n this."

"I'm telling you, them Lymans ain't in there!" Marsh Crisp insisted for the third time. "We're cooking ourselves for damn-all nothing."

The whole episode had begun to turn sour, Hannibal recognized, screwing the lid back on his canteen. In a flash of clarity he understood the Lymans would win the feud because they had the most men, the most guns, the most time. The Lymans had a ranch and cattle; their property made them favored citizens.

For a time the feud had seemed important to Hannibal, as if something significant hung in the balance and it mattered who won. Since learning of Etta's death the war with the Lymans appeared futile, as pointless as everything else seemed to be.

Rolling back on his stomach, Hannibal stared at the adobe house and absently fingered the scars on his forehead.

He couldn't return to Colorado. Judge Horace Mockton had been after Hannibal and his gang for years. The judge would have doubled his efforts following the Leadville robbery. Texas was out because of the Wells Fargo holdup. As for Wyoming, there wasn't anything in Wyoming worth stealing, nothing there but crude settlements and cash-poor ranchers.

California? Right now, with the sun sucking the moisture out of his bones, the effort to reach California seemed daunting, too arduous to contemplate. Kansas? He was never going back to Kansas.

"Piss on this!" Jumping to his feet, Hannibal jerked down his hat brim, then strode toward the Lymans' ranch house, shooting at the chickens scratching in the yard. Behind him, he heard Crisp swear, then the boys scrambled to follow, firing at chickens or the Mexican lanterns swaying in the mesquite trees.

They had almost reached the yard fence when a broomstick poked out of the door, waving a white towel. When the shooting stopped, a woman's head cautiously appeared. Wide-eyed and shaking, she edged into the doorway.

"Nobody here, señores," she called in a quavery voice.

"Who the hell is that?" Hannibal growled. She was a breed, a mix of Indian, Mexican, and white. Her shiny black hair was piled on her small head like a glossy crown. They were close enough to see her dark eyes, creamy skin, and rosy mouth. Her youth and beauty made something ache inside Hannibal's chest.

Marsh Crisp released a low whistle. "Hooee! I wouldn't mind having a piece of that."

"She's Josiah Lyman's woman," Billy commented, his eyes hot. "I seen her in town."

Josiah Lyman owned a ranch, a herd, a house, and a beautiful woman. He was respected, a favored businessman, a success. Fate had smiled on Josiah Lyman; he had everything a man could want.

A jealous rage exploded inside Hannibal's head. It wasn't fair that destiny had dealt Josiah Lyman aces and had given Hannibal Cotwell a pair of deuces.

Through a crimson haze he sighted on the woman and fired, narrowing his eyes as a red blossom unfurled across her white blouse. She staggered backward and collapsed inside the doorway.

Marsh Crisp swore. "Now why'd you go and do that for? Hell. We could of had some fun with her."

"He has to lose something." Lyman didn't have scars disfiguring his back or scars rising on his forehead. There was no price on Josiah Lyman's head. Lyman didn't worry about amounting to nothing, or wasting his life. Men tipped their hats to Josiah Lyman.

Well, now Lyman would get a taste of how it felt to stand under the lash. Except killing Lyman's woman wasn't enough. He wanted to burn the ranch, slaughter the cattle, and spread the earth with salt. Even that wouldn't be enough. He wanted Lyman to see a noose in his nightmares, wanted to steal Lyman's life and smash it.

Billy Jones exchanged a look with the kid who didn't talk. Soon they too would drift away as Burt had done. Hannibal stared at the silent adobe house and the dead chickens in the yard, and he considered killing Billy and the kid who didn't talk.

Before he reached a decision, Crisp spat and made a disgusted sound. "Well it looks like we roasted our butts for nothing. Might as well head on back."

Hannibal stared, his gaze narrowing. Crisp was too cocky by half, forgetting who made the decisions, looking at Mattie when he thought Hannibal didn't see.

"We sure oughtta. Company's coming." Billy Jones shaded his eyes and pointed to a coil of dust approaching from the south. Spinning on his boot heels, he sprinted toward the draw where their horses were hidden. "There's a lot of 'em."

As they lashed the horses into a gallop, Hannibal cast a glance over his shoulder, watching half the Lyman gang peel off toward the ranch house. The second half swept past the yard in pursuit. This possibility had been anticipated. Hannibal and the boys rode hell-bent for leather to a preselected gulch, jumped from their mounts, and hurried into positions above a road that dipped between two rock outcroppings.

The ensuing gun battle was short and sweet with the Lyman gang taking the worst of it. At the finish, Hannibal watched with hard-eyed pleasure as the diminished opposition scattered across the range, racing back toward the ranch. They would return with reinforcements, but for the moment Hannibal could enjoy an unqualified victory.

He descended into the draw and counted three dead men before he holstered his gun with a grunt of satisfaction.

That's when he noticed he'd taken a bullet in the left shoulder.

Crisp and the boys emerged from the rocks, wiping sweat and dirt off their faces. Crisp nudged one of the dead men with his boot before he inspected the blood gluing Hannibal's shirt to his skin.

"Guess you know this hammers it. The marshall ain't going to ignore three dead men and a dead woman. 'Spect we need to be moving on as soon as you get that shoulder tended to."

Hannibal had located a bolt-hole not far from the Holborn ranch. The new hideout was primitive, intended only as a temporary stopover, but it would buy them time to make new plans. He gave the boys directions, ordered Crisp to fetch Mattie, then pressed his bandanna against the hole burning in his shoulder. He felt the ache now and his entire left arm had begun to tingle and go numb.

Arizona, he decided, as he swung into the saddle. Arizona was the only place left where no one wanted to hang him. The thought of hanging made him wince where getting shot had not. Hanging was the worst thing, the thing he most feared.

*   *   *

Mattie Able had dug bullets out of men before and most likely would again. Glancing at the tray beside her, she checked to see that she had everything she needed. As soon as Hannibal was drunk enough, she'd begin. Sitting back in the chair beside the bed, she fanned her face with an old newspaper and shoved sweat-damp hair off her forehead, inspecting her surroundings.

With each move, she sank a bit lower in the world. The Holborn ranch was deteriorating under the blistering sun, but it had been a palace compared to this. The walls of the new hideout, only a shack, were mesquite logs chinked with crumbling mud. The roof was sun-bricked sod. Inside were two dark rooms and a dirt floor, an adobe oven like the Mexicans used, the cot Hannibal sprawled on, and a couple of unsteady, hand-hewn chairs.

"The only time an outlaw lives rich is immediately after a big holdup," Hannibal said, watching her face. "And then only if he's stupid and wants to call attention to himself."

"Keep drinking that whiskey." Mattie nodded at the bottle he clutched against his chest. "This newspaper is three weeks old, but there's an article that'll interest you."

"Where'd you get a newspaper?"

"Every now and then Marsh brings a paper from town. Want me to read the article?"

"Just tell me what it says," Hannibal ordered, raising the whiskey bottle to his lips and swallowing heavily.

Mattie smoothed the paper over her skirt. "Your brother was convicted of killing a man and stealing the dead man's horse."

"He was framed," Hannibal said flatly. "Trace is no killer, and he isn't a horse thief. Anyone who says differently is a goddamned liar."

"He was sentenced to hang in Denver, but he escaped when a bounty hunter burned down the jailhouse. He's still coming, Hannibal."

"Don't start anything, Mattie. Just shut up."

Standing, Mattie started cutting his bloodied sleeve away from his shoulder. "Tell Trace the truth," she said quietly, pausing to gaze into Hannibal's whiskey-hot eyes. "Tell him it was Etta who betrayed him, not you. Tell him you never would have touched her if she hadn't seduced you first."

She couldn't tell if he was listening. After the second bottle of whiskey his eyes had glazed over.

"It was me who taught Trace to shoot," he muttered, his voice furred and thick. "Do you ever think about hanging?" he asked abruptly when she leaned over him.

"Can't say that I do." After wringing a cloth over the basin, Mattie washed the bullet wound and bent closer to inspect the damage. He was fortunate. The bullet had not struck bone and she guessed it would be relatively easy to dig out.

"Well, I think about it. . . . Hanging is the loneliest, ugliest, most painful way there is to die."

Easing back, Mattie studied him in surprise. Hannibal never talked about hanging. But for him, Mattie knew, the true horror of Etta's death was that she had chosen to hang herself.

"Keep drinking," she ordered.

He swallowed deeply, then scowled at the back wall. "When the law does it, they hang you in public with strangers watching. No one cares about the man being hanged. The spectators come for entertainment." He raised the whiskey bottle again. "If the hangman doesn't do it right—and often he doesn't—you strangle. Slowly."

Mattie placed a hand on his brow, smoothed back his damp hair. "Don't talk about this now."

"That's the loneliest death in the world, dying in front of strangers. It's worse than dying alone." He stared at her. "I should have been hanged years ago."

"Not you. You'll die of old age in your own bed." But that was a lie. For a man like Hannibal, there was nothing at the end of the ride but a rope and a noose. Looking away, Mattie tested the blade-point of a narrow kitchen knife against the tip of her forefinger.

Hannibal frowned at the blade. "That's the worst. Dying in front of strangers with none of them caring and no one wishing it was different and no one knowing who you were or might have been." Lowering his head, he stared into the neck of the bottle. He'd had enough whiskey to pass through indifference and anger and progress to melancholy. "Trace . . . he's the only one who ever believed in me or saw anything good in me. The only one. Maybe

Etta. But Trace . . . he never turned his back on me. Never did."

Stung, Mattie pulled away and glared down at him. "How about me? I never gave up on you or turned my back."

"And how did I repay him? I stole his wife." His amber eyes struggled to focus on Mattie. "I don't care what that damned letter claimed, Etta would have gone off with me if I'd have taken her. That's what she wanted. She begged me." He stared at her, clutching the whiskey bottle. "Don't ever want m'brother t'know we both betrayed him. Better if 'e thinks it was just me. Not her too."

Anger flashed in Mattie's dark eyes. "That's right, you damned fool. Go ahead and protect Etta's sainted memory even now!"

Hannibal's eyelids fluttered. "For Trace! Give 'im his wife's memory in payment for never giving up on me."

"I expect he's given up on you now!" Mattie snapped, turning in a whirl of skirts. "I'm going to get the boys to hold you down." Angry, hope running out of her like sand out of a sieve, she stormed outside, stepping into a blaze of late-afternoon sun. Shading her eyes, she looked at Marsh Crisp, who, leaning against the wall of the shack, was cleaning his fingernails with the blade of a cavalry pocketknife.

"He's almost drunk enough," she announced. Marsh nodded. After a minute, Mattie added, "Thank you for them newspapers. Reading helps pass the hours, especially as slow as I read. Where's Billy and that kid who never says anything?"

Marsh glanced up, letting his gaze linger on her perspiration-soaked bodice. "They left. Said they wouldn't ride with no woman-killer."

Surprise lifted Mattie's eyebrows. For a minute she thought Billy and the kid who didn't talk blamed Hannibal for Etta's death. But that was ridiculous. They didn't know about Etta. "What are you talking about?"

After Marsh related how Hannibal had killed Josiah Lyman's woman, Mattie's knees collapsed. Shocked, she sank to the ground and stared at miles of cactus, sage, and hot, dry emptiness.

"My ma was wrong," she whispered. "Some men treat animals better than they treat women." She rested her forehead against her upraised knees. "He just ain't no good. He's bad through and through. Long ago, something went awful wrong inside his head."

Marsh gazed at her curiously. "Why do you stay with him?"

"There ain't no choice." Hot tears welled in her eyes. "I love him. A woman can't choose who she loves."

"Maybe you can't choose about loving, but you got a choice about living," Marsh said after a minute. A wave of his hand encompassed the shack and the barren, heat-baked desert beyond. "A fine woman like you deserves better'n this."

"Why do *you* stay?"

Crisp shrugged. "He's a legend."

"You hate Hannibal, don't you?" Mattie stared up at him. "You're just waiting. You ain't going to be happy until you take everything that's his. Well, that makes you a fool because Hannibal ain't got nothing except that legend and you can't take that away from him."

"I'm just saying if you was my woman, you wouldn't be sitting in a shack in the middle of the desert."

"I ain't never going to be your woman, Crisp. You get that through your head. And you ain't no Hannibal Cotwell. You ain't never going to be no legend." Her eyes narrowed and she thought about Josiah Lyman's woman and the blood spreading across her white dress. "Come inside," she said when she couldn't stand the image another instant. Wearily, she pushed to her feet. "You hold him down until he passes out. I'll dig out the bullet."

In the morning, Mattie eased a fresh shirt over Hannibal's bandaged shoulder, then adjusted a sling she'd sewn before last night's sunset faded. "It hurts right now," she said, "but I seen this before. In ten days, you'll be using that arm like you never got shot at all."

"This isn't the first time I've taken a bullet." Hannibal shifted his arm in the sling, then found a comfortable spot against the pillows she adjusted behind his back. "Crisp and I are leaving for Nowhere, Arizona. We'll head out tomorrow morning."

"I figured."

He met Mattie's eyes. "I'm not taking you with me."

Mattie sat on the edge of the cot and took his right hand, holding it gently in her lap. The heat and her thoughts had kept her awake most of the night. Near dawn she had decided not to go with him even if he offered to take her.

"I wish you hadn't shot that woman," she said softly. Usually she could justify the things Hannibal did. But she couldn't overlook his shooting a woman for no reason. "You shouldn't have done that."

"I know."

She listened hard, but she didn't hear regret in his voice. There was no remorse in his steady gaze.

They sat in silence, baking in the dry heat, listening as something skittered across the sod roof.

"We could go to California or Oregon," Mattie suggested eventually. Even to her, the proposal sounded halfhearted, nothing more than a polite gesture. She loved him, that hadn't changed, but there was no future with a ghost.

Because she knew it was unlikely that she'd ever see him again, she saw him clearly now, and she locked his image away in her memory. He was pale and tired, but still as ruggedly handsome as the day she had first seen him. He was the only man who had ever made her heart beat faster. Usually she didn't notice the scars on his forehead or the eyelid that sagged. But today she acknowledged all his flaws.

"I'm going, and you're staying," Hannibal repeated. But he said it gently like he knew they would never see each other again, and maybe he regretted that.

Mattie clasped his hand. "There's something I been thinking about," she said in a low voice. "Remember how you told me about that Wells Fargo box? Buried by the big boulder in the south pasture out at the Holborn place?"

Hannibal stared at her, then swore. "What the hell! Do you write down every damned thing I say when I'm drunk?"

"What I was wondering . . . " She lifted her head and gazed into his frown. "Well, could I have the money in that box? Sort of like a good-bye present so's I can buy me a fresh start? I ain't saying you owe me anything," she added hastily, "I'm just saying I'd sure like to have that money."

"Since you know where it is, it seems to me you could take it any damned time you wanted to." He glared·at the sod roof. "You might as well."

Mattie spread his hand on her thigh and flattened hers over it. "You're sure?" she asked in a low voice, moved that he wanted to provide for her. That's how she decided to look at it.

"I've got boxes buried all over the Southwest," he said, sounding irritated as he did when caught in an act that might be considered kind. "I won't miss that one."

She nodded, lacing her fingers through his. "Maybe I'll stay in Santa Fe for a while. Maybe open a high-end house. I always wanted a place of my own." Lifting her head, she gazed through the mesquite branches where the chinking had fallen out. The winters would be easy here. The Santa Fe Trail brought a steady influx of customers to town. "Maybe Big Sal and Fat Annie would come and work for me."

Hannibal's gaze turned inward. He didn't comment.

She looked down at their joined hands. "Hannibal? When Trace shows up in Santa Fe . . . you want me to tell him you went to Nowhere, Arizona? Or do you want me to lie?"

A shrug lifted his shoulders, followed by a wince. "Suit yourself. He'll find me sooner or later."

"I know you're thinking ahead, worrying about a shoot-out."

His laugh reflected genuine amusement. "You think Trace could get the drop on me?"

"I think you're eating yourself alive worrying that you'll have to kill him." She watched as his face shut down. "If Trace knew the truth, nobody would have to kill nobody." Her dark eyes pleaded. "Hannibal, for God's sake. Tell him you never would have touched Etta if she hadn't slipped into your bed."

His look was incredulous. "How did you know that's what happened?"

"Deep inside, Trace knows who and what Etta was. A man knows his wife. He'll recognize the truth if you'll just tell him! He's your brother. He'll want to believe you, and he will! Just *please*, tell him the truth."

She peered into his stony expression and felt her heart shatter within her chest. He hadn't been the same since she told him that Etta claimed he raped her. Something in Hannibal had died that night.

Lifting his hand, she placed a kiss in his palm, then stood and blinked at the tears filming her eyes. Silently, she pinned on Big Sal's black hat and hoisted the bundle containing a clean petticoat, her best shawl, and the small items she counted among her possessions.

"I'll ask Marsh to take me as far as the road."

"Don't pick an outlaw." Hannibal watched her tuck up a strand of auburn hair. "Hold out for a man who can give you a house and a piece of land. Use some sense next time."

For an instant, she saw a flicker of the man she had fallen in love with, the man who had rescued old Mick from the cowboy's torments.

"Hannibal?" Drawing a deep breath, she offered him the only farewell gift she had to give. "If I ever hear they're going to hang you . . . "

His eyes narrowed. "I won't hang. I've decided that."

"But if they do get you, I'll come. I'll be there in the crowd so's it won't be only just strangers. I'll tell them all how you saved old Mick, and I'll cry for you. You won't be alone up there with nobody to cry and wish it didn't happen."

They gazed at each other for a long moment, then Mattie stepped outside the shack and lifted her hem to her eyes. She'd tell them about the lash welts scarring his back and how he had provided for her when he didn't have to. She'd tell them that once he had been loved. And that he had a brother. She'd tell them that no man was born bad, that once upon a time even the worst outlaw had been a small boy afraid of the dark.

As for grieving, she was crying already.

The next morning, an hour before dawn, Hannibal and Marsh Crisp rode away from the shack without a backward glance. As happened so often, Hannibal knew he was leaving with a posse hot on his heels. One day his luck would go sour and some tin badge would become a footnote in history, remembered as the man who had finally captured Hannibal Cotwell and strung him up.

That's how destiny had it planned, but it wasn't going to happen that way. Hannibal Cotwell wasn't going to die in front of strangers.

CHAPTER
* 13 *

The Santa Fe River cut through town south of the plaza, cooling the scorched air piled against the Barren Hills. At least, that's what the locals claimed. Sweltering newcomers were more apt to notice the constant flow of horses and freight wagons that kicked up a haze of dust thick enough to trap the heat close to the ground.

Pausing near the plaza, Trace mopped the sweat from his brow and examined what was called the Governor's Palace. The residence was a one-story adobe rectangle that a multitude of windows and a broad shaded porch could not make attractive.

The plaza spreading before it, however, was leafy and pleasant. An outdoor market operated at a thriving pace. Indian and Mexican women, occupying opposite sides of the square, did a brisk business selling trinkets to travelers fresh off the trail. Music drifted from open-faced cantinas, the smell of roasting chilies and stewed chicken spiced the air.

"The telegraph office is that way," Sam announced, scanning the throng crowding the market. "I'll meet you back here."

Trace wanted to caution her about wording her telegram to the judge. The judge should know who sent the message and what they were asking, but it shouldn't make sense to anyone else. But as he watched her walk away, he thought better of it and said nothing.

Exactly when he had begun to trust her was difficult to pinpoint, but he had recognized the change during the train ride and the long stage journey that followed. What bothered him was the unconventional notion of trusting a woman to cover his back and negotiate his future. It puzzled him that when he forced himself to regard Sam as a male, he unquestioningly relied on her judgment and trusted they would function as a skilled and efficient team if trouble arose.

The difficulty was, he saw her as a woman more and more often, a unique and fascinating woman.

A strange moment had occurred during the last leg of the journey to Santa Fe. He had watched Sam trying to sleep as the stage bounced over terrain never intended for wheeled vehicles, and he discovered himself seriously attempting to visualize her dressed in satin and ribbons for an evening at the opera.

What shocked him was the realization that it no longer mattered what she wore. Sam Kincade was fascinating and desirable even when she wore trousers, a poncho, and her ragged man's hat.

He enjoyed her conversation, the illumination of

her smile, and the way her eyes sparked when she was angry. He admired her honesty and integrity, her courage, and her uncompromising self-reliance. None of these qualities depended on gender, but he was keenly aware of her femininity. In particular, he couldn't stop remembering how soft and yielding her mouth had been when he had kissed her.

Trying to thrust all distractions from his mind, Trace decided that right now he needed to concentrate on finding Hannibal. He pushed back his hat and scanned the cantinas opening onto the plaza, trying to guess which Hannibal might frequent. His first item of business was to learn if Hannibal was still in the Santa Fe area.

To begin the search, Trace chose an establishment more Americanized than the others. He walked in out of the punishing sun, stepped up to an ornate bar, and ordered a Mexican beer.

"A Southerner, am I correct?" a voice inquired after the bartender had served Trace's beer. "I'd guess the accent as originating in New Orleans."

Trace slid a wary gaze toward a gray-haired man standing at the rail near painted bowls of piñon nuts, olives, and red peppers. The posture was military, the eyes as sharp as a scout's. "I don't believe we've met, sir."

The man moved closer, pushing a glass of tequila along the bar. "The name is Major Addison T. Allerbee. Retired." His shoulders stiffened beneath the memory of epaulets. "I'm proud to state that I served under General Robert E. Lee throughout the entire tenure of that vain but valiant effort." He studied Trace. "But you aren't interested in old war stories."

"Maybe another time," Trace replied, watching the bartender and hoping for a word in private.

"Perhaps you would favor me with your name, sir. I prefer to know with whom I'm drinking."

"Andrew Marshall," Trace said, offering the alias under which he and Sam were registered at a small bed and board situated near the outskirts of town.

"Ah," the major murmured, a faint smile curving beneath the waxed ends of his mustache. "You can't have been in town longer than a day or I would have noticed. I'm continually on the alert for fellow Southerners. A gaming man, are you?"

Trace lifted his glass to his lips. "Why would you assume that?"

"It's an amusement of mine, deducing a man's occupation through observation. I'd say you're a gambler based on the way you're dressed and the keen manner in which you've been observing the game at the table against the wall. I believe I detect a professional interest."

Trace placed his glass on the bar. "Suppose I told you I'm a boot maker."

"I don't think so."

Trace shifted to meet the major's eyes. "Maybe I'm a shopkeeper, or a bounty hunter."

The major smiled. "Certainly not a shopkeeper. And definitely not a bounty hunter, not with clean fingernails and without manacles in your pocket." Enjoying himself, the major smiled broadly. "Manacles are heavy, Mr. Marshall. They drag a man's pockets out of shape. Your pockets are as flat and smooth as your tailor intended. Moreover, bounty hunters dress sturdily, prepared for rough action. Your clothing is travel weary and I'd guess you've endured a rain storm or two, but the cloth is fine, the cut superb. That suit began expensively and was hand tailored. So no, Mr. Marshall, you could not be a bounty hunter."

Trace stared.

"If you wish to observe a genuine bounty hunter, Mr. Marshall, you need only to glance into the plaza. There are three bounty hunters there now. Two you will spot easily. The third, who is their prey by the by, is not as easily identified."

"Who are you?" Trace asked in a low voice.

"The third bounty hunter is but a boy, yet famous and successful nonetheless. He is clever enough to hide himself among other boys his age. Notice the young men beside the benches, particularly the handsome lad with battered hat and poncho. He's watching everyone in the plaza without appearing to do so. The other bounty hunters, those looking for him, don't see him because they are searching for a pair, a boy traveling with an older man, a gambler."

Trace lifted his beer and took a long swallow.

The major kept his gaze on the plaza. "If this boy bounty hunter and the gambler wish to escape detection, they should split and go their separate ways. Each should take pains to alter his appearance. The telegraph has made our world smaller, Mr. Marshall.

Descriptions are sent far and wide, information is exchanged daily."

"Why are you telling me this?" Trace asked quietly.

"I'm a fellow Southerner, Mr. Marshall, from New Orleans as I suspect you are." Frowning, he turned the tequila glass between his fingers. "Years ago I knew a woman named Annabelle Du Bose, a woman, incidentally, who had eyes much the same honey color as yours. To my great misfortune, Miss Annabelle wed a man named André Cotwell. Before I learned Cotwell had died, Miss Annabelle had remarried, a man named Charles Harden."

Allerbee. Finally Trace placed the family and recalled the Allerbee mansion in the Garden District.

"It's passed my thoughts that Hannibal Cotwell and the Trace Harden whom those bounty hunters seek may be connected to Annabelle Harden. Odder things have happened. Often I have wondered what happened to Miss Annabelle and how that dear lady fares."

Trace swung toward the plaza, immediately finding Sam among the boys pitching pennies against a shopfront. Seen through the major's eyes, she stuck out like a joker in the deck, more wary and wiser than the other boys. To Trace's eye, she didn't even look like a boy. He wet his lips and swallowed.

"Mrs. Harden died earlier this year," he said after a moment.

The major removed his hat and placed it against his chest. "I'm sorry. She was a lovely and great lady."

Trace fingered his beer glass, his lips tight, waiting until the bartender returned to the far end of the counter. "Since you're so interested, perhaps you would know if Annabelle's son, Hannibal Cotwell, is in Santa Fe or nearby."

The major studied him for a full minute. "Annabelle's sons did not turn out well, did they, Mr. Marshall? According to print accounts, one son is a felon on the run and the other is an infamous outlaw. Both are said to be killers."

Trace ground his teeth and his expression hardened. "Any information concerning Hannibal Cotwell would be greatly appreciated." He met the major's sharp eyes. "Mr. Cotwell commissioned a pair of boots which I'm obliged to deliver."

"Boots." The major's laugh sounded like a short bark. "I've heard mention of Hannibal Cotwell in connection with a local feud. The last I heard, he vanished." His smile faded abruptly. "Your client left several dead bodies behind, Mr. Marshall. One was a woman."

Briefly, Trace closed his eyes. "I need to find him."

"Yes, to deliver a pair of boots." Curiosity flickered in the major's eyes. "There's a woman at the Toro Blanco who may know something about Cotwell. The bounty hunters seem to think so, although she isn't telling them anything. Her name is Marguerita, Maria, something like that."

"I'm obliged for the information, sir." Trace tossed a coin on the bar and turned to leave.

The major called softly. "This town is not safe for Cotwell, Harden, or the young bounty hunter, Mr.

Marshall. One cannot turn around without bumping into a lawman or another bounty hunter, each of them seeking to claim the bounties and make his reputation. Should you chance to encounter a clean-shaven gambler with a southern accent traveling with a hard-bitten eighteen-year-old boy carrying a Colt on his hip, you'll earn enough to leave the boot business merely by mentioning their whereabouts to the nearest lawman."

Trace met his eyes. "I can assure you, sir, that Trace Harden never killed a man. He did escape from jail to avoid hanging for an offense he did not commit, an act made possible only by an honest and honorable young bounty hunter."

"If that is true, then I wish the fugitives luck."

They were going to need it, Trace thought grimly as he strode into the plaza feeling as conspicuous as a face card in a run of numbers.

He passed Sam without speaking, giving her a pre-arranged signal to return to their quarters at once. Walking through the plaza and into a side street where he had earlier spotted a row of small emporiums, he felt the sweat pouring out of him. Every eye appeared to measure him against a wanted poster.

As he turned into a shop showcasing ladies' accessories in a tiny window, he wondered how Hannibal could have lived on the run for so many years.

Sam was sitting in a rickety chair aiming her pistol at the door when Trace entered. The shutters were closed and the air inside the room was hot enough to bake an egg. But Sam was taking no unnecessary risks. She'd closed the shutters because the town was crawling with lawmen. When she saw Trace, carrying several packages, her eyebrows lifted and she lowered her gun.

"Has the heat boiled your brains?" she demanded, watching him toss the packages on one of the beds. He returned to the hallway and reappeared with enough additional parcels to cover the second bed as well. "Half the population is looking for us. Our posters are plastered over the telegraph office and outside the marshall's quarters. I spotted at least three bounty hunters while I was waiting for you. They're looking for Hannibal and they're looking for us."

"You were supposed to be soliciting information about Cotwell." Her lip curled. "Instead, you went shopping?"

Trace dropped into a chair and fanned his face with his hat. "We've got two choices, Sam. Either we split up—"

"We agreed to take Hannibal together!" she reminded him sharply, feeling the bottom drop out of her stomach.

Suddenly she remembered the quiet despair of riding alone, felt it for a moment like a dagger in her heart, recalled the bleak friendless solitude of her previous existence. Panic flared in her eyes.

"Or we disguise ourselves."

"What kind of disguises?" she asked after a minute, her voice strained. Whatever he had in mind, it would be a thousand times better than splitting up. Whenever she jumped ahead to that inevitable moment when Trace left her to face an empty future, despair tightened her chest.

"The marshall and the bounty hunters have our descriptions, so we need to make some changes. I need to grow a beard and mustache, dress like a banker, and avoid all gaming establishments. And you . . . " His eyes traveled slowly from the man's collar showing above the slit in her poncho to her corduroys, then down to her scuffed boots.

The criticism and blatant speculation in his gaze brought Sam's nerves quivering to full alert. Grabbing one of the packages, she shook it open and stared in disbelief as a lacy white petticoat tumbled out. A smaller package revealed stockings and blue garters. Digging through the parcels in horrified frenzy, Sam discovered a corset, a camisole, more stockings, high-heeled slippers, and two dresses with so much yardage and so many frills that for a moment she was speechless.

When her shock receded, she gingerly picked up a hairy thing resembling a small dead animal and turned it in her hand. "What the hell is this?"

"Surely you know about false hair. There should be some pins in the same packet." Trace wiggled his fingers at the back of his head. "You pin it on at the back, or on top. You need some hair, damn it. There's also powder and rouge in there somewhere."

With a snorting sound, Sam tossed the hairpiece on the bed, then stalked to the shutters, peering out between wooden slats. "I won't wear petticoats," she said finally. "I can't do it."

"Tricking you out as a woman is the best possible disguise."

"Listen, Harden. Even when I lived with Preacher Moss and his wife, I didn't wear that kind of frippery," she said, jerking a nod toward the bed. Her frown settled on the corset, a frothy confection of lace and ribbon as mystifying as lightning. "Even if I was willing, which I'm not, I wouldn't know how all that fru-fra goes together or how to behave once I hung it on me."

Trace leaned forward, elbows on knees. "You can't grow a beard, Sam. So how do you disguise yourself? Consider this. Suppose there are, say, two hundred boys of about the right age in Santa Fe. Maybe a hundred are Indian or Mexican. Of the remaining hundred, let's say fifty are local and known to the lawmen. Let's say another thirty are fresh off the trail and can prove they aren't you. That leaves about twenty boys who are possibles. That's a small group to hide in."

An unhappy crease deepened between her eyebrows and a sinking, panicky feeling tightened her chest. Sam's scowl settled warily on the clothes billowing over the cotton bedspread.

"I see your point," she admitted with deep reluctance, grinding her teeth. She detested the inescapable logic. But the silly clothing strewn across the beds would make her invisible to the lawmen. He was right about that.

A burst of relief eased the lines drawing Trace's mouth. "No one is searching for a banker and his wife. The bounty hunters will look right past us."

"Damn it. I hate this!" She glared at the frilly clothing.

A peculiar and provocative ambivalence slowly crept over Sam's mind, muddying her objections. Suddenly something wild and rebellious burst inside and shocked her to her toes. She realized that a secret corner of her mind burned with curiosity and yearned to try on the women's clothing. Part of her actually longed for a small peek at how she might have looked if her life had veered down a different path. And she wanted to observe Trace's reaction, she thought, sliding a glance toward him. Biting her lip, she mopped the sweat from her brow, annoyed by the direction of her speculation.

"I've spent five years of my life being a man," she said, sounding defensive. "I've done that because it was the only way I could go after Hannibal. But there are other reasons too. I prize freedom and I don't want to be at the mercy of men. Men kill women. Plus, a woman's life is stuffed with can'ts, don'ts, and shouldn'ts. Women don't own a smidgeon of independence or power! I don't want to be one."

Raising a dark eyebrow, Trace nodded toward the women's clothing. "Are you claiming the instant you tie on those petticoats, you'll suddenly become weak and incapable of making a decision?" A challenge flickered behind his steady tiger eyes. "Isn't that investing a lot of power in a few yards of cotton and lace?"

It sounded ridiculous when he stated it aloud, but that was indeed what Sam believed. She was sure there was something about petticoats and stockings that robbed a woman of her ability to act in her own best interests. A woman in petticoats became subservient, passive. Her options narrowed drastically. She could be raped and shot in front of her young daughter. She could be held prisoner in her home and end by swinging from a rope in the attic.

But outside the door, there were bounty hunters and wanted posters. Santa Fe was crawling with lawmen.

"Is there any other choice? Do I really have to wear this stuff?" she asked desperately. Immediately, disgust twisted her mouth. God. She hadn't yet donned a single item, but already she was looking to a man to make her decisions.

"It's only temporary. Once we finish our business here, you can dress however the hell you want."

A sigh eased out of her chest as she contemplated the dainty tasseled boots tossed near the pillow. The heels looked impossibly high. Never in her life had Sam been this close to a corset; she didn't even know if the camisole went over or under it.

"If I agree . . . " she said miserably, dragging out the words, despising the idea, "what's our plan?"

Trace dipped a handkerchief into the water basin and mopped his face. It had to be ninety degrees in the shade, if a patch of shade could be found.

"We can't be seen together looking as we do now.

I'll take our new belongings to the Mission Hotel and check us in as a honeymooning couple."

A burst of scarlet heated Sam's cheeks and she turned aside so he wouldn't see.

"I'll leave an envelope at the desk informing you which room we're in. We'll take all meals in our room until I've grown a full beard and you're comfortable with skirts. Then we'll renew the search for Hannibal."

"That's a long delay," Sam remarked, considering. She studied his face, trying to concentrate on his jawline and not on how handsome he looked with his hair tousled and his collar opened. "How fast does your beard grow?"

"We'll be able to leave our room at the end of a week."

The negative side of the plan was the delay and the necessity for Sam to tog out as a woman. The positive side was that when they finally emerged from their hotel room, they would be completely altered in appearance. They could proceed without fear of discovery and capture. There was really no decision to make.

And there was another positive, Sam thought. She'd have Trace all to herself for an entire week.

"I guess I have to do it," she agreed in a low voice, glaring suspiciously at the multitude of women's garments.

The plan worked as smoothly as a new watch. Sam called at the desk of the Mission Hotel and was given the envelope Trace had left for her. Once she learned their room number, she waited until the lobby was crowded, then walked through unnoticed to slip up the staircase and down a gaslit corridor. When she darted into room 202, Sam Kincade, bounty hunter and outlaw, vanished.

"This isn't a room," she marveled, peering around in open-mouthed awe. "It's a suite."

"I'm a civilized man, Kincade. As I believe I mentioned, when you travel with Trace Harden, you travel first class." Approaching a side table in the living room, Trace removed a bottle of red wine cooling in a silver bucket of river water. "Wine or brandy?"

She tossed her hat toward a horsehair sofa and pulled the poncho over her head. Immediately, she felt cooler. Trace, she noticed, had peeled to his shirtsleeves, which were rolled to his elbows, and his tie had disappeared. Already a dark stubble shadowed his chin and jaw.

"Wine, I guess. But in a minute." First, she explored the suite, inspecting heavy dark Mexican furniture, Indian rugs, and vivid wall hangings. The suite featured a private water closet, which delighted and amazed her. There was only one tap, which produced an erratic flow of tepid water, but it was possible to have a bath anytime she liked without ringing for someone to carry up a tub and buckets of water to fill it.

In the bedroom, Sam opened an armoire and found her new clothing and Trace's new clothing hanging inside. But her eyes continued to stray toward the single four-poster. The combination of her clothing hanging beside Trace's, the massive bed, and finding a frilly nightgown sent Sam's thoughts churning down strange paths.

Swallowing hard, she returned to the living room, closing the bedroom door firmly behind her. Not looking at Trace, she sat in a striped chair and tasted the wine he'd placed on a small table. It slipped down her throat like liquid flowers, reminding her of Clarion's in Denver and the dinners with the judge.

Trace sat in the chair facing her, his long legs elegantly crossed on an ottoman. It occurred to Sam that this was his natural milieu. The only time she had seen him as comfortable was at the poker table in Pueblo, relieving the coal cart and his friends of their purses.

"You didn't tell me, did the judge respond to your telegram?"

"I was just thinking about the judge," Sam admitted, wondering if it meant anything that they often shared the same thoughts. "I returned to the telegraph office while you were setting us up here."

"And?"

"It appears the judge will accept our bargain. He's heard about Hannibal ambushing some ranch hands here in Santa Fe, and killing a woman." She watched Trace turn aside, and knew how difficult it was for him to hear about his brother's crimes. "If we guarantee the judge will receive the credit for bringing in Hannibal . . . well, you and I are insignificant compared to the favorable press he'll garner for being the mastermind behind killing or capturing Hannibal. The only sticking point is Edwin Snow."

Trace rolled his eyes. "What the hell does Edwin Snow have to do with the judge obtaining a pardon for us?"

Sam's chin jutted. "I don't want to get this all worked out . . . deliver Hannibal's body, restore our names . . . then get shot down and scalped by one of Snow's hired thugs! As part of our deal, I want the judge to force Snow to call off his manhunt."

Exasperated, Trace waved his wine glass. "Snow's hired guns aren't going to recognize you. They're looking for a boy."

Sam leaned forward and stared. "If you think I'm going to rig myself out like a woman for the rest of my days, you've plum lost your mind, Harden. This disguise is only temporary!"

"It's your choice," Trace said, frowning.

"Damned right it is. And getting Snow to call off his gunslingers is part of our deal with the judge. It is not negotiable."

"Is the judge willing to risk offending his banker?"

"He's thinking about it. He needs the credit for Hannibal's death or capture to offset the debacle of your escape. I'm confident he'll agree to all our terms."

"You're positive we can trust your uncle to keep his end of the bargain and persuade the governor to issue us pardons?"

"Since your escape, the judge's odds of winning reelection don't look favorable. I trust him to recognize that receiving credit for Hannibal's demise will go a long way toward improving his chances. I told him he'll get the credit when we get our pardons." She tilted her head. "Did you find out if Hannibal is still in Santa Fe?"

Standing, Trace stretched and walked to the window. From this view, he could see a dusty line of freight wagons winding toward town along the Santa Fe Trail. "It's a safe bet that Hannibal has moved on. A woman named Marguerita may have some information. I'll call on her as soon as it's safe to leave the room."

"There's only one bed," Sam blurted. Heat pulsed in bright circles on her cheeks. Despite trying to concentrate, throughout their conversation she had continued to see the four-poster in her mind, experiencing a strange tingling whenever she glanced at the tanned skin exposed at Trace's open collar.

His shoulders tightened; otherwise he gave no indication that he too might have been thinking about the four-poster.

"I'll sleep on the sofa."

"Good," Sam breathed, praying she didn't sound as disappointed as she felt. Appalled that she could possibly regret his choice, she jumped to her feet, confused and suddenly flustered. "I think I'll try out that bathtub."

He studied her with his dangerously speculative eyes. "You do that."

*   *   *

When Sam emerged from the water closet, draped in a thick Mexican towel and feeling calmer, she scanned the bedroom, then stopped short and frowned.

"Where are my clothes?"

"Gone," Trace called from the living room. "You might as well start practicing wearing women's clothing. The sooner you get accustomed to heels and hems, the better."

Her anxiety returned full force. Cursing, Sam clutched the towel to her breasts and wheeled toward the open armoire. A glance confirmed that Trace's new trousers would be too large in the waist and too long in the legs to fit her. She was stuck.

"How do I know you bought everything I'm supposed to have?" she shouted angrily, glaring at the armoire's contents.

"Believe me, Kincade. I know what women wear. Your undergarments are in the bureau, petticoats and dresses are in the armoire. If you need help . . . call me." She heard the smile in his voice.

After shoving back a wave of dripping hair, she jerked open the bureau drawers and stared inside in dismay. Sinking into a chair, Sam leaned forward and covered her face with a hand.

"It's too much," she whispered. "I can't do this."

"Yes you can," Trace answered from just outside the door. "Remember, Sam. You're still you regardless of what you're wearing. And, as you said yourself, this is only temporary."

"I'm going to look ridiculous."

"Does it matter?"

That was the worst part. It did matter. If she was going to disguise herself as a woman, then she yearned to be a beautiful and desirable woman. She wanted Trace to look at her and see a woman as lovely as Etta had been. Sam wanted this so badly that she hurt inside with the certain knowledge that it couldn't and wouldn't happen.

Hesitantly, she approached the cheval mirror and made herself peer into the glass, examining herself with a hypercritical eye. It seemed to her that her skin was too sun-pink for fashion. Her figure was too slender, too boyish. Her hair . . . impossible. Hopeless. She stared at the cropped strands dripping near her jawline and felt a sinking despondency.

"Is there any whiskey out there?" she shouted, feeling as depressed as she could recall being. She hated her hair, her body, her legs, her nose, her mouth, her chin, her—

There was a pause before Trace's answer came. "Respectable women don't drink whiskey. I'm placing a glass of wine on the floor and I'm going to push it through the door."

Sam closed her eyes and pressed her fingertips to her temples. The very changes she dreaded had begun to surface. Already the don'ts had begun: the complete erosion of her independence and freedom could not be far behind.

CHAPTER
* 14 *

Sam's problems mounted.

The stockings smoothed over her legs with little trouble, but it required twenty frustrating minutes to figure out how to twist the tops around the garters securely enough to hold them up. The pantaloons with the silly lace ruffle just below the knee presented no great difficulty. The corset mystified her. It was a beautiful garment, constructed of satin and lace, rose-colored ribbon, and strips of whalebone that Sam suspected could squeeze the life out of a person. She stood in front of the glass and positioned the corset against her body, studying how the cups would clasp her breasts and gently push them together and up. A pink flush stained her cheeks. After five years of flattening her breasts and trying to make them vanish, it seemed wildly peculiar to now don a garment designed to enhance them.

In fact, she couldn't do it. Not because she didn't want to, but because she couldn't reach the laces that ran up the back. After several futile attempts, Sam ground her teeth and accepted that she would have to request Trace's assistance.

"Are you still there?"

"Yes."

She thought for a moment. "I'm going to open the door a crack. You reach through and lace up this corset thing, all right?" She finished the last of the wine in one long swallow. It was her fourth glass on an empty stomach, and she was starting to feel tingly and lightheaded.

"I'm delighted to be of service, Miss Samantha."

She listened for sarcasm, but didn't find it. But calling her Miss Samantha, that was a jolt. Another defeat. Of course he had to call her by a female name. But she didn't have to like it.

"I thought we were posing as a married couple," she said sharply. "Shouldn't that be Mrs.?"

Pressing her lips together, she cautiously approached the door and opened it wide enough that he could get his hands through, then she pressed the corset against her breasts and turned her back, expanding her rib cage so he couldn't lace her too tight. The crimson pulsing in her cheeks spread down to her throat and up to her hairline.

"In the South, married women are often referred to as Miss."

For a long moment nothing happened and Sam's nerves jumped to the surface of her bare skin. She felt naked and foolish and vulnerable. She kept telling herself that he had seen her in her altogether when he nursed her through the snakebite. But it didn't help.

"Just lace me," she demanded finally, desperate to get it over.

"You have a beautiful back," he remarked in a strange thick murmur.

Sam swallowed hard and stared at the four-poster. She didn't recall any of the saloon Venuses being painted with their spines showing. It was always their fronts that men were interested in. Maybe Trace was trying to tell her that her front side wasn't worth praise. Or maybe he really believed her back side was attractive. A light dew of perspiration appeared on her brow as she struggled to decipher what might possibly be "beautiful" about the back of her shoulders or her spine.

His fingers brushed her skin as he caught hold of the corset laces, and an involuntary shiver raced through her body. Sam continued to stare at the four-poster, but now she was remembering his long, elegant fingers, recalling the way his hands tapered and the shape of his nails.

Behind her, he cleared his throat and edged the door open a little farther. "Is that too tight?"

"No," she said in a strange voice that sounded as if she were choking. One warm hand pushed against her waist while the other drew the laces tight. Then he threaded the ends through another eyelet and his hand scalded her waist again. The push-pull movement brought her back against his body. It felt as if she were standing near a stove that radiated a strange and compelling heat that surrounded her and plunged deep into her flesh. The pleasant scent of starch and strong soap filled her nostrils, and a scent she would have recognized anywhere as belonging to Trace alone. A nuance of bay rum and cigar smoke, a hint of leather and something faint but exotic that made her think of felt tables and a new deck of cards.

"The pantaloons pull up over the stomach part of the corset," he explained, his voice husky. "Just a minute. I think the ends of the corset laces should tuck inside."

Warm fingers smoothed across her bare shoulders, leaving a fiery echo. A hot tingle spread across her skin.

By the time she could breathe again, Sam realized he had finished lacing her and she also realized that the door was full open and she was almost standing against him, not touching, but close enough that she was acutely aware of the tension crackling between them.

"I don't know what comes next," Sam whispered, swallowing and staring straight ahead, afraid to move a muscle.

"The camisole."

She felt his hands hovering above her upper arms like a hot shadow, then heard his teeth grind together and the rustle of shirtsleeves as he dropped his arms. Willing strength into her knees, Sam drew a deep breath and made herself walk toward the bureau. Trying to pretend that he wasn't watching, she lifted her arms and slipped the gauzy camisole over her head. She heard a low groan emanate from the doorway.

The sound made her close her eyes briefly. Had he groaned with pleasure at the sight of her? Or with despair at how hopeless she was? Quickly, Sam glanced toward the mirror, needing to see whatever Trace was seeing.

She stood paralyzed, unable to believe what her eyes beheld. Her mounded flesh swelled above the lace cups of the corset. Her waist nipped down to a small hourglass curve, then flared into hips defined by pantaloons that fit tightly enough to reveal a smooth shapely line of buttocks and thighs. Thin white stockings emerged from the pantaloon ruffles, molding her calves and small feet.

From the neck down, she resembled one of the naughty French postcard paintings that men sometimes passed around saloons. Lace and ribbon. A sensual curve of breast and buttocks.

"My Lord," Sam breathed, blinking at herself. She'd had no idea that she would turn out to look so provocative.

Trace wiped a hand across his brow and collapsed into the chair just inside the door, staring steadily at her image in the mirror. "My Lord," he agreed hoarsely.

From the neck up was another matter. Sam squinted at her short mop of hair that had dried in a curly tangle, and she examined her tanned cheeks. "I need powder," she whispered. "And my hair . . . do you know how to fix my hair?"

A strangled sound rasped against Trace's throat. "I don't know anything about women's hair."

Spinning, Sam flew to the bureau and threw things this way and that until she found the false curls and the packet of hair pins. It was crazy, but she had to know how she would look as a full woman. After brushing her curly hair until it crackled and gleamed, she pulled it straight back and secured it with the pins. There was supposed to be some frizz on the forehead, she thought that was the fashion; but she didn't know how to create a frizzy fringe. Giving up on frizz, she pinned the fall of false curls on the back of her head, considered, then adjusted it higher and anchored the curls in place.

"The color match is good," she murmured, standing back to study herself in the glass.

"I don't believe this," Trace said in a thick voice.

Sam stared. "Neither do I."

She stared again into the mirror, inspecting an image that no one could possibly mistake for anything but female. The corset and false curls created a magical concoction of feminine mystery and illusion. With the help of some scraps of lace and a hank of hair, she had metamorphosed into a slim version of a saloon Venus, curving and alluring, rosy-fleshed and tempting.

Her eyes sparkling with amazement, Sam pulled out the seat before the vanity and found the small box of trinkets Trace had remembered to include. Leaning to the mirror, she held one set of earrings to her lobes, then another, turning her head this way and that, lost in the miracle she was creating.

Trace watched with smoldering eyes. He could recall hundreds of times when he had become aroused while observing a woman remove her clothing. This was the first time he had become powerfully aroused while watching a woman put clothes *on*. He would have thought such a thing impossible.

Later, he would remember this unique experience and laugh. Right now, he watched her don a pair of pearl ear drops and practice a smile in the glass. He wanted to throw her on the bed and tear off the undergarments she had so carefully assembled. He wanted to touch her all over, and stroke her, and caress those small swelling perfect breasts, and tease his fingertips along the inside of her strong thighs until she gasped his name and begged him to take her as he burned to do.

When she had the pearl drops secured, she turned from the vanity mirror with excitement dancing in her blue eyes and she threw open the armoire. "I want to see the whole thing," she said eagerly, trying to decide between her two gowns.

Trace couldn't speak. His mouth was dry, and his eyes felt as if they were burning. His body was on fire. He could not take his eyes off of her small curvaceous form, a vision in lace and ribbon, and garters and stockings.

Sam slid her feet into satin slippers, then, after two attempts, managed to drop an evening gown over her head and tug it into place. Lifting the curls from the nape of her neck, she presented her back and asked him to fasten the hooks.

"I don't know how women get dressed by themselves," she murmured, craning her neck to see the mirror.

"The women who wear this type of gown employ a lady's maid," he said, fumbling with the hooks running up her slender back. "I can see you need a more extended wardrobe. I'll order more dresses."

When he finished with the hooks, he stood behind her and they both gazed into the mirror. To Trace's amazement, Samantha Kincade had emerged from her ragged cocoon a spectacular butterfly. She was simply one of the most beautiful women he had beheld. The blue shimmer of the gown deepened the blue of her eyes to a crystal glow. It sculpted her breasts and waist like a second skin. When she gasped and swayed, her hands flying to her mouth, the skirt moved gracefully like the cup of a bell.

"Oh Trace." Her whisper was almost inaudible. "I had no idea it would be like this. I didn't . . . I never dreamed . . ."

He stared at the creamy flesh swelling against a delicate ruffle edging the bodice of the gown. Her waist was so tiny, he could have spanned it between his hands. Until now, he hadn't realized how small she was. Even wearing heels, she stood beneath his chin.

Something shy and anguished darkened her eyes. "Am I . . . do you think . . . ?"

"Not a soul will recognize you," he assured her in a voice that sounded like a growl. He started to touch her, but was afraid of losing control if he did. "You are absolutely beautiful."

"Do you mean that?" she asked uncertainly, searching his eyes in the mirror's reflection.

"I mean it," he snapped, instantly regretting his tone of voice. She was so fragile in these first moments, so desperate for reassurance.

Frowning, she turned away from her image. "Why do you sound so angry all of a sudden?"

He wrenched his gaze up from her cleavage and stared at her mouth. "You figure it out," he said gruffly. Forcing himself away from her, he strode to the living room and poured three fingers of brandy, which he drained in one deep swallow.

Sam followed and poured a brandy for herself. "I can't read your mind, Harden. If you have something to say, spit it out." Eyeing him, she tilted her head and tossed the brandy down like a man, then wiped the back of her hand across her lips.

Suddenly Trace laughed. She might look like a vision. She might have transformed herself into the most desirable woman he had seen in years. But she was still feisty and forthright, still a creature of habits more male than female. She was still Sam Kincade.

And he wanted her with an intensity that made him ache.

Sam hid in the bedroom when a valet brought supper to their suite, setting a table beneath the window where they could enjoy a breath of cool air.

"You can come out now," Trace called after the valet departed.

Sticking her head out of the bedroom door, Sam looked around, then emerged wearing a wrapper over her undergarments. She had earlier removed the blue gown and had taken off the false curls when the pins began to give her a headache. Her thick, jaw-length dark hair bounced against her cheeks as she moved to the table and examined the array of dishes.

The false curls appealed to a conditioned concept of what constituted female beauty, but Trace surprised himself by liking her short hair. It moved when she did, capturing the sunset in a shining cap. The sobering realization occurred to him that he liked just about everything about Samantha Kincade. Right now, he especially liked the way the wrapper curved over her breasts and accented her waist and hips. He couldn't stop imagining the lacy corset and ruffled pantaloons underneath.

When he extended a chair for her, she gave him a startled look that clamped into a frown. "Don't do that. It makes me feel peculiar."

"Detail determines the success or failure of a disguise. You need to become accustomed to the courtesies extended to women. And for God's sake, stay alert so that *you* don't pull out a woman's chair, or offer her your arm."

Making a face, she sat down and lifted the cover off of her plate. A frown tugged her brow. "I can't tell you how strange it feels to wear a corset." She buttered a roll, reaching for the jam. "Mrs. Moss, the preacher's wife, insisted that corsets were the devil's instrument. She said they wrecked a woman's insides and gave her female troubles. I don't know about that, but if you'd laced me any tighter, I'd have trouble breathing, let alone eating. Maybe for everyday, you only have to wear the camisole."

"Sam," he lowered his knife and fork. "Underwear is not a suitable dinner topic."

Her eyebrows rose. "Who's going to hear? It's just us."

"We're practicing, remember? That's what this week is about."

She put down her fork and scowled. "There's no reason to get in a lather. Why in the hell are you so upset all of a sudden? For all your blather about living a civilized life, I think hotels bring out the worst in you."

"Ladies don't swear."

Her eyes narrowed. "Ladies probably don't stab their dinner partner with a fork either, but that's what's going to happen to you if you don't stop telling me what to say, what to drink, how to eat, what to wear, how to walk, and all the damned rest of it!"

"Do you want these disguises to work or don't you?"

"That's why I've been practicing with this stuff!" She pointed a jabbing finger at the powder and rouge on her face. "But there's a limit to how much criticism I can stand in one day! So just shut up, Harden, and stop ordering me around like I was a . . . a woman!"

"You are definitely a woman," he confirmed quietly, studying her across the table. She had been a pretty boy, but she was a beautiful woman. The transformation deeply disturbed him.

Warily they examined each other above the light flickering from the center candles.

"I told you petticoats change everything," Sam said suddenly. To Trace's astonishment tears welled in her eyes. Abruptly she pushed back from the table and stood up. "Oh hell!" Her mind spinning, she ran into the bedroom and slammed the door behind her.

The hotel was dark and silent, the only sound a drunken cowboy singing in the street beneath the windows. Trace stood beside gently fluttering curtains and gazed at the night sky, sipping brandy from a crystal snifter.

After three days of not shaving, his beard was filling in nicely but had reached the itchy stage. Idly, he scratched his jaw, then drew on his cigar, the tip glowing red in the darkness.

He knew why he couldn't sleep.

This was not like camping on the trail, or sharing a room during the long stage journey. Then, if he opened his eyes and looked at Sam, he saw her wearing long johns in need of a wash, or a man's shirt and denims. That was before he had begun to hunger for her with a constancy that was almost painful. He had experienced flashes of desire on the trail, but nothing as powerful as what he now felt.

Rubbing his forehead, he turned back into the room and sank into a chair. Drawing on his cigar, he listened to the faint squeak of the bedsprings as Sam rolled over in her sleep. She was driving him crazy with wanting her.

Everything she did seemed unique and exciting. The new way she walked, taking small steps so as not to trip over her hem; the way her swaying skirts drew his attention to her hips. The charming way she leaned to the vanity mirror, practicing with powder and rouge and demure smiles. The special way she held her fork, the provocative tilt of her small head.

Leaning forward, Trace rubbed his eyes.

To pass the time they played cards in the mornings, read to each other during the long hot afternoons. As a male, her voice had seemed ordinary, nothing remarkable. But her voice was husky for a woman, pitched low, the kind of contralto that arrested a man's notice and caused him to think of rustling sheets and low, sultry whispers. He found himself waiting for her to speak his name, noticing that no one else used quite the same inflection as she did.

God help him, he was suffering an aching attraction for a tough little bounty hunter who had captured countless ruthless outlaws. He was lusting after a strange hybrid woman whose single-minded purpose in life was to gun down his brother.

That thought brought him up short. He had no

right to judge her on that count, as his purpose echoed hers. Until he met Sam, revenge was the only thing that had occupied his mind from the moment he had found Etta hanging in the attic. The quest for vengeance had brought him west.

Leaning back in his chair, Trace stubbed out his cigar.

The end was in sight. He felt it inside. That being the case, it wasn't Sam he should be thinking about. It was Etta. He needed to remind himself why he was searching for Hannibal and why Hannibal had to die by his hand.

He stared toward the window, but looked into the past.

In the beginning he had desired Etta, he remembered, though never with the powerful fierceness with which he desired the woman sleeping only a few footsteps from where he sat.

His passion had died within a year, once he understood Etta considered sex a duty, a means to achieve a greater end. Sex was the coin of the marriage realm, something bartered for something gained. Or withheld if refusal suggested greater advantage. Sitting in the darkness alone with the truth, Trace closed his eyes and asked himself if he had ever loved her.

Perhaps. In the beginning he had noticed only the veneer, her charm, her accomplishments, the kindness she displayed in welcoming Hannibal into their home.

But quickly he had grasped that Etta's actions

were motivated solely by self-interest. He didn't entirely fault her; self-interest was a protective device. But it also led to a need to control. He suspected Etta's desire to marry him had been an act of rebellion against her family, just as he guessed her charm and calculated kindnesses were an investment in an expected return.

In retrospect, Etta's manipulations were all directed toward getting what she wanted when she wanted it. Fury erupted when she encountered an obstacle she could not surmount.

Trace had been one of those obstacles. He could be pushed only so far. He didn't bend to tears or cajoling or other forms of manipulation. Despite Etta's wishes, and later her accusations, he had been unable to make her the center of his existence as she demanded. He wouldn't permit her any contact with his gaming establishments and neither tears nor tantrums budged him.

Thinking back, Trace could recall cold, silent weeks when they had not exchanged a single word. Frequently he had resided at his club, seeking a period of peace and relief from Etta's demands.

He tried to recall if he had kissed her good-bye the day he departed for New Orleans, the last time he had seen her alive. He doubted it, since he had departed in the middle of a violent argument. He remembered Etta watching him board the train, her face stony and her eyes cold.

"You'll be sorry." Those were the last words she spoke to him.

"You were right," he said aloud.

As he sat alone in the hot darkness, vivid echoes resonated through his thoughts. He heard Etta screaming that the only person who had ever touched Trace's cold heart was his brother. She referred to Hannibal as her rival, shouting that she hated him, that she would never permit Hannibal inside her home again.

But she had. And she had suffered and died because of it. Trace dropped his head in his hands.

Guilt spiked his chest. If only he had taken her with him to New Orleans, if only he had returned to Kansas City immediately after settling his mother's estate, if only he had never invited Hannibal to think of their home as a safe haven. If, if, if.

"What happened during those two weeks?" he whispered hoarsely, staring into the darkness as if the shadows held answers. "And what happened afterward?"

From the first, he had understood that Etta's exhortation to forgive Hannibal was intended to incite and inflame. Her plea that he forgive Hannibal was a fraud. She had died wanting him to kill his brother.

It impressed him as sad that Etta had known him so little. He would have gone after Hannibal without her attempt to manipulate him. No man could rape Trace Harden's wife and live.

But there were so many unanswered questions.

Why hadn't Etta defended herself? When did she discover she was pregnant, and how did she inform Hannibal? Had Hannibal lived in Trace's house longer than two weeks? Or had Etta written him about her pregnancy and received a reply?

And finally, the question that cramped his stomach and brought anguish to his eyes: why had Hannibal done this terrible thing?

After a lifetime of love, trust, and loyalty, why had Hannibal betrayed him? Trace dug his fingers through his hair. In the past, Hannibal had treated Etta with courtesy and respect. There had never been a hint of insult. Only with her had Hannibal conducted himself as the man he might have been.

Anger and pain burned Trace's eyes. Hannibal's betrayal was the most catastrophic event of his life. It preyed on him worse than Etta's death, worse than losing his father and mother, worse than the time in Denver when he had believed he would hang. Nothing in his life, no injury, no disappointment, no devastation, equaled the anguish of knowing his brother had raped his wife. He could not feel more pain if Hannibal had twisted a dagger in his chest.

Trace gazed unseeing at his shaking, clenched fists. He would kill Hannibal for what he had done to Etta. But when Hannibal died, a piece of Trace would die with him. No man destroyed his brother without surrendering a portion of his soul.

He hated Hannibal as much for forcing this tragedy on them both as he hated him for causing Etta's death.

By the end of the week, Sam and Trace were gritty-eyed from lack of sleep. Their nerves were frazzled from the heat, and the tension between them strained tempers and sharpened their awareness of each other.

Although the hotel suite was larger than Sam's small house in Denver, she found herself continually bumping into or brushing up against Trace. Each time it happened, she reacted as if she had been scalded. Her nerves twitched and she couldn't catch her breath for minutes afterward.

After weeks of talking about everything and anything, conversation suddenly dried in Sam's throat. The same seemed to happen to Trace. Occasionally she discovered they were sitting on the edges of their chairs, staring at each other without speaking. When these taut, feverish moments occurred, Sam usually jumped up and fled to the bedroom to examine the new dresses Trace had ordered through the hotel. Behind her, she would hear him curse and suddenly erupt into a flurry of activity.

Sam didn't know what was happening to her. Or maybe she did know but couldn't bring herself to admit it. Everything conspired to make her agonizingly conscious of Trace as a man and herself as a woman.

It began in the mornings the instant she opened her eyes and found herself alone in the big four-poster bed, gazing at the empty pillow beside her. Then came the exciting fluttery moment when Trace laced her into her corset, and when he sometimes watched her assemble her womanly persona, donning her gown, earrings, hairpiece, and powder.

Next the valet delivered their breakfast, sliding an

arch smile toward Sam and all but exchanging a knowing wink with Trace. Heat flooded her cheeks when she imagined what the hotel staff whispered about the honeymooning couple in room 202 who had not emerged from their suite in a week.

After breakfast, Sam practiced walking in her heels and skirts. Sometimes Trace took her arm and they pretended to stroll. In the afternoons, they play-acted, trying to anticipate situations they might encounter, responding as would a banker and his wife.

Sometimes they read aloud to each other. Sometimes they played grim, cut-throat poker. Occasionally, Trace spoke about growing up in New Orleans and Sam spoke about her parents, straining to remember.

Then came supper and the lessons addressing how a woman seated herself and daintily used her cup and her utensils.

Finally, when the sun sank, Sam fled to the bedroom and away from smoldering amber eyes and wide lips and long slender fingers and heavy thighs and the scent of starch and perspiration and wine and man. She fled the fever of being near him but discovered she brought the heat into her bed, where she lay tingling and agitated as she listened to his restless movements in the next room.

She didn't know how much longer she could bear this.

"If I don't get out of this suite soon," she said, interrupting her pacing to throw Trace a despairing glance, "I'm going to lose my mind."

Trace looked up from a game of solitaire spread across the table beneath the window. His new beard and mustache were neatly trimmed, framing his lips, filling out his face. Now when Sam gazed at him, all she saw were his patrician nose and smoldering tiger's eyes.

"I agree," he said after a minute, sweeping up the cards. "We're as ready as we're going to be. Fetch your gloves and bonnet, Miss Samantha. We'll tour the plaza and purchase some souvenirs to recall our honeymoon."

Neither of them smiled at the thin joke. Before they left the room, Trace tucked some coins into the purse that dangled from her wrist. "In case you see something you want to buy."

Angry amazement flared in Sam's blue eyes. "I didn't come to Santa Fe to shop for doo-dads, Harden. In case you've forgotten, we came here to kill Hannibal Cotwell! Which, by the way, is taking a whole lot longer than I anticipated!"

"Believe me, I haven't forgotten," he answered sharply. "But we aren't going to kill Hannibal tonight. Tonight we're going to test our disguises."

She made a face at the silly little purse swinging against her skirts. "And I don't like you doling out money as if you're some high and mighty prince distributing largess among the peasants."

His eyes glittered. "If you'll recall, I used your poke as a stake to win the money we've been spending. I owe you. The money I just gave you is your own."

"Oh." She glared at him, trying to figure out why both of them were so angry.

Extending his arm stiffly, he opened the hotel door. "Are we agreed on the conditions of the test?" Sam nodded. They had laid their plans two days earlier. "Then we're ready. Try to remember that you're a lady, and ladies don't swear."

They made it down the staircase, through a lobby crowded with people dressed for dinner, then out onto the boardwalk and another half a block before Sam drew him into the doorway of a storefront and gripped his arm.

"We're in trouble. My disguise isn't working!" She chewed her lip, peering past him into the street. "Did you notice all those people staring at me?" Her gloved fingers opened and closed. "Lord, I feel naked without my Colt!" Frantic, she patted her skirt where her gun would have hung. "They know who we are!"

Trace heard her out, then his scowl broke into a wide smile, and his hands framed her shoulders. "Calm down. Sam? Listen." Leaning, he peered beneath the brim of her straw bonnet. "No one has penetrated our disguises. They're staring at you because you're a beautiful woman." His smile widened. "No one in that lobby noticed me. All they saw was a stunning woman."

She searched his face with an uncertain expression.

Patting her hand, he tucked it around his arm and drew her along the boardwalk. "It's all right."

Sam wasn't convinced. Trying not to trip over her hem, she watched from the corner of her eye, noticing the people they passed slide a glance past Trace and focus on her. A dozen men smiled and tipped their hats before they reached the plaza. Sam frowned uncomfortably. She didn't recall attracting this much attention in her entire life. It made her feel squeamish. She had always tried *not* to attract attention.

"The wrong kind of attention," Trace corrected, as if he had again read her thoughts. The longer they remained together, the more frequently they seemed to finish each other's sentences and complete each other's thoughts. Trace patted her glove and held her arm possessively against his side. "Relax. We're doing fine."

He certainly seemed relaxed, Sam thought sourly. From bowler hat to tan jacket to trousers to the conservative lace-ups on his feet, he appeared every inch a banker. But he still moved like Trace Harden, she noticed, with arrogant confidence and a challenge in his tiger eyes that caused men to step out of their path. And the tense hardness of the muscles beneath her fingertips didn't relax until they entered the plaza.

They strolled the perimeter, pausing here and there to inspect the Indian pottery and rugs offered for sale, using the moment to scan the evening crowds.

"Over there," Sam said between her teeth, inclining her bonnet. "That's Pete Durkem, a bounty hunter out of Dodge City. The man he's talking to is the marshall."

"Just the men we want to see," Trace commented pleasantly. His eyes narrowed slightly and he squeezed her hand against his side.

Sam hesitated. "I've been drinking with Durkem. We've swapped stories." Not wearing a pistol was the hardest part of being a woman. She felt utterly defenseless. If Durkem recognized her, her only option was to meekly surrender. "Damn!" She swung a hasty look of apology up to Trace. "I mean, drat!"

He laughed, but it was a tense mirthless sound. "Right now, your own relative, the judge, wouldn't recognize you. But we'll find out for certain in a minute."

They strolled toward Pete Durkem and the marshall, and with each step Sam's heartbeat accelerated. Her chest expanded against her corset stays until she thought she couldn't breathe. She was utterly convinced they would be apprehended in mere minutes.

"Excuse me, gentlemen," Trace interrupted smoothly. "I left my watch in our hotel room. Might I inquire the time?"

Sam felt Pete Durkem's eyes settle on her while the marshall consulted his pocket watch. Forcing herself to complete the test, she raised her lashes and met his puzzled expression.

"Evenin', ma'am," Durkem said, lifting his hat.

"Evenin', sir. It's hot tonight, isn't it?" Pretending to shrug at the heat, Sam let her shawl fall open across her cleavage. She turned her head to gaze at Trace and let Durkem see the false curls peeking beneath her bonnet, and also to permit him a good long look at her breasts. How she knew this handy trick, she couldn't have explained, but she did.

"Thank you, Marshall," Trace said after learning the time. He smiled, tipped his hat, and they moved on. When they had advanced a few feet, he spoke from the corner of his mouth. "Slowly, don't rush. We'll take another turn around the plaza, see if anything develops."

Blood pounded in Sam's temples, her fingers shook. This was the first time she had faced a dangerous situation unarmed. Six months earlier, she had spent an entire evening in Pete Durkem's company, had matched him beer for beer, tale for tall tale. Yet her heart now soared, certain he had not recognized her.

There had been one instant when she knew Durkem thought he should know her, and wondered if they had met before. Holding her breath, Sam had watched him consider and then dismiss the possibility.

A heady feeling of raw power exploded through her small frame. Her head tilted at a jaunty angle and she fought to suppress a shout of triumph. Pausing, pretending to examine a Mexican bowl, she and Trace exchanged a smile of victory. Sam's eyes sparkled like Catherine wheels, flashing light and excitement.

"He didn't recognize me!" she marveled.

Amusement and irritation flickered in Trace's gaze—along with something else that made his eyes glow like amber beacons. "I doubt Durkem spent two seconds looking at your face. You all but thrust your cleavage at the bastard."

A frown dampened Sam's delight. She had never heard Trace use that tone of voice before. She tried to pin down the emotion motivating his growl. She heard anger and pride and possession, accusation and an uncharacteristic uncertainty.

Good Lord. She blinked, then stared at him. Her mouth dropped open. Trace Harden was jealous.

CHAPTER
* 15 *

They dined at a restaurant unequal to Clarion's, but the finest public establishment Santa Fe had to offer. Soaring and feeling invulnerable in her disguise, relaxing in the mounting certainty that her former self had become invisible, Sam could not resist playing with this new toy called femininity. She wanted to test its strength and revel in an inherent power that she had never suspected.

Quickly she discovered she possessed the exhilarating ability to turn men's heads. A few women stared at her too. Their appraising eyes swept over her bonnet and gown. Sam returned their glances and secretly compared her frills to theirs, grateful for Trace's unerring knowledge of fashion. Thanks to his taste, she could hold her head high in the world of hems and trimmings. She didn't question why this should matter. She simply felt a savage burst of pleasure that her new self could compete favorably with other women.

Discovering the language of female body posturing simply amazed her. By leaning forward Sam could make the waiter dart a glance at her bosom. She could draw attention to her hands if she moved them slowly with delicate, graceful movements. If she tilted her head a certain coquettish way, her earrings danced flirtatiously and the false curls bounced on her shoulders. If she became the least careless, a flash of ankle drew immediate admiration.

"You haven't said three words," she remarked to Trace after the waiter removed their plates and served thick Mexican coffee topped with a half inch of cream. Until now she'd been so fascinated with her small experiments and surprising discoveries that she hadn't noticed his silence.

Leaning back in his chair, Trace squinted at her above the candles, watching flickering shadows define her cheekbones. "Don't you think you're overplaying your hand?"

"I beg your pardon?" Sam said in her best ladylike manner. She believed she was playing her role quite well, actually.

Trace scowled. "There isn't a man in this room who doesn't believe you're flirting with him. You've turned the waiter into a fumbling idiot." He nodded toward the archway where a bearded man studied them intently. "That man with the limp has been staring at you for twenty minutes."

She couldn't help it. A broad smile of delight

curved her lips. "Do you really think so?" She wouldn't have believed she could enjoy this so much. It was amazing.

Trace considered her through narrowed smoky eyes. "I know being female is new to you and undoubtedly you're making interesting discoveries. But may I remind you that honeymooning wives do not treat every man they encounter as a potential conquest? As a favor to my pretended status, will you please stop dipping your cleavage and fluttering your damned eyelashes?"

"What? I'm not doing that!" A blaze of embarrassed color bloomed on her cheeks.

"You know you are. You're doing it on purpose." Standing, he walked around the table and moved her chair so she could rise, dropping her shawl over her shoulders. The back of his fingers brushed the nape of her neck and a paralyzing shudder raced down Sam's spine. She drew a deep breath, then remembered to take his arm, feeling the muscles rise as hard as when they had entered the plaza.

Suddenly she was tense too, feeling herself the object of undeserved and confusing criticism. Silent and defensive, she let him escort her out of the restaurant and into the heat of the evening. Lanterns swayed in the trees surrounding the plaza, flickering like painted stars; guitar music strummed from open-faced cantinas. Couples stood whispering in the shadows.

"It isn't necessary to throw a dazzling smile at every damned man who looks at you!" Trace snapped, almost dragging her into the side street that led to their hotel. "Or show him a glimpse of ankle!"

"I didn't!"

"As a male, you seemed reasonably modest," he continued angrily. "As a female, I swear you're absolutely brazen!"

"What? I am not!"

It felt uncomfortable and unnatural to mince along, clinging to a man's arm. In fact, Sam didn't recall ever walking this close to a man. She could inhale the spice of Trace's bay rum mingling with the rose water he had given her, and occasionally their hips bumped like bolts of heat lightning striking together. With every step they took, she became more and more aware of his height and his solid, elegant body.

"The next time we go out in public," he continued, still berating her, "I insist that you wear a dress with a higher bodice."

"I've had enough of this. I'll wear whatever I damned well please!" The old Sam rejected any man issuing orders in her direction. The new Sam didn't like it either.

Trace's arm brushed the side of her breast like a flaming log and Sam jumped. When he looked down at her, the angry sparks blazing in his eyes shot a tingle straight to her toes.

Abruptly Sam comprehended what was happening now and what had been happening between them for several weeks. An acute awareness of each other had begun long before now, but the mysterious fascination of the corset and stockings, the rustle of silk and petticoats, had seduced Sam into an experiment ending in the full realization of her sex. Willing or unwilling, Trace responded to the experiment as well. Sam's transformation, conscious and unconscious, affected them both. It had heightened their perception of the similarities and differences simmering between man and woman.

Tonight Sam was all woman, vibrant and resonating with an emerging feminine knowledge, power, mystery. And Trace was all man, virile and forceful in his masculinity, instinctively protective and possessive. The tensions tugging between the two pulsed primitive and raw, as old as the hills above town, as urgent as a gunshot.

Sam stopped dead a few yards from the hotel entrance, staring up at Trace's bearded face in shocked realization.

All her posturing and flirting, all the glimpses of ankle and shifting of bosoms, all the sparkling glances and effervescent smiles had been for Trace's benefit. She hadn't cared if anyone else noticed as long as he did.

She wanted him.

She looked up at him, stared into his dangerous tiger eyes, and her body trembled. Suddenly she craved the sensation of his hands on her skin, yearned to drink passionate kisses from his sensual lips. She wanted to see him rise over her, rampant and raging with a man's need, wanted to cup his buttocks in her palms and pull him between her thighs.

She wanted him now, right now. And she had wanted him for a long time.

"Oh my God," she whispered, stumbling, her eyes fixed on the brooding, angry curve of his lips.

Trace caught and steadied her. "Watch your step, it's bumpy . . ."

Then he saw her pale face and quickened breath emerging from parted lips, saw her breast rising in a struggle to capture the next short gasp. Abruptly his anger vanished. He gazed deeply into her wide eyes, then his narrowed gaze dropped to her lips.

"Don't look at me like that, Sam," he warned. "Don't practice female wiles on me. I swear to God, when you look at me like that I—" He bit off the words with obvious effort.

"Oh, Trace," Sam whispered helplessly. "I've wanted you since the first time you asked my opinion."

Waves of male heat surrounded her in a shell of mounting desire. Light-headed, she swayed toward him, sensing his answering need and his immediate arousal. To prevent herself from falling, she hastily raised a glove and steadied herself against his chest. His muscles were rock hard. The touch of him seared her.

A low groan sounded above her bonnet. Trace caught her hand and clasped it hard against his waistcoat.

"What are you doing, Sam?" he asked in a low voice that sounded as if he were in pain.

When Sam gazed up at him, her expression helpless, his eyes had narrowed and were smoldering with a look that was dangerous and exciting. She swallowed, unable to speak above a whisper. "I don't know, I just . . ."

"Don't tease me," he said hoarsely, tracing the contour of her lips with his stare. "You already have me half crazy." He stepped closer until his hips pressed against her skirt, letting her feel the hard arousal between his legs. "You're playing with fire, Sam."

A rush of white-hot dizziness overwhelmed her and she sagged against his body with a soft moan.

"That time you kissed me. Remember? I can't get it out of my mind. I think about it all the time. I've been wanting you to do it again."

He gripped her arms above the elbows, peered beneath the brim of her bonnet. "I don't dare kiss you again. If I do, I won't be able to control myself. I won't stop."

"I think about you all the time," Sam admitted softly, leaning against him. "I can't get you out of my mind!"

"I can't think about anything but *you*," he replied. "I keep remembering you naked, the way your hips curve and the sweet hollow of your waist. I dream of you waking and sleeping." His fingers tightened on her arms. "I can smell your scent long after you've left the room. I remember the taste of your mouth and the feel of your breasts against my chest."

Briefly Trace closed his eyes, then stared at her again, two points of fire blazing between his dark lashes. "So stop this, Sam. Or I'll start to believe what you're saying with that soft rosy mouth and those blue, teasing eyes."

"I want you," she said simply, her voice a tortured whisper.

She had always spoken as directly as a man, said what she meant. And she did so now, trembling on a dusty side street in Santa Fe, her body aflame.

"I want you to take me to bed. I know how it feels to look like a woman. Now, I want to know how it feels to be one." She dropped her face into her gloved hands. "Oh God, Trace. I'm burning inside. You look at me and my skin catches fire. The sound of your voice ignites a blaze in my stomach. I don't know what's wrong with me, or why I feel like something inside is about to explode. No," she said, waving a glove, "I do know why. I'm afraid to be a complete woman, but I'm eager too. I want to know! I can't stand this torture another minute. I'm going crazy inside!"

They had both forgotten where they were. Neither noticed the irritated pedestrians stepping around them or the horses and wagons rattling past in the street. They stared at each other with dawning recognition.

Trace opened his fists, then in a motion that was fluid, powerful, and urgent, he scooped her into his arms and wordlessly carried her into the hotel and through the lobby.

The hotel clerk peered past the post-dinner crowd who had paused to gape, then hurried forward, wringing his hands together. "Mr. Marshall! Your wife, is she ... does she require medical attention?" Hovering, he followed them to the staircase.

Aflame with embarrassment and heart-pounding anticipation, Sam hid her face against Trace's chest. Her heart was thudding so loudly that she hardly heard Trace's growl.

"Get out of the way."

He carried her to their room and set her on her feet in the darkness inside the door. They stood for a moment, trembling but not touching, peering through the shadows into each other's faces, searching for assurances, for evidence that the heat boiling inside was real.

Without looking away from Sam's expectant face, Trace threw his hat aside, untied the ribbons beneath her chin, then pushed her bonnet to the floor. Her shawl dropped from her shoulders as she lifted her arms, hesitated a moment, then encircled his neck. She gasped as she stepped against the hard length of his body and felt the contour of flesh and bone mold against hers.

She thought her knees would collapse when his mouth came down fiercely on her lips and his hot hands enclosed her waist, pulling her roughly against him.

There was nothing tentative about Trace's possessive kiss. It was the hard, demanding kiss of a man who had waited to the breaking point, who had waited beyond the sensibility of give and take, whose body rose rampant with the powerful urgency of instinct and primal forces.

Anything less would have failed to match the wild storm raging in Sam's breast and thighs. The decision to experience the full range of womanhood had been made. She was free to surrender totally, to give of herself and take for herself without hesitation or modesty or second thoughts.

She returned his kiss with an equal ferocity that she was only dimly aware of, pressing urgently against his heat and power, matching passion with passion, yearning to melt into him, wanting to fill herself with him, wanting to become him. When Trace's tongue plundered her mouth, Sam moaned and gasped with the hot thrill of tingling sensation, thinking dizzily that she might actually faint for the first time in her life.

In a blur of passion they moved into the dark bedroom, pulling frantically at their clothing, kissing, touching, tearing off petticoats and shirt studs, stockings and trousers. The dim starlight at the window glowed on their nakedness and they tumbled onto the four-poster, wrapped together like a single writhing being.

Because she was inexperienced, Sam expected him to penetrate at once, to plunge immediately and deeply inside and satisfy the hot craving that pulsed through her body with every racing heartbeat. But Trace pinned her with his lips, his hands moving, stroking, caressing, teasing her in places no person had ever touched, making her sob and cry out and thrash beneath his hips and thighs until she was gasping, pleading, blazing with a hot wet heat that she feared would consume her.

"Please," she murmured mindlessly, her head thrashing across the pillow, her fingers sliding and pulling at him. "Please."

"Are you certain about this, Sam?" he asked in a hoarse voice she scarcely recognized.

The question almost made her laugh. If he left her now, she was sure she would die from the passion he had aroused in her. "Please," she begged, licking her lips and groaning when he kissed the old scar on the side of her ribs.

When Trace finally moved above her, gently opening her thighs with guiding fingers, he stared into her eyes, then thrust deep. Sam cried out once before she arched her back and lifted to meet him. His fullness swelled inside of her, satisfying the terrible demanding emptiness, replacing it with strange thrilling new sensations. An electric tension quivered along her thighs, urging, compelling her to draw him deeper into her.

And to Sam's delight and joy, they moved together as if they had orchestrated each touch, each movement in advance. There was a tempo to their kisses that each understood, a rhythm they heard deep in their minds. Together they accelerated toward a crescendo, climbing on waves of sensation and emotion until Sam gasped for breath, her hands flying over his shoulders, over his face, and she felt as if her small body could not contain all the wondrous explosive feelings.

There was a moment to gaze into his eyes, a moment when his kiss seared her lips, then her mind erupted into a blissful, fainting darkness before contracting sharply inward in a glittering shower of rain and fire. Sam trembled violently, then relaxed, trembled again and gradually subsided into boneless languor as a feeling poured through her as if warm molasses melted inside her skin.

Beneath her shaking fingertips, she felt the muscles gather under Trace's shoulders and tighten into rock as his body shuddered, then convulsed. He crushed her against his chest; his head sagged to her breast and she heard him gasping for breath.

To her surprise, the weight and heat of his spent body felt glorious, and Sam experienced a pang of disappointment when he rolled onto the bed beside her, his body as slick with perspiration as hers. Still gasping, Trace turned his head on the pillow to look into her soft eyes.

"Did I hurt you?"

"Hurt me?" For a moment the question puzzled her. There had been one brief flash of pain, only an instant that was swept away on tides of emotion and fiery urgency. "No," she said, her blue eyes serious. "You didn't hurt me. I liked everything you did." Gazing deeply into his eyes, Sam felt the night breeze tiptoe across her damp nakedness. "Tell me something," she whispered, unable to look away from him. "Is it always like this between men and women?"

Lazily, Trace ran his palm from her waist to her hip, turning her to face him fully. "Like what? What was it like for you?"

"You know how it is when you've tracked a man over several hundred miles and you finally catch up to him?" She combed her fingertips through his beard, surprised by how soft the hair was. "You get him in your sights and you know something is about to happen. Your heart starts slamming against your rib cage and you begin to sweat because you don't know if it's going to be successful or if it's going to turn bad. Then you pull the trigger and something wild explodes inside. It's like a geyser erupting or Fourth of July fireworks. It's like you grow taller, so tall that your mind stretches over the universe and gathers in the stars. What we did just now . . . it was like that, only more. More. Is it always like that?"

Trace laughed, then pulled her close, fitting her body into the curves of his. She felt him stirring again against her thigh and she moaned softly. When he kissed her, his mouth was tender, and this time she remained aware enough to notice his mustache brushing her cheek.

"No," he answered gruffly, "sex isn't always wonderful. Sometimes it's indifferent or ugly." For one brief instant, ghosts from the past hovered nearby. Then Trace shook his head and smiled into her eyes. "Sometimes it's better than wonderful."

Her eyebrows lifted in surprise. "Better?" What

they had experienced together had wildly surpassed Sam's expectations. She couldn't imagine anything better.

"Lie back and let me show you," Trace whispered gruffly against her lips.

Before he finally released her and let her fall into a blissful exhausted sleep, Sam experienced shock, amazement, heart-pounding urgency, discovery, and utter joyful satisfaction such as she had never dreamed possible.

When Sam awoke shortly before dawn, she blinked at the tousled head on the pillow next to her and felt her heart lurch and then sink. Moving carefully so she wouldn't wake him, she slipped out of bed, found Trace's discarded shirt on the floor, and hastily pulled it over her nakedness. Tiptoeing, she moved through the shadows and quietly closed the door behind her.

In the living room, she curled up on the cushioned window seat, facing into the sunrise and letting the dawn glow pink and gold on a face clouded by confusion.

What had she done? What sort of insanity had befallen her last night? Sam pressed her fingertips against her temples, trying to sort out thoughts that whirled like bits of wind-borne confetti.

Viewed one way, what had happened between her and Trace had been exciting and wonderful. But in a larger way, bedding a man represented a monumental defeat, crushing an image of herself that Sam had labored for years to construct. Tilting her head back, she closed her eyes with a soft groan.

Now she was changed in mysterious ways. The part of her that remained a terrified eleven-year-old standing in boy's overalls watching a ruthless outlaw abuse her mother was grateful to discover that sex did not have to be brutal and deadly, or casual and indifferent.

But, another part of her deeply resented her weakness in surrendering to a surprising and powerful need she had not previously acknowledged.

For years, Sam had considered herself passionless, untouched by the physical urges that drove the rough men with whom she associated. Since she knew she could not satisfy such urges and had no desire to do so, she had banished sexual needs from her consciousness. She hadn't realized suppressed desires could stack up like kindling awaiting a match.

And yet, discovering herself as a woman had been electrifying, joyful. She hadn't imagined the existence of such sensations; she wouldn't have believed she could take pleasure in anything female. But she had. Oh God, she had.

A groaning sigh collapsed her chest. Who was she really? Where did she fit in a world that had spun upside down? She gazed out of the window trying to see where her future might be.

She and Trace hadn't found Hannibal yet, but they would. Her professional instinct told her the final confrontation was drawing near. The revenge that had driven her for so many empty years would finally be satisfied.

And then what? Could she adopt skirts and petticoats on a permanent basis? Would she attempt to set aside the unfeminine habits of the last five years and become the woman she might have been? She wasn't sure that was possible anymore. More likely she would return to what was familiar, the lonely role of a sexless being in boy's trousers drifting through the west searching for meaning and a future that was always out of reach.

Dropping her chin, Sam thrust her fingers through her hair and shook her head against the confusion clouding her thoughts. Who was Sam Kincade? Yesterday she had believed she knew the answer. Today, she didn't have the faintest notion.

"Having regrets?" Trace inquired softly.

Sam jumped and whirled to see him sitting in the striped wing chair, watching her, his fingers tented beneath his short beard. The sight of his bare feet exposed beneath his trousers unnerved her. Somehow his naked feet seemed more intimate than his bared chest. A flush of color warmed her cheeks.

"No regrets," she answered slowly, turning her face back toward the rising sun. Biting her lower lip, she hesitated. "But I guess I didn't know it would change me."

"Change you how?"

Because his steady examination made her uncomfortable, Sam pulled her knees up and tugged his shirttail down over her bare legs, wondering if the sight of her naked feet made her seem vulnerable too. Feeling vulnerable was a new and uncomfortable experience, one she suspected went part and parcel with a female persona.

"I don't know exactly," she said, still speaking slowly, trying to figure it out as she spoke. "I feel good about what we did, but upset too. I'm confused and I feel different inside." She lifted eyes brimming with turmoil.

"Like a woman?" he asked quietly. A burst of sunlight filled the room, making his amber eyes translucent and coaxing copper highlights from his tousled hair.

"I don't know. I feel lost, Trace. I don't know who I am anymore. Or who I want to be. It's as if I'm straddling a dangerous river and can't move in either direction." They stared at each other. "Trace? What will you do after we kill Hannibal? Will you return to Kansas City?"

He shook his head. "I've been thinking about San Francisco."

"Will you ever remarry?" Instantly Sam bit her tongue, appalled that she had asked such a suggestive question. She ducked her head, letting her short hair swing forward to conceal her expression, wishing she could fall through the floor. Yet she wanted to know his answer.

Moving to the window seat, Trace sat beside her and tried to take her hands in his, but she slapped him away, too embarrassed to meet his gaze.

"Sam, listen to me." Watching her, he paused as if

gathering his thoughts. "What happened last night was wonderful." Gently he cupped her chin and tilted her flaming face up to his. "I don't want to mislead you. I'm fond of you, Sam, very fond of you. But I don't plan to marry again."

"Why not?" Sam whispered. Her mind raced frantically; her lips were saying things her brain desperately did not want to say. This conversation could lead to nothing but humiliation.

His thumb gently stroked her jawline. "I'm not a good husband. Etta was raped because I was not there to protect her, and because I exposed her to Hannibal. What good is a husband who can't . . . or won't protect his wife? What kind of a man is that?"

"A man who was out of town on business," Sam said tartly. She gazed deeply into his eyes. "I don't need a man to protect me. I can outshoot any man I ever met." Embarrassment and despair gripped her stomach. She was almost begging him to invite her to go to San Francisco with him.

His lips tightened. "I'm glad you don't need me or any other man."

"Well, I don't." She swallowed. "But I might want one anyway."

After a pause, he raised his hands and tightened his fingers on her shoulders. "I don't want to take advantage of you. If you don't want to repeat what happened last night, then we won't. But if you do, then you have to understand that I'm not offering marriage. One woman died because I failed her. It won't happen again."

Anger flared in Sam's eyes and again she slapped away his hands. "You're a damned fool, Trace Harden."

He stiffened abruptly.

"Remember the cabin? If you hadn't been there, Edwin Snow's hired gunslinger would have killed and scalped me. Doesn't that count for anything?"

A frown hooded his gaze.

Sam slid from the window seat and crossed the room, turning back to face him. "It doesn't count in your mind because you were thinking of me as a man. Well, surprise. You protected a woman. And you didn't fail me. Just think about that, damn it. If it wasn't for you, I'd be dead!"

Whirling on her bare feet, she ran into the bedroom and slammed the door, threw herself on the bed, and burst into a storm of weeping. When the tempest passed, Sam flung her arms wide on the bed and stared red-eyed at the ceiling.

With great disgust, it occurred to her that since she'd met Trace, she was behaving more and more like a woman every day. The next thing she knew, she'd be throwing a tantrum because her hair didn't curl properly.

Sickened and thoroughly revolted, Sam flopped on her stomach and pushed her face into a pillow that smelled like bay rum.

"I wish I'd never met him!"

That wasn't true, of course. Trace Harden had blown into her life like a whirlwind and had spun her into something new and unsettling and secretly exciting. But she felt frightened because she didn't know the rules and she didn't know where all these changes would lead.

Most important, she was worried to death that she was falling in love with him—or, worse, that she already had.

"I'm going out," Trace announced, stepping to the mirror in the entryway to adjust his tie and straighten his hat.

Sam glanced up from the book she was pretending to read. This was the first they had spoken since her blowup in the morning. Lunch, along with most of the afternoon, had passed in utter silence.

"Where are you going?"

"I told you about Major Allerbee. He suggested a woman at the Toro Blanco may know where Hannibal is hiding out."

Elated by the prospect of action, Sam tossed aside her book and started to rise. "I'll fetch my bonnet and gloves."

"Sam, the Toro Blanco is a whorehouse."

A wave dismissed his objection. "I've been in a whorehouse before."

"Really?" Sudden amusement erased his frown. "Someday I'd like to hear that story."

"I was waiting for a friend," she said sharply.

"Regardless, you can't come with me." An eyebrow lifted and his glance swept the lace at her throat, then dropped to the ruffles flouncing her hem. "Things have changed."

Frustrated, Sam struck the arm of the chair with her fist. "Another female rule, one of the can'ts! Since I gussied up in skirts all I've been hearing is can't, don't, shouldn't!"

"Do you really want to visit a whorehouse?"

The question caught her up short, as did the sobering answer. There was nothing in a whorehouse except acute discomfort. Moreover, since Trace had trusted her to negotiate with the judge, she should trust him to solicit information without her hovering at his elbow.

"I'll wait here," she conceded, sourly and without grace. "That's what women do, isn't it? Wait for men."

After Trace departed, Sam paced the length of the suite, muttering and lost in thought. After several minutes she stopped abruptly as it suddenly occurred to her that she no longer wobbled on her heels or tripped over her hem when she walked. Nor had she realized that her hair was now long enough to tuck smoothly into the false hairpiece, nor that she seldom complained about wearing her corset.

Shock swept the strength from her knees and she fell into the nearest chair.

Good God. The unthinkable had happened. She had become a woman! She didn't know whether to laugh or cry.

*   *   *

"Marguerita?"

The woman turned in a swirl of lace and ruffled Mexican skirts, and Trace found himself facing Mattie Able. As she had darkened her hair and eyebrows and adopted Mexican dress, and now wore a mantilla, he hadn't been certain it was Mattie until he gazed directly into her handsome dark eyes.

Mattie nodded once, recognition twitching her lips. "I've been expecting you," she said quietly, turning her head toward the parlor. Her glance swept a room crowded with heavy dark furniture and portraits of voluptuous nudes. A bored-looking Indian girl fanned her cheeks, listening to a stunning halfbreed complain about the afternoon heat. Most of Mattie's girls were still asleep upstairs.

"As I was saying before we were interrupted," Trace said with a humorless smile, "where is he, Mattie?"

"My office is in the back," she answered, her ruffled skirt flaring as she turned toward a narrow corridor. After they entered her private study, Mattie watched with pride as Trace inspected the best furniture she had ever owned.

"Congratulations," he offered, flicking a finger through the silk tassels that swung from a lampshade. "You appear to have prospered since we last spoke."

Mattie seated herself behind the desk where she laboriously kept her accounts. She liked the image of herself as a businesswoman. "It's hard to fail in this business. There's a constant source of new customers coming in off the Trail every day."

Trace took the chair in front of the desk and crossed an ankle over his knee. "I assume you've seen Hannibal, and you've told him that Etta is dead. Now where is he, Mattie?"

She clasped her hands on top of the desk and drew a breath. "You're going to kill him, aren't you?"

Opening his jacket, Trace removed a pouch of gold pieces and placed it on her desk. A dangerous look flickered in the eyes that reminded Mattie so much of Hannibal. "Where is he?"

Mattie's hands were shaking and she lowered them to her lap. A deep breath strained the lace that barely covered her bosom. "I paid Alf at the Dogtown hotel to read that letter you carry, and he told me what it said. But it ain't true." Her chin lifted. "Hannibal never raped your wife."

Ice frosted Trace's gaze. "You don't know anything about it."

She leaned forward, her eyes intense and begging him to hear the truth and believe. "I know more than you think. I know Hannibal loved Etta. From the minute he met her, he worshiped the ground she walked on. The damned fool still does. He loves you too and it's tearing him to pieces knowing what he done! But it wasn't rape and he don't regret it, Trace. He loved her. And she was clever enough, plain bad enough, to make him believe that she loved him back."

The laugh that burst from Trace's throat shocked

them both. "You'd know how ridiculous that sounds if you knew how Etta always ridiculed Hannibal. She disliked him intensely."

"I don't doubt it. She sent you to kill him, didn't she?" Mattie considered him with a shrewd expression. "But I'd say she hated both of you."

Trace stared. "I don't want to discuss my wife. Tell me where I can find Hannibal, then I'll leave."

"Hannibal never would have touched her if she hadn't come into his bed. That's the truth, that's how it happened."

"You're lying," he said flatly.

Tears welled in her dark eyes. "Please. I'm begging you. What happened was not Hannibal's fault! Etta made him do it, then she lied to set the two of you against each other. This is her doing."

Eyes glittering dangerously, Trace rose to his feet. Fury rocked his voice, shook his body. "Hannibal raped my wife. He betrayed my trust. He destroyed thirty years of . . ." He stopped. "Did Hannibal ask you to tell me this pack of lies?"

Mattie drew back from the look on his face. "I'm telling you because I'm trying to right what Etta set wrong. It's *wrong* to turn brother against brother!" A tear of anger and frustration tracked through her powder and rouge, followed by another. "Hannibal is going to die sooner or later. You got to know that. He'd going to hang or get himself gunned down. All I'm saying is, you don't have to be the one who pulls the trigger. The one who done wrong by you both already hanged herself. Let it end there."

Shaking with fury, Trace stood over the desk, flattening his palms on the surface, leaning forward until his face was only inches from hers. He snarled between his teeth.

"I've never struck a woman, Mattie. But I swear, if you don't tell me where Hannibal is, and tell me right now . . ."

She stared at him through a film of tears, then dropped her head and answered in a hopeless whisper. "He's waiting for you at Nowhere, Arizona."

Without a word, Trace pushed back from the desk and strode out of her office.

Mattie sat as still as stone for several minutes before she hurled the Judas pouch of coins against the wall. She watched with dulled eyes as a shower of gold rained over her Indian rug. Then, feeling a hundred years old, she dragged herself out of her chair and went to her room to cry until she could cry no more.

Afterward, she dressed in mourning because a good man was going to die. Then she said a short prayer for Trace Harden.

CHAPTER
* 16 *

Nowhere was the hottest damned place on the planet, Hannibal decided, mopping a red bandanna over his throat and brow. Deep sun-baked cracks scarred the earth. Heat waves shimmered and distorted and made a man doubt his eyesight. Last week, a horse had fallen over in front of the general store, dead from standing in the heat.

On the positive side, Nowhere's marshall was good for jailing drunks and breaking up the fights around the town well, but he wasn't good for much else. Hannibal was almost certain Brown recognized him, but capturing or drawing against a notorious killer wasn't written on the marshall's backbone. When Hannibal had ridden into town to wet his whistle at Nowhere's only saloon, the marshall had skedaddled, finding urgent business elsewhere.

But the marshall was capable of sending a telegram. If Brown hadn't already summoned an outside posse, he would eventually. He might lack the grit to confront Hannibal directly, but he sniffed opportunity when it rode into his backyard. Undoubtedly Brown was feverishly scheming to find a way to link his name to Hannibal's capture without actually endangering his yellow hide.

Hannibal spat at the dry sandy earth, then fired another shot at a three-fingered cactus, honing his skill by shooting off preselected spines.

Every instinct warned him to leave Nowhere. He hadn't evaded capture all these years by acting stupidly. He knew when to move on. Standing up out of a crouch, he let his fingertips stray to the scars on his forehead. The net was closing, he could feel it. If a posse didn't get him first, Trace would.

Narrowing his eyes against the white glare, he scanned a horizon bare of all but cracked earth, cactus, and low, dry brush. The blazing sun bleached all color out of the landscape. During the day everything appeared gray or brown. In the evening, rusty sunsets bloodied the skies.

Nowhere, Arizona was as close to hell as a man could get and still pretend he was alive. Thinking about it almost made Hannibal smile. Penny novels portrayed the outlaw life as exciting and glamourous. On those rare occasions when he'd read such fiction, he had laughed out loud.

"When are we leaving this hell-hole?" Marsh Crisp asked, joining Hannibal behind the rancho. He hooked his thumbs in his belt loops and watched Hannibal aim and then shoot at the cactus. "There ain't nothing in this place to hang around for. Not even a bank to rob." He cast a contemptuous glance toward town, a collection of adobe boxes baking in the sun.

"Where are the boys?"

"Jake's inside taking a siesta. Grass-Eye rode to town to eyeball that horse for sale."

Hannibal nodded, then shot a fist-size chunk out of the left finger of the cactus. Jake had joined them recently. Grass-Eye had appeared two days out of Santa Fe and stayed when he learned he was riding alongside Hannibal Cotwell. There were always men who hoped some of the reputation would rub off. Their names and faces blurred in Hannibal's memory.

"When are we leaving?" Crisp demanded irritably.

"When I say so."

Hannibal was beginning to suspect that belligerence was just Crisp's way. He wasn't sure any more that Crisp plotted to take over his outfit. Crisp had, after all, stuck by him when he got shot and the last set of boys lit out. Lately he'd surprised himself by wondering if he and Marsh Crisp were friends. He hadn't decided if he welcomed that kind of responsibility.

"When's that gonna be?"

Hannibal rubbed the shoulder where Mattie had dug the bullet out of him. Sometimes he missed her. "I'm waiting for somebody."

"Who?"

Hannibal let his eyes settle on Crisp's heat-red face. If he wanted it to, his gaze could make a man back off muttering apologies. Today, because he was feeling mellow toward Crisp, he deliberately chose a reply rather than a snarl. "Not that it's any of your business, but I'm waiting for Trace Harden."

Crisp acknowledged the answer with a nod, trying not to look too interested. "Should I know who Harden is?"

Hannibal whirled, dropped to one knee, and fired, sending fleshy bits of cactus spinning into the hot air. "After I've talked to him, we'll leave."

Crisp kicked at a rock. "Well, I hope he gits here soon, then. The boys are restless, wanting to move on."

Hannibal shrugged. "Take them into town tonight. Get them liquored up. Let off a little steam."

"You ain't coming?"

"I have some thinking to do."

After supper the boys left for town. Hannibal carried a warm beer out to the front porch and sat on a sagging step, watching a scarlet sky burn away the remaining daylight.

Even the nights were hot in this godforsaken place, fit only for scorpions and vipers and thick-shelled remnants of a distant era.

There was something fitting about Nowhere lining up as the site of Hannibal's final showdown. It satisfied something desolate and solitary inside him. Listening to the minute rustlings of small poisonous creatures, Hannibal decided that Nowhere offered a foretaste of hell. Not that he'd expected anything different. He had earned his place in the flames.

Tossing his hat aside, he tilted his head and let the warm beer trickle down the back of his throat.

He had to decide what he was going to do about Trace.

Trace was not a gunslinger, and he had never killed a man. In a gunfight, Trace would get shot. Hannibal didn't want to kill his brother, but once a gun was in his hand and a fight threatened, instinct would overtake him as it had before. At the finish, he could add murdering his brother to his list of crimes.

Leaning back against the steps, he rubbed his forehead and frowned at the bloody sky.

If he told Trace the truth, he made a cuckold of his brother and sliced away his manhood. The truth blackened Etta's character, and Trace would learn that his wife had not loved him. Instead of grieving the loss of a beloved, Trace would condemn his wife as a liar and an adulteress, a cheat and a willing partner in betrayal. Etta's memory would forever be tarnished.

But if he told the truth, there was an excellent possibility that no one would get killed. It was the difference between a love affair and a brutal assault. Trace would hate him for what he and Etta had done, but Hannibal knew his brother's character well enough to know there would be no gunfight.

The second alternative was to support Etta's letter. But if he let Trace believe that he had raped Etta, the only possible result was a shoot-out. Either Hannibal would kill his brother, the likely outcome, or the lie would force his brother to kill him. Etta's reputation and her memory would remain intact and unblemished. There would be no scandal; no one would ever learn that she had preferred her husband's brother in her bed. Trace could blame Hannibal solely. That must have been Etta's intention, or she wouldn't have lied with her last breath.

But if he supported her lie, then his brother would die.

The dilemma revolved endlessly through his thoughts, as it had since he'd learned of her accusation.

"Why?" he whispered, tilting his head to watch the sky shade toward inky red.

Why had she betrayed their love and accused him of raping her? He had asked that question a thousand times but no answer had come to him. She must have known that the worst thing that could happen to him or to Trace was to turn against each other. All he could come up with was that she must have been out of her head at the end.

And it was his fault because he'd refused to take her away with him. His fault because he'd left her to explain her pregnancy without him by her side. His fault because he had loved his brother more than he had loved her.

When the moon rose like a cold white ball, he saddled Gringo and rode alone across the desert floor. He didn't see the spiny cactus or smell the sage, didn't hear the rustle of night creatures preying on one another. His thoughts had turned backward, wandering the shady lanes of New Orleans, remembering the swamp deer bounding through the back bayous. He remembered tracking possum and treeing fat coons. Remembered the boy with eyes like his who trailed after him as if he were a hero, shouting: Hey Hanny, wait for me!

For the first time since childhood, moisture stung his eyelids. "I'm waiting, little brother . . ."

CHAPTER
* 17 *

Sam baked inside an oven of women's trappings. Her traveling costume, composed of numerous undergarments, layers of petticoats, a shirtwaist, a dark skirt, a short jacket, and a hat with a veil, was slowly cooking her.

After blotting her handkerchief against damp temples and cheeks, she lifted her hem and drew Trace away from the stage driver who was securing their trunk to the boot of the stage. Proper behavior be damned; she drew off her sticky hot gloves and touched bare fingertips to his sleeve.

"Do you recall the bearded man with a limp who was watching us in the restaurant the night before last?" she asked uneasily.

Trace hadn't been himself since visiting the Toro Blanco. For a man, he was unusually talkative, but the night before he'd been distracted and withdrawn.

Speculation was driving Sam crazy, his silence activating insecurities she hadn't known she possessed.

A dozen times it hovered on the tip of her tongue to inquire if she had annoyed him. Disgust stopped her from asking. And pride had prevented her from inviting him into her bed again when it seemed obvious that he'd forgotten her presence.

"Trace?" she repeated impatiently. He stood with arms folded across his chest, legs planted wide, his gaze focused on a distant point that only he could see. "Hey!"

"Sorry." He frowned down at her. "Did you say something?"

Tilting her hat brim sharply to the left, Sam indicated a man leaning against a tree at the edge of the plaza. "Do you see that rancher? He's very interested in our departure."

"What rancher?"

When Sam darted a quick glance across the street, she discovered the man with the limp had vanished. A troubled scowl pursued her lips.

"Maybe I was mistaken," she said slowly, not believing it. The man with the limp had displayed extraordinary interest in their preparations for departure. The question was: why? If he had been a bounty hunter, Sam would have recognized him. And he wasn't wearing a badge. That left Edwin Snow's hired gunslingers to consider. Except, she had a distinct impression that his main focus was Trace.

Spitting tobacco flakes off his tongue, the knight of the reins tossed a pair of steps before the stage door and assisted a stout woman inside, followed by an elderly gentleman. He tipped his hat to Sam and extended a dust-darkened hand. "Ma'am?"

Hesitating, she glanced toward the plaza, then back to Trace. There were a dozen questions she wanted to ask, but she settled for a brisk nod and stepped forward. "Let's go."

The stage interior was hot but the seats were wide enough that the four passengers were not sitting thigh to thigh. The elderly gentleman tipped his hat to Sam and inclined his head to Trace. The stout woman settled a lunch basket at her feet, then studied her companions above the edges of a fluttering fan.

The driver cracked his whip and the stage lurched back on its springs, then bucked forward. Trace caught Sam before she was flung to the floor; the elderly gentleman retrieved his hat from atop the lunch basket.

"They *will* make a flourish," he complained, placing his hat firmly on his lap. "As we'll be traveling together for several days, allow me to introduce myself. I'm James Goodnight, riding the full distance to California to enter business with my son." An expectant smile settled on Trace and Sam.

"Mr. and Mrs. Andrew Marshall." Trace's manner was polite, but an undertone announced that he had offered all the personal information he intended to reveal.

The stout woman brushed dust from a plain gray traveling skirt. "I'm Mrs. Wallace Callen, from La Junta. Recently widowed," she added, casting a side-long glance toward Mr. Goodnight. "Where in California does your son live?" she inquired after a minute of silence in memory of her departed husband.

It was the last moment of silence they were fated to enjoy. Mrs. Callen felt compelled to fill every blessed second with conversation. She complained of the dust kicked up by the horse's hooves, fussed over closing and opening the leather shades. She called on Jesus to rescue them from the broiling heat, informed them in stupefying detail of every hot day she had ever experienced. She spoke at eye-glazing length about her children and discussed the virtues and many faults of her recently departed husband.

Early on, Trace shut out the sound of Mrs. Callen's voice as he would have ignored the persistent buzzing of a troublesome fly. Turning his head to the window, he peered at the barren, baked landscape. Sam shifted and fidgeted on the seat beside him, gripping the strap as they bounced around the stage interior like dice shaken in a cup.

Gradually his surroundings faded and blurred into the heavy furnishings cluttering Mattie Able's office. Her voice replayed in his ears, insisting that he listen.

As he had during the long night behind him, he asked himself how much of Mattie's conviction was based on Hannibal's revelations and how much on wishful thinking. Would Hannibal have discussed Etta with Mattie? Would he have told her the truth?

Mattie's claims blew through his mind like a cold wind chilling the fire of his temper.

What rolled in his stomach like bile was the knowledge that if Mattie was correct, if Etta had seduced Hannibal instead of being a victim of rape, then some of the puzzles contained in her letter were solved.

Closing his eyes, Trace leaned his head against the back wall of the stage and fingered the pages folded inside his waistcoat pocket.

Whatever Hannibal claimed when Trace confronted him, rape or a romance as Mattie claimed, his relationship with his brother could never again be the same. He and Hannibal would face each other over guns. For that, he was more than sorry. Anguish clawed his chest.

To set this final confrontation in motion, Etta must have hated them both.

Reaching into his waistcoat, he removed her letter and rubbed the pages between his fingers as knots rose in a line along his jaw. Her face floated in his memory.

Slowly, he tore the letter into pieces. Pushing his fist out of the window, he opened his hand and watched the bits of paper trickle through his fingers into the wind and blowing dust.

When he glanced at Sam, he discovered her staring at him, her blue eyes as round as buttons. "I'll tell you about it later," he said shortly, taking her hand.

Sam nodded and glared over at Mrs. Callen, who had stopped talking long enough to glower disapprovingly at their clasped hands.

Trace returned his gaze to the window and noticed that the terrain had altered, becoming more rocky and not as flat or featureless.

"As I was saying," Mrs. Callen continued.

Sam leaned forward, eyelids narrowing into threatening slits. "Shut . . . up."

Mrs. Callen's eyebrows soared toward the feathers quivering on her hat brim. An angry plum-colored flush rose from her collar. She crossed her arms over an ample bosom and huffed. "Well! I never heard such rudeness!"

"One more word, Mrs. Callen"—flashes of the bounty hunter gleamed in Sam's narrowed eyes—"and I will personally fling you out of this coach. I'm in a bad mood, do you understand? So shut up. Do it now."

Shock pursed Mrs. Callen's lips and she swung toward Mr. Goodnight for support. But that old gentleman had closed his eyes and leaned his head back, a smile on his lips.

Now the only sound in the coach was the rattle of harness and wheels, the rusty squeal of the springs, and the leather shades flapping against the window frames.

Smiling, Trace patted Sam's hand.

What was he going to do about her? That question also troubled his thoughts. He had believed making love to her would satisfy his curiosity and his passion, would diminish his fascination. But it hadn't. He suspected there was no getting Sam out of his system. Without his being aware of when or how it had happened, Sam Kincade had become integral to his life.

With nothing to do but bounce around the inside of the hot dusty coach, he had time to ponder how greatly his ideas of women had altered since he met Samantha Kincade. Sam had shown him that a woman could be a desirable companion, could pull her own weight, could hold herself to standards of integrity as rigorous as any male's. She had shattered his image of the ideal woman by showing him how shallow that image had been.

From all outward appearances, Etta had been the ideal woman for her time. But inside, Etta had seethed with a poisonous fury that Trace doubted he would ever understand.

"What was that?" Mr. Goodnight gasped, bolting upright and clutching his hat. "Was that a gunshot?"

"Damned right it was." Sticking her head out the stage window, Sam peered ahead through coils of roiling dust. "Damn!" Her hands slapped at her waist, seeking the Colt she was not wearing. "Three masked men," she shouted. "It's a holdup!"

"Oh no! We're stopping!" Mrs. Callen gasped.

Trace leaned to the window. Dust billowed around the coach, obscuring his vision. He turned inside to Mr. Goodnight. "Are you armed, sir?"

"You mean a gun?" The old man was as flustered and frightened as Mrs. Callen. "No!"

Trace exchanged a look with Sam. "You saw three men?" She nodded confirmation.

They were outgunned. If the stage driver believed

the situation hopeless enough to brake for the robbers, and he wasn't putting up a fight, then for Trace to instigate a gun battle would endanger everyone. There was no sensible alternative but to submit and hope they all emerged alive to continue their journey.

"Damn, damn," Sam muttered, striking the seat with a gloved fist as the stage rocked hard and shuddered to a halt amid a swirling ball of dust. "I should have worn a gun!"

Mrs. Callen gave her an appalled stare.

A masked face loomed in the window before the door flew open. "You!" The bandit snarled at Trace. "Outside. Your wife too." Dark slits swept over Mrs. Callen and Mr. Goodnight. "You two stay put. Don't move a muscle lest you want it shot off."

Trace stepped outside first, then extended a hand to assist Sam, who slapped furiously at her skirts. They stood in the settling dust and returned the stares of the masked men inspecting them. Again Trace considered drawing his gun before he rejected the thought as foolhardy. When the bandit leader ordered him to drop his pistol at his feet, he reluctantly did so.

"That's them all right," the leader grunted. "Kryder, you take the woman, I'll lead Cotwell's brother." He stared hard at Trace, the eyes above his mask glowing with hate. One of the men roped Trace's hands behind him and shoved him up into the saddle atop a sweat-lathered roan. The leader leveled a critical glance on the man struggling with Sam. "Having trouble, Kryder?"

"She's a goddamned wildcat!"

Sam had time to curse the entangling petticoats that deflected the knee she aimed at his groin, time to land a satisfying punch in Kryder's belly, then his fist slammed into her temple and the sun winked out.

Sam regained consciousness slowly, gradually becoming aware that she lay sprawled on the tile floor of a courtyard shaded by a leafy tree covered with dusty pink blossoms. Her hat was gone, and so was her beaded purse. Groaning softly, she sat up and blinked hard, trying to clear her head.

When she saw that Trace had been tied to a chair placed near a fountain splashing in the center of the courtyard, it became instantly clear that she needed her wits about her and fast.

First to consider was the sobering fact that the bandits had removed their masks. Outlaws didn't expose their faces if they feared being identified later.

Anger swelled Sam's chest as she recognized the leader, the bearded man with the limp. Damn it. She should have trusted her instincts, should have insisted they delay their departure until she had learned his identity and why he was so interested in them. Should-haves got people killed, she thought bitterly, staring down at her petticoats. A month ago she wouldn't have made a stupid mistake like this.

After scanning the courtyard and counting the guns present, she understood the odds were heavily weighted against them.

The man with the limp stalked forward to stand in

front of Trace. "See the way I walk?" he demanded in a dangerously low voice. "Your son-of-a-bitch brother shot me. I'll limp for the rest of my life. He killed my woman, my cousin, and one of my men."

Trace returned Josiah Lyman's stare, but he didn't speak.

"I knew who you were the minute I laid eyes on you in the restaurant. You got them same cat eyes like Cotwell. Decided right then I'd save the law the trouble of hanging you." Lyman spat on the court-yard tiles, his face twisted with hate and anticipation.

"What're we gonna do with the woman?" asked the one called Kryder. He leered at Sam, licking fat lips. "Seems like she needs some taming."

"Cotwell's going to pay for killing Maria," Josiah Lyman snarled. "The price is his brother and his brother's wife."

"If you think killing us is going to cause Hannibal a minute's pain, you're wrong," Trace said sharply. "My brother and I hate each other."

Lyman's laugh emerged as a menacing growl. "What do you take me for, some crack-brained east-ener? You think I'll swallow any tall tale that falls out of your lying mouth?"

"I'm telling the truth. I've sworn to kill Hannibal. He knows it. Kill us, and you'll be doing him a favor."

"Then it looks like this is Cotwell's lucky day, as-suming you ain't lying. Which I ain't assuming." Turning, he swept a tight glance over Sam's bosom, small waist, and flaring hips. "You can thank your brother-in-law for what's about to happen to you, Pretty."

Desperately aware that she was utterly defenseless, Sam slowly pulled to her feet. Wide-eyed, she stared into Lyman's hot eyes and her mouth dried and her mind spiraled backward. Her heartbeat accelerated to a drum roll as the courtyard walls wavered and became the walls of her father's office in Cottonwood, Kansas.

This was how the nightmare had begun that hot afternoon twelve years ago: outlaws leering at her mother with the same slack-jawed, brute animal expressions. Even the words were similar. *Hannibal Cotwell had swept the papers off her father's desk and said: You can thank your husband for what's about to happen to you.*

Horror and paralysis locked Sam's body. Sour-tasting saliva flooded her mouth and her hands shook uncontrollably. She couldn't move, couldn't think. A silent scream shrieked through her mind.

For twelve years she had half-expected and feared this moment. She had known it would inevitably arrive if ever she donned petticoats and skirts. This was a woman's fate.

Josiah Lyman moved toward her, his hands opening his belt buckle, a violent smile twitching his beard. A powerful shove pushed Sam toward a doorway leading into the house.

"Leave her alone!" Trace shouted. "She isn't part of this. Hannibal has never met her, he doesn't know who she is." Bucking and straining, he battled the ropes binding him to the chair.

Limp with destiny, Sam didn't attempt to fight. Her mind had locked onto the past and her knowledge of woman as victim, learned that day so long ago. Resistance was pointless, she knew that. Like her mother before her, she couldn't win. First came the rape, then came the gun barrel against her forehead. The only difference was this time there would be no terrified and impressionable eleven-year-old witness.

Numb and stumbling beneath the force of Lyman's hard shoves, she reeled into a dim room furnished with a bureau and a single cot. When Lyman threw her on the cot, she sprawled like a straw doll. Her shocked mind began to retreat, frantically seeking a place to hide from what would follow.

"Pick up your skirts and pull down your drawers."

Eyes stark with terror, she stared at Lyman as he stepped toward her, fumbling with the buttons on his trouser front. His features shifted and blurred and transformed into the face of an outlaw with tiger's eyes, scars on his forehead, and a drooping eyelid.

Hatred burst Sam's heart, shooting poison throughout her body. This man and his vicious lust had destroyed her family and altered the course of her life.

Past and present shattered her mind, mixing together in explosive nightmarish images. She was eleven years old, weeping and pleading and shaking with fear. She was lying on a cot, paralyzed by fate.

She was dressed in fishing overalls, praying that Cotwell would not hurt her mother. She was frozen, waiting for the man leaning over her to rend and tear and brutalize. The shock and pain of a bullet ripped into her side. She heard the violence in Hannibal Cotwell's hot quickened breath.

Reaching down, he tore open her jacket, then ripped her shirtwaist, exposing her camisole, corset, and a cringing swell of breasts.

Sam stared blindly up at him, her arms limp at her sides. From what seemed an immense distance, she heard shouts coming from the courtyard, the noise of breaking pottery and men's angry curses.

Trace.

Even bound and powerless, it sounded as if Trace was mounting a hell of a fight.

Something stirred through her paralysis and gathered deep in Sam's eyes, coming alive and gaining force. Trace was battling to resist while she had given up before the fight began. She had surrendered to the past, waited passively for history to be repeated. She was so damned certain a woman had to be a victim, so convinced that Cotwell couldn't be stopped, that she wasn't even resisting.

She bared her teeth. Fire blazed in her eyes. She had waited twelve endless lonely years for this moment. Now that she had finally found him, had finally reached the end of her long quest, was she going to let fear win? Was she going to let Cotwell rob her future as well as her past?

History could mimic, but it didn't repeat.

"Not this time!" she snarled as Cotwell reached for her.

He had destroyed her and her family once; he would not do it again.

"You're finally going to pay, you son of a bitch!" He'd made a mistake by throwing back her petticoats. Now, she was free to kick, and kick she did, hitting him as hard as she could in the crotch, throwing a surge of energy and strength behind it. The toe of her boot crumpled at the impact.

The air rushed out of him like sour wind as he gasped and doubled over. As he collapsed, Sam jumped to her knees and struck him in the nostrils with the heel of her palm, hitting him hard enough that she heard his nose shatter in a series of dull crunching noises, thrusting bits of sharp bone into his brain. Blood gushed from his nostrils and mouth.

Cotwell was dead before he struck the floor.

Panting and shaking with exhilaration, Sam stared over the side of the cot. He was dead! Finally, finally, she'd taken her revenge, had kept her vow to her mother. Wiping at tears of relief, she remained on her hands and knees, peering down at him in a blaze of victory.

His face wavered and shifted form. Shocked, Sam watched Hannibal Cotwell fade and disappear and become Josiah Lyman. Rocking back, she covered her face and breathed deeply, gulping air until her hands steadied and her head cleared. Reality returned in a bitter rush. She had not killed Hannibal Cotwell.

But she had narrowed the odds against Trace and herself by a third.

Senses sharpening, Sam climbed off the cot and stepped over Lyman's body, staring down at him and wishing with all her heart that he was indeed Hannibal Cotwell. Fortunately, he had gone down with so little resistance that the noise in the courtyard had covered any sounds he had made.

Sam pulled the gun out of Lyman's holster, checked the chamber, then quietly approached the door. She allowed herself one full minute to steady her thoughts and prepare herself. Then she threw open the door, dropped into a crouch, and fired twice, fanning the hammer.

The first shot struck Kryder between his small pig eyes; the second shot hit the remaining bandit in the chest, two inches left of dead center. Surprise widened their eyes, then they crumpled to the tile floor of the courtyard.

Sam fell against the doorjamb, the gun smoking in her limp hand. Dizzy, she pushed back a wave of hair and wiped the sweat from her forehead.

She had not been raped. She and Trace were not dead. A strange weightless feeling soared through her body and imaginary wings sprouted between her shoulder blades. If she spread her arms, she thought, she could fly away.

"You're absolutely amazing, Kincade."

Trace lay on his side, his cheek against the tiles, still roped to the chair, surrounded by fragments of broken flowerpots. A red lump bloomed on his forehead, and his lower lip was cracked and bleeding.

"I would have sworn they held aces and we had deuces."

Sam went to him and knelt, clumsily working the knots in the rope. When he finally stood and shook the cramps out of his muscles, Sam threw herself into his arms, starting to shake.

"Oh God," she whispered, pressing her face against his chest. "It was like I was eleven years old again, scared and helpless and powerless."

Trace held her tightly, kissing the top of her head, her hair, her temples, her eyelids. "Helpless and powerless," he murmured, shaking his head and glancing at the dead bandits.

"I went crazy. I thought I was my mother, but it was me at the same time. And I thought Lyman was Hannibal." She searched his eyes, then ground her forehead against his chest. "Why didn't she fight him? It couldn't have ended worse than it did, but she would have died knowing at least she tried, that at least she put up a struggle! But she gave up. She just . . . she gave up!"

Trace smoothed tangled strands of hair toward her false curls. His jaw worked. "Christ, Sam. I couldn't do a damned thing." Self-disgust roughened his voice. "What the hell good is a man who can't protect the woman entrusted to his care?"

Gripping his lapels, Sam continued pressing against him. "I thought I'd killed Hannibal," she whispered.

"If you'd depended on me, we'd both be dead."

Sam lifted her head and frowned. "What are you saying?"

Gently, Trace eased her away from him. "There should be horses in the barn. I'll saddle a couple and we can get the hell out of here." He glanced at her torn shirtwaist. "Maybe you can find a fresh blouse in the house."

"Trace?"

He wiped the back of his hand across his lips, looked at the blood on his fingers, then strode rapidly away.

Inside the house, Sam eventually located a back bedroom and a trunk of women's clothing. She chose a white shirtwaist, wondering if it had belonged to the woman Hannibal had shot and killed. After washing her face and hands in a basin of water, she found a mirror and gazed into the glass, intending to repair her hair.

Instead, she paused, holding the mirror before her face. Somehow, she looked different. Examining herself, puzzled, Sam struggled to identify what had been altered. When finally she understood what she was seeing, tears welled in her eyes and spilled down her cheeks.

Always before, she had seen her eleven-year-old self when she gazed into a mirror. Peering out of adult eyes had been a terrified child, hiding from maturity. Now, the child was gone. A woman's face gazed back from the glass. Dashing the tears, Sam examined this new face, so like her mother's. Her inner shell cracked and fell away. Old fears and childhood terrors leaked from the fragments of shell and drained away. For the first time in twelve years, the bullet scar on her side did not feel like the most significant part of her anatomy.

Dropping the mirror, she bent forward and covered her tears with her hands.

Her long search had ended.

It had never been Hannibal Cotwell that she sought, it had been herself. Sam understood that now. All those years, she had been seeking the woman in the mirror, the woman hiding behind a terrified eleven-year-old child dressed in boy's overalls.

The child remembered, and the child feared the weakness of women, the helplessness, the exploitation. But the woman in the mirror gazed back with self-reliance, strength of will, the obligation and the power to resist being victimized.

"I'm free," Sam whispered, pressing her palms against her eyes. She felt the wings flutter on her shoulder blades, felt herself emerging victorious.

Exhilarated, wanting to share her freedom, she ran out of the house and flew toward the barn, shouting Trace's name.

At first she didn't see him. She noticed the horses saddled and waiting just inside the barn, but her eyes required a moment to adjust to interior shadows after the glare of the late-afternoon sun.

When she finally spotted him, her face lit and she ran forward. Then she halted and her heart skipped a beat.

Trace sat on the side of a hay mound, his head dropped in one hand, his other hand holding a gun. When he looked up at her, pain swirled in his amber eyes.

"Etta hanged herself. You came within minutes of being raped and murdered. What the hell good am I?"

CHAPTER
* 18 *

Give me the gun, Trace."

"I failed both of you." Disgust twisted his lips and he shoved a hand through his hair. "I don't have the right to call myself a man." His stare cut past the sunbeams falling through the barn slats. "You asked if I planned to marry again. . . . What woman would want half a man?"

Sam drew a breath, then kicked her hem out before her, storming toward him. "You self-pitying idiot!" she snapped. "What is the matter with you? You're sitting there holding a royal flush, wishing you had a pair of threes!"

He frowned at her. "What are you talking about?"

"Me! That's what I'm talking about!" She pounded her fist on her chest. "I'm your royal flush, you damned fool! Lady Luck gave you a partner with brains and ability, a woman able to think for herself and defend herself. And yes, defend you too if the cards fall that way! When I needed you, you

328

were there for me. Is it so damned unthinkable that I might be there for you when the situation is reversed? Would you rather have had me helpless and brutalized? Would you rather have seen us both murdered? Would that have made you feel more like a man?"

"Stop it, Sam."

"It's not your job to save me or any other woman from every lousy situation that might arise. Your manhood is not dependent on weak women! Women are responsible for themselves, Trace. I am never going to sit back and wait for some man to rescue me. Not if there's something I can do in the meantime. If saving my hide and yours wounds your sense of manhood, well that's crazy and just too damned bad!"

His chin jutted beneath cold eyes. "Etta—"

"Etta had choices! Just as I did with Lyman. Each of us did what we could, each of us made decisions." Straightening, she placed her fists on her hips and narrowed her eyes into angry slits. "My mother didn't have a choice about what happened afterward, but Etta did. She could have chosen to live with the memory of Hannibal's violence. She could have trusted that you would understand and accept her pregnancy. She could have relied on her own strength and resilience. Are you so arrogant that you think her death was your fault? *Etta* made that choice. *Etta* decided to drop the rope around her neck. Not you! You are not to blame for her death.

And Etta's choice didn't have a damned thing to do with your manhood!"

Silent, intent, Trace examined her face. "Something has changed . . ."

Dropping onto the hay beside him, Sam drew a long breath, then took his hand in hers. "Listen to me. A woman doesn't have to submit quietly to whatever happens any more than a man does. There are choices about what happens before, during, and after."

Trace continued watching her face. She hoped he was listening.

"We all choose what kind of man or woman we'll be. I didn't understand that before today." Sudden moisture shimmered in her eyes. "Oh Trace . . . I can be a woman and still be me!" She dashed a hand across her eyes and peered earnestly into his face.

Trace studied her pleading expression. "I don't understand what changed your thinking." He hesitated. "But I'm glad."

"Me too," Sam said simply. She smoothed her skirt and smiled. "I'm going to be fine with this woman thing."

Dropping his head, he inspected the gun in his hand, spinning the chamber. "Suppose Etta was not raped," he said at length, speaking slowly. "Suppose she went willingly to Hannibal's bed." Another silence elapsed, during which he turned the gun between his fingers.

Raw vulnerability was etched across his features. Sam caught a quick breath and understood she could destroy him with a careless word, understood that he had placed his manhood in her hands to accept or reject.

"If that's what happened," she said slowly, "then the fault was with Etta, not you."

Reacting instinctively, Sam reached for the tiny buttons running down the bodice of the shirtwaist she had found in Lyman's house. Her gaze dropped to his lips and she issued a low sultry challenge.

"You don't think you're a whole man? Well, let's see . . ."

Standing in front of him, she tossed aside her jacket before she finished unbuttoning the shirtwaist and pushed it to her waist. Her fingers moved over her breast, tracing the curve. Wetting her lips, she toyed with the hook at the waist of her skirt, glancing at him through her lashes, recognizing the heat rising in his stare, hearing his low involuntary groan.

Dropping back on the hay, she stretched languorously, then raised a knee and let her skirts slide to her thigh. She lifted a leg and smoothed her fingertips along the curve of her stocking, ending at the garter on her thigh.

"Shall I stop?" she asked in a throaty whisper. "Or is there a man here?"

"Where did you learn to behave like this?" he demanded hoarsely. The gun dropped unnoticed from his fingers. Gold flecks blazed in his hot tiger eyes. "Damn it, Sam. Is this what you think being a man is all about?"

"It's certainly part of it." Closing her eyes, she

arched her throat, lifting her breast, and smiled. "It's part of being a woman too. When it's our choice." She peeked at him from the side of her eyes while trailing her fingertips suggestively along the curve of lace edging her corset. Her lips parted. "It's too bad you're only half a man," she murmured, letting her voice sink to a husky whisper. "Right now I desperately want a whole man."

His lips came down on hers, hard and hot and as possessive and demanding as the hands grabbing her waist. Sam fell against the haystack, her arms going around his neck, and she kissed him back, hard, her lips opening beneath the insistent pressure of his.

The explosive sensation of their kiss was like a spark set to kindling. Raw passion detonated between them and an urgency that sizzled in their mingled breath electrified each frantic touch. Kissing, stroking, tearing at each other's clothing, they rolled on the haystack, gasping, challenging each other, teasing and taunting with words and fingertips until both trembled with desire and shook with the force of their need for each other.

The high emotion of the day released in cataclysmic eruption, in a contest of domination and refusal to be dominated. Sam teased him without pity, whipping his passion, and her own, into frenzy, but wiggling away before he could penetrate her, gasping from long breathless kisses, from a desire that shook her body and seared her flesh.

Pushing her roughly against the hay, Trace captured her wrists and pinned them above her head.

The weight of his body crushed her into submission. His lips hovered a fraction of an inch above hers, his breath emerging in controlled gasps, but he drew back when she tried to kiss him.

Sam moaned and thrashed beneath him, wanting him with a passion so powerful and consuming that she could not have controlled it if she had tried. Like his, her body was bathed in perspiration, her panting lifted her breasts in quick hot gasps. Every nerve flamed and her body screamed for release. She thought she would die if he didn't take her, now, now, now.

"Trace, I beg you . . . please!"

But he continued to tease her into wildness, almost touching his lips to hers but not quite, dodging when she thrashed to reach him, letting her feel the strength and power of his erection against her body, but playing her game and not allowing her to draw him inside. His bare chest brushed teasingly across the aching tips of her breasts, his skin was wet and burned against hers. One hand firmly pinned her wrists above her head, the other mercilessly tantalized the contours of her mouth, caressed the side of her breast, stroked her hip, fanned the flames of her desire until Sam thought she would disintegrate in a shower of flaming sparks.

"Please," she panted, lunging, trying to capture his lips with hers. "Trace, please! I need you so much!"

As if she had spoken magic words of release, he thrust into her and she arched against his body, accepting him fully, crying out with joy. This time she knew what to expect, knew to wrap her legs around his hard buttocks and draw him deeply into her center. She knew how to meet his deep and urgent need, knew how to pace the urgency driving them both. She knew where to kiss him to make him groan and grind his teeth and when to surrender herself to the tides of sensation that swept her toward ecstasy.

Later, exhausted and damp, they lay on the hay mound, wrapped in each other's arms, legs entwined, surprised to notice the shadows had lengthened.

"In my humble opinion," Sam offered in a happy, drowsy voice, "you are man enough for ten women." She loved the lingering musky scent of their lovemaking, loved the solid strength of the chest beneath her cheek. Most of all, she loved the way Trace made her feel like a wildly desirable woman. Right now it was impossible to believe that once she had yearned for whiskers and had wanted to be the toughest bounty hunter in the territories. Warmed by the glow of their lovemaking, the idea of wanting to be male seemed unthinkable to Sam, a peculiarity from someone else's life.

Trace rested his chin on top of her head, his fingertips lightly caressing her bare shoulder. "What you said earlier," he murmured gruffly. "Some of it goes against the grain, but . . . all of it makes sense."

Sam knew the admission came hard. Tilting her head, she gently explored the lump on his forehead with the tips of her fingers. "You scared me," she confessed quietly. "When I walked in here and found you with your head in your hands and a gun, I thought you were considering . . ."

Genuine shock darkened his eyes and he drew

back to stare at her. "Suicide?" A thin smile curved his lips. "I'm not the type to fold a hand until the last card has been played. No, I was thinking about Etta."

"Which reminds me, why did you tear up her letter?" Sam dropped her head back to his shoulder and wondered if there would ever come a time when Etta didn't rise between them like a malevolent ghost. During the past weeks, she had begun to despise Etta Harden. Etta's poison had survived her death.

Holding her loosely in his arms, Trace related his conversation with Mattie Able. "That's what I was thinking about. If Mattie's speculation is correct," he finished, gazing up at the barn rafters. "Then every word of Etta's letter is a lie."

By the time he finished speaking, Sam was wide awake, sitting with her arms clasped around her knees, frowning down at him. "Do you believe Mattie is correct? Do you believe Etta seduced Hannibal?"

His troubled gaze swung toward her face. "I don't know. I think it's possible."

"What are you trying to say, Trace? Are you telling me that you no longer want to kill Hannibal?"

"I'm not sure anymore." Sitting up, he leaned forward and buried both hands in his hair. "I thought Etta hated Hannibal. But maybe she hated me more. Maybe she hated me enough to seduce my brother."

"Mattie wasn't there," Sam stated flatly. "But even if her conjecture is right, Etta and Hannibal betrayed you. Hannibal could have refused to be seduced by his brother's wife!"

Trace met her blazing gaze, his own eyes steady. "If Hannibal tells me Etta came to his bed willingly

. . . then I can't kill him, Sam. I won't forgive him; I'll never see or speak to him again. But he's my brother. I won't kill him."

"I will!" Sam responded hotly, her eyes narrowing. Her fingernails dug painfully into her bare legs. "I *know* Hannibal is a rapist. I *saw* him rape and murder my mother!"

Tense and moving apart, they studied each other's drawn expressions. "If there was no rape, I won't let you kill my brother. If Etta lied about what happened . . . then we ride away and leave Hannibal to the law."

"No!"

Grim-lipped, Trace reached for his jacket and removed a deck of cards. "Draw."

"This isn't something to decide by a cut of the cards. Killing Hannibal is not negotiable. It's what we came to do, why we're here. Please, Trace, try to understand. I'm almost free, but I have to fulfill my vow to see Hannibal dead. If you can't or won't kill him, then by God I swear I will!"

He reached for her hand, but she pulled away. "Don't put Hannibal between us, Sam. Don't make me choose between you and my brother."

"Then don't ask *me* to choose between you and the vow I made as my mother was dying."

"Earlier you insisted that being a woman is about making choices. You have a choice."

"And I made it," she snapped. "Years ago."

"You can remain trapped in the past, or you can move forward."

"I don't have a future until the past is settled! I've

found myself, Trace. But I have to find Hannibal before I can move on. I have to finish it!"

They peered at each other through deepening shadows, abruptly aware of the dying day and their nakedness. Standing, Sam turned her back to him and stepped into her pantaloons. She considered her corset, then glanced at the waiting horses and tossed the corset aside. A hard ride lay ahead, and she would be more comfortable without lacing. Discovering a corset in the haystack would pose a small mystery to whoever found Lyman and his men.

When they were dressed and prepared to depart, Trace helped Sam into her saddle. She permitted it even though she didn't require assistance. For a moment he stood beside her, his hand on her boot.

His beard was short but thick enough to make reading his mood difficult. He kept his gaze carefully expressionless.

"I don't know where you and I are in all of this, Sam." A rusty shaft of sunlight made his eyes gleam like an animal's. His tight gaze swept her features, settled on her parted lips. "We're both trapped until we finish our business with Hannibal."

"Will you hate me if I kill him?" she asked in a whisper, staring down into his eyes.

"From the first, we agreed that I'd be the one to pull the trigger."

"But if you can't? Or won't?"

A tense moment passed as they stared into each other's eyes.

"I won't let you kill my brother. You may have to choose between him and me." Turning, he walked toward his horse, swung into the saddle, and urged his mount into a trot through the barn doors.

"I've hated Hannibal Cotwell a lot longer than I've loved you," Sam whispered, in a voice so low that she knew he didn't hear.

Sam watched him go with her heart filling her eyes. She loved him with an ache that filled her completely. There would never be another man for Sam Kincade, she knew that. Something deep inside had been waiting for Trace Harden all of her life. She suspected she had been born with his name written on her heart, and she knew she would die with his name on her lips.

But depending on what happened in Nowhere, Arizona, she might have to live her life without him. She had to accept that her future might be as empty and lonely as her past.

Blinking back stinging tears, Sam dug her heels into the horse's flanks and cantered out of the barn, following her heart.

Once again, Hannibal Cotwell would decide her future.

Four days later, sunburned and swaying in their saddles, white-lipped and silent with fatigue, they rode into Nowhere as the sun was sinking into the desert. A gleaming copper sky bathed the ramshackle collection of low, adobe houses in umber shades of dilapidation. An old Mexican, as wrinkled as the cracked earth, sat on the ground with his back against the well stones, smoking a cigarillo. Otherwise, the town appeared deserted.

Trace reined alongside a square of sand and brown grass that might have been intended as a plaza when the town was new. After handing Sam his canteen, he inspected a short row of storefonts, mopping the rivulets of sweat that cut dusty tracks down the sides of his face.

"First a bath. Then a shave," he said grimly, scratching his jaw.

"If you shave, the town marshall might recognize you," Sam reminded him, summoning the energy to speak.

"It doesn't matter anymore."

After wetting her handkerchief, she closed her eyes and wiped her face and throat. Her bodice was soaked and salty with sweat, sticking to her skin. She longed for a bath, clean clothing, and a bed to fall into for twelve hours.

"It's almost over," Trace said in a taut voice, leaning on the saddle horn. The dying sun spread bloody shadows across the adobe boxes. Removing his hat, he pushed a hand through sweat-damp hair. "Do you see anything that looks like a hotel?"

Sam thumbed back the man's hat she had found in Lyman's house and studied the collection of logs and mud bricks. Dying towns didn't have much need for hotels.

As if the old Mexican had rung a silent alarm signaling that strangers had arrived, a few people appeared in shadowy doorways. Eventually a man stepped into the dusty haze overhanging the street and walked toward the plaza, one hand resting lightly on the butt of the gun protruding at his hip. The badge pinned to his vest gleamed red in the sunset fanning the western sky.

Trace tipped his hat. "'Evening, Marshall. My wife and I are seeking accommodations for a day or so. Perhaps you could assist us."

The marshall's gaze lingered on Sam's sunburned cheeks, inspected her dust-caked skirts, then swung back to Trace, noting their single saddlebag. "Traveling light, aren't you, mister?"

"Too light," Trace agreed, not offering more. "We need clothing, food, and a bath. First, I want to get my wife settled. She needs rest."

Sam resisted raising an eyebrow. She was exhausted, but of the two of them, she was more accustomed to long punishing rides than Trace. The miserable scorching journey had proved an ordeal for both, but it was Trace who suffered more from the unrelieved hours in the saddle. When they had halted for a few hours of sleep during the coolness of the night, his legs were so cramped he had hardly been able to walk.

"Doña Martinez might have a house to let," the marshall suggested after a pause, studying them with ill-concealed curiosity. "Her daughter cooks and cleans."

"We'd be obliged if you would lead the way."

Sam touched her heels to the mare's flanks and

they followed the marshall down the main street, aware that inquisitive eyes followed their progress.

"Don't get many strangers here since the silver played out," the marshall called over his shoulder. "How long you folks plan to stay?"

"Until we conclude our business."

The marshall nodded as if he hadn't really expected Trace to reveal much information. "That there's the cantina," he said, jerking the brim of his hat to the left. The soft strumming of a guitar drifted from an open-faced adobe. "You can put up your horses at the stable. On the right, at the end of the street."

As they passed the cantina, a man stepped to the boardwalk holding a tin mug of beer. He was youngish, but cold-eyed, a type Sam recognized at once. She would have wagered the clothes on her back that his face stared out of a wanted poster.

"Who is that man?" she asked in a low voice, speaking to the marshall, who had dropped back to walk alongside her horse.

"His name is Marsh Crisp, ma'am." The marshall's gaze darted toward Crisp, then away. His lips turned down. "Take my advice and steer clear of that one."

A prickle lifted the small hairs on the nape of Sam's neck and she sat straighter in her saddle. She'd first heard Crisp's name in Leadville when the old miner talked about the robbery of the assay office. If Crisp was here, so was Hannibal Cotwell.

Elation burst through her mind and adrenaline

pounded through her body. Impulsively she tugged the reins of her horse, her thoughts racing.

Hannibal might be inside the cantina.

Trace dropped back beside her, a warning flickering behind his golden eyes. "We're exhausted. Tomorrow is soon enough."

Nodding, Sam relaxed her hold on the reins. He was right, of course. With an effort she resisted glaring back at the man leaning against the wall of the cantina, watching them.

Sensing her tension, the marshall peered up at her with a frown. "Do you folks know Crisp?"

"I've never seen him before."

Sly satisfaction hooded the marshall's gaze. "He ain't going to be around much longer." He spat in the dirt. "We'll see who owns this town when the posse gets here."

"A posse?" They hadn't arrived anytime too soon. "When will the posse arrive?"

The marshall opened his mouth, then snapped it shut as if realizing he was talking too much. "Shortly," was all he said.

Marshall Brown led them to Doña Martinez and lingered while Trace arranged for a rental behind one of the whores' cribs. The marshall tipped his hat to Sam and departed reluctantly, his curiosity unsatisfied. Doña Martinez, a sharp-eyed matron of uncertain years, assured them her daughter Estrella would arrive within the hour with food and bath water.

"And clean clothing," Trace instructed, dangling a pouch of clinking coins from his fingertips.

"I'll want men's denims and a loose shirt," Sam instructed evenly. "A hairbrush and fresh undergarments."

Doña Martinez nodded assent, her expression unchanging. Rental opportunities didn't present themselves frequently. Sam suspected Doña Martinez would have agreed to anything they requested.

It was surprisingly cool inside the rental's two adobe rooms—and cooler yet after Sam opened a back window to encourage a cross breeze. Gazing past the whore's crib, she noticed more people moving in the street now that the sun had set. The drift of frying tortillas mingled with odors of dust and furniture polish, rodent droppings, and a fruity scent she couldn't identify. The guitarist in the cantina played a melancholy tune that made Sam ache inside. From somewhere nearby, she heard a woman sob.

"He's here," Trace remarked quietly, standing in the doorway, smoking and watching the shadows lengthen across the desert. "I can feel him."

"Crisp will pass the word that you've arrived." Dropping onto a wooden chair, Sam closed her eyes and let her head fall backward.

It could end in so many different ways.

Hannibal's men could kill them before they exchanged a single word with Hannibal. Or they could find Hannibal, kill him, and still get shot themselves. Crisp wasn't going to stand idle while they confronted Cotwell. And there were worse possibilities.

Sam opened her eyes and studied Trace's silhouette in the doorway. "What did you mean when you said you wouldn't let me kill Hannibal?" she asked softly. "Would you shoot me, Trace? Because that's what you'll have to do to stop me."

He exhaled, the smoke from his cigar hanging in the night air like a ghostly feather. "During all these months I haven't allowed myself to think about what it means for one brother to kill another."

"Would you kill me, Trace?"

He turned into the room, but the shadows were too deep for Sam to read his expression.

"When we were children, we used to speculate what we would do if one of us suffered a mortal wound. We agreed not to let the other die in prolonged agony. Do you understand what I'm saying?"

His voice rasped from his throat, raw and strained. When he spoke of Hannibal, the south deepened in his voice and became more pronounced. "I was the youngest. I took that discussion and our agreement very seriously. Way back then I came to terms with the possibility that I might have to kill Hannibal if circumstances warranted. At least I thought I did. These are not the circumstances I imagined. But if I have to I can pull the trigger. Understand that, Sam.

"It will be the worst thing in my life, but I can live with killing him if I have to. Understand this, also. I don't excuse what Hannibal became or how he has chosen to live his life. But he's my brother."

"Could you live with killing me?" Sam whispered.

He flipped the cigar out of the open doorway, then leaned against the jamb, frowning at the darkness. "No," he said finally.

Sam's breath ran out of her body like water through a sieve. A sob escaped her throat and she ran to him. "Oh God, Trace. What are we going to do?"

His arms came around her, crushing her against his body. He held her so fiercely that she felt his heart pounding against her chest. His lips moved in her hair. "Will you kill me if I stand between you and Hannibal? Could *you* live with it, Sam?"

"Oh God." Anguish clawed at her mind when she thought of aiming her pistol at Trace. She gripped his lapels and implored him with wild eyes. "We could ride away," she suggested frantically, hearing panic spiral through her voice. "We could end it here, now. All we have to do is ride away."

Trace's hands framed her face. "You know that won't work."

He was right. She'd come too far to ride away and pretend she could live without confronting Hannibal.

"If we don't finish this, we'll resent each other for the rest of our lives. No, Sam. You have to cut this final tie to the past before you can go on. And I have to know what happened between Etta and my brother."

Tears spilled down her cheeks. If they retreated, she would bitterly regret it for the rest of her days. They would end by blaming each other, hating each other. It might end that way anyway, depending on what happened. Now she understood why they could not discuss the future. In all likelihood, they had no future together.

Estrella arrived with food and two boys carrying

buckets of tepid bath water. Sam ate without noticing what she put into her mouth. They bathed, drank more of the sugary limeade Estrella had brought, and Trace shaved his beard and mustache while Sam watched without comment. Then, their weariness thrust aside, they made love slowly, tenderly, each acutely aware that this might be the last time they held each other in their arms.

Afterward, Sam rested with her head nestled in the hollow of his shoulder, her hand lightly on his waist. "I love you," she said softly, inhaling the pungent sharpness of the thin dark cigar he smoked.

"I know."

At another time it would have offended her that she had become so transparent. But this was not the moment for false pride, or for contemplating the changes occurring within her.

Sam closed her eyes and pressed her cheek against his warm skin. "I'll delay as long as I can, Trace. But if you don't shoot . . ."

He hesitated, then answered in a voice that told her he was dying inside. "We don't know what will happen. Right now, you need some rest."

"You need sleep too."

"In a while."

Trace stubbed out the cigar and wrapped his arms around her, holding her close to his body. Long after Sam dropped into an exhausted sleep, he remained awake, staring into the darkness, his mind wandering through space and time to remember two young boys and shouts of laughter that rang through the back bayous. He remembered his brother fighting his battles until he was old enough and big enough to fight them himself. He remembered thinking Hannibal was ten feet tall, remembered trying to walk like him and talk like him. Hannibal had been his hero.

Tears stung his eyelids.

Hannibal sat on his horse facing town in the starlight. His chin dropped to his chest and he rubbed his forehead, surrendering to a flood-tide of memories. Near dawn he made his decision, roused himself, and turned back toward the dark rancho.

Tilting his head, he watched the sun rise.

CHAPTER
* 19 *

The tension between them was as heavy and oppressive as the heat mounting outside. Sam's throat grew tighter each moment and speaking became difficult. Neither she nor Trace had been calm enough to eat the tortillas or fried beans and sausage that Estrella had brought them for breakfast. Sam paced from one thick adobe wall to the other; Trace leaned in the open doorway, smoking another cigar and grinding his teeth, his fist opening and closing at his side. The minutes dragged as the sun climbed higher in the sky.

"You have a revolver and Lyman's rifle, right?" Sam asked again, pacing past him for the hundredth time.

"Yes."

Lightly she touched the handle of the gun in her hip holster, seeking reassurance and finding precious little. There was no way to anticipate how many men would be arrayed against them. But it was certain that she and Trace would be outnumbered. The possibility of emerging unscathed seemed slim. Before nightfall one or both of them would likely be wounded or dead.

Her own death didn't frighten Sam, but she couldn't bear to consider a world without Trace Harden. Making herself sit in one of the uncomfortable wooden chairs, she tried to relax her muscles and force her thoughts onto a more optimistic path.

"Will you be leaving for San Francisco after . . ." she waved a hand, letting the sentence trail.

Trace kept his gaze fixed on the heat waves shimmering above the barren horizon. "Have you thought about what you'll do?" he asked after a pause.

"I don't know," she replied in a low voice, turning aside for fear that he might glimpse the moisture filming her eyes. "I know I can't return to bounty hunting. That's over. My days of passing myself off as a male have ended."

The future loomed before her like an abyss.

When Sam attempted to visualize herself in ten years, assuming she survived the upcoming gunbattle, she saw a woman growing older in solitude and silence, alone as she had always been. No man appeared in her mental picture. Few men would accept the kind of woman she was discovering herself to be, independent, self-assertive, uninhibited, bluntly honest, prickly, and occasionally short-tempered. It didn't matter. The only man she would ever want was Trace Harden.

But after today, there would be little possibility of

a future together. He would never be able to forget that Sam was the woman who had killed his brother. He would understand her reasons, just as she would understand when he was unable to pull the trigger— and she predicted that would happen. But he would never be able to forgive her.

When it came to Hannibal, Sam had no choice. The night before she had dreamed again of those devastating few minutes in Cottonwood, Kansas. Once again she had wept and begged Hannibal not to hurt her mother. Once again she had watched him shove the gun barrel against her mother's forehead and pull the trigger. And once again she had screamed in pain and shock as a bullet seared into her own side.

When she'd awakened this morning, she had known it would be Sam Kincade who killed Hannibal Cotwell. She would do it even if it meant that Hannibal's men would riddle her body with bullets. She would do it even if it meant that Trace would hate her all the rest of her days.

"Sam?"

Blinking hard, she gave her head a shake, then looked up to discover Trace standing in front of her chair.

"There are things I want to say while there's still time, before everything changes."

But time had run out. A sudden shadow blocked the scald of sunlight streaming through the door. Trace spun and Sam leapt to her feet.

"Are you Trace Harden?"

Tense, hands on their guns, they stared at the man in the doorway. "Who wants to know?" Trace growled.

"Marsh Crisp." Stepping into the room, out of the glare, Crisp noticed Sam and removed his hat. "Ma'am." A cold speculative flicker stirred the gaze he ran over her loose shirt and down the denims that molded her hips. His lips tipped in a faint smile before he returned to Trace. "Cotwell's been expecting you. You're to come with me out to the rancho." When Sam reached for her hat, Crisp frowned. "Cotwell didn't say nothing about no woman."

Stepping between her and Crisp, Trace gripped her shoulders, speaking urgently. "Stay here, Sam. This is difficult enough. Let me do what I have to without worrying about you."

"You know I can't do that." She gazed into his eyes, silently begging him to understand. To forgive. "This is my fight too."

Trace released her so abruptly that she stumbled and almost fell. "Our horses are at the stables," he informed Crisp, then swung their saddlebag over his shoulder. They wouldn't be returning to the adobe rental. Without glancing at Sam, he strode out the door.

"I'm with him," Sam said grimly, her expression daring Crisp to object. Crisp shrugged and nodded, and stepped aside to let her precede him out the door.

He smiled at the gun on her hip. "You know how to use that thing, little lady?"

"Well enough that I wish I had two."

He laughed, and he continued to tease and flirt with her during the walk to the stables. Coldly, Sam turned his comments aside, wishing she could cuff him and claim the bounty on his hide. But Crisp's behavior underscored the finish of her career as a male bounty hunter.

What she wore today wasn't substantially different from what she had worn during her days of masquerading as a boy. But something profound had altered in her face and in the way she carried herself. Loving Trace had made her into a woman.

"Is it a long ride?" she asked when they were mounted and following the dirt road that led into the desert. Crisp rode beside her. Trace followed two lengths behind.

"'Bout two miles," Crisp answered, tugging his hat brim to shade his face. He jerked a thumb over his shoulder. "Who is he?"

"Cotwell didn't tell you?"

"I know Cotwell's been waiting for him." When Sam didn't comment, Crisp added. "Whatever business he's got with Cotwell must be damned important. I've never seen Cotwell so agitated."

"Is that right," Sam answered tersely, her gaze fixed on a ramshackle collection of low adobe buildings that drew nearer with every hoofbeat.

Crisp glanced behind them, his gaze sliding past Trace and settling on the town. "We'll be leaving once this meeting ends. Not a minute too soon if you ask me. That pissant marshall is up to something."

When Sam didn't reply, he sighed and patted the

neck of his horse. "So, what's your name, little lady?"

The gaze Sam turned on him was glacial. "Shut up, Crisp. Do it now."

He examined her expression and his eyebrows lifted. "Who the hell are you two?"

Pulling up on her reins, her fingers tense, Sam dropped back to ride beside Trace. He met her glance and nodded once, but he didn't speak.

Prompted by professional habit, Sam checked his hands, noticing they were reasonably steady. Anguish burned in his eyes and his jaw was clenched, but he held his turmoil in check.

"Listen to me," Sam said quietly. "I've thought about this. I should be the one who kills him. Not you."

A familiar combination of heat and tension gathered inside her body, and a rush of adrenaline tingled just beneath her skin. It was always this way before a gun battle. Strange chemicals seared her stomach, blending excitement, anxiety, expectancy, caution, and a prickling nuance of fear that sharpened her senses.

Eyes fixed on the approaching buildings, Sam unconsciously flexed her trigger hand, rolled her head on her shoulders, tightened her muscles, then forced them to relax. Now she could clearly see the weathered gate and a wooden porch protruding like a pouting lip along the front of the main house. There wasn't a tree in sight, not a scrap of shade. The yard was bare dirt fringed by sage and cactus.

Her shoulders twitched when Trace spoke, his voice taut and hoarse.

"If he raped Etta, I'll kill him."

Sam ground her teeth together, tasting dust and grit, and forced her jaw to release. "The first man you kill shouldn't be your brother. If you do it, you'll hate yourself for the rest of your life."

"If I *don't* do it, I'll hate myself for the rest of my life." His gaze burned her.

"If you can't, Trace . . . I'll give you every opportunity . . . I'll delay as long as I can . . . but Hannibal isn't going to walk away. Not today."

"You won't have a chance against him. He's a professional gunslinger," Trace snapped, staring at her. His fingers wrapped the reins so tightly that his knuckles had turned white.

"So am I."

Never had his measuring amber stare reminded her so strongly of a tiger's. He jerked his head toward Crisp and directed her attention toward two men walking from the corral toward the house, watching the road as they climbed the porch steps.

"If you draw on Hannibal, those men will cut you down without a second thought. For God's sake, Sam. What he did to your mother happened a lifetime ago. If you ride away now, you'll have a chance. You have your whole life in front of you!"

They rode past a lizard sunning on the gate post and entered the yard. Sam felt her pulse beating steadily beneath her ear. "I've spent twelve years waiting for this moment, dreaming about it, getting ready for it," she said, speaking between her teeth. A wave of stage-fright shuddered through her body, passed, and left her calm inside. "I think you and I have known from the beginning that neither of us is going to ride out of here."

Trace touched her arm before they reined to a halt in front of the porch. When she met his eyes, she read regret, admiration, respect, and something else that he hadn't let her see before, something that made her heart soar and made her feel like weeping at the same time.

"I'm proud to have known you, Samantha Kincade." His voice was low and husky, saying goodbye.

"I'm proud to have known you, Trace Harden," she whispered.

They held each other's gaze while Marsh Crisp dismounted and turned his horse into the corral before he started toward the house. When he reached the porch, Crisp removed his hat, wiped his sleeve across the sweat shining on his brow, and shouted. "Cotwell! Harden's here."

Mouth dry, eyes narrowed, Sam urged her horse forward, positioning herself between Trace and the men leaning on the porch rail. At the moment Hannibal's boys were merely curious, unaware that the morning was about to turn lethal. Sam wished to God she had more firepower than the one single-action revolver resting on her hip. When she looked at Trace, his gaze was locked on the door of the house. He'd forgotten her.

They waited.

When a stocky form appeared in the doorway, Sam's heart lurched and rolled over in her chest. Her pulse accelerated, pounding at her throat and wrists. Tiny hairs rose on the back of her arms and her body stiffened as Hannibal Cotwell stepped onto the porch. Slowly he came down the steps, his gaze fixed on Trace.

All these years Sam had remembered him as a huge man, an ugly giant, a brute whose ruthlessness lay revealed in gargoyle features. It shocked her to discover he was none of those things. Hannibal was shorter than Trace, barrel-chested and bandy-legged. Despite the scar that pulled his eyelid and the old scars nested on his forehead, Sam realized with a second shock that Hannibal Cotwell was a ruggedly handsome man. He was an older, coarser version of Trace, the dark side of the same coin, but he would be powerfully appealing to a certain kind of woman.

"You know why I'm here," Trace said hoarsely when Hannibal stopped in front of his horse. His accent had thickened to the extent that Sam didn't immediately understand his words.

"Mattie told me about Etta's letter." Hannibal's shoulders squared and he hooked his thumbs inside his gun belt.

Trace drew his revolver and the men on the porch straightened abruptly, their eyes swinging to gauge Hannibal's reaction. Sam's fingers curved on the handle of her pistol, and her muscles tensed for swift action. When she looked at Hannibal, his resemblance to Trace unnerved her, the same tiger eyes, the same expression around the mouth, the same quiet voice and accent. For one terrible instant, she wondered wildly if she would be able to kill a man so like the one she loved.

The barrel of Trace's gun steadied directly on Hannibal's chest. Only a quick hand-signal from Hannibal prevented the men on the porch from drawing their guns. Exchanging puzzled frowns, they lined up at the porch rail, palms resting uneasily on gun butts, sharp eyes squinting. The tension in the yard wound tighter. The sun blazed on taut mouths and wary expressions.

"Etta hanged herself," Trace said, each word like a gunshot. His pistol didn't waver, the barrel pointed steadily at Hannibal's chest. "I have to know. Is it true what she said in her letter? Did you rape my wife?"

Hannibal pushed back his hat and narrowed his eyes against the scorching white glare. The corners of his mouth twitched in a half-smile, but when he spoke, his voice was as strained and tight as Trace's. "And if I did, little brother?"

"Then I'm going to kill you."

"You don't have the guts." Hannibal's smile widened. "What was it you used to say? You preferred to make a killing with cards rather than guns."

Knots rose like stones along Trace's jaw. He cocked the hammer on the pistol. *"Did you rape my wife?"*

If Sam hadn't been watching closely, she would

have missed it. Briefly Hannibal's eyes closed and a look of deep pain convulsed his features. When she blinked and stared again, the expression had fled, leaving her uncertain that she'd seen anything.

His shoulders rolled back and his chest expanded in a swaggering posture. "What if I did? She was asking for it!" he snarled, his eyes glinting yellow in the harsh sunlight. "They're all whores," he snapped, flicking a contemptuous gaze toward Sam.

Rage stiffened Trace's body. The gun barrel shook. "Draw!"

Instantly the men on the porch tensed and their hands gripped the gun butts extending from their holsters. Hannibal raised a palm in their direction, then crossed his arms over his chest and grinned. Only the sweat flowing from his temples and trickling down his throat betrayed his intense emotion.

"If I draw on you, I'll kill you." He squinted up at Trace. "I'm giving you a chance. Take your new woman," he tilted his hat toward Sam, "and ride out of here."

Rigid with tension, Sam stared at him, straining to understand his strange mix of belligerence and coaxing. Hannibal's words and his posture goaded Trace to pull the trigger. Yet his refusal to draw, the arms crossed over his chest, bewildered her. Sam couldn't get a fix on what she was witnessing.

"I didn't want it to be true," Trace whispered, his lips white. Pain and fury burned in his eyes. "Draw, goddammit!"

Planted in front of Trace's skittish horse, arms

firmly crossed over his chest and away from the heavy gun on his hip, Hannibal watched Trace intently as if no one else were present.

"Hannibal, for God's sake! Draw! Defend yourself!"

Hurting inside at the sick pain she heard in his voice, Sam watched the conflict claw Trace's ashen face. At this moment he was more transparent than at any time since she had known him. She read his emotions as if they were written across his sweating forehead. Rage and regret and anguish shook his body. Etta was there too, and sorrow for what she had endured. And a devastating bewilderment as to why Hannibal had done this thing. Trace's teeth were clenched so tightly that Sam doubted he could have spoken. He quivered with the urge to kill Hannibal, Sam saw that. He believed Hannibal deserved to die for raping Etta and causing her death, for betraying the one person in the world who had cared about him.

But Trace Harden was not a cold-blooded killer. He was a good and decent man who could not fire at a brother who refused to draw in his own defense. Fury and frustration knotted his jaw. His hand shook uncontrollably, and the barrel of the heavy .44 sagged. He ground his teeth together and fought a growing resignation.

"You never did have any guts," Hannibal sneered, grinning.

"Draw, damn it!" Trace shouted furiously. The gun

jerked up and he fired into the ground inches in front of Hannibal's boots.

In rapid response, a second shot exploded from the porch and Trace's pistol flew out of his fingers. As Sam whipped out her Colt, Trace made a soft sound and drew his bloody hand tight against his chest.

Before Sam's gun cleared the holster, Hannibal had spun and dropped into a crouch.

"That's my brother, goddammit!" He shot Crisp between the eyes and watched coldly as Crisp toppled over the porch rail. "Jake, Grass-Eye. Get out. This is between me and my brother. You too," he snarled, swinging toward Sam.

Jake and Grass-Eye peered at Crisp's sprawled body, then backed away from the porch rail. They exchanged a glance and looked toward the road, did a double-take, then the one called Grass-Eye shouted at Hannibal.

"Riders—headed this way! If that ain't a posse, I never seen one!"

Hannibal pushed to his feet and dropped his gun into the holster. Licking dry lips, Sam stared at him. Never in her life had she seen anyone draw and shoot that fast. Now with Trace wounded in the right hand, all they had was her. And, as good as she was, as much as she wanted him dead, Sam knew she couldn't match Hannibal's skill.

Hannibal glanced toward the shroud of dust kicked up by the riders, then he turned back to Trace, forgetting Sam and the men on the porch.

"I raped your wife. That's what you came to hear,

now you've heard it. So what are you going to do about it?"

Sam thought surely she was wrong about the desperation edging his voice.

"Why?" Trace stared at him. "Etta welcomed you into our home. She never made you feel unwanted. She treated you with respect. I trusted you with her."

Hannibal narrowed his eyes. "You always had it all. The attention, the gifts, the charmed life. Then the big house in Kansas City and the servants and the beautiful wife. Well, I took something for me. I figured it was about damned time you shared a little something. Maybe this didn't have anything to do with Etta. Maybe this had to do with resenting you all of my frigging life!"

Cradling his bloody hand against his chest, Trace stared white-lipped into eyes identical to his own, studying his brother's face. A minute passed in such utter silence that Sam heard her heart pounding.

"You're lying, Hannibal. You didn't rape her, did you." Trace said finally, softly. It was a statement, not a question. "It was like Mattie said. You loved her."

"Aren't you listening?" Hannibal swore. "What the hell is it going to take? I'm not what you think I am, I never was. All my life you've been trying to hang your values on me, seeing something in me that isn't there. I'm not you! I was bad from the start. Our mother knew that. Your father knew it! Why the hell can't you see it? I deserted from the army, I've robbed stages and trains, I've killed two dozen men.

I've raped a hundred women. And I used you. You think because you feel some kind of brotherly loyalty that I feel it too. Well, you're wrong. All you were to me was a safe place to hole up when the heat was on!"

Trace just looked at him.

"I raped Etta and laughed at you while I was doing it. I paid you back for all the times I took the lash and you didn't. Now get the hell out of here before I kill you."

Now was the moment, Sam knew it. Trace was not going to grab the rifle and kill Hannibal. Every instinct screamed at her to do what she had come to do, what she had vowed to do twelve years ago and had thought about every day since. She shook with the urge to kill him. But, she had promised Trace that she would delay until the last possible instant. Grinding her teeth together, shaking and sweating, she made herself wait. She would give him one more minute.

Trace shook his head. "I don't know why you're saying these things. I don't believe any of it. I've always known when you were lying. Etta came to you willingly, didn't she?"

Fury erupted in Hannibal's eyes. "Do you think a fine lady like Etta Harden would have lied with her dying words? Do you think she would have demeaned herself or betrayed her own husband? Do you think she was an adulteress?"

"Was she, Hannibal?"

"She was the finest lady I ever knew! An angel!

When she rejected me, I beat her and I raped her." A glance darted toward the approaching riders, then toward the rifle in Trace's scabbard. "You want a demonstration?" Hannibal demanded, swinging his attention to Sam. He walked to her horse and stared up at her with eyes so like Trace's that Sam caught an involuntary breath. For an instant she felt paralyzed.

An instant was all Hannibal needed. His hand darted out so swiftly that Sam had no time to react. He dragged her from her horse, wrenching her gun from her hand as she fell at his feet, taking it from her as easily as he might have taken coins from a blind man's cup. With a flip of the wrist he tossed her gun toward the porch, then slapped her horse's flank, sending the mare side-stepping toward the corral.

It happened so unexpectedly and so rapidly, with so little effort on Hannibal's part, that Sam was stunned. One minute she was cocking her gun, the next instant she was sprawled in the dirt at his feet, unarmed, her heart slamming around inside her chest.

"Leave her alone!" Trace's voice emerged harsh and raw.

Bending, Hannibal stared into Sam's eyes and for an instant the agony in his gaze made her gasp. If he hadn't held the winning cards, she would have sworn that she gazed into the eyes of a dying man. Then he ripped her shirt open, exposing her breasts. A callused hand fondled her roughly.

"I always wanted what you had. You had everything and I had nothing." He glanced down at Sam with eyes that didn't see her, then he backhanded her across the face hard enough that her head cracked to the side and her ears rang.

A shot exploded and time appeared to stand still. It seemed that Hannibal continued to look deeply into her eyes for several minutes, although it could only have been a second or two. But it was long enough for Sam to watch his pain fade to relief.

A long sigh eased from his lips, then he fell to the side and away from her, clutching his chest. Sam had a split second to dart a glance toward Trace, who sat on his horse holding Lyman's smoking rifle in his left hand, his face twisted with grief. Then she snatched the gun out of Hannibal's holster and rolled, fanning the hammer and firing toward the porch until she emptied the gun.

In the ensuing silence, Sam lay flat on the hot earth, chest heaving, her breath emerging in shallow spurts.

When she cautiously sat up and wiped the sweat from her eyes, the explosions still ringing in her ears, Jake was crumpled on the porch, and Grass-Eye had slumped over the rail. Sam's fingers twitched on the gun, hot in her hand. Holding her torn shirt together, she slowly pushed to her feet and looked around for Trace.

He sat on the ground behind her, Hannibal's head cradled in his lap, his bloody hand caressing Hannibal's cheek.

"I forgot you could shoot with both hands," Hannibal whispered, looking up at him.

"No you didn't," Trace said in a strangled voice.

"I should have remembered. It was me who taught you how to shoot. Remember that day? It was autumn, almost cool." He gripped Trace's hand. "All those things I said . . . I didn't—"

"Oh Christ, Hanny." Moisture shimmered in Trace's eyes. "I didn't want it like this."

A pink froth bubbled on Hannibal's lips. "I wanted it this way. Didn't want to hang in front of strangers."

"Goddammit!" With a trembling hand Trace smoothed Hannibal's hair back from the scars on his forehead. He blinked hard. "Oh Christ."

"I'm sorry I did it, Trace, sorry she died. I always . . . Etta, she . . ." Hannibal whispered, his eyelids fluttering, sinking. A convulsion shuddered along his stocky frame and he tried to cough. The pink froth deepened in color. "She fought like a wildcat . . . she . . ."

"She loved you, Hanny. I knew it the first time I saw her look at you." Gently, Trace rocked back and forth, his eyes wet.

"She . . ."

Biting her lips, Sam spun away from a scene too private to witness. She walked toward the gate to meet the horsemen sweeping down on the rancho.

Hannibal hadn't recognized her. She hadn't told him her name or reminded him of that day so long ago in Cottonwood, Kansas. Now it was too late.

Somehow it didn't matter. As she watched Trace holding his brother in his arms, she thought about revenge. She wondered, for the first time, if perhaps her mother would have hated it that Sam had wasted so many years poisoned by thoughts of vengeance. If her mother had been able, maybe she would have advised Sam to grieve, then accept, then find the strength to move on.

Sam looked at Trace still cradling his brother in his arms and talking softly.

There was no satisfaction in watching Hannibal die. None whatsoever. She wished she had understood that years ago.

Raising both hands, suddenly exhausted, Sam waited for the posse, signaled them to halt.

"It's over. Cotwell's dead," she informed them, lifting her voice into a swirling cloud of dust. The men had already spotted the bodies in the yard. She drew a deep breath and tried to straighten her spine. "The credit goes to Judge Horace Mockton in Denver. The judge set this trap and Cotwell fell into it."

"Who are you?" the posse's leader demanded. A hard gaze swept the bodies on the front porch and Hannibal's crumbled form, then swung toward Trace, who stood beside his horse, his forehead pressed against the saddle.

"My name is Sam Kincade, and that is Trace Harden. My instructions are to order you to telegraph Judge Mockton at once. He'll explain everything." She stood aside as the horsemen trotted into the yard.

Marshall Brown reined beside her, pausing to wipe the sweat from his face, looking down at her.

"Are you crying? Do you need medical attention?" He glanced at her hands gripping the edges of her torn shirt, then back at her face.

"No," Sam whispered, blinking hard. "I'm not crying."

"If you two really are Trace Harden and Sam Kincade then I'm going to have to take you in."

"I know."

He stared at a glimpse of cleavage. "You sure you're Sam Kincade? You sure don't look like no boy bounty hunter to me."

"I'm Sam Kincade," she confirmed dully. "But I'm not a boy. Most of my life has been a lie."

Marshall Brown slowly gazed across the bodies sprawled in the yard. "What the hell happened here?"

"Two brothers," Sam whispered. "And a bad woman. A man who didn't want to die by a stranger's hand. A man who drew the joker in the deck. And someone who should have known that revenge is the shabbiest of human emotions. That's what happened here."

CHAPTER
* 20 *

Marshall Brown kept Sam and Trace locked in his stifling jail for ten days while he traded telegrams with Judge Mockton in Denver. Not coincidentally, the judge's delay in confirming their pardons allowed time for members of the press to congregate in Nowhere.

For two excited days the town boomed. The cantina had to send to Prescott for additional barrels of whiskey and beer. Beds were let on double shifts. And the telegraph office hummed with activity as newsmen wired sensational dispatches to a dozen newspapers, some located as far east as New York City, some as near as Santa Fe.

The story combined the elements newsmen dreamed of: a ruthless and notorious outlaw, an escaped felon, brother against brother, a woman bounty hunter disguised as a male, a master plan devised by a scheming judge seeking reelection. The story offered glamour, pathos, politics, a bold and pretty girl, and a shoot-out beneath the blazing sun.

If an Apache raid hadn't occurred sixty miles to the south, sending the newsmen scurrying in that direction, it was anyone's guess how long Marshall Brown would have kept Sam and Trace in jail. But with the newsmen having departed as suddenly as they arrived, and a telegram in his hand from the governor of the Colorado Territory confirming their pardons, Marshall Brown grudgingly conceded he had to release them.

After ten days of languishing in the gloom of the adobe jailhouse, the stark desert sunlight shocked their eyes. They wore the same clothing they'd worn when Marsh Crisp had come to the door of Doña Martinez's rental house. Trace needed a shave, and they both needed a bath.

Marshall Brown followed them out into the sun. He shoved a telegram toward Sam. "This here is from a judge up in Denver."

Sam smoothed out the paper. Thanks to widespread newspaper articles, it was addressed to Miss Samantha Kincade. YOU GOT YOUR PARDON STOP SNOW MORTIFIED AND MOVING BACK EAST STOP DON'T EVER COME BACK TO DENVER STOP. She crumpled the telegram and shoved it in her pants pocket.

The marshall jerked a thumb toward the cantina across the street. "You're entitled to a drink and a free meal before you leave."

They glared at him, then turned as if they had discussed it beforehand and started walking toward the stables at the end of the dirt street.

When they were alone, Sam slid a concerned look toward Trace. This was the first time they'd been able to speak without someone listening.

"Are you all right?" Nowhere's jail lacked separate facilities for women prisoners. Therefore, Sam had been incarcerated in the cell next to Trace's. For ten days she had watched him torture himself, and she knew he'd slept only a few hours.

"Telling yourself you can live with something isn't the same as actually doing it," Sam added softly.

Trace didn't answer for a full minute. "At the end Hannibal reminded me that years ago we'd agreed to . . . he said it was his choice. He planned it."

"I've thought about that day a lot," Sam said, walking slowly. "Hannibal wanted you to kill him. Maybe he didn't want the posse to get credit for catching him, maybe it was a pride issue. Maybe he didn't want to hang. Who knows? But he goaded you, made you shoot. I think he decided what would happen between you two, and he made sure it happened that way."

"Maybe."

They arrived at the end of the street and paused, standing side by side, gazing through the heat waves toward the low buildings hunched on the horizon. Newsmen had scavenged the buildings clean. No trace remained of Hannibal and his men or the final shoot-out.

"I'm not right with it yet. It's going to take a long

time," Trace said, looking across the cactus and sage toward the rancho. "I think he lied. I don't believe he raped Etta."

Sam kicked a rock ahead of her boot. "Etta claimed he did. And Hannibal supported her accusation. For whatever reason, that's what each of them wanted you to believe."

"I'll never know for sure."

"Does it matter?" Sam asked curiously, studying his profile.

For a long moment Trace continued to gaze into the sun-white desert as if watching that final day repeat itself in the glare. Finally he shook his head. "It's over now."

They stepped into the shade beneath the roof of the stable. Their horses were saddled and waiting near the stalls; otherwise the stable was deserted.

"Well," Sam said awkwardly, feeling her stomach fall away. Mentally, she'd been rehearsing this moment for days, steeling herself not to betray the anguish of saying good-bye to him.

Now that the long lonely return across the desert was almost upon her, she tried to stiffen her backbone and remind herself that she hadn't expected anything else. Where she was heading, she hadn't decided. It didn't matter anyway. But the loneliness of going there cut her adrift and hollowed out her insides.

"I guess this in where we part company." She thrust out her hand for a farewell shake, and found the fortitude to give him a wobbly smile. "Good luck in San Francisco."

Ignoring her outstretched hand, Trace leaned against his horse and lifted one dark eyebrow. "You're saying good-bye?"

His lean, elegant body still impressed her as patrician even though he was badly in need of a bath and clean clothes, just as she was. Both of them looked terrible and smelled worse. Sam hated it that his last memory of her would be dirty and smelly.

"Well, what did you expect?" she asked, dropping her hand and rubbing it along the seam of her denims. She sounded angry, mad at the world. "We've concluded our business. It's time to move on. You've got your plans . . . and I've got mine."

"Is that right?" he asked curiously, watching her run a hand down her horse's flank. "And what exactly are your plans?"

Growing uncomfortable beneath his steady gaze, she frowned and transferred her attention to her saddle, fussing with the rawhide strings securing a bedroll. "That's none of your business."

A faint smile twitched Trace's lips. "In my opinion, you don't have any plans."

Sam's chin came up. "Well, I didn't ask your opinion, now did I?" Turning aside, she gave a hard jerk on the cinch girdling her horse, making sure her saddle wouldn't slide. Then she checked her canteen, sniffing the warm brackish water inside.

"I've been thinking about your future. I've been picturing you overseeing a gaming hall. It seems to me that you have certain qualities that could prove useful in that position."

Sam's heart lurched in her chest. Her knees wobbled. Slowly, she turned to face him, her gaze narrowing in speculation.

"I don't want to misunderstand what you just said. Are you offering me a job?"

Folding his arms across his chest, he smiled at her soiled shirt and grubby hat. "What would you say if I was?"

Sam considered, studying his dancing eyes and trying to decide if he was laughing at her or if he pitied her.

"I don't know," she said finally, doubtfully.

Being a woman wasn't an easy thing. A woman's heart got in the way of practicality and common sense. More than anything, she wanted to stay with Trace. But her newly discovered female persona rejected a mere job offer. The new womanly Sam wanted woman things, and that meant something more than a job.

"And here I thought you were fond of me. I thought you'd jump at the offer." Smiling, Trace reached inside his coat pocket and withdrew the familiar, worn deck of cards. "If you draw the low card, you come to San Francisco and be my partner in the best damned gaming establishment on the West Coast. Agreed?"

Eyeing the cards with suspicion, Sam frowned and bit her lip. "I swore I was not going to cut cards with you again," she said, stalling, trying to figure out what he was doing.

Trace fanned the cards between his fingers. "Aren't you curious how Lady Luck would decide?"

She was almost positive he was teasing. On the other hand, if she abandoned her nonexistent plan and accepted his suggestion, she could stay with him a little longer. And putting the decision to Lady Luck would save her pride. A shrug collapsed her shoulders and she released a sigh. "What the hell. Shuffle."

His right hand had healed but was still stiff. But a shot-up hand never stopped a professional gambler. Trace managed a blurring shuffle using his left hand, then extended the cards. "Draw."

They gazed at each other, both recalling the last time he had urged someone to draw. A glow of pain flickered in his eyes before he controlled his expression. "It's all right," he said quietly.

Sam nodded, wet her lips, and plucked a card from the deck. The moment passed.

"It's a deuce," she said, staring down at the card. "I don't know why I agreed to this. I never win."

"Looks like you're going to San Francisco." Without glancing at the cards, Trace cut an ace and flipped it up for Sam to confirm.

"Wait a minute." Fists on hips, Sam tilted her head and stared hard. "You cheated."

"I never cheat."

"Is that so? Well, shuffle those cards again. The

stakes just went up. This time we'll cut for what I want!"

"And what do you want, Sam Kincade?"

They stood close enough that she felt his body heat and her own sudden warmth. She wanted to caress the jail-stubble darkening his jaw, wanted to feel his arms wrap around her. Knowing she didn't have to say good-bye made her want to spin in a circle and shout with joy. But first, there were higher stakes to decide.

"All right," she said in a low voice, rubbing her hands on her shirt. "If I draw the low card again, I'll manage your place and that's it. But . . ." Crimson burned on her cheeks as she raised defiant eyes. "If I draw the high card . . . then you have to marry me. Are you willing to play for those stakes?"

"Ah . . . high stakes indeed." Something stirred deep in his tiger eyes. It might have been laughter, might have been resistance. Sam was too agitated to decide.

"Go ahead and get it over with. Cut," she demanded.

"In case Lady Luck decides I have to marry you, then let's agree on one rule right now." His gaze traveled along the contours of her trembling mouth. "No more pissing and moaning about what kind of woman you are. You're a hell of a woman."

Sam nodded slowly. "And no more complaining about being half a man. You're man enough for me, more man than anyone I ever met!"

"If you should feel compelled to rescue me sometime in the future . . ." He grimaced and sighed. "I'll try to let you do it with a minimum of complaints."

"But you have to promise *not* to rescue me unless I ask you to. It's my choice."

"Agreed," he said wryly. "Is there anything else we should discuss before we put the decision to Lady Luck?"

Sam was so nervous she could hardly speak. It annoyed her that Trace didn't seem the least unnerved at the prospect of letting luck decide such an important life-shattering matter.

"As long as you know that you're never going to have a conventional wife." She licked her lips and wrung her hands, staring at the cards in his hand. "I'll try to be what you want, if the cards fall that way, but I'm always going to swear a little, drink a little, and want to raise hell every now and then."

"Just be yourself, and we'll be fine."

"Just shuffle the cards, will you, damn it?"

With a flourish, Trace performed a one-handed shuffle, then fanned the cards between his thumb and fingers, smiling at her frown. "Draw."

She reached for a card, hesitated, let her fingers hover above another. Swallowing, she made a fist, flexed her knuckles, and bit down on her back teeth. Swearing softly, she wet her lips and glared at him. "I changed my mind. I'll take the job. That's all I want."

"Too late, Kincade. The stakes are set. The game's in play. Draw."

Trembling, embarrassed and feeling stupid that

she had suggested this, Sam closed her eyes, then snatched a card and pressed it against her breast, afraid to look.

"What is it?" Trace inquired politely.

"I'm not going to look until after you've drawn."

Casually, he selected the first card his fingers touched.

"What did you get?" Sam asked breathlessly, hating herself for sounding so eager and anxious. She couldn't help it. For a moment she squeezed her eyes shut, then tilted the edge of her card and risked a peek. She gave a shout. "I drew an ace!"

Without glancing down, Trace lifted his card between two fingers and spun it to face her. "Damn all if I didn't draw a deuce." A grin spread over his lips and he laughed. "Looks like Lady Luck wants us to get married."

Sam paused and tilted her head, narrowing her eyes. "You know," she said thoughtfully, her periwinkle eyes sparkling with joy and suspicion. "It seems strange that we drew the same two cards as before . . . but of course, you don't cheat. Do you?"

"Never," he insisted, smiling.

"Trace," she said softly, not daring to let herself believe they would arrange their future based on a cut of the cards. "You already married one woman you didn't want to be married to. I won't hold you to this." In fact, she didn't want it this way. She didn't want Trace to look at her across a breakfast table and think he was stuck with her because of an unlucky draw. Her pride had taken a beating lately, but she still had a little left.

Trace caught her arm and spun her hard against his body. His fingers cupped her chin and lifted her face so he could look into her eyes.

"I swear, Sam, you act more like a woman every day! Listen to me, you little idiot. What do you think I was about to say to you before Crisp interrupted us?"

"I don't know," Sam whispered, staring at his beautiful, sexy mouth. The hard length of his body pressing against hers made her suddenly feel wild inside, dizzy with wanting him.

"I was going to tell you that I love you! That no matter what happened at Hannibal's rancho, you and I were going to survive and we were going to be together for the rest of our lives because I can't imagine a life without you. I was going to tell you that you're brave and wonderful and beautiful and you drive me crazy and sometimes I'd like to throttle you. I was going to tell you that I'd like to show you Paris and Rome and see them fresh, through your eyes. I'd like to build you a big mansion overlooking San Francisco Bay and fill it with children who have two parents and are loved equally. I want to see you with long hair and with gray hair. I want to see your face the first thing every morning and the last thing every night."

Sam gripped his lapels and sagged against him. Tears of blinding happiness stung her eyelids.

Then she kicked him.

"Damn it, that hurt. Why'd you do that?"

"Because you didn't tell me this earlier!" She thought a minute, then she kicked him again. "And that's for letting me think you didn't love me and for scaring me with the cards! You had me believing our whole future hung on the cut of a card!"

She grabbed his face between her hands and kissed him hard and passionately, her body melting against his. "And that," she added softly, speaking against his lips, "is because I love you more than anything else in this world."

"Ah, Sam," he said, smoothing back a strand of hair that had dropped out of her hat. "My sweet, feisty, one-of-a-kind Sam." Wrapping his arms around her waist, he smiled down at her. "It's never going to be dull with you."

"Let's get out of here," Sam said, circling her arms around his neck. "The sooner we get to a preacher man, the better. But first . . . kiss me, mister. Do it now!"

He kissed her until her knees gave way and her breath steamed and she was shaking and weak with loving him. He kissed her until she forgot about the sun and the heat and the long arduous ride ahead of them. He kissed her until the last faint traces of the boy bounty hunter burned away and it was all woman that remained.

And when they rode out of Nowhere, Arizona, riding so close that their legs touched, their faces glowing in the sun, Sam's heart soared. Never again would she ride the prairie alone or feel like the loneliest creature in God's creation.

In finding herself as a woman, she had found a man.

And this time when she brought him in, she was going to keep him.